THE SILENCE GAME

Many thanks to
Alain Poitevin (French translations)
Annika Peter (German/Saarlandisch translations)

harry.james.books@gmail.com

Twitter   @HarryJamesBooks

To Laurant, for the kindness and the coffee

1

The heavy brass knocker rapped three times on the oaken door.
I pictured him, looking up, switching off the television, then
striding through the hushed interior of the house to answer it.
His face, behind his usual imperious righteousness, would be lit
with excitement and anticipation.
He would walk with that arrogant, straight-backed gait of his
across the stately blue carpet of the living room.
Through the double doors with their ornate handles.
Out onto the smooth stone floor of the hallway.
Past the broad polished golden oak stairway.
Past the ancient Comtoise clock, telling everything it had seen

tock.......

tock.......

tock.......

I pictured the black hairs on the pale fingers of his feminine hand
as he reached for the iron ring of the handle, watched them grip it.
I heard the clack as he twisted it and threw the door wide open.
"Mister..."
The Beretta shoved against his throat cut him off.
The first hollow point it spat punched through his neck above the
larynx and obliterated his brain stem.
He was already dead as the second, a professional nicety, blew
his left eye out of its socket.
His blinded corpse stood for a moment open-mouthed, as if
shocked at the piss that was darkening its trousers, then collapsed
backwards.

The room was silent, the curtains to my left just a lighter smudge in the darkness. I lay there, playing that game where you guess what time it is before looking. I guessed six-thirty. When I checked, it wasn't even five.

So there I was. Wide awake.

And once I'm awake, I have to get up.

I primed a mug with coffee and stared down at the courtyard two storeys below. It was raining again, that kind of fine, almost invisible drizzle that lays on your face and itches.

The faux Victorian lamps that lit the wet paths between parking areas shivered in the wind and threw a sickly glow over the paintwork of the cars closest to them.

It was nine days before Christmas.

Not that it mattered.

I carried the mug into the living room and sat down at the coffee table, pulling the remote control from where it had slid between the cushions the night before. The TV flickered into life and 24-hour news waved a collage of events at me.

Whimsy, corruption, earnest reporters ducking stray munitions, gormless celebs and grinning winners, the usual mindless jumble of non-information.

I hit the mute button and flicked through channels.

In the dusty ruins of somewhere, kids in snide football shirts danced jigs around a reporter as he talked to the camera. Behind the dancing kids, half a dozen men slouched in the back of a battered pickup, proudly posing for the world with their third-hand AK47s. The reporter mouthed a sincere conclusion and the picture switched back to an over made-up woman in the studio.

I sat back and sipped my coffee as she blathered in silence.

Then my heart missed a beat.

Susan was right there in front of me, just feet away.

I sat there transfixed for a few seconds before turning the sound back on. She was being interviewed on a windswept hillside. Behind her, against a scudding slate grey sky, a wind turbine droned like a lost bomber on a moonless night, its blades scything down through the air over her head. She raised her voice to compete with the mournful howl it made.

Her hazel, almost amber eyes were earnest, her eyebrows arched. The wind kept pulling her hair from under the loosely knitted hat she wore, trying to cover her mouth with it as she spoke.

Her left hand fought a running battle with it, while with her right, she gestured at the blades as they swung down towards her.

She was explaining how wind turbines were bad for the environment.

Or something.

I took a swig of coffee.

Looking at her there, it was as if only months had passed since I'd seen her. It wasn't of course.

It was - what, now? Twelve years?

No. Thirteen.

I smiled through a blur of tears at the plucky tilt of her chin as she spoke, at the shape of her eyes. Her eyes had lost nothing. They still had that innocent half-roundness to them.

The nodding reporter asked her a final question as her name came up in the caption.

Susan Booth.

As she raised her hand to control her hair, I looked for the glint of gold on her finger. It was empty.

I drank the coffee down and went back out into the kitchen to make another. On the way past the broad desk that served as my office, I tapped the laptop awake. It whirred softly into life while I made my refill.

I set the new coffee down next to it and logged on, and half an hour later, I was bang up to date about Susan and the man she was married to.

There was nothing unusual about this. Nothing creepy. I do it for a living every day of the week. Background information.

The difference was that this time it was for me, and it wasn't about investigating anybody. It was about closure. Letting go. Moving on.

In knowledge lies wisdom, and all that.

I could have turned the work down, of course, but instead, I said nothing and tried to treat it like any other job. Just another solution to someone else's problem, because in the end, that's what I'm paid to do: solve people's problems.

Years ago, they used to call it being a shamus, a private eye, but these days there's more to it than just following people around. These days you have to know more. Be willing and able to do more.

Fifty-quid a day strings who've watched too much Colombo are ten a penny, of course. You'll find one online, or in your local rag, but you won't even get me out of bed without a Monkey up front, and you won't find my number in a newspaper or on a website.

I have a good clientele, and I get recommended – which is saying something when what you do is secretive and highly personal.

Mostly though, I still work for the man who started me off, businessman Malcolm Denning. I say businessman - he's probably a worse villain now than he was when he stiffed clubs for their takings.

But Malcolm was always more than just your average hood. Malcolm has intelligence, and he made his early winnings work for him. Nowadays, he heads international companies, not long firms, and gets cringing respect from the law rather than having to dodge them.

Let's face it: if they can, they'll dodge him.

He's respectable now, and respectability - that's what it's all about.

You can be corrupt as fuck, the sickest pervert – just make sure you stay respectable.

If you're respectable, you'll be protected. If you're protected, you can do what you want. Just think about it: in our Septic Isle these days, we elect the obviously corrupt to govern us, and we do it in the full knowledge that even if they were caught red-handed, they'd just smirk and carry on.

But there it is.

Respectability is everything, and the people who ask Malcolm Denning to solve their problems would rather die than lose it.

Turning to Old Bill would be the last thing they'd do.

Not only are they useless, they're clumsy; they don't respect respectability. Besides, getting Plod involved means you're leaving the club, once and for all. You can't be a grass and be respectable.

So they bring their problems to Malcolm Denning, and he gives them to me.

Then one day, he handed me a job involving Susan.

Like I say, I could have turned it down.

But really, I didn't fancy explaining to Malcolm why. Especially when, although he didn't know it, it was because of Susan I'd met him in the first place.

And anyway, let's be honest: once I knew it was her, I was like a moth to a fucking flame.

In knowledge lies wisdom, yeah?

Right.

You see, Susan was off the leash for the first time. She was studying at the local University, and I was the bit of rough she picked to slum it with for a while.

I used to paint her as cold and selfish, arrogant even. Now, I know that while she could be all those things, she was just blessed with more self-confidence than me. She was educated, intelligent, and her parents were loaded.

It helps. Sure, I could blame my background. When your view of life is narrowed by always just scraping by, and you come from a world that would rather kick you than show kindness, it's easy to kick out yourself. But that's not what screws you. What screws you, is when you can't get past having a shitty outlook on life.

Susan always seemed to know what she wanted, and more importantly, she seemed to know how to get it. Me? I didn't know where to start.

We were eighteen and twenty-two, and looking back, all we seemed to do was fuck or argue.

Well, make love.

It was never just fucking, and we did more than argue. We talked. And I mean, we really talked.

About everything.

She would lend me her course books. Books on history. Books on politics. She showed me things I'd never heard of before, made me see things that I couldn't see before.

I began to understand how our lives aren't so much shaped by what we can do, but more what we can't, the things we're not allowed to do by others.

The trouble was, though, as she opened my mind, she rubbed in how far behind her I was. So far behind, I would never catch up. I didn't even have a basic education, let alone a degree. I could never be the equal she needed. I would never be someone who could achieve things, someone she could be proud of.

I was convinced that the axe was going to fall, one day, so I tried to control the situation by treating her off-handed, like I didn't care.

I can see it all clearly now, of course.

Twenty-Twenty hindsight, and all that.

Back then, though, I didn't get it. I couldn't see it was my fault. How that ingrained shitty outlook stopped me trusting, and in the end, she had enough.

I remember, it was a Friday, and instead of meeting her where I'd promised, I was acting cussed. Sulky.

That's what I could be like. It was how I proved she cared.

So after a welter of texts, she drove to the block of flats I lived in and parked up, and then she rang me.

No, she wouldn't come up there, I should come outside. She had something to tell me.

I threw on a jacket and went down.

Down the flights of cold concrete steps because the lift was fucked again, reading the familiar graffiti, breathing in the stale piss and cigarette smoke before stepping out into evening air.

I walked across to her little blue hatchback. She stood leant against it, her hands deep in the pockets of the long dark coat she wore.

"Well? What do you want, Susan?"

"What do I want?"

"What do you want Susan. I mean, what do you want from me?"

8

She shook her head, then she laughed, a little strangled noise.

"You are such a fool, Danny."

I shrugged.

"Is that it?"

She stared at me, then, she just seemed to crumple inside.

I saw her lips quivering, watched as the half-round hazel eyes I loved with all of me filled and spilt tears down her face.

In a moment, she would soften and lean against me.

I would keep my hands in my jacket, not giving her the tenderness she wanted. Not until she gave in properly. It was a scene that we had played out so many times recently.

That day, though, would be different. It was like she had something else on her mind, and this bullshit with me was just too much trouble.

She stared at me. Not at my eyes, at my shoulder.

"Yes. Yes, Danny, it is. It."

She turned and opened the door of her car.

"I will post your things, Danny. I'm sorry."

She pulled the door shut after her and started the engine.

I didn't react.

No fucking way, would I react.

The car lurched and stalled as she reversed out of the parking place. She started it again.

I watched her drive away.

Then I did what I always did. I pushed it all down inside of me, so deep I couldn't see it anymore.

If I couldn't see it, I couldn't feel it, and if it cried out I smothered it, buried it, stamped it into silence.

I went to the pub.

I ended up at some dingy flat strewn with kid's clothes, with some girl whose name I can't remember, and her eager, vinegary sex had felt like a parade right up until the moment I'd started to come. Then Susan was there, all around me.

Then, it felt exactly what it was.

I left her there with part of me I'd never get back, and began walking home in those empty haunted hours before dawn, when London gives up pretending that it's vibrant and exciting and sits sulking at its wretchedness.

9

Squalid, soulless buildings split the chill wind, scattering it into breezes that chased swirling carousels of litter.

The stench of thrown up curry slid from a darkened doorway. Shattered glass in a sparkling carpet around a bus stop.

A hundred yards ahead of me, the dark worm of an unlit train clattered and squealed across a bridge towards Neasden, where the puke and piss and blood of another Friday night would be swilled out of it.

I hunched my shoulders and dropped my head, trying to stop the cold from getting inside my Harrington.

I was frozen.

I was hungry and I was tired, but most of all, I was angry.

Angry with Susan. Angry with life.

Above all, I was angry with myself.

It was more than anger. I fucking despised myself.

I was so many miles away, head down, and so completely lost in the blackest thoughts, that when I turned the corner into a narrow side street, I walked straight into a fight.

Two men were attacking another bloke who had his back to me.

He was tall, fair-haired and wearing a beautiful petrol blue suit, and he was, as they say, a proper handful, landing solid hits on both men even as they moved in close and forced him down onto the pavement.

Even then he wasn't finished.

One of them tried to kick him in the head, but Blue Suit swung his feet around and took the man's legs away from under him. The man fell, an ugly back-flip, and the kerb split his head open.

Straight away Blue Suit was back up on one knee, and something glinted in his right hand.

He stood up, pointing a snub-nose gun, and suddenly it seemed like the whole filthy city fell silent and watched.

The bloke in the gutter curled slowly into a ball, his head in his hands.

The other backed away, staring at the gun, but Blue Suit wasn't pointing it at either of them.

Another man had stepped out of the darkened doorway of the club we were outside. He stood there in the dirty ochre of the street lights, silent, dark-suited under a Crombie coat, like some brutal undertaker.

Blue Suit broke the silence by cursing at him, shards of words that slapped against the cold pavement and echoed along the brick walls.

The man began walking towards him.

Ten feet.

It was like he didn't see the gun.

Eight feet.

Like he didn't care if he got shot.

Six feet.

He took another step forward, even as Blue Suit thumbed the gun's hammer back and pointed it straight at his face, screaming at him.

Four feet.

I saw him smile, dark hair pushed back, eyebrows raised, his pale eyes never leaving Blue Suit.

Blue Suit took a step back away from him and walked straight into me.

Don't ask me why I did it, because to this day, I still don't know.

The best I can come up with is that I was past caring, I no longer gave a shit about anything, but I didn't want, on top of everything, to watch some geezer's head blown off in front of me.

So at the moment Blue Suit backed into me and pulled the trigger, I'd grabbed the gun with my right hand, and instead of firing, the hammer chewed down into the web of flesh between my finger and thumb, and as it did, the man in the Crombie stepped forward and hit Blue Suit full in the face.

The blow sent us both over backwards, and I fell onto the ground with Blue Suit on top of me. The man stepped forward and stamped down between Blue Suit's legs, and that was the beginning of the end.

The other bloke joined in as well, both of them stamping and kicking into Blue Suit while he lay half on top of me, and within a few seconds, I felt his body going limp.

His grip loosened on the gun and I pulled it away from him, still clamped into the flesh between my thumb and finger, watching the blood drip from my hand onto the pavement.

In the end, in less than a minute, Blue Suit was just dead weight. They rolled him off me.

I looked up at the man in the Crombie.

He was standing over me, pushing back the dark hair from his forehead with one hand and offering me the other. I took it, and he pulled me upright, and I nearly keeled straight back over again. I hadn't eaten since midday, and the loss of blood from my hand on top of everything else had finally got to me.

He held me up and allowed me to lean against him as he freed the gun from my hand.

Then he spoke, and his voice was low, almost gentle.

"Come on. Let's get you in the motor."

He helped me into the back of a Mercedes parked a few yards down the street.

He got in the passenger seat in front of me and we sat in silence, watching the other two making their way to the car.

Blue Suit lay half in the road, a clothes shop dummy after a looting. What was left of the beautiful suit was now wrapped around him, a sleeve torn away, its back split and showing a long gash of crimson lining.

The bloke with the cracked head was put in the other side of the car to me with blood running through his fingers and in streaks down his arms.

His mate got in the driver's seat and started the car's engine.

"He still breathing?" Crombie asked.

"Yeah. He'll live. Where to? Manny's?"

"Yep."

The car lurched away from the kerb on full lock, then straightened up and we pulled away.

Crombie spoke without looking at me.

"What's your name, son?"

"Danny."

"Danny what?"

"Danny Massey."

It was the first thing that came into my head.

It was Susan's name.

"Malcolm Denning."

Then, a moment later:
"Thank you."

Manny was a private doctor of some sort whose kitchen became an improvised A&E.

Malcolm Denning watched silently as he worked on us. He was maybe forty years old, lightly olive-skinned. His face was even featured under straight blue-black hair that was thinning slightly at the temples. I'd heard of him, of course. Who hadn't?

The hearsay was lurid, and under the street lighting his face had matched his reputation, but now, as he leant against the back door in Manny's kitchen, watching everything and sometimes seeming lost in his own thoughts, he looked more like an Italian history teacher than a violent villain.

Only his eyes gave the game away, and only then, if you were wise.

They were gold-flecked grey, with a softness that you would never expect given his reputation. There was no anger in them. No sneering. No veneer of viciousness.

Malcolm Denning didn't need to put on an act.

When you looked in his eyes and saw that quiet calm, almost placidity - if you had even half a clue about how the world worked, you'd know not to fuck him around.

An hour or so later, as dawn spilt dew over the cars parked around the centre of the flats, the Mercedes dropped me home.

Malcolm Denning's window slid down as I stepped out of the car's warmth into the frigid air. "I'll be in touch, Danny." he said quietly.

He spoke without looking at me, as if he was thinking about something else.

I shut the door and the Mercedes pulled away, leaving me stood shivering in the roadway with the sparrows arguing amongst themselves.

A few days later a different Mercedes slid alongside me as I left the flats. A sullen black face stared out at me from the passenger window, checking me over.

"Danny Massey."

I'd forgotten I'd used the name Massey.

"Who?"

He rolled his eyes at me.

"Get in. Mister Denning wants to see you."

I got in.

There was no point in doing anything else. They might not know my proper name, but they sure as fuck knew where I lived.

After a quarter-hour of stony silence, we pulled into a transport yard pockmarked with oily brown puddles. The driver steered the Mercedes slowly across the broken surface and stopped near a Porta-Cabin surrounded by stacks of pallets.

He told me to follow him, and led me through the maze of pallets to the door of the cabin, then motioned with his thumb for me to go in.

I stepped inside and he pulled the door shut behind me.

It was only mid-morning, but already the air in the cabin was thick and humid, a fug of diesel, coffee and stale cigarette smoke stitched through with the sharp disinfectant of wood sap from the pallets.

A voice spoke from inside a door on my left.

"Danny?"

"Yeah."

"Come through."

I took a step forward, and I could see him through the open door.

He was sitting at an unpolished desk in the grimy office that took up the left-hand half of the cabin. His back was against a grey wall that was bare except for a calendar featuring a kitten and a chick.

The kitten looked at the chick.

The chick studied something on Malcolm Denning's shoulder.

Malcolm Denning's grey-gold eyes studied me.

"Come in and shut the door."

I took a step inside, pushed the door shut behind me and stood there, waiting. I knew what was coming. I knew the script. I'd been rehearsing it all the way there:

"You never saw anything the other night, did you?"

"Don't know what night you're on about Mister Denning. Haven't been out for ages. Not been well."

"Good lad. I'll get them to drop you home (because we know where you live). Here's fifty quid. Have a drink."

He nodded at a blue plastic chair. "Sit down."

I sat down, and as I did, he laid a thick stack of money half out of an open plain white envelope onto the desk between us.

He said that it was a grand, and it was mine.

Which hadn't been in the script.

Then he offered me the kind of opportunity that blokes my age in films always grab with both hands, then they morph overnight into shiny suited wise-guys, driving flash motors and living the good life.

Or some old bollocks like that.

But this wasn't a film.

It was me and Malcolm Denning, sat in a Porta-Cabin in one of the many shithole corners of London that time and honesty had long forgotten, and while I wasn't an angel, I wasn't anyone's idea of a gangster.

Least of all my own.

I'd already seen enough of life to know that there is always someone harder than you are, and there's always someone nastier than you are, and that facing someone who's got their beak full of bugle makes the fact that you might be able to look after yourself completely fucking moot.

Once someone's chugged up, they're no longer rational.

Just like Blue Suit, they don't give a toss about odds or reputations. They're super-human, indestructible, and common sense no longer comes into it. Outside of Hollywood, being a two-bob gangster is a short and usually tragic career.

It wasn't one that I wanted, however bad things might be.

So.

I thanked Malcolm Denning politely, and then, I told him the truth: I wasn't like that, Mister Denning. I wasn't the kind of man he needed.

Really.

He frowned at me for a second, then stood up, picking up the money from the desk and tucking it slowly into the envelope, walking around the desk until he stood over me.

Outside through the mesh-covered window, a pair of forklifts rattled around on the greasy potholed surface, loading an unmarked curtain-sider. I'd already worked out that I couldn't make it out of the yard, so there was no point in trying.

Malcolm Denning looked down at me.

If there was no escape, there was no point in being scared.

His eyes narrowed, and his face turned a little side-on to me.

Whatever happened, happened. All I could do was stay respectful.

"You know how many no mark little cunts, would have bitten my hand off for the chance I've just offered you?"

He stared down at me, waiting for me to say something.

I kept schtum.

He nodded, almost to himself. "Then when they weren't up to the job, they'd be liabilities. More trouble than they're fucking worth."

He held the envelope out to me. "Take it son, and no strings."

I decided it would be rude to turn down a grand from Malcolm Denning for stopping his face being blown off, so I took it from him with a solemn thank you.

"You might not think you're hard son, but - you're no coward. It takes more bottle to face yourself, than any other cunt you will ever come up against."

He put his hand out.

I stood up, my chair scraping on the dusty floor, and shook it.

"Get in touch if you ever think I can help you, Danny. And I mean that. You come in here, and you ask for me, and if I'm not here, you ask for Garry Sneed. Got that?"

I nodded. "OK. Thanks, Mister Denning."

He showed me to the door, but then he stopped, dipping his hand into the pocket of his coat and then opening it in front of me. On his broad palm lay the snub I'd stopped from being fired at him.

"It's a Smith and Wesson 56. From the seventies."

He motioned to me to take it from him. "It's old but it works, and it's clean. No numbers on it, nothing." I took the little gun from him and weighed it in my hand. "We've got enough toys, you keep it." He winked. "Call it a souvenir."

To be honest, I'd always liked guns. Not for what they could do, but for the engineering and ingenuity that went into them, but this was the first time I'd ever held a real one.

"Well, why not?" I thought. I slid it into my inside jacket pocket.

He smiled and winked, no doubt thinking he had me on a firearms charge if I ever pissed him off.

I smiled back, unable to imagine even me being that fucking stupid.

He led the way from the office, calling to the driver who'd brought me there and telling him to take me wherever I wanted to go.

I had him drop me home.

I hid the Smith & Wesson in a shoe at the bottom of my wardrobe, then walked into town, bought some new trainers and got a haircut.

I banked the rest. I didn't know what I wanted to do with it yet, but it felt like I was ahead for once, and all I knew was I didn't want to piss it away.

A week later, the same Mercedes was waiting as I left the flats. The same face stared up at me, but this time it grinned.

"Danny Boy. Malcolm wants to see you."

He motioned to the back door. I got in and pulled the door closed. The Mercedes sat its rear down and we swept away.

When we got to the yard, Malcolm Denning was waiting in the sunshine at the door of the Porta-Cabin. He led me into the office and sat down in his usual place behind the desk.

Behind him on the calendar, the chick still studied his shoulder.

17

The kitten was still wondering why it had a primaeval urge to rip the chick's neck open.

"I heard you lost your job." It was a statement, not a question.

"Yeah. Few weeks back now."

He nodded, opened a drawer beside him and slid a folder onto the desk.

"Never mind. I've got something I reckon you can help me with. It's straight, and no trouble. There's a ton up front now, and another two when you've cracked it. You interested?"

I nodded. "Sure."

He pushed the buff folder across the desk to me, and as I looked through the handful of photographs it held he explained what he wanted.

On one level it was straightforward - someone was knocking off a married woman, and he wanted proof they were at it, but there was a catch: the bloke in question was Trevor Halland, an Edinburgh copper who had transferred down to London a few years back.

He'd got himself pretty well known, with a rep as a bit of a nutter. I'd heard of a couple of people who'd taken a hiding from him after they'd been pulled.

But according to Malcolm Denning, Halland had also been small-time bent while he was in uniform. Now though, he'd made it up to CID, and Malcolm Denning wanted something good on him. Something that would make sure the scales were tipped in his favour.

Which is where I came in.

It would be tricky, but it would be another three hundred quid. Besides, it sounded like an interesting way to make money, as long as I kept my wits about me.

"Now -" said Malcolm Denning, after we'd gone through it all and I was happy with what I'd have to do, "- you'll need some wheels."

He led the way outside and we stood by the Porta-Cabin's door in the afternoon sunshine. He nodded at a dark blue Golf parked across the yard.

"Reckon that'll do you?"

Then he elbowed me and grinned.

18

"Keys are in it, it's insured any driver."
Then he leaned close to my ear and whispered.
"Go on Danny. Go and get me a result."

So Malcolm had explained to me, that rather than follow
Halland, I should stake out the woman instead.

That way, when Halland turned up, he would have his mind on
other things and be less likely to be paying attention.

So I did as he said, and I followed her here, there and fucking
everywhere for a few days. To the shops. To the doctors. Out with
her mates for coffee.

It was useful experience. I learned how to follow a car at a
distance. I worked out various ways to watch someone without
making it obvious. I fucked right up and lost her a few times.

In short, I thoroughly enjoyed myself.

I worked out that her old man worked shifts, and left home
around midnight, so I started sleeping down the road from her
house, parked up in the Golf with a sleeping bag over me, just in
case Trevor Halland paid a nocturnal visit. He never did, and it was
a waste of time and energy, but I consoled myself that I was always
on point whenever she went out.

Then after a few days going unwashed and unshaven, and
beginning to feel a bit feral and not liking the way I smelt too
much, I finally hit the jackpot.

I followed her out of town around ten o'clock, and caught her
meeting up with Halland at one of those managed forest places
with woodland walks.

I'd bought myself a nice second-hand Canon with a 200mm lens
for the job, and I snapped them walking hand in hand into the trees.

Then, after stalking them through the best part of a half a mile of
undergrowth, bingo: I scored a series of crystal clear shots of DC
Halland, laying back in the bracken while the woman played his
bagpipes.

When I handed over the pictures to him, Malcolm Denning had grinned at me like a Cheshire Cat.

"Fucking lovely job, Danny," he said, and pushed my money across his desk to me. "So how would it be if I asked you to do this kind of thing for me again?"

I nodded. "Sure, be happy to."

"Good." He smiled. "Well then, you look after the Golf for me."

He took a compliment slip out of the desk drawer and passed it to me. "That's our place in Wycombe. Go over there and see Garry Sneed. I'll give him a ring and get him to sort out the paperwork on it for you." Business over, he stood up and held out his hand. "Look after yourself and stay out of trouble. I'll have something else for you in a week or so."

I said thank you very much, Mister Denning.

And I meant it.

On the way to High Wycombe, I pulled the Golf over into a lay-by.

It had been over a month since I'd seen or heard from Susan, and although it was more by luck than judgment, it felt like I'd turned myself around.

I had wheels. I had money.

We could go away for a weekend, have a decent time by way of me saying sorry.

More than anything else, I wanted to show her that I'd learned my lesson. I'd thought about it. I knew it had been my fault. It had been me, creating problems out of nothing, because I was frightened. Because I was vulnerable. Scared because I'd never felt I could offer her anything, and that one day, whatever I did, she would see it, too, and leave.

I wanted to explain it all to her, how the more you loved, the more afraid you became, the more you trusted, the further you ran away.

Most of all, I wanted to prove to her that now I could respect myself, I could respect her.

I rang her number. It rang off.

I rang again and got the same result.

I detoured off the A40 and drove to her University. They told me she'd left.

No, they didn't know where she'd gone. They assumed home.

I tried her phone again.

It was switched off.

After half an hour of feeling sorry for myself about it all, I decided to pick my bottom lip up and get on with life.

She might have the arsehole with me right now, but I'd been given a chance to be someone she didn't need to be ashamed of, and the last thing I should do was allow her having the hump with me to wreck it for both of us.

One of us had to play the grown-up.

Sooner or later, we would get back in touch, but for now, if I wanted to be someone she could feel secure with, someone worth being with when we finally met up again, then I had to push her out of my mind and run with the chance I'd been given.

I found the place in Wycombe after about twenty minutes of searching. It was a three-storey brick-built warehouse unit tucked away behind a furniture factory.

The yellow shutter door to the warehouse was down. Next to it was a door with MDH Logistics RECEPTION across its obscured glass panel.

I pushed it open.

Inside, a flight of cast concrete stairs ended beside a yellow-painted fire door. Under the stairs was a small kitchen area, a cheap white melamine unit with a sink set in it, and next to that, a small wooden table with a tray of upturned mugs and a kettle.

On the right was a chest height reception desk.

Behind it, the top couple of inches of a gold-brown loose corkscrew afro bobbed.

I walked to the desk and looked over.

Under the hair was a magazine.

Thin white cables fell from under the corkscrew curls and ended in a music player that lay beside the magazine. The slim body under the afro twisted rhythmically from side to side on a swivel seat.

"Hallo?"

Nothing.

The corkscrews still bobbed and the body still twisted.

I dropped my hand over the counter. The afro moved back and a pair of startled grey gold-flecked eyes stared up at me from under it.

I raised my hands and grinned.

"Sorry."

Slender hands pulled the earbuds out and lay them on the desk.

I smiled.

The grey gold eyes smiled back.

"Sorry." she said, "We're closed now. I'm just waiting."

"I was told to ask for Garry Sneed."

"Oh. I see. I think he's out the back." She stood up, and I caught a glimpse of pale coffee cleavage. "I'll see if I can find him for you. Who are you?"

"Danny. Danny Massey"

"OK, well, wait here."

She walked out from behind the desk and opened the yellow fire door. She was more than half her height in legs, and the legs ended in a beautiful little backside that wriggled inside her jeans as she walked.

I reminded myself: it was Susan's choice.

I was free to do what I wanted with who I wanted, and this seemed as good a time to start as any.

I checked my blurred reflection in the glass of the entrance door, decided I'd do, struck a pose against the reception desk facing the fire door and waited for her to come back.

I was still posing when she came in through the entrance door behind me.

"He says to wait," she said.

She walked past me and got back into her seat behind the desk. "He'll only be a few minutes."

"OK. No probs."

She looked up at me and smiled with even white teeth. I grinned back, my mind blank.

"You from round here then?"

It was crap, but it was a start.

"Yes, sort of. We live near Missenden."

I didn't have a clue where Missenden was, but I was sure I'd be able to find it.

She kept her face to me. I took it as encouragement and mentally kicked myself up the arse. She was only about eighteen. I was the one who was supposed to know how this went.

"So, what's with Missenden then?"

"It's a village. About five miles from here. Where are you from? London?" the grey gold eyes had deep black pupils and they smiled when her lips smiled.

She had a cute little chin that gave her face a kind of elfin look under the curls.

23

"Yeah, London." I was playing at home now: London jack-the-lad versus wide-eyed yokel. I leant my arms on the countertop. "You get up London often?"

"Not much."

"Ah, you should babe. There's some great places. You like clubbing?"

"I expect I would, but I've never been." The wide grey eyes were suddenly sad. "There's a couple of clubs in Wycombe, I think." she added.

"Blimey." I winked at her. "Don't you ever get out?"

She said nothing. Her smile faded, and she looked at me with a hopeless look on her face.

"Well then, tell you what. How do you fancy coming out with me? We can go uptown and..."

The seal to the fire door clacked as it was pushed open. I straightened up and stood away from the counter. A tall man with close-cropped sandy hair stared at me. I turned to face him.

His pale blue eyes took me in for a moment, then: "You Danny Massey?"

I thought about putting my hand out, but he only kept the door half-open with his foot and didn't come into the room. "Yeah. Mister Denning said I should come and see you. About the Golf."

"Oh yeah, right. I forgot about that." he put his head round the door to her: "Nats, can you go up to my office, and go into the vehicle drawer. There's a Golf - " he looked at me. "It's on a P innit?"

"Yeah. P 88 LBW"

"What he said. Can you bring the file down for me, sugar?"

"Sure." she got up.

"I'll be back in a bit," he said to neither of us and let the fire door spring shut.

She was only gone a few minutes. I heard a door upstairs close, then her trainers were pattering on the rubberised surface of the stairs as she came back down. I leant back into my pose and waited for her. She smiled as she saw me. I grinned at her and winked. I could see she was blushing slightly as she laid a buff folder on the countertop and sat back down.

The phrase shooting fish in a barrel sprang to mind.

"Are you buying the Golf then?"

"Nah. I'm just kind of - looking after it."

As if on cue, the fire door clacked open and Sneed poked his head in again. "Cheers Nats. Bring that with you and come through, matey."

I gave her a smile as I went. "See yer."

She smiled back. "Bye."

I followed Garry Sneed through the fire door and out into a warehouse, past rows of stacked pallets and into a glass-fronted side office by the steel shutter. "Take a pew, chap." He waved the folder at a brown metal framed chair and leaned against the desk in front of me. "So what am I sposed to do with this?"

"I don't know. Mister Denning just said to come over here and you'd sort it out."

He opened the file. "OK. Well." he frowned. "I haven't actually spoke with him about it, so I'm not clear if he wants it put in your name or not. I'll have to ask him, but we can forget that 'til Monday now. He's away for the weekend. Anyway -" he turned through the papers in the file. "- Ticket runs out in a couple of weeks."

I waited.

"Rents until next year, so you're alright there." he closed the file. "Tell you what to do. Take this with you and keep it safe. Monday, take it over the MOT station that's on the old tickets. Get them to stick it through. Don't worry about money; they won't want anything off you. By the time you've done that, Malcolm will be back and I'll have spoke to him about it. Bring it all back in on Wednesday, about five o'clock, and we'll sort it all out."

I nodded. "OK."

"Come on then." he got up off the desk. "I'll throw you out this way before you get yourself in trouble."

I followed him to the steel shutter.

He pressed a button and the shutter clattered and squealed as it began to rise. He put his face close to me and spoke to me over the noise.

"Just a tip matey, if you're going to be in and out here. Play nice with Natalie. She's the apple of his eye, and he is very protective.

25

You know what I mean?" His eyes held mine, their almost white lashes unblinking.

I nodded. "Yeah. Thanks."

The door was high enough to walk under now. He hit another button and the motor stopped. He put his hand out to me.

"By the way, never tell anybody that I said this to you because it never happened, did it. But thanks for what you did, matey." I shook his hand.

He waited until I was outside before hitting the button.

"See you Wednesday," he called over the noise of the shutter.

When I went back to Wycombe the following Wednesday, Malcolm and Garry Sneed went upstairs and left me in reception with Natalie, saying they'd be down for me in ten minutes.

This time I didn't pose.

"I didn't realise you were Mister Denning's daughter."

She looked glum. "Yes."

I got the impression she wanted to say more. It wasn't hard to guess what. I probably wasn't the first bloke that Sneed had warned off.

"So do you work here full time?" I offered.

"Sort of. For now. I start college in September. So until then, I'm just helping out. There's not much to do, to be honest."

"Magazines and music?"

"That's about it."

"Could be worse." I smiled.

She smiled back. The grey-gold eyes were black pools again.

"So what are you going to take at college?"

"Media Studies. I want to get into TV."

"Oh right. Doing what?"

"Well, presenting, really. I've got an idea for a children's show. But that's a long way off."

"What's that about then? The kids' show?"

"Oh. Just an idea." she gave me that helpless look again.

I was pretty sure that she didn't want to tell me in case I passed it on to Malcolm.

"Fair enough. I'd be interested if you want to tell me."

"I'm not sure yet. Not about you -" she added quickly. "- about the idea."

"Nah, it's OK. I understand. I work for your Dad. It's no problem."

She looked at me, then she leaned close to the countertop and whispered. "You understand how it is?"

"Yes. I think so." I whispered back. "But let's not worry about it, eh?" I winked at her. "It could be worse."

"I believe you." she was still whispering "I'm sorry. What you asked me, the last time you were in, whether I would go out with you. I know Garry heard. I'm sure he has the place bugged. He hears everything. You didn't get in trouble, did you?"

I grinned at her and whispered back again "No, course not. He just said you were Mister - your Dad's - daughter, so watch it."

"I am. And I understand why he is like it. But I'm seventeen next week for God's sake." She said, rolling her eyes.

I put my finger to my lips. "What day's your birthday?"

I reached over the counter and took a pen and a piece of paper.

"The 23rd"

"Ah right. Virgo, eh?"

"Yes."

"I'm a Capricorn." I wrote on the paper then held it up in front of her:

Have you got a mobile?

She rolled her eyes and shook her head.

I lay the paper back down on the counter again and wrote on it, then held it up to her:

BOLLOCKS

She laughed, and as she did her white, even teeth showed between her lips and the grey-gold eyes with their deep dark pupils danced under the gold-brown corkscrews.

I pulled onto the clean-swept herringbone blockwork of the MD Holdings car park, locking the X3 and checking my reflection as I approached the tall black glazed entrance.

Grade 2, neat and tidy. Slim-cut 3-button deep navy blue suit, set off by heavy-soled English brogues, and a turquoise and white mini checked shirt, its top button open, the way a button-down collar should be worn.

These things matter.

You know what I'm saying.

The doors parted and I walked into the deep, high ceilinged reception with its black marble floor like the still surface of an underground pool. A broad open-stepped staircase swept upwards in front of full-height windows on the right.

A plain off-white wall ran down the left-hand side, the stainless steel doors to a lift their only feature.

Next to the lift lounged Weasel Brannigan, looking dapper in a sharp charcoal lounge suit over a cream polo shirt.

He wore the suit jacket open.

Its three buttons hanging just higher than their holes showed anyone who cared he was that he was a left-hander, and he was carrying.

Which was unusual.

He tipped up his head to me as I strolled across to the far wall and the two women sat behind the wide teak reception desk.

The elder of the women, Mary, had worked for Malcolm several years now.

The younger one I hadn't seen before. She was early twenties, with pink glossed rosebud lips under an auburn sixties bob. Her kohled eyes watched me slyly as I walked up to the counter.

Mary smiled saucily at me over gold-rimmed glasses.

"Hallo, Danny, what can I do for you?"

I told her I was early, but Mister Denning was expecting me.

Early was good. Malcolm liked early.

"Of course. Just hold on." She picked up a telephone, pushing a button on its keypad with a well-manicured finger.

I glanced at Auburn Bob. She was busy finding something out in the car park far more interesting than I'd ever be. I showed her a mohair shoulder and winked at Mary as she waited for the phone to be answered. She smiled back, showing a bite of white teeth around the tip of a pink tongue, then straightened her face as she spoke into the phone.

"Oh hallo, Jackie. Mister Massey is here to see Mister Denning."

She looked at me over her glasses again as she spoke, her pupils wide within narrow rings of pastel blue. "Yes, of course, Jackie."

She pressed a button and lay the phone down on the desk. "You can go right up, Danny."

Weasel lifted himself off the wall as I walked toward him.

"Alright Josh?"

"Alright Dan. How's tricks?"

"Been worse, mate. Got a sec?"

He followed me into the lift and I thumbed the button.

I let the doors slide shut before I poked under his arm.

"What's with the tool?"

He gave me a look like I didn't miss much.

"Got told to carry a few days after Crimble."

"What is it?"

"Sig Compact, 357."

"229?"

"Yeah."

"Sweet".

"Noisy little cunt, but it shoots nice. I'll speak to Malcolm, see if you can come down the bunker one evening next week and have a go."

"Yeah, I'd like that. Thanks."

The lift slowed.

"By the way -" he nodded, smirking at the still-closed door of the lift. "- your best mate's here."

The lift door slid open onto the polished sandstone floor of a semi-circular room.

Softly lit, it was divided by a pair of ceiling-high teak doors.

On either side of the doors, suede settees followed the curve of the walls. Above each of the settees, scenes from mythical Greece were cast into bronze friezes a metre or so high.

Trojan spearmen, Triremes on the high seas and the Minotaur made up most of the left-hand frieze, while on the right-hand side, handsome Perseus held Athena's shield in one hand while the Gorgons snaked head rolled its eyes in the other.

I elbowed Weasel. "Catch you in a bit." and walked out onto the sandstone.

Under the head of writhing snakes slouched Trevor Halland, his arms stretched along the back of the settee, his thick fingers tapping noiselessly.

Below his broad, flat baby face with its almost pretty doll's eyes, a bluebottle green tie shimmered down a pricey looking white silk shirt. The shirt mushroomed over the waistband of bit-too-tight trousers. Detective Inspector Halland had obviously had a jolly good Christmas, with lots of Sticky Pudding.

"Well now. Look what the cat dragged in. Good to see you again, Danny." he lied.

He bared his teeth at me as I sat down under the Minotaur. I knew it wasn't a smile, and he knew I knew it wasn't a smile, but it served in case anyone was watching the output from the cameras.

"Trevor." I nodded at him. "How's it going?"

He nodded back.

"All good, Danny, all good. So, why haven't we seen y' around for while? Have y' been away?"

"No such luck, Trevor. Are you keeping busy?"

"Arm always busy, Danny," replied Halland, nodding sagely at me.

"All work and no play, Trevor." I winked.

"Aye, that's me, Danny. That's me."

He bared his teeth at me again and scribbled something in his mental copper's notebook. Everything got totted up with Trevor Halland. Every little sleight, however real or imagined. Then, if and when an opportunity ever presented itself, it could all get paid back out with compound interest.

Or compound fractures, depending on the circumstances.

Trevor Halland was a pig, in more ways than one. He was also a clever pig. There isn't much on God's green earth lower than bent Filth, but behind the too-bright blue and long dark lashes of Halland's eyes, there ticked a well above average detective brain.

His ambling walk, and the languid tone that remained of his Midlothian accent disguised a very real intelligence.

I was under no illusions that somehow, even if it was only down to his copper's gut instinct, Halland knew that I was the reason he was Malcolm's creature these days.

That's not to say Halland minded being Malcolm's creature.

He didn't – he thrived on it.

What he minded was that Malcolm had the upper hand. That it wasn't him in control.

I smiled back at him.

I had no illusions about Halland or the phoney respect he always showed me.

Without Malcolm, he'd have me eating through a straw.

Just for old times' sake.

One of the tall teak doors opened and Malcolm's secretary Jackie stepped between us like an unwitting umpire.

"Mister Denning will see you shortly, Inspector Halland."

She turned to me, and I saw Halland's eyes fall to her backside, the tip of his tongue on his lower lip.

"Come in, Danny." She smiled.

I winked at the sneer Halland gave me and followed her through the doors.

Malcolm was speaking to someone on the phone.

The room was in half-darkness, as it always was unless a meeting was taking place at the long walnut table that dominated the first half of it.

The only lights on were the ones above Malcolm's desk, and the only windows that didn't have their blinds drawn were the two behind him.

He waved to me to come into the pool of light and sit down. I shook my head and raised my hand like it was OK, he should take his time with the call, and waited in the gloom by the table, enjoying the feel of my shoes on the thick pile of the plum coloured carpet.

Jackie stepped into the light from the alcove she worked in off to one side of Malcolm's desk.

She picked up a cup and saucer from his desk and pointed at it.

I shook my head and raised my hand again. I couldn't drink too much ground coffee without getting the jip for hours afterwards.

She knew that, but she always offered anyway.

As the call ended, she brought Malcolm's coffee and laid it on the desk beside him.

"Right you, come here." He pointed at a leather seat. "How have you been? All good?" He stood up and put his hand out to me, his eyes smiling.

"Bearing up, thanks. Did you have a look at the stuff I dropped in on Festler and his monkeys?"

"Yeah, thanks. I've got another angle I want to talk to you about on that, but I'll see how some other stuff plays out first. Let's talk about it when you're in next week."

Next week meant next Wednesday.

Unless something cropped up, Wednesday was my "day in the office". Not that I did anything while I was there. It was just a regular day that I'd show my face at MDH and pick up anything that wasn't urgent.

At the moment though, things were just rolling along. No dramas. Well, not at MDH, anyway.

I liked it like that. It let me get on with private clients.

"Sure." I said.

He took a sip from his coffee.

"Sneedie's on his way up. He's got a flight to Germany today, but I told him to bring your money up before he goes."

Wednesdays were also when I picked up any bunce I had coming.

"Great, thanks."

"What did you get up to over Christmas?"

"Not much." I grimaced.

He mimicked my expression. We both hated the festive season. He leaned back in his chair and looked sideways at Jackie through the door of her office.

"Still, my gorgeous secretary has booked us a dirty weekend disguised as a skiing holiday, so it's not all bad."

I couldn't see her, but I expect Jackie was rolling her eyes at him. That, or pretending to ignore him.

I heard one of the teak doors open and Malcolm looked over my shoulder. "Here he is."

I turned in my chair. Garry Sneed sauntered across the carpet towards us, a beige Mac over one arm, an envelope in one hand and carrying an old-fashioned looking dark brown leather briefcase in the other.

"Have I missed anything?" he asked.

"As if we'd start without you." Malcolm dead-panned.

"Probably." Sneed pouted and dropped the envelope in my lap. "For services rendered."

"Count it." Malcolm widened his eyes.

I grinned and slid the envelope into my inside pocket.

Sneed dumped the briefcase beside me

"Dan, couldn't ask a favour, could I, matey? Fancy taking me over the airport?"

"When do you need to go?"

"About half an hour."

"Sure."

"I'd grab Weasel but he's busy."

"No worries."

I got up and nodded at the vacant chair to Sneed.

"I'll let you two talk and wait for you downstairs."

"Don't forget you have Inspector Halland waiting."

Jackie spoke from the entrance to her office.

Malcolm grunted.

"What's he here about?" asked Sneed.

"Ah.. " said Malcolm enigmatically.

"Bye, Jackie," I said.

She smiled at me and went back into her alcove.

"See you soon, Malcolm." I put my hand across the desk to him and he stood up and shook it.

"Take care, Danny." he winked.

"Be right down, Danny," said Sneed.

"Just whistle," I said, and walked back across the plum carpet to the door.

"Watch out for Mary," called Malcolm as I left.

I cheesed a faux frightened grin at him and pulled the door to.

Outside Halland still slouched under Medusa. I walked past him to the lift

"That didn't take long." he sneered as I pushed the call button.

The door slid open and I stepped inside. I thumbed the down button and winked at him as the door slid shut.

"Like one of your fucks then, Trevor."

5

Weasel was back to leaning against the wall when I got out of the lift.

"That is a fucking nice whistle," I said, eyeing his suit. "Where'd you get it?"

"Geezer Sneedie knows. He was working in Saville Row, but some Kitchens bought the place out and he couldn't get on with them, so he's started up on his own."

"How much?"

"Three, cash."

"Very nice. I'll tap Sneedie up for his number."

"You taking him over the airport?"

"Yeah. Lucky me."

He nodded past me. "Eyes right, the princess."

I looked around.

Natalie was walking slowly down the broad stairway across the other side of the building. She was with a suave looking character whose body language said he was done talking business, and now he was onto trying to chat her up.

Even from that distance, I could tell that he was boring her.

But then, I do know Natalie better than most people.

The shy awkward girl I'd first met was long gone.

She'd done college and she'd got into TV, and she'd made her dreamed-of kid's show, and then gone even further.

So there she was: rich, beautiful and famous, and having men flannelling her was par for the course.

A bloke had to be pretty special to get beyond flannelling her, though. Malcolm's vetting service kicks in after any second date, and it's very efficient.

I should know.

I'm it.

A couple of times when she was younger, back when she was still doing the kid's show and had first got her own place, she'd kicked back against what she saw as Malcolm being overprotective.

It hadn't taken her long to work out that some men – to be honest, it was most men - were being kept away from her. She sussed that I would be doing the keeping away, and when she got tired of trying to talk sense to Malcolm about it, she came to me and we cut a deal.

If she really liked the bloke, she would let me know, and as long as I didn't find out he was a complete arsehole, I would let him through the net. I might even tidy up around him a bit for her if I thought it needed doing.

That way, even if Malcolm checked up on my check up the bloke didn't look too bad.

She was happy, the blokes were happy.

Me?

I tried not to think about it.

Financially, I did alright out of it, because showbiz can be a shitty little game, and some of the men she saw were only too happy to have their loose ends tidied away.

That way, rivals couldn't use them.

Some of them eventually became my clients in their own right.

That said, I hadn't had to vet anyone for the best part of five years now.

Nats has got MDH to play with these days, and it's far more interesting.

She'd noticed me now, and as she walked across the black lake with Mister Chatty, she pointed down at the floor. This little signal meant "Stay here, I want a word with you.", so I said ta-ta to Weasel and went and waited for her by the reception desk
.

Mary wasn't there.

I ignored Auburn Bob watching me from under her eyelashes.

Natalie shook the man's hand, saw him out through the doors into the car park and then headed over to me.

"Hello." She kissed my cheek. "How are you?"

"Fucking awful." I winked.

"Glad to hear it. Come and have a cup of tea."

"Nothing for me, but you carry on."

We walked across to a seated area under the staircase.

36

"I've got a favour to ask," she said as she worked the vending machine.

"No shit."

She pulled a face at me over her shoulder. "What are you up to on Saturday?"

"Evening?"

"Yes."

"Washing my hair, unless it's something exciting. What have you got?"

"An awards dinner, for journalists. We're sponsoring a couple of them. Plus, I want to do some catching up. I was going to go with Colin, but he's had to pull out. He's got to go on another table."

"Who's Colin?"

"Colin Luscombe. Writes for the Daily Mail."

"That's nice."

"What is?"

"That someone at the Daily Mail can write."

She frowned at me and took a sip from her plastic tea cup.

"Colin is nothing like you'd expect, believe me."

"Go on."

"No point if you're in one of your sarky moods."

I grinned at her. "Go on."

"Pig."

I bowed slightly.

"Thank you."

"So. Will you take me? Please?"

It sounded pretty dry, but she had asked nicely. I supposed we'd have a crack, whatever happened. We usually did.

"Yeah, alright, you win. What time and where?"

"Your place. I'll let you know on the time."

I was sure she would.

I was also sure she wouldn't arrive when she said she would, but that was Nats.

After she went back upstairs I hung around and waited for Sneedie, watching reps come and go and trying to catch the new girl watching me so I could ignore her some more.

Even that got boring after a while.

Mary came back.

Weasel still leant against the wall.

Time crawled.

Then Halland burst out of the lift and stomped across the foyer. His face was red and scowling and he was cursing under his breath.

Weasel caught my eye and grinned.

I grinned back at him, but I couldn't help noticing the new girl out of the corner of my eye.

She didn't hide, as such. She couldn't. But she didn't once look directly at Halland, which would have been only natural. She could hardly miss six foot something of red-faced angry geezer exploding across the calm of the foyer.

Instead, she almost ducked out of sight as he stormed through, like you might when you see someone you want to avoid talking to.

It was more of a tiny unconscious reaction than anything else.

Body language, if you like.

It was a curious thing, and it pricked my interest.

I was starting to run through the possibilities when Sneed appeared out of the lift, still carrying the Mac and the briefcase, and now pulling a black hardshell suitcase behind him as well.

He went across to the desk and spoke briefly to Mary, then we met up with each other by the main doors.

"Sorry, Dan. Business."

"Don't worry about it. What terminal you need?"

"Three."

We got out to the car and he threw his coat on the back seat.

He put the briefcase in the footwell while I lifted the suitcase into the back.

I started the car.

"What times the flight?"

"2.40."

"No probs."

He seemed to be busy thinking so I let him alone.

It was fine by me. I had my own thoughts to think. About the new girl, and about Saturday with Natalie.

We were coming off the M4 before he finally broke the silence.

"What you up to the weekend?"

"Not much. Escort duty for Nats on Saturday. She just nailed me."

"Oh. Right. What's that about?"

"She's got some do she wants me to take her to. Some award dinner thing."

He sniffed. "Does Malcolm know you're taking her?"

"Dunno. Why?"

"OK, listen Dan, under your hat, OK? There's a few sparks flying. So keep your eyes open."

"Who with?"

"Ah, just some old shit."

Code for "Mind your own business."

. Fair enough.

"Is Nats involved?"

"Nah, course not. Nothing to do with her."

We drove into the dirty unnatural light of the airport tunnel.

"Do you think it would be better to blow it out? Try and talk her out of going? Just in case?"

He went quiet again and stared out of the window.

"Well, give me a clue, eh? what would you do?"

"I dunno. Ah, fuck it Dan. Don't worry about it. If he doesn't want her to go, he'll tell her. Then it's nothing to do with you if she makes you take her, is it?"

We got through the tunnel and I pulled around the inner roads.

"I expect it will be OK." he continued. "Just thought I'd let you know, that's all. Where's this do at?"

"I didn't ask. Uptown somewhere I spose. They usually are."

"Ah, well. Don't worry about it then."

I laughed at him. "I fucking wasn't until you turned up."

He grinned.

"Well. I'd be a cunt if I didn't say anything, wouldn't I?"

"Yeah, well, thanks for the nod. How long you in Germany for?"

"Not sure yet. Just a few days."

He pointed at a space behind a parked bus. "That'll do. I can get across from there. Stay in the motor, I'll get me own stuff out."

I pulled over. He lifted his case out of the boot and set it on its wheels by the kerb, then took his Mac and the briefcase from the back. "Let me know if you need picking up on the way back, yeah?" I said while he shrugged the Mac on.

"Yeah, will do, cheers. Take care, matey."

He slammed the door and I pulled away.

I put a call in to Malcolm. He was tied up with something, but he rang me back twenty minutes later.

I asked him what he knew about the new girl on reception, and his answer was a flat nothing. He asked me why, and I filled him in about how she'd reacted to Halland's exit earlier in the day.

"What do you think? She might be Old Bill?"

"I don't know Malcolm. It crossed my mind they might have slid her in to keep an eye on Halland. Do you know who took her on?"

"No idea."

"Has Jackie got her file?"

"Jack's not here, but I suppose so. I'll get her to pull it out. Pop over about four and pick it up."

When I got back to MDH, Mary was working the desk alone.

I waited while she took a couple of calls, then asked her who the new girl was.

"Oh. Sophie." she looked at me along her eyelashes. "Bit young for your taste, isn't she?"

"Well you don't want me, so I figure I'm free." I pouted.

She gave me a finger and a bored smile.

"Where is she?"

"Upstairs this afternoon. She's helping Robin in accounts."

I leaned closer to her across the counter.

"What do you know about her?"

She raised her eyebrows.

"Oh, I see-eee, it's official. Well, not much, hun. She's a temp. She's - OK. She's a bit - standoffish, but she's no trouble."

"Where's she from?"

"Harrow. No wait, she's from -" she thought for a moment "- Ealing, I think she said. But she lives in Harrow. She shares a house with a couple of other girls. Nurses, from the hospital."

"Any idea who took her on?"

She shrugged. "I expect Garry did. I've got my holidays coming up, and we'll need cover. It gives her a few weeks to get up to speed."

"OK, fair enough. I thought I'd better have a sniff round. Keep it under your hat though, OK?"

"Of course."

"Where's your holiday?"

"Malaga. Have you ever been?"

"No, but I hear there's plenty of Germans like it."

"Yes, you get quite a few Germans go there. Nice people. And it's very beautiful in places. Not all bars and piss-heads."

"Sounds great. You'll have to take me one day." I winked at her and drummed my hands on the counter "Can I go up? Malcolm's expecting me."

"Course you can. Off you go." She smiled.

Weasel nodded to me. "You back again?" I buttoned the lift.

"Yeah, need to sort something out for Malcolm. You had much to do with that new bird?"

"What? Little Miss Snotty?"

"Yeah."

He sucked his teeth. "Not much. Said hallo, that's about it. Not exactly chatty, is she."

"No. She gave me the dirties as well, but listen, Josh, watch yourself around her. Nobody seems to know how she got here, and I caught her acting a bit funny earlier. I need to have a dig around and find out what she's about."

"What d'you think she is? Filth?"

The lift door slid open. I stepped inside and thumbed the up button.

"Don't know mate. But until I've had a chance to dig her out properly, best keep your guard up."

"Yeah. Sure. No probs."

Malcolm let me into the office. The file was waiting for me on the conference table. I opened it and looked through the half dozen sheets it held while he watched me. Nothing jumped out at me as being strange. She was twenty-four. Single. On a temp contract for six weeks, via an agency in Greenford, and as Mary had said, she lived in Harrow.

"Take it with you if you want." said Malcolm.

"No, it's OK. I'll take a shot with the phone of a couple of pages. Long as I have her address and her car that will do me for now. I'll go over and see what her house is about. Mary says she told her that she lives with a couple of nurses, so getting in while she's at work might not be straightforward. Depends what shifts they're on. But anyway, I'll see what I can find out."

"Better safe than stupid," said Malcolm. "She gets to see a lot of people going in and out, and if she is Old Bill and she's been told to snoop on Halland, D.I.'s don't come cheap bent double."

"Leave it with me," I said. "I've tipped off Weasel to watch himself. Oh, and Mary said the girl is working in accounts today? Not my call, Malcolm, but I think it might be better if she didn't get around too much til we know what she's about."

"Yeah, good point. I'll make sure she stays put on the front desk."

I nodded and he patted my arm and went back to his desk.

I took my photos and left.

6

Sophie Calder finished work at five, and ought to be home by around six latest, so I hammered the X3 through the traffic and was waiting down the road from the address on her file by five-thirty.

I sat and waited, watching the house and finishing a Big Mac I'd grabbed on the way.

I was still there an hour later, and the house was still in darkness.

I gave it another half hour and decided I'd gone off half-cocked.

I could have sat there all night like a dope, freezing my bollocks off, while she'd gone to some boyfriend's place and got poked.

I drove home, hit the sack and re-read half a book about Stalingrad until I nodded off.

Thursday started wet and icy cold, and I waited until midday before I went out and fired up the Doblo van I kept as my mufti wagon.

Dirty, white and a bit tatty in places, it looked exactly what I wanted it to be: an anonymous tradesman's van. A few quids worth of stick-on sign, and I was instantly anything, from a plumber to pizza delivery.

The badge on the back door said 1.4, but under the bonnet was a remapped 1.9JTD that would try and slip the clutch in third if you went too silly at it.

I took it over the ton once, just to prove that it could do it. Once was enough though. There are far more interesting ways to commit suicide.

Satisfied that everything was in order transport wise, I went in for some lunch then got into some work clothes, topping them off with a faux fur trapper hat that I wore with its earflaps down.

Happy that I looked like a nondescript nobody, I made myself a flask of coffee and set out for MDH.

I parked the van outside an industrial unit where I could see the cul-de-sac that led to MDH and waited for her to leave work. Just after five, the little powder blue Hyundai she drove nosed out into the traffic and I set off after her, half a dozen cars behind.

Surprise, surprise - she didn't head for Harrow.

Instead, she turned off at Uxbridge, then in Uxbridge towards West Drayton. A mile or so later, she turned right at some lights and drove down a road towards an industrial area.

Half a mile on and she turned off into a narrow cul-de-sac on the right.

I pulled over a hundred yards further on and waited, watching to see if she was trying to gull me and would drive out again.

After ten minutes, I got out of the van and walked past the end of the road.

Her car was parked on the left-hand side, but it was one of those pokey little Victorian side streets with more houses than parking places, so which house she'd gone into was anybody's guess.

I went back to the van and turned it around, drank some coffee and gave her an hour, then decided she was probably in for the night.

I could wait and see if she came out, or I could call it a wrap and come back first thing in the morning. Cold gnawing my bones and the thought of a hot shower decided for me.

At six the next morning I reversed the Doblo into the start of Sophie Calder's road and set the van's door mirror so I could see her car.

It was parked where she'd left it the night before, and covered in a thick layer of frost.

I turned the heater to recirculation and let the screen and side windows mist up. When they were nicely fogged, I wiped a narrow slot clear for myself.

I let down the seatback, pulled the trapper hat almost over my eyes and settled down to wait.

An hour later, a grey Mondeo turned into the road and drove slowly down between the parked cars.

It stopped and Sophie Calder got out, closed the door without speaking to the driver and let herself into the third house on the left.

Just like that.

No kisses, no conversation. Out, and straight indoors.

The Mondeo's reverse lights came on. I started the Doblo, put the heater on fresh air to clear the screen and got out of the van.

I slid the side door open and ducked my head inside, pretending to be sorting something out.

The Mondeo edged past me, the driver looking over his shoulder and concentrating on reversing. He was thin-faced with a gingery blonde goatee beard and a blue woollen cap pulled down almost to his eyes. He looked as if he might be tall and narrow-shouldered. He didn't appear to take any interest in me.

I fiddled about in the back of the empty van, watching him through the windscreen as he waited for a couple of cars to pass before reversing out of the cul-de-sac. That was all I needed to see: which way he was going. I waited for him to pull away, slid the door shut and got back in the van.

I let a car and a Vito van pass in front of me and pulled out after him.

At the junction with the main road, he was waiting on a red light to turn towards West Drayton.

He had two cars ahead of him.

The Vito pulled up behind him. I pulled up behind the Vito just as the lights went green.

We all began moving, and it was all going great until the Vito driver had a fit of humanity and let a woman with a pushchair and a toddler cross in front of us.

The Mondeo pulled away on the main road as the lights changed to amber. The Vito pulled off, with me stuck up its tailpipe as the light went red.

The Vito turned left a quarter mile later, and now I could see the Mondeo ahead. I dawdled along and allowed two cars to put themselves between us.

He carried on through Cowley towards Yiewsley, then went left towards Heathrow.

I was well behind him, but some gut instinct told me he was on to me.

After another mile, he confirmed my hunch by pulling a Magic Roundabout on me. I was ready for him and let it play out. There was no point in doing anything else.

He went right the way round, while I took the turning off and watched him come up behind me in the rearview mirror.

The straight dual carriageway ahead gave him no excuse not to overtake me, so I dropped the Doblo into second and let it crawl at 30 on the inside lane. He sat there behind me while other traffic passed us.

So that was that.

Game over.

Rather than waste my time doing a grand tour of West London, once we got on the Uxbridge Road I drove into a garage and pulled up as if I needed fuel.

He drove straight past with his face ahead, but I could tell his eyeballs were on stalks, peering between the pumps and trying to see my face.

All he got was the top of the trapper hat.

I gave it a minute for him to either clear off or come back, then got out and tanked up the Doblo while musing to myself.

We both knew it was a score draw

We'd both got each other's numbers, although mine was registered to Danny Gregory at an address in Hastings, and I'd eat my furry trapper if his turned out to be genuine.

So who was he then?

There was an outside chance that he was just a jealous boyfriend that thought he was being clever, of course, but that didn't wash.

Only someone who knew how to tail would have twigged me in the first place, let alone worked themselves in behind me.

But if he knew enough to turn the tables on me, why not just go in the opposite direction at the roundabout? Even if he'd followed me to get my number, he could have done that before we'd driven a hundred yards. Then he'd turn off, and I was screwed, driving the wrong way up a dual carriageway while he put miles of side roads between us.

Instead, what he'd done was rank amateur, which he clearly wasn't.

It was by the by now, anyway.

The important thing was I knew that Sophie Calder didn't live where she'd told MDH she did.

When I got home I got on the laptop, and to save me having to eat the trapper, the Mondeo didn't exist on the DVLA database. The most obvious reason for that was that Sophie Calder was part of a police op.

CID could put a set of moody plates on and log them on the system, then they'd be left alone if ANPR pinged them. That still left the question of why Sophie Calder left her car in Uxbridge and got dropped back to it in the morning.

Perhaps she was just driving to Uxbridge and waiting for him, then he picked her up, leaving the Hyundai sitting at a false address all night. If I'd come back later the previous evening, it would have still been sat where I'd seen her leave it, and I'd assume she was home.

But then, why the second false address? They could have pulled that stunt at the house in Harrow, and not have blown her using a dodgy I.D.

Not much made any sense, but it wasn't often much did make sense when it came to Plod. Their ops were either so incompetent they were laughable, or so bloody arcane and intricate you fell asleep trying to fathom them out.

But the fact was, I had an itch I couldn't scratch over this one.

Some sixth sense about "What if they weren't police, and were trying to make me think they were."

I slapped the lid down on the laptop and sank what was left of my coffee.

I didn't need to do anything else for now. Whoever it was she was working for, it was their move. They'd pull her out, or leave her in. In the meantime, I needed to find out who at MDH had taken her on.

I was back at MDH at midday.

Mary was alone on the desk.

"Where's our mystery girl?"

"She rang in with a cold."

"Oh right. Sounded rough, did she?"

She looked at me curiously.

"Well. She sounded bunged up."

I pinched my nose. "Gan I thee Malcolm?"

"I'll ask." she said, frowning.

When I got upstairs, Weasel was lounging on the settee under Perseus.

"You alright, Weaz?"

"Yeah, bored. Needed a change of scenery."

"Malcolm in with anyone?"

"Nope." He stood up and went over to the lift. I waited for him to get in and the door to close before rapping the door with my knuckles.

Malcolm let me in and we sat down at his desk with Sophie Calder's file between us.

"Well?"

"She's a wrong'un. I'm just not sure what kind, or where from."

"How do you know?"

There was no doubt in his voice. He just wanted filling in.

"She doesn't live where she says she lives. She lives in Uxbridge. Or at least, that's where she went back to after work last night. Then around seven this morning she got dropped back there by a geezer in a Mondeo with moody plates."

"Boyfriend?"

"Didn't look like it. Just a normal goodbye between them this morning, like two colleagues. No tension, no passion. He dropped her off outside and she went indoors."

"And?"

"I followed him. He went up towards Harlington, then he pulled a stunt on me and ended up following me back towards Hillingdon."

"He followed you?"

48

"I know. Makes no sense. Maybe he's stupid, maybe he wanted me to think he's stupid. Or maybe he doesn't give a fuck either way. Anyway, I pulled over into a garage and he went past trying to check me out, then disappeared."

He looked at me carefully.

"What do you think she is, Dan? Old Bill?"

I pulled a face.

"Gut feeling? No."

"What then?"

"Don't know, Malcolm. I can't put my finger on it. I just don't think she's Police."

He nodded.

The next part was going to be the most difficult, and I wasn't looking forward to it. "Do you know who took her on, Malcolm?"

"Doesn't the file say?"

"No."

He shook his head. "No. I don't know."

I knew I was going to talk out of line, but someone had to point out the obvious. It was part of my job to pull the short straw.

"Well, it seems to me, realistically, that we've got a choice between Sneedie and Jackie."

His eyes came up, but he didn't look at me. He stared through me, at what was behind me, and I knew it was the two people who stood on the thick plum carpet around the deeply polished surface of the table, with its neat chairs, and it's cream blotters and silver and cut glass decanters.

The two people he trusted more than anybody in the world.

One could destroy him financially, and see he spent the rest of his life in a cell.

The other could do that, and much, much worse.

There was no point in making cooing noises about everyone making mistakes. You didn't let someone into the firm that could sit there and scope it out.

And if did, you didn't do it by accident.

I'd saved Malcolm's neck, but by the time I'd done my first three months, I was nailed on for at least half a dozen things that would have seen me inside, and inside I'd have spent every day of my life meeting friends of Malcolm's that nobody sane would ever want to meet anywhere, let alone in a prison cell, with a Screw outside making sure nobody interfered.

It didn't matter that I'd saved his life.

That was gone. The past.

Loyalty today was what mattered.

Loyalty to him, and loyalty to what, by sticking together, we all gave to each other.

He focused his eyes on me. He was pissed off, but behind the split flint stare of old was something else. It was the look his eyes had in them the first time I'd seen him, and these days, I knew what it was.

I eased out a slow breath.

"There's one other possibility Malcolm. That Mary took her on. She says she didn't, but that might be because she's worried I'm checking her out, and doesn't want to get in the shit. Mary doesn't - isn't —" I thought about what I was trying to say. "She can be a bit naive. The agency this bird is from could be a front, and they've come in and schmoozed her, and when she's got a holiday coming up, she's just gone ahead and sorted it out."

His face was expressionless.

We both knew that Mary could have done it. I was only stating the obvious. The point was that someone should have overseen what Mary had done.

It seemed like a good minute before he slowly nodded his chin half an inch. Then he laid the file gently and precisely down on the desk.

"Check it out and let me know."

"I will. I'll drop by as soon as I find anything out." I stood up.

He nodded at me. "Yeah, OK. Have a good weekend Dan."

"And you, Malcolm."

By the time I got out of the lift, normal service had been resumed.

I wished Weasel a good weekend and strolled over to the counter. Mary was fiddling with a packet of paper, re-stocking the printer. She had good legs and a tidy figure that looked a good 10 years younger than her fifty-two, and the dark skirt she was wearing cut in nicely around her buns. "You having fun, blossom?"

She looked up. "Just getting stuff ready for Monday. I can't stand coming in and it's not all ready to roll."

"I know exactly what you mean, babe." I lied. I had a cleaner who came by twice a week for an hour while I watched. The dishwasher went on when I ran out of plates. The only things I kept organised were the files I kept on people and my best clothes. I leaned against the counter and whispered to her. "Fancy a drink next week, Mary?"

Her hands stopped shuffling papers and she stood stock-still for a half-second, then she looked at me over her shoulder, her eyes a mixture of shock, doubt and frustration.

Shock fell at the last, and Frustration beat Doubt by a couple of lengths.

"Mm," she said. "Why not? That would be lovely."

"OK, deal." I grinned. "How are you sorted Wednesday?"

She mentally sifted through her diary. Right between feeding her cats and watching Netflix, she had a window.

"Wednesday? Yes, OK." she smiled.

"OK, Wednesday it is. Give us your address and I'll pick you up. About 8.30, OK?"

"OK." She leaned across the desk, scrawled her address on a piece of printer paper, and handed it to me. I took it from her and made a show of checking it. "You know where it is?" she asked.

Her eyes over the top of her glasses were - limpid pools, I think the old poets used to call them.

"I'll find it." I folded the paper and tucked it in my jacket.

Of course I knew where she lived, and I knew how she lived.

I knew who her ex-husband was. I knew he left her for a woman half his age. I knew her daughter's name. I knew the names of her two Siamese cats. I knew she was a distant cousin of Sneedie, which is how she'd got her job at MDH in the first place.

I also knew she had two maxed-out credit cards and a car loan she was behind with, thanks to some arsehole she met on a dating site a year after her husband left, and I knew there had been another half dozen two-bob gigolos and fuckwits who she'd thrown her knickers at during the first few years after he'd left, including one who'd blacked both her eyes and put her off work for a fortnight.

I knew lots about him.

I knew he'd done it before, to other women.

I'd helped persuade him that a fresh start in a new town would be an inspired idea - the sort of inspired idea that can come to anyone when four men in balaclavas kick them awake in their bedroom at three a.m.

I don't enjoy violence, but watching a pig like that, sobbing and begging in a bed full of his own blood and teeth, that isn't violence.

It's speaking the only language they understand.

There are a lot of women like Mary out there.

Nice women. Good women.

Then somebody breaks them. And once their self-esteem is broken, like sharks smell blood in water, it's like every no mark loser for miles swims up and takes bite after bite out of them, until in the end, there's nothing left.

On the surface, Mary was happy and confident, a good looking, intelligent woman any decent man would be lucky to have.

But scratch the surface of that veneer of self-respect she'd rebuilt, and she was a shipwreck waiting to happen, a storm away from capsizing again.

But that was Mary's problem, not mine.

My problem was MDH.

It might employ seventy-odd people, but at heart, it was still a family firm. And families look after their own.

That Mary was a part of the family could only be allowed to carry so much water. In the end, the greater good was more important than any of us.

She closed the printer and looked up at me.

The gold-rimmed glasses twinkled under the black-blue of her eyes and her cheeks had little spots of colour that weren't blusher.

"See you later." I winked at her. "Have a good weekend."

I walked away across the inky glistening pool of the lobby floor, through the tall doors that hissed me goodbye and out into the icy evening air.

The weather was changing.

You could feel it.

Soon the days would turn colder, and we'd have snow.

I hoped Mary hadn't done anything stupid, but in the back of my mind, I was already working through scenarios where she could have, and reasons why she might have.

I stopped myself.

Next week was next week.

Tomorrow was the do with Natalie, and that was enough bullshit to worry about all on its own.

7

I'd have put money on Natalie's cab arriving half an hour early.
She rang the bell while I was still in the shower.

I let her in, dripping wet and naked, just so I could watch her
ignore that I was dripping wet and naked.

She smiled sweetly, kissed my cheek and walked straight past
me into the flat.

She was used to my shit by now.

She wore her hair loose in tawny shoulder-length corkscrews,
with a beige short-jacketed trouser suit over a low cream silk
blouse. She looked good enough to eat.

I left her in the lounge flicking through TV channels and finished
showering and dressing.

I'd heard nothing from her since we'd met at MDH except a
single text telling me when she would be over.

I'd heard nothing from Malcolm either, and the closer it got, the
more what Sneedie had said about something kicking off, together
with Weasel carrying, had started to nag at me.

But he had a point, about just doing as I was asked and letting
them sort it out between them. We both knew how getting dragged
into anything between Natalie and Malcolm usually worked out.

On paper, anyway, whatever happened - if anything happened - I
could hand on heart say it was nothing to do with me.

But that didn't make ignoring it right.

I came back out into the lounge linking my cuffs.

"You seen your Dad?"

"No. Why?"

"Just wondered. I was half expecting a call from him about
something."

She flicked through more channels.

"No. I've not seen him."

I grunted, straightened my cuffs and pulled my suit jacket
sleeves just so. "Are we ready?"

"Yep." She turned off the TV and got up.

"So. Will I do?" I asked.

She let her forearms rest on my shoulders and wrinkled her nose at me. "Probably."

"Thank you. And you, look... almost passable, Miss Denning."

"Do I really, Mister Massey?"

"Yes, you do, Miss Denning. Just about."

The place was full of close-packed white-sheeted round tables, all dimly lit with pastel blues and reds.

Around the tables, the often dull and sometimes almost interesting were perched, earnestly paying coy homage to each other.

We wove our way through table after table full of townhouse socialists, all busily virtue-signalling to anyone who'd listen about how appalling it was that people didn't want to share their lives with any old soul who floated up to Europe rolling their eyes.

I knew I would have to be on my guard.

Not because there was any kind of threat in the air, but because I realised with a sinking feeling that on past form, it would only be a matter of time before I forgot myself and I got caught sneering at some be-jewelled cod communist as they chirruped about how they would simply love to be able to take in refugees - if only they didn't need the spare bedrooms for Tarquin and Jemima's friends on sleep-over.

Trying my best to remain detached to avoid having to grate my teeth at too many of them, I traipsed dutifully along at a distance from Natalie until eventually we were shown to a table a couple of rows back from the stage.

Only one couple sat at our table, a young Indian looking bloke in his late twenties and his pretty partner.

She stared demurely down at the tablecloth, while he was looking all around him. Either he was in awe of people, or anxious they were going to be on their own.

When he saw us being ushered towards them he jumped up and greeted Natalie with a warm smile, holding both her hands as she spoke to him.

His partner looked like she might cry.

When I arrived a few seconds later, I was introduced to Suresh, who did something that sounded mind-numbing at the BBC, and his wife Meena, who whispered hello to us both.

While Natalie and Suresh caught up with each other and forgot about us, I thought I'd try to cheer Meena up, and complimented her on how lovely she looked in the sari she was wearing.

I thought she might smile and say thank you, but instead, she looked distraught.

I gave up after that in case I gave her an aneurism, picked up the menu card and pretended to study it.

It was the usual tripe you get at over-priced restaurants everywhere - the kind us hoi polloi get spared unless we deserve it for showing off.

I supposed I'd have the steak, and it would be half the size of a cigarette packet with a couple of runner beans artfully arranged near it.

Never mind. I could always pick up a kebab on the way home.

A cover band climbed up on stage, gurning around them like ventriloquist's dummies.

Nobody took a blind bit of notice, and they duly began trolling out eighties and nineties hits at a volume people could still chatter at each other over.

A smatter of muffled applause followed each song, and the overall effect was a Millennial version of a tearoom string quintet, and by the end of the third song, even the singer had stopped pretending to be cheerful.

They crept off stage after another half dozen numbers and a tall blonde bloke with expensive-looking teeth leapt up in their place and started trying to pull the evening together.

Lame gag followed in joke, but at least he stopped the bods at the tables talking about themselves, and gradually they began laughing and remembered why they were there.

I leaned across and asked Natalie who the joker on stage was. Her reply got lost in a round of applause. He was obviously famous for something though, which shows you how much television I'd watched in my life.

The starter came and went, and then the first of the awards were presented. Short films flashed onto screens hanging above the stage, followed by the obligatory faux tension before a golden foil envelope got opened and somebody trooped up to grin and bow and thank everyone.

During breaks in the proceedings, various people would arrive at the table and there would be hugs and kisses and back-slapping.

I did the best I could to appear interested during the introductions, but I was already bored stiff and the whole deal was making my teeth itch.

I looked around me at the sea of self-satisfied faces hanging in the lurid light of the table lamps.

It wasn't like most of them had ever really achieved anything.

Here and there you'd see a face you recognised, someone who'd done some spectacular work or bravely covered a conflict or opened up corruption, and a few tables away I spotted the staffers of a satirical magazine that was always worth its salt, but apart from that, most of them were more likely to break their necks than a story that changed the world.

Journalists?

Maybe one in thirty of them got close.

The rest were newsreaders, no different to Natalie had been.

Showbiz without the show, as she called it.

The idea for the children's series she'd had when we'd first met she'd nurtured and worked at until it bore fruit. She became a kids' TV presenter, "Nat'lee Dread", for which she affected a scatty, away with the fairies persona as far from the real Natalie as it was possible to get.

Bottom line, she'd done what she was always going to be able to do - profit from her good looks, but more importantly, from her drive and intelligence.

And she'd done it for herself, on her own terms.

Then, when she'd had enough, she had put down Nat'lee Dread like she was a drink she'd finished, and moved over to news reading.

Once again, she had done it for herself, working at it and learning by doing.

She could have walked into a top slot anywhere on the back of being Nat'lee Dread. She knew all the right people, and what doors she couldn't open Malcolm would have. Instead, she'd started in a lowly regional slot and worked her way up.

But Natalie wasn't a journalist, and she never pretended to be.

She was a talking head, just like most of these people here were, even if they did kid the public that politicians cared what they thought.

They didn't.

Mainstream newspapers and journalism seemed to have systematically bled themselves of anything that might upset the order at the top, and the internet was now making them as redundant as their lack of guts deserved.

Underneath these "stars" were the real journalists.

Independents and bloggers. People who still believed in truth over political tribalism, and that quaint old idea that someone elected was there to serve, not help themselves.

A lantern-jawed woman with dyed crimson hair, famous for her sneering tirades at men, was holding court a few tables away. A woman the size of a small house with a Grade Three crop was paying her rapt attention. A pallid looking man with a wispy musketeer's beard sat next to her, nodding enthusiastically.

You asked yourself: what had she actually done? What had she actually achieved?

The answer was fuck all except sell a grotesque image of herself on the back of identity politics.

Loud laughter broke from a table just behind me. Someone was already half-cut and giving it large. I looked around out the corner of my eye.

A big-built silver-haired man wearing a silk-collared tuxedo was mouthing off, telling some story or other. A scrawny looking bird sat next to him, all bony chest in a little black dress she shouldn't have worn ten years ago.

On the other side of him, a thickset bloke about my age with slicked-back hair hung on his every word, waiting to cackle with laughter and nod on cue. Then he pushed the older man's arm to grab his attention, pointing. The older man turned in his seat and looked.

I followed their gaze. Across to my right, a waiter was leading a couple through the tables. Out of the corner of my eye, I saw the scrawny woman talking to the silver-haired man. He put his hand up and waved away what she was saying.

The couple were getting closer, and the kindest thing you could say about the man was he looked insignificant. Thin faced, maybe in his late fifties and wearing round tortoiseshell glasses, he was dressed in a tuxedo that looked three sizes too big for him.

Behind him, the woman he was with had turned away to speak to someone.

All I could tell was she was short with a mass of dark hair in what I suppose was a grown out bob. She wore a sleeveless blue dress, some kind of dark turquoise colour.

By now, the waiter was standing at our table and showing the gent to a spare seat.

Laughter erupted from the table behind.

The gent thanked the waiter and waited for the woman to arrive. Seeing him closer, fifties was being kind; he was closer to sixty-five, and he didn't look too well. He had that pasty undertone that people get when they've been ill a long time.

While he waited he laid his hands on the back of her chair, and like the rest of him, they were too thin to be healthy. The skin on them was mottled, and veins and sinews showed along his long bony fingers.

I wouldn't give him six months.

The waiter gave a courteous little nod and moved away, leaving the man standing alone, gripping the chair back as the woman finally arrived.

More laughter peeled out from the table behind me, and she looked around, startled. It was like she'd been tricked into sitting with us and wanted to move somewhere else, but the man motioned to her to sit.

He pushed the seat in behind her and she settled and put a small clasp bag on the table. She raised her hand, moved her fringe out of her eyes and looked up. Under the mop of dark hair was an oval face, with a proper nose, not big, not a button, over a mouth perhaps a bit too wide to be perfect.

Her eyes under her dark brows were the clearest sea green, wide-set and just a little almond-shaped.

I nodded to her.

She smiled at me nervously, then looked away.

The old gent she was with sat down next to her. Suresh stood up and went to his side. He half stood again, and they shook hands. The girl turned to greet Suresh, and I watched her breasts move within the silk of her dress, her small hand resting on the tablecloth, the set of her chubby arm as it met her elbow, her small even white teeth when she spoke

Laughter bellowed from the table behind.

"I need a piss," I whispered at Natalie and got up.

"Oh really? is that what it is..." she smirked up at me through her lashes.

I gave her my best sarcastic smile.

I passed the table where all the laughter was coming from.

The silver-haired man was holding court again, the man with the slicked hair nodding along.

Two other younger herberts sat at the other side of the table, smirking, waiting for the punch line. A pair of identikit Jemimas sat between them, peering into a mobile phone together.

"Completely wrong! Completely!" the silver-haired gent called out, then his voice dropped and he spoke in a whisper while prodding at the tablecloth with his finger.

As I reached the loos and pushed the door open, the laughter bellowed out again.

When I came back they'd been served some food, and silver-hair was busy stuffing his face. As I walked past him he glanced up at me with a pair of watery blue eyes that showed too much white under them.

The scrawny woman next to him sat twirling the stem of her glass.

When I reached my seat, the girl was talking to Natalie, her arms propped on her elbows, a half-full glass of wine in her hand, nodding and smiling. I sat back down again, sensing her eyes on me.

" - it wasn't right what she did, but that kind of overreaction is par for the course," said Natalie.

I tipped some mineral water into my glass.

Natalie was banging on about someone, I assumed a mutual friend.

I looked across at the old bloke. He was listening intently, nodding at what Natalie said.

I looked at the girl. She nodded at Natalie. The sea-green eyes looked at me for a moment, then quickly back to Natalie.

"But as we both know Natalie, the problem is that there are never any tangible repercussions." the man began.

His voice was dry, little more than a hoarse whisper, like every educated vowel was being forced out of him. "They appoint who they like and control reportage of any adverse reaction to the appointment. The consequence is to make redundant the -"

Bellowed laughter from the table behind blotted out the end of his remark. I turned a bit so I could see them better.

The geezer with the slicked hair was raising his drink to someone.

"It's all Greek to me!" he shouted and emptied it.

The two younger herberts behind him laughed.

The older man cackled and patted him on the leg.

I looked back to our table and noticed that the girl was looking down at the glass she held, no longer appearing to listen to the conversation.

The fringe of dark hair had fallen across her eyes.

She must have felt me looking at her because she looked up at me.

I winked at her, and she looked quickly away at the man she was with as he spoke. Then she looked back at me, stroked her hair away and smiled. I smiled back, tilting my glass towards her.

She looked at Natalie as Natalie put her hand on my arm. "I'm sorry, I need to introduce you. Danny, this is Richard Hemming of Auspex magazine. Richard was with the Beeb when I started there, although sadly he was just leaving at the time."

He held out a bony hand. "Hi, Danny."

I reached across and shook it. It was like gripping a bundle of twigs.

"Creative differences I'm afraid." He smiled a tired smile in Natalie's direction.

"And this is Phillipa Phapetis." Natalie continued. "Phillipa writes for Auspex, among others."

"Hallo Phillipa." I raised my hand. I wasn't going to try reaching across the table to her.

She nodded and smiled at me again. "Hello."

As she spoke, the lights dimmed and the compere strode back onto the stage. He began waffling about more prizes that would be awarded and telling more in-jokes.

People around the tables began applauding or laughing. There would be a group of three awards in a few minutes, then a break, then on to a further three, then a break and then some final award that was supposedly important.

"Are you up for anything Richard?" Suresh asked Hemming.

"I shouldn't think so." the dry voice wheezed. "You know, they normally tip you off beforehand."

Suresh nodded.

Laughter broke out from the table to my left again.

I glanced over. The scrawny woman was slapping at the older man with a table napkin.

The Compare left the stage to a smattering of applause and some banter from people he knew. The whole thing was starting to drag again.

"Everything OK?" Natalie asked.

"Yeah, sure babe. How about you?"

"Yes. It's such a shame Colin couldn't make it though.

I would have liked you to have met him. He's a lovely guy, and very funny."

"What's the old guy Richard's magazine about?"

"Politics. Quite dry stuff." She glanced across at him. Her eyes softened for a moment, then it was gone. She turned back to me. "He's a man out of time, really. Tilting at windmills. Very anti-establishment."

"Far left?"

"God no. Old school Liberal. He's had a thing about how politics has become corrupted and removed from ordinary people as long as I've known him. It's why he left the Beeb. Well, let's be honest, he was forced out. I don't think he's very well. He's lost a lot of weight since I last saw him."

"Who's the Phillipa Phapetis woman? she works for Hemming?"

"Yes, she works for Richard. She does other stuff, freelance, an occasional column in the Guardian. I don't know her that well. I've only met her a couple of times, out and about."

I felt her looking at me. "Oh, and I think she'd rather eat you than ice cream," she added. "My turn for a pee."

She got up, said a few words to Suresh and walked away through the tables.

I stared at my drink, then looked up at the girl.

She was listening to Richard Hemming talk but must have felt me watching her. She turned and looked at me from under her hair then went back to listening.

More laughter peeled out from the table behind.

The geezer with the slicked hair had stood up and was walking, swaggering, towards our table.

I caught him out of the corner of my eye as he approached.

The older man was calling to him: "Toby, Toby", but he ignored him.

When he got to Suresh and Meena, he stopped and laid his hand on Suresh's shoulder.

"Excuse me. Is there anyone by the name of Fat Pieces here?" then:

"Ah! There you are!" he held both his hands wide to Phillipa Phapetis. "Oh! And Richard Lemming! What a fantastic surprise." He clasped his hands together in mock happiness.

"Miss Fat Pieces, I just wanted to say that we are all -" he paused and swung his arm around towards the table he'd come from - "so pleased you could make it here tonight. The evening wouldn't be the same without your arse - I'm sorry, your art - to laugh at, and I just want to say -" the silver-haired man was now behind him, but instead of moving him away, he was leering, egging him on. "- that the next time you want to print a story about a member of my family,-" his voice rose "- make sure, that you aren't fucking lying."

Suresh stood up.

"Now OK, you've said what you wanted to say, now go back - "

Slick Hair turned on Suresh: "Go back? Why don't you fucking go back, and mind your own fucking business."

63

Silver Hair nudged Suresh. "Sit down and stay out of it."

Slick Hair turned back to face the girl. "OK, Fat Pieces? So let it be a fucking -"

Richard began to get up, and as he did Slick moved from beside Suresh and pushed his face into his.

"And what now? Are you going to make a speech, professor?" He shoved Richard back down in his seat.

And that, was enough.

"Oi. You. Silver bollocks."

The older man stared around at me, looking shocked that anyone would dare speak to him like I had.

"Yeah, you. Get your fucking monkey away from here. Now."

Bollocks to embarrassing Natalie.

Some people are just cunts.

You know what I mean?

Bullies.

Slick had turned around now, but my eyes never left Silver Bollocks.

"Don't make me get up," I said.

Slick moved alongside him.

"And 'oo the fuckin' hell are you?"

His accent skittered between Tunbridge Wells and Wapping, a public school wannabe football lad.

I bet he could parrot the whole fucking script of Green Street.

"Never mind who I am, cunt. Go back to your fucking table."

"I think Toby has a point," said Silver Bollocks, pulling himself up and trying the old imperious bullshit. "Who exactly do you think you are?"

"He's an extremely good friend of my father's."

Natalie spoke from behind him, then pushed between the two of them and walked back to her place.

She rested her hands on the back of her chair and faced them.

"It's Desmond Dannecker, isn't it?"

Silver Bollocks looked shifty.

She took her seat again. "Would you like me to tell my father you asked for a personal interview, Mister Dannecker?"

"And who's your fucking father?" said Slick.

"Shut up." said Dannecker, grabbing his jacket sleeve. "Back, now." he hissed and dragged him away.

"I can't take you anywhere, can I?" Natalie whispered to me as she sat down.

I looked at her.

She gave me a look along her lashes. "Sir Galahad."

I shrugged and looked across the table.

Both Suresh and the girl were talking to Hemming.

His complexion was like wet pastry.

"The old geezer doesn't look too good."

Natalie got up and walked around to him.

She bent her face close to his and spoke to him, her hand on his shoulder. The girl looked up at her and shook her head. Natalie looked across to me, motioning me to come.

She spoke quietly to me.

"Richard's really unwell, Dan. They came by public transport. Would you mind if we gave them a lift home?"

"Course not, babe. Now?"

"Yes, please."

I dug the X3 out of the underground car park across the road, brought it around to the entrance and stood leant against it, waiting for them.

Some jobs-worth flunky in a comic uniform left the door, strutted up and told me to move it.

I took a tenner out of my wallet, screwed it up into a ball and dropped it at his feet.

"Your tip. Now fuck off."

He looked around, picked it up and scuttled back to his place in time to hold the door open for someone. A tall blond man stepped outside, pulled a cigarette from a silver case and lit it.

He looked at me, nodded, and then walked across the pavement towards me.

When he was stood in front of me, he put the cigarette between his lips and stuck his hand out to me.

"Colin Luscombe. Daily Mail," he said.

I stood away from the X3 and shook his hand.

"Danny Massey."

He nodded. "Friend of Natalie? Boyfriend?"

"No. Just a friend. She mentioned you."

"Yeah, I was sposed to be on your table." he grinned, showing large white teeth. "Shame I wasn't. Looks like you had more fun than most of us."

"Yeah, well. No need for it was there."

"No." He took a pull on his cigarette. "That's why I wanted to thank you. Neither of them deserved that. Specially poor old Dickie. Booth has friends in some very low places."

"Booth?"

"Stephen Booth. The MP. You've heard of him?"

"Vaguely. What has he got to do with it?"

"Take it you don't know what it was about?"

"Not a scooby."

"Ah, right. Well, Booth is suing Auspex about a story. There's plenty about Booth that needs attention, but, you have to be careful. He's very well protected. From what I hear, Phillipa fucked it up. Now it's open season on Auspex."

"A story about what?"

"Oh, there are all sorts of stories about Booth, but nobody is silly enough to print them."

"Like what?"

He looked at me thoughtfully.

"You seem - interested. What do you do, if you don't mind me asking?"

"Let's say I work for Natalie's father."

I saw his eyes widen slightly.

"Oh, right. That is interesting."

I didn't ask him why.

"What kind of stories are there about Booth?"

"Well, like - between ourselves Dan, OK?"

"Sure."

He took another pull on the cigarette, his hazel eyes studying me carefully as he did, like he was making up his mind whether to trust me or not.

Then he smiled.

"OK, between ourselves. For instance, Booth makes a big play of being the perfect Shires MP with a doting dutiful pipe-and-slippers wife. Like some parody of a married couple from the Fifties, you know? Course, the blue-rinsers and Tufton-Buftons lap it up."

He looked around himself, checking if we were being watched.

It was all a bit theatrical, like he was about to plant a bomb with "BOMB" written on it or something.

And then, he did.

"Well, a few months back, I got sent pictures of Booth's missus at the family home, at it with a black guy."

He stood back and dropped the stub of his cigarette and stood on it.

"Where did they come from?"

"I'm guessing, but via Phillipa, I think. Someone wanted to send them to her, but they're not Auspex material. Auspex is a serious mag. Or was"

"How'd you mean, was?"

He shrugged.

"They're fucked, Danny. Booth's broken them. That's what happens. Money and influence."

"So what happened to the pictures?"

"Gone. Destroyed. At least, I assume so. I had to hand them in."

"So what else have you got on this Booth?"

He stared at me a moment.

I could tell he wanted to ask why I would want information on an MP that I only vaguely knew of. It was a fair question, and it was just as well he didn't ask.

I wasn't sure myself.

"Well -" he began. Then he got out another cigarette and lit it. "I have a few bits and pieces I could maybe share with you. But you realise, Danny, that this Auspex thing is a warning to everybody else as much as anything. If I send you stuff, and I need to think about it before I do, even if you are friends with Natalie, even then, it will be only partial. I'll redact anything that could point it back to me. You understand?"

"Sure, I understand. You think about it, I'll give you my email. You send me what you want on a moody account. Then there's no way back to you."

Again, he looked at me as if he'd like to ask me why, but then he worked it out.

Or thought he did.

"OK. That's what we'll do. What's your email?"

I pulled a silver clip out of my inside pocket and handed him a card.

He studied it for a moment.

"You're an Estimator? What does an Estimator do?"

"An Estimator hands out cards to journalists with bullshit printed on them. I'm a P.I., Colin. The only genuine things on that card are the phone number and the email."

He grinned his toothy grin at me. "Alright mate, I get it."

He shook the card at me and stowed it in an inside pocket, then his face was serious.

"It might take a week or three, but I'll look at what I've got, and I'll send you what I think might be useful," he said, "but Danny - a word to the wise, OK? Don't get too involved with Phillipa Phapetis. She can be a proper loose cannon, mate, and she's got a lot of people's backs up by going after Booth. Well, not for going after him, but for going after him but not getting him. There are a lot of knives out for her. Make sure you don't collect one for yourself."

"Fair enough Colin. But do me a favour. If you see Natalie, we haven't spoken,"

He nodded and we shook hands."Sure."

He clapped me on the arm and moved back towards the entrance. The flunky held the door open for him.

He took a last drag on the cigarette then flicked it away and went inside.

A few minutes later, Natalie and Phillipa Phapetis appeared with a shaky looking Richard Hemming supported between them.

As he stepped outside the cold air hit him, and he stopped and gulped at it like a fish until they gently moved him towards the car.

We piled them into the back seat and set off for his house in Dulwich. Richard let the back window down a bit and let the breeze dance through his thinning hair. The girl sat behind Natalie. I watched her in the mirror, staring out at the passing streets.

"So then, what was all that about?" I asked nobody in particular.

I heard Richard clear his throat behind me and waited.

He ended up saying nothing.

Then the girl spoke. "It was about a story we - I - " she trailed off.

I looked at her in the mirror.

She was looking at her hands. Then she looked up into my eyes in the mirror.

"What story?"

Richard cleared his throat again, and this time he spoke, his voice not much louder than the hiss of the tyres on the wet street coming in through his window, and so quiet that in places what he said was carried away and lost altogether.

"It was a story that Phillipa worked .... regarding expenses... owning a house" Then he gave a short cough and fell silent

I was none the wiser.

Natalie laid her hand on my arm. I glanced at her and she shook her head, telling me to leave it.

I watched the girl as she stared out of the window. Tears glossed her eyes and were laying wet on her cheeks. She wiped them angrily away with the heel of her hand.

"Not far now, Richard," Natalie said, looking back at him.

I glanced at the sat nav.

Less than three miles.

With luck, he might even make it.

We saw them into a villa down a narrow street in Dulwich, then headed back out west.

"Well, that really was a splendid evening Miss Denning. I can't wait for you to invite me out again."

She took most of a minute to answer.

"I'm sorry." she said quietly.

"Don't be daft, Nats. It's OK. We did what we had to do. It's early yet. Do you want to go back there?"

"Why? So you can lamp that idiot Toby in the toilets?"

"Thought never crossed my mind."

"I'm sure it didn't." She blew out a long breath. "No, let's - oh, I don't know."

We drove in silence for a mile or two.

"You hungry?" I asked.

"No, Dan. Not really."

"Want me to drop you home?"

She watched the traffic for a while.

"No. Take me back to the Hidey Hole. I'll probably be OK by the time we get there."

"OK, Hidey Hole it is."

She tipped the seat back a bit and closed her eyes.

I left her to it. The Hidey Hole was a one-bed flint-built cottage in the back street of a village not far from Beaconsfield. Unlike Natalie's flat, it was off the MDH books, bought on a mortgage she had taken out in a false name that I'd set up for her.

She paid the mortgage from an account held in the same false name, one that she only ever paid cash into. The Hidey Hole was the place she could be where Malcolm wouldn't find her. Provided of course, he only ever asked me to find her.

We were out on the M40 before I tried breaking the ice again.

"What was it all about earlier? I couldn't make out what Richard was saying."

She took a deep breath. "There was a story that Phillipa wrote, a couple of months ago now. Richard ran it, but it didn't stand up. The man involved brought a case against them that will ruin Richard. Richard has tried to settle out of court but the man is having none of it. He's out to finish Richard. It's revenge, pure and simple. Richard has been a thorn in the guy's side for years, but this time it looks as if he's come unstuck, and Auspex is finished."

"And it's a relative of that Toby?" I asked innocently.

"Yes. An MP. Booth. He's a vile piece of work."

"Booth?"

"Stephen Booth."

"Seriously?" I was hamming it now, but it suited my purpose.

"Yes. Why."

I shook my head. "Unreal."

"Why?"

"I knew his wife, years ago."

"Really? What, as in "knew, knew"?

I gave her an old-fashioned look.

"Knew. In a way, she's how I met your Dad.

"Seriously?"

"Seriously. I'd split up with her the night I ran into them and matey pulled a gun on him."

"What? He's never said anything about a gun. Was he shot?"

That bit wasn't meant to happen. It was my turn to go quiet.

"Well?" she insisted.

I couldn't believe that Malcolm had never talked to her about it. "You seriously don't know, Nats?"

"No."

"Well then, ask your Dad. If he wants to tell you, then he can."

She wasn't going to let me off that easy.

"Come on Danny, tell me."

"No Nats. It wouldn't be honourable."

"Oh for God's sake. You boys and your honourable bullshit."

"Nothing wrong with being honourable."

I looked across at her.

She was staring at me. I looked away and kept my eyes on the road.

When she spoke again, her tone was softer, more intimate.

"Tell me, Dan. He trusts you. He trusts you with me for God's sake."

"No. And that's why."

"But you've told me now, so I'll have to ask him."

"Fair enough. You crack on."

"But, I can't." She slid her hand onto my thigh. "Go on. Please."

"Nope."

Her hand travelled up to my crotch and gave me a gentle squeeze.

I wouldn't look at her, but I knew she was grinning.

"If your father could see us now, he'd be disgusted."

"If my father could see us now, he'd have Weasel shoot your balls off."

"I hope you'd talk him out of it."

She gave me a harder squeeze. "Not unless you tell me what happened."

I said nothing.

She gave me another squeeze, one that made me flinch, and then she laughed.

"I'm not sure it would do much good. I don't think he'd understand the concept of fuck-buddies where I'm concerned."

I had my doubts as well.

8

She'd never really known her mother.

She was six when Essie and Stephen had been killed.

She'd never known her father, either, but you can say that about most people, because he hides himself. From most people because it suits him to, and from Natalie because he couldn't help it.

And so, sometimes, I got the ugly little feeling inside that all she'd ever known was me.

From the first time, knowing it was the last thing we should do, and especially the last thing I should do, I was part of her life in a way that meant I could never leave it unless she told me to.

But if I was trapped, it wasn't her fault.

Sometimes, being trapped weighed too much, and that was my fault too. I started it. Even if it was always going to happen, I allowed it to, knowing full well she would always be in control.

She would start seeing someone else and I would take my cue, back away, give her space. Then at some point she'd ring me, tell me it was going wrong. He was getting too heavy, bla bla bla. Any of the reasons a woman decides she wants out.

What could I do?

Just my job.

A quiet word outside someone's front door, at six in the morning when they were half-asleep, would usually do the trick. The name was enough.

"Mate, just thought I ought to let you know, best walk away before you make Baby Jesus cry."

"What?"

"You're making Natalie unhappy mate, and I don't want it to get back to her Old Man. Know what I mean?"

Only once did anybody need treatment.

A packet in his jacket at a wine bar and a word to Halland.

A tug on his way home for having a brake light out, then "And, what's this then, sir?" and him staring bug-eyed at the bugle shaken in his face.

Grade A and family TV shows don't mix. One career, gone.

It could have been worse - a bit more in the bag would have been supply.

That would have really fucked him.

But he didn't deserve a stretch.

It was just love.

Love makes men stupid.

Some party, in the big office upstairs at the warehouse, the kind that would just happen out of nowhere. The same old faces. A celebration, some job or other, some result.

Talk and laughter, the air full of good weed, drink, expensive perfume and aftershave.

Some of the girls fire up the PA and put music on and dance, all high hair and hot pants, Uggs and micro skirts, swaying away, laughing and slapping at each other and singing along to Britney Spears and the Streets while the men bragged and joked and schemed, then after a while, someone, usually Sneedie, would make a show of chucking whatever was playing on the floor, and then the low slow heavy rock-steady bass and toppy shicka-shick, miss-shicka would start throbbing all gritty out of the big matt painted speakers, and the old faces would get up, fists up and shoulders swaying, one miss, a-two miss, one miss, a-two miss or grab their lady, rocking them round, grinding together, painted nails on the pleats and neats of handmade silk Sherman copies, and the younger faces would grab a sort and start rocking too, John Coady, rest in pieces, all swagger and gob, always riding for a fall, Andy Pearson, Donny Lacey and the rest, even Weasel, watchful and serious even back then, all of them knowing it would be a fucking good night and Malcolm and Sneadie and Croxie and Dave Pace and the rest would be still be at it, swaying half dancing, chanting Cry Tough and shit talking, even as dawn licked the darkness from the wet windows.

And over there, in the corner, there was Nats.

And me, in another corner, dusting someone else's ash off my suit sleeve, watching her, until she walked slowly across to me, her body in time with the sweet slabs of silence in the music.

We sit and talk.

Just us and the racket everybody else there was making.

After that, it started.

It never became anything.

It never ended.

It just was.

Does Malcolm know?

I've never asked him.

He's never asked me.

That way nobody has to lie.

It is, what it is.

Whatever the fuck it is.

I slid out of bed and looked back at her, her arms under her pillow, her hair loose and everywhere, the smooth skin across her shoulders, nut brown in the half-light.

I'd almost finished my drink of milk when she pushed the kitchen door open and turned the lights on. "You alright?"

"Yeah, just fancied a drink."

She slid into the seat next to me and pulled the collars of her robe together at her throat. "Can't you sleep?"

"Yeah, I'm fine. Couple of minutes, I'd've been back."

She breathed a sigh, got up and walked to the fridge, and brought a bottle of water back to the table. It hissed as her slender fingers cracked it open. She took a long drink from it then screwed the top back on and put it on the table to one side of her.

"You've got your thinking face on." She accused me.

"I think you think I think more than I do."

"Pish. You never stop. What is it this time?"

"Wasn't thinking." I shook my head. "I'm just sitting here drinking milk. It's you who's thinking I'm thinking."

She unscrewed the bottle again. "Phillipa Phapetis."

"What about her?"

"That's what you were thinking about."

I gave her a look.

"Behave yourself."

"I saw the way you looked at her." she watched me through her lashes, her eyes half-closed.

I stared back, shaking my head slowly. "Go and dig somewhere else, lil' doggie."

"What were you thinking about then?"

"You."

"Oh yeah," She chuckled. "This I can believe."

"I was, actually." I drank the last of the milk down. "About your Dad, and how little you know him."

"Does anybody?"

"You're not anybody."

"Sometimes I wonder about that."

"As I said, how little you know him."

"He's cold on purpose. I know that. He keeps his distance, from everyone. Not just me. That's why I don't take it personally. It's just how he is."

"He's vulnerable. To you, I mean."

"I get that. I just find it hurtful at times. Like the thing with the gun you said about earlier. These are things that I should know."

"No, they're not, Nats. They're nothing to do with you. They're not even anything to do with him anymore. He's moved on from that shit. Left it behind."

"Can't you see, though? You know these things, I don't. And I'm his daughter. You're..."

She left it there, and we sat in silence for a few minutes.

"What's he really like, Dan?"

"He is what he is. What you see."

"But he's not like he is to me, with you."

"How do you mean?"

"Come on. It's obvious. Everybody sees it."

"Everybody sees what? I'm just another one of the bods. I do my thing, and as long as I'm useful, I'm useful. If I stopped being useful, I'd be out on my ear, just the same as everybody else. Well, probably not quite the same as everybody else, because I know where bodies are buried."

"What do you mean by that?"

I shrugged. "I know too much. I couldn't just pick up my P45 and get wished a bright new future."

"You mean..." she looked genuinely startled.

I looked at her and shrugged. "That's how it would have to be."

"You mean you'd be..."

"Probably."

"I wouldn't let him."

"That's nice of you, but I doubt you'd know anything about it."

"Of course I would. He wouldn't be able to keep that a secret from me."

I chuckled.

"What's so funny?"

"You worry me sometimes. Why do you think a geezer like Desmond Danneker tonight, climbs down in public when you mention your Dad?"

"Well. He knows a lot of people. He could cause problems for Danneker. Some of the MDH businesses advertise with the group Danneker's paper belongs to."

"Oh, well. That's probably it, then."

She pursed her lips and wrinkled her nose.

"No, it's not it, is it."

"No, it isn't Nats, but it doesn't matter. It doesn't concern you, or me. It's your Dad's business what pricks like Danneker think of him."

"I sometimes wonder if men ever leave the playground."

She got up and went to the fridge and came back via the drawer by the sink, carrying some jellied fruit thing in a plastic pot and a teaspoon.

"I mean, take Danneker. What's he really got to be afraid of? That Dad will have him - beaten up or something?"

She rolled her eyes and peeled back the lid on the fruit thing, letting a sniff of pineapple escape.

"And if he did, Desmond would go to the police and Dad would end up in court and probably jail." She scooped at the fruit and took a mouthful. "I mean, it's ridiculous."

"And what if your Dad knew something about Danneker that would stop him going to the police?"

She swallowed another spoonful. "Like what?"

"It doesn't matter. Imagine, your Dad has something on Danneker that would stop him getting the police involved if your Dad whacked him. Then what?"

She shrugged.

"But that's it, isn't it. Like I said, playground stuff. Everything comes down to some kind of physical threat, like little boys pushing each other, 'Do as I say, or I'll punch you in the mouth'."

"Yeah, I suppose that's the psychology behind it. But then most of us – men, I mean – have taken a pasting at some point, so we're not keen on getting another one."

"Animals." She scraped at the last of the fruit thing. "There's no right or wrong, there's only 'I'll smack you in the mouth', then someone gives way rather than stands up for themselves."

"Or their principles."

"Yes."

"Or their honour."

"Ah, you and your precious honour again. So honour boils down to you being honourable so Dad doesn't have you beaten up. That's not honour, that's you being scared of being beaten up. Honour is you being happy to be beaten up, rather than disclose a secret or let somebody down."

"Ah, I see. So someone has to be a victim, to have honour."

"Smart arse." She dropped the spoon into the empty pot. "That's not what I'm saying, and you know it."

"It is what you're saying. There's no such thing as honour for honour's sake. Honour can only be achieved if you are punished for being honourable."

"Well? I'm right, aren't I?"

"No. You're talking bollocks."

"No, I'm not. Honour is about respect. Like you said earlier, it wouldn't be honourable of you to tell me about Dad and that gun thing, but that's because you respect Dad."

"Yes."

"So if you didn't respect him, you would tell me."

"No."

"Yes you would, because you wouldn't feel threatened, and the only reason you respect him is because you feel threatened. You only call it being honourable to make yourself feel good about it."

She held her hands open as if she'd explained the be-all and end-all of life.

I sat and stared at her, then laughed.

"Fuck you, Nats, I'm not telling you about it."

She pulled a face at me. "Pig."

"Buttering me up won't work either."

She put her tongue between her lips and narrowed her eyes. "I've got margarine. We can try."

She lay with her head on my chest, her corkscrews loosely tied back with a thick band, her hand gently tracing shapes on my chest.

"Do you think if you left, Dad would actually have you..."

"Topped?"

She nodded.

"I'm fairly sure it would look like an accident."

"How can you be so calm about it? How can you even keep doing it? You're trapped."

"Life is full of traps. Every job is a trap until you find a better one, then that becomes a trap as well. Just a trap you like better. I like my trap. It's the best trap I've ever had."

"I wouldn't let him, Danny."

"I can guarantee, you'd know nothing about it."

"Of course I would. You wouldn't be there anymore."

"So what would you do? I wasn't there anymore, I disappeared, so you'd accuse your Dad of having me topped?"

"But I would know, from what you've said."

"You knowing, and you proving, are two different things. Besides which, if – if – I went, it would be because I threatened MDH in some way, and you, my darling, are MDH, or pretty soon will be. Would you really throw MDH away because I stepped out of line? I mean, not just your future, or your Dad's freedom, but the jobs of everyone there, all the little people who rely on MDH to pay their way. You'd chuck all that away because I'd threatened it and your Dad had stopped me?"

She slid her hand around my neck. "I don't want to think about it."

"Then don't, because it's not going to happen."

"You'd never fall out with him? Never argue with him, if you thought he was doing something wrong?"

"He leaves me alone to get on with what he gives me to do. It's not my place to argue with him about what he does."

"But what if you did?"

"I wouldn't."

"What if I threatened MDH, and he told you to ruin me. What would you do then?"

"You wouldn't threaten MDH."

"What if I took up with someone who threatened MDH, and it didn't matter what you did, I sided with them, and threatened to blow everything open if you, Dad, didn't allow me to be with him?"

"I'm glad you get it now."

"What?"

"Why I wouldn't ever tell you what you don't need to know."

"Oh, I see. So you don't trust me."

"Don't be bloody stupid woman. Of course I trust you, but what you don't know can't hurt anybody. Even you can see that."

"So it's not honour, it's that you don't want to tell me in case I used it against MDH if you disappeared."

"Or you took up with some wrong 'un."

"Or I took up with someone you didn't approve of."

"Nothing to do with me. Like I said, I'm just a bod, doing my job."

"That's nice."

"Natalie, what the fuck do you want me to say? I can't help how you and your Dad are. I can't help that we both work for MDH. I can't help what my job is. I can't help, that if you went off the rails, I'd have to protect MDH. But it's all hypothetical, because you're not going to go off the rails, are you."

"No. Because you're here, aren't you. Whenever I snap my fingers. So another man that might lead me astray won't happen."

I kissed her hair.

"Come off it. I'm here because I want to be."

"Oh, don't worry. I wasn't suggesting for a moment that being my free male hooker was just another part of your job."

"Now that, was a shitty thing to say, wasn't it."

She shrugged, then rolled over and turned her back to me.

I lay and stared into the gloom for a minute, then rolled over the other way.

If you're arguing with a woman, you've already lost.

9

My phone ringing in the darkness woke me up.

I lifted it from the bedside cabinet, saw who it was and let it drop.

It was Monday and only just gone seven, but Malcolm liked to start early. He would miss all the traffic, be in his office by six, sort out the day and then be gone by mid-afternoon.

I made myself get out of bed.

I'd need coffee inside me before I spoke to him.

I scratched my way out to the kitchen, put the minimum of water into the kettle and loaded a mug.

Twenty feet below me, the courtyard was a sparkling carpet of frost. Misty yellow halos shimmered around the lamps. Here and there in the darkness above the parking lot, oblongs of light hung suspended, as other people, no doubt staring at the crystallised sleeping cars like me, made their first coffee of the day.

I sat down on the couch, took a sip at the still too hot coffee and called Malcolm's number.

It rang three times before he answered.

"Danny."

"Malcolm."

I sounded wide-awake and fully focused.

I doubt he was fooled.

Could I come in for ten-thirty? He had a job for me.

The traffic was better than I'd thought it would be, and it was just past ten when I rolled the X3 into MDH.

Only Sophie Calder was on the desk when I arrived. She did her thing with the phone without eye contact.

I looked across at Weasel. He nodded at me.

Cleared to go, I walked across to the lift.

"Alright Dan."

"Alright, mate."

"What's new?"

"Not a fucking lot. Same old same old."

"Did you ring the bloke about a suit?"

"Fuck no. I forgot to ask Sneedie about it. You got the blokes number?"

"Yeah. I'll text it to you later."

"Cheers, catch you in a bit."

Perseus was still giving the Gorgon grief, but at least Halland wasn't there, and I didn't have to stare at the walls for long before Jackie showed me in and pulled the door closed behind me.

"Danny. Come in, sit down." he pointed to the broad leather chair. "How you keeping?"

"All good Malcolm thanks. How's yourself?"

I sank into the chair's cold leather.

"I'm good mate. Looking forward to a few days away at the end of the week."

"Where you off to?"

"Austria. That bit of skiing I said about. Not really my thing but Jackie likes it."

He slid a buff folder across the desk to me.

"Got someone who needs a hand, Danny. He's involved in a bit of a marital situation. It's delicate, because of who he is."

I picked up the folder.

"His wife is a lot younger than him and she's playing away, which wouldn't be such a problem, cos she seems to have her head screwed on about it. But looks like the bloke involved hasn't."

I opened the folder as he spoke. There was an A4 envelope with a stack of photos in it.

"He's making noises. Silly threats. The husband is worried it might get out of hand and cause him problems."

I slid the photographs out of the envelope and my blood ran cold.

"The boyfriend needs to find himself a new hobby, Dan. Think you can sort it?"

I pushed the stack of photographs back inside the envelope and closed the folder.

I looked across the desk at him. "Sure."

"Geezer needs a slap, to be honest, but the husband doesn't want any blowback. Name is Stephen Booth. He's only a back-bencher, but he has a lot of clout and fingers in a lot of pies."

I nodded. The file was making my hands itch.

I took a mental deep breath.

This was what I did. Be professional.

I looked out of the window behind Malcolm, out over the low roofs of the modern industrial estate, to the brown roofs of the housing estate beyond them, to the grey-green hills of the Chilterns rising behind them, fading, merging with the dirty grey sky into an unseen horizon. I dropped my gaze to Malcolm.

"Is this the husband asking, or someone else watching his interests?"

"Third-party."

I knew better than to ask who.

If Malcolm had wanted me to know, he'd have told me, and for that matter, the third party could be just an intermediary, a meaningless red herring in the scheme of things.

"So, this Stephen Booth knows about his wife playing away, but just lets it happen?"

"Looks like it."

I looked into Malcolm's eyes.

Instinct told me there was something neither of us was being told.

Normally that wouldn't bother me. I was paid to do a job, not to think about why I was doing it, but I thought back to the meeting with Luscombe and his warnings about Booth and his contacts. I'd heard nothing from Luscombe in the meantime, and it hadn't surprised me. But here I was, with the very photographs he'd told me had been taken away from him because they were such a hot potato. Photographs of Susan, which in the end would mean that however I achieved what the client wanted, Susan would be involved. That she might end up a victim of what I needed to do.

Malcolm tilted his head and looked curiously at me. "Do you want the job, Danny? I can get someone else if you're busy."

I stared back at him.

No Malcolm, I didn't want the job. But I didn't want anybody else doing it. I kicked any doubts I had into the future.

"No problems, Malcolm. I was just thinking it's not straightforward. Strikes me, it will need to be subtle. Subtle takes time."

He nodded. "Subtle is important with this Dan. This fella can be a right pain in the arse to me if it gets fucked up."

He sat back in his chair. "Nothing serious, or I'd have blanked the thing. I only do favours for these fuckers because they're useful. But still. Play it low key until you know more about the background, and we'll speak about it after I get back from skiing. Pop and see Sneedie on the way out and he'll sort you out the usual up front."

It was my cue to let him get on with other things.

I stood up to leave, conscious that the file felt damp in my hand.

Half an hour later I was thoughtfully cruising back to the apartment. The Monkey in my pocket felt good, but the folder filled with photos of Susan and a tall, good-looking black bloke? That put a look on my face that would've made people who knew me well ask what the fuck was up.

Luckily, people who knew me well were few and far between.

I passed as my usual cheerful self with fit little Cathy from downstairs, who was coming out of the complex as I arrived.

She smiled and waved at me as I let her through first after the gates finished swinging open, an anytime-you-like Danny greeting, waved me from under the top of her Mazda.

I lifted my fingers from the steering wheel in salute and grinned gallantly back as she drove past, just as if I would, Cathy, definitely, if only you didn't live downstairs.

Which let's face it, was true.

But not today.

Today my head was full of Susan.

Again.

After years down there, deep inside me where I didn't have to look at any of it, she was back. I'd thought the episode of seeing her on the TV had put it in order and finally, I'd closed the book on it all.

Hearing about her and the photographs from Luscombe had only piqued my curiosity, or so I thought.

I realised now that had just been me, kidding myself.

I drove in and swung the car's nose round into my parking space.

The gates were still clanking through their closing ballet as I pushed open the door to the block.

Ignoring the open lift, I climbed the stairs to the top landing and let myself in.

I walked through into the kitchen, tapping the laptop out of its sleep on the desk as I passed, started myself a coffee then laid the beige folder open on the kitchen top, spreading the photographs out and studying them as the kettle heated through.

There were nine of them in all, and they seemed to have been taken in series from some distance away, all within the space of what appeared to be a minute or two.

The angle they were shot from was low, waist height, maybe even lower.

One was of almost the whole back of the house, with Susan and the man showing through the glass of the patio doors. Seven of them were taken closer in, expertly focused and stopped so that what could have been images obscured by reflections on the doors were instead starkly detailed studies.

The interior of the house had been captured as if it were a stage set, the principal actors clearly defined within it. It was a top-quality job, by someone who not only knew exactly what they were doing.

Someone who had probably been hidden out for a while, perhaps days, just to get exactly the shots they wanted.

But the question was: what exactly was I looking at here?

Blackmail shots? And if so, who exactly was being blackmailed?

Booth? But if, as Malcolm had been told, Booth already knew Susan was having the affair, then he couldn't be blackmailed.

OK, Booth was a well-known xenophobe and if his surface was scraped, a nailed-on racist. There'd be sniggering about his wife sleeping with a bloke with a suntan, let alone a black geezer.

But beyond that? It might lead to a divorce, but that was hardly the end of the world politically.

Susan might take him for a few bob?

That didn't add up. Susan didn't need his money. Her family were well off.

If anything, Booth was worth less. For all his upper-crust pretensions, in reality, he was a career politician who'd had a brief desk job in the Army and had then pretty much ponced and kick-backed his way through life.

So what exactly did he stand to lose from a divorce?

"Not much." seemed to be the only logical answer.

I went through the photographs again.

Had Booth set Susan up?

The quality of the photography, the stakeout and the sheer time it would have needed all meant that someone had thrown a lot of money at the job.

But why would Booth bother with all that, when if he wanted out, he could just leave a tape recorder under the bed?

So the questions remained: if they were blackmail, who was blackmailing who?

And to what end?

And why had Malcolm been given these exact photographs? They could have given him any old snapshot of the bloke to pass on. Even a decent description and an address would have been enough unless he had a twin brother.

I sipped my coffee and stared at the photos, willing them to tell me something. Anything.

They tried.

One thing missing on the otherwise perfect shots was a time-stamp.

Even though digitised photographs were open to simple doctoring, it was still usual for photographers providing evidence pictures like these to leave the time-stamp on the shot.

I took the photos into the lounge and rummaged in the drawers of the desk until I found a magnifying glass.

Within seconds I'd found what I'd hoped would be there: on the back wall of the room, only two thirds in shot, was the face of a clock.

One by one I checked the other photographs for the time on the clock, arranging them across the desk in the order they'd been taken.

When I'd finished, three things became obvious. The fond goodbye was a happy hello, the actual goodbye was brief and less than loving, and while there were less than six minutes between the first seven photographs, there was almost an hour and a half between the seventh and the eighth.

A ninth photograph was a landscape shot of Susan and the man, cropped at the waist and blown up to A4 size directly from what I'd originally thought was the happy hello. Slim and good looking, he stood two or three inches taller than Susan. Allowing for any heels she wore, that would make him around my own five-eleven.

I turned the photograph over. Printed across its back was a name, Gavin Durrant. An address in West London, a vehicle registration and a mobile number.

I propped the photo up beside the laptop and typed the address into the search bar.

In a few seconds, I had confirmation that the address existed, and a short while later I'd confirmed that Gavin Durrant was listed on the electoral roll.

It looked like he was a private tenant. The Land Registry listed the house as belonging to someone called Harris.

I made a note of the title owner's name on the photograph under Durrant's, and then went to the DVLA site and typed in Durrant's registration number. It matched back to a blue Audi A6 estate. Tax and insurance were current.

I knew the area Durrant lived in pretty well, and flint built detached country houses they weren't, so I began trying to track down the Booth's address, which as I expected proved to be a lot more difficult.

I ended up with a house registered to an S. Booth in a small village called Whistbury in Booth's constituency.

From there, it took me a few minutes to find the property on Google Earth and satisfy myself that the house could match the scale and design of the one in the photographs.

It also confirmed my initial impression that nobody had hung around behind the house and got lucky.

The shots had to have been taken from within the property, and in such a way that nobody in the house would know the photographer was there.

From the size and shape of the Booths garden, and the angle of the patio doors in the photographs, they were odds-on to have been taken from a point not far inside the garden's rear boundary, where some outbuildings lay along the border with the next house.

Logically then, the photographer had been within the nearest section of outbuildings to the house.

That meant they had to have been moving in and out of the outbuildings, and given the kind of security MP's had to have on their homes, where cameras and flood-lighting were normal, it was nailed on to have been an inside job.

That meant either Booth, or Susan.

But if Booth was on the face of it the victim, why would he source photographs in order to blackmail himself?

That left Susan, or, perhaps, as an outside possibility, Gavin Durrant. But how far-fetched was it that a bloke who lived in a West London shithole could afford to hire an expert photographer who would be willing to break into an MP's garden, with all the security an MP's house would have, and stake his wife out for days on end?

Once again, it came back to the same row of questions, and the same row of blanks.

I panned back out to study the local geography. The Booth's house was one of a row of about twenty that ran along one side of a road. Each had a front garden around fifty yards deep, while the backs were around a hundred long, varying in width, but usually between thirty to forty.

Running past the end of the gardens, sometimes partly hidden under trees, was a dirt track wide enough to take a single vehicle.

Beyond the track, open land was divided into fields. From their size and the fences between them, most looked likely to be paddocks.

I got Durrant's address on satellite view. It was a typical West London cut through, and though I didn't know the street, I knew the area.

The houses were broad fronted thirties London Brick semis and terraces, once upon a time respectable homes, built for the middle classes between the wars.

You could guess the ones still owned by older folk. Their gardens were tidy, with neatly shaped grass lawns scorched pale lime by the high summer during which the satellite shot had been taken.

Most other houses had front gardens that had been laid to block paving or tarmac to serve as drives. On the drives sat family cars, vans, here and there a Range Rover or Mercedes bought cheap because of age or a thirsty engine.

The front garden of Gavin Durrant's house looked more like a breakers yard than a drive. I counted four parked up, and more vehicles lay in an alleyway that ran down the side of the house.

Behind the six houses of the terrace that ended with Durrant's was a service road. On one side of it the short back gardens ended, along the other were garages, their mix of grey asbestos and rusted iron roofs half-hidden under trees.

I zoomed in on Durrant's house, went to street view and ran through the selection of vehicles parked on his drive.

A Renault Espace that had once been pillar-box red had crawled into the far corner to die. Its panels had faded varying shades of pink and the paint on its bonnet had peeled away to the white fibreglass underneath.

Parked hard against the Espace was a dirty brown Hyundai hatchback.

Next to that, backed almost onto the open front porch of the house, sulked a gold Toyota, its bonnet and wings buckled by a collision. With grille and headlights gone, it stared at Google's camera like a toothless skull.

Down beside the house, on a driveway that met the end of the service road, an ageing grey Transit van lay half-hidden by nettles.

A blue motorbike sat in front of it. Its front wheel had been removed and its rusting front forks rested on a concrete block. Orange foam spewed from a split at the front of its seat.

There was no sign of a blue Audi estate, but that didn't mean much.

I moved back out of street view and re-checked the vehicles again; the Espace still sat in its corner, but the brown Hyundai was gone, and in its place was a small yellow van or MPV with some kind of red estate parked next to that.

What was almost certainly the gold Toyota was parked diagonally across the garden. It had either had a shunt or been repaired between the shots being taken. To the side of the house, the motorbike was nowhere to be seen, but the Transit didn't look to have moved, and a large silver saloon was parked behind it.

I shut the lid to the laptop.

Tomorrow morning I'd go and have a proper nose around, and see what Gavin Durrant had to say for himself.

Morninton Road was modern West London in all its glory. What had once been a tree-lined avenue of genteel homes was now a decrepit cut through, a red brick and patched up pebbledash transit camp, over-filled with everybody from everywhere.

I drove as quickly down the road as I could without knocking the bottom out of the Doblo on the speed bumps. If anyone was watching, I wanted to look like someone in a hurry cutting through, not someone on a recce, but my eyes were taking in everything.

I saw the red Espace in the corner of Durrant's garden fifty yards before I reached the house. Parked diagonally across the drive was a blue Audi estate. Recce completed, I drove slowly around the block, then came back into the street and parked a hundred yards or so before Durrant's house.

Down a turning on the right almost opposite me was the entrance to the service road. I gave it a couple of minutes, picked up a clipboard from the passenger seat to deter nosey parkers and walked down the side turning and straight into the service road as if I had official business there.

Then I stopped and took my bearings. Down the right-hand side were the garages, hung with a mixture of metal doors and older wooden ones.

From the grass and nettles that grew in front of them, it looked as if only a couple were ever used.

On the left ran the back fences of the houses, all pretty uniform lapped timber of varying ages, all about six feet high.

I opened the clipboard, pulled a pen from my pocket, and began walking slowly down the alley, looking up at the roofs of the houses, checking the gardens and pretending I was making notes.

Nobody was out in any of the gardens, but a woman was peering at me suspiciously from an upstairs window. I waved to her and showed her the clipboard. She nodded and disappeared.

Nobody living around here would want to see an official.

Eventually, I stood outside the gate to Durrant's back garden. A light was on upstairs in what I guessed from its pebbled glass was the bathroom. I stood on tiptoe and glanced over the fence. A scruffy overgrown grass area lay in front of patio doors that would open into an untidy looking room, and next to them, a kitchen window.

No lights were on, and through the kitchen window, I could see right through the darkened house to the small segments of glass set into the top of the front door.

I pushed at the gate. It shifted under my hand but didn't open.

I moved on around the corner.

The alley was still blocked by the grey Transit. Its back doors were open and a jumble of tyres half-filled its insides and lay scattered on the ground behind it. Grass and nettles grew through and around them.

I closed the clipboard and walked slowly back to the Doblo.

From the back of the van, I took a small power screwdriver and a handful of three-inch screws and stuffed them into the pocket of my coat. I went back to Durrant's back gate and drove three of the screws through the edge of it into the frame.

Back in the Doblo again, I settled down to warm myself through for five minutes before I knocked Durrant up, sipping coffee from a flask I'd brought with me.

Vehicles passed both ways and slowed for the speed humps, but none seemed to pay any attention to either me or Durrant's house.

Coffee finished, I put a miniature recorder onto record and tucked it in my coat's breast pocket, sat a grey flat cap on my head and put on a pair of thick-framed glasses.

I waited for a woman pushing a pram to pass, then picked up the clipboard again and walked across to Durrant's house.

I knocked on the door, opened the clipboard and waited.

Nothing.

I looked around the doorframe for a bell but found none.

I knocked on the door again.

Two women walked past chattering to each other.

I kept my back to them, staring down into the open clipboard.

When their voices had faded, I leant sideways and peered through the yellowed net curtains of the bay window next to me.

Flat-pack wooden cabinets. A fantasy painting on the wall over the fireplace of a naked woman staring out over a lake. A television flickered in the corner, showing some daytime rubbish.

I straightened up and looked around me slowly, casually checking left, then right.

The street was empty.

I ducked forward, pushed the flap of the letterbox open and peered through it into the house.

Ahead of me, the hallway led into the kitchen.

Moving my head left, I could see in through the open door into the living room on the right.

An empty brown velour couch with a coffee table in front of it. On the coffee table was a plate of something half-eaten, a mug beside a packet of cigarettes.

I moved my head right.

Durrant lay on his back at the foot of the stairs, his head lolling backwards, his shirt black with congealed blood.

His throat hung open like a wide toothless smile and his left arm hung through the bannisters.

Three of his fingers had been broken backwards.

I let the flap drop quietly.

I smudged it with my knuckle where I'd touched it, took a step back, closed the clipboard, and walked with my head lowered back to the Doblo and started for home.

I rang Malcolm's office phone as I drove. Jackie answered.

"Is Malcolm there Jackie?"

"Sorry Danny, there's only me today. He won't be in until we get back from Austria now. Can I help?"

"It's OK Jackie. It'll wait. Have a good trip."

10

I brought up the satellite view of Susan's house on the laptop again and spent some more time studying the track that ran behind it.

The boundaries to the gardens were either hedgerows or fences. The track ran almost exactly east to west, curving a little to follow the road, with the houses running along the south side of it.

Further east along the road, there was a sports field with a parking area, and the track ran along the back edge of the sports field. I ought to be able to find a way onto it from there.

An hour or so later I'd parked at the sports field and pushed through a gap in a hawthorn hedge onto the track.

Feeble sunlight dripped from a sky that promised snow.

I pulled the collar of my reefer close under my chin and began to trudge towards where the houses began.

Barely wide enough for a vehicle, the track was more a muddy bridle path where riders travelled side by side, and over time their horses had cut two parallel paths on either side of a largely un-trodden centre.

I was able to walk along the grassy island rather than paddle through the mixture of horse shit and shallow puddles on either side, but occasionally someone would have ridden alone or crossed over to allow someone to pass, and for a distance, the middle would be as chewed up and sticky as the tracks.

I was glad I'd changed into boots before leaving.

The path ran around the shallow bowl of a valley.

To my right, it was bounded by a three-strand wire fence that hung loosely from greyed timber posts.

Beyond the fence, a field of close-cropped stubble fell away until it faded into a shroud of mist. To my left, low hawthorns pushed through the rusted strands of dilapidated fencing.

As I walked the hawthorns thickened, becoming an unkempt hedgerow around shoulder height dotted with occasional trees, and that in turn became part of a copse that ran alongside the path.

I pictured the image from the laptop in my mind: in a few hundred yards, the copse would peter out and the houses would begin.

I could see the path widening slightly as it reached the houses and curved around the valley, where small buildings began to appear from within the mist. Scratch built stalls and chassis-less horse boxes were tucked into the corners of small paddocks enclosed by split rail fences. Far ahead of me in the distance, a horse almost as grey as the mist raised its head and stretched its neck as it shook itself.

A white terrier about the size of a large cat sprang from within the copse thirty yards ahead of me and began barking as it bowled along the track directly towards me.

It was less than 10 feet away, and I'd planted my feet and teed myself up to kick it away when a voice called from within the trees.

The terrier stopped as if an invisible lead had pulled it to heel.

It looked back the way it had come, then sidled up to me with its stub of a tail flicking uncertainly from side to side.

I stood and allowed it to sniff around my feet for a moment until it followed a more interesting scent across the path and into the weeds.

It cocked its leg against nothing in particular, pissed less than a spoonful, then launched itself nose down off the path into the stubble field after another scent.

As I began to walk again, a woman emerged from the copse ahead of me.

"I'm so sorry about that. He's quite harmless really. He's all noise."

As she spoke she smiled apologetically and tucked a loose strand of dyed auburn hair under the grey fur ushanka she wore.

"No problem." I smiled and walked past her.

"Are you from around here?" she asked abruptly from behind me.

I stopped.

"No, I'm not."

As I turned to face her I scanned the interior of the copse, searching the dark shadows beneath and between the slender beech trees and the straggling clumps of last summer's brambles.

It looked to be empty.

I smiled, looking deeply into her serious-looking blue eyes.

"No, I was just passing through and fancied stretching my legs. How about you? You live around here?"

"Yes, further along. We're just on our way back."

"We?"

"Casper and me. That's Casper."

She motioned at the terrier, who was following another random scent across the stubble.

"He always makes a bee-line for the copse. There are rabbits in there. If I don't go in and get him out he'll stay in there all day until I do."

She made a face as if to say, "What can you do?", then finished weakly:

"It's a bit of a game we play."

I looked at her wryly

"I see." I grinned.

"I'm sorry," she said quietly. "Please don't take the mickey"

"As if I would."

I smiled and winked at her, and began walking towards the houses again. She followed, and within a few paces was walking alongside me.

I smiled at her.

"I've never been out this way before. It's quite beautiful."

A copse of mostly leafless trees clambered up the opposite side of the valley, smaller trees gradually giving way to larger ones as they got nearer to the sky, until at the top, large oaks and elms paraded along the ridge into the distance.

"You're very lucky if this is your view."

"It's not bad, is it. Where do you live?"

I watched Casper, who had stopped dead and begun sniffing the air.

"London." I lied.

"Oh really? Whereabouts?"

"East."

"I see," she said, stuck for something else to say. I knew she wanted to ask "which part", but wasn't sure I wanted to play.

Which I didn't.

I was busy trying to work out where Susan's house was.

We walked on in silence, with her beside me pretending to be absorbed in what the terrier was doing.

Then, some sixth sense or other ran its fingers down my back. I stopped and half turned and looked back along the track.

Its emptiness mocked my instinct.

I carried on walking.

"So what do you do?" she asked.

"I'm an estimator,"

"An estimator? What do you estimate?"

"I estimate liabilities, whether X will become Y, or Z. It's all to do with trading of imports and exports, currency risks and derivatives and so on."

"I see!" she said as if she understood completely.

I'd have been surprised; I was fucked if I did.

"And what about you?" I asked, "What do you do?"

Her voice had a hollow note to it when she answered.

"Oh. Not much really."

"No kids?"

"Yes, two. Boys. Both at university."

"Doing what?"

"John, he's the eldest, is taking Chemistry at Warwick, and Kevin is reading English at Cardiff."

I smiled genially at her and she caught my eye but looked quickly away.

"So what's your name? I'm Joe."

"Jane."

We were now almost at the houses, and while we walked I was busy trying to get a feel for how the back gardens lay.

"It must be a pretty close-knit community here, Jane?" I offered casually.

"Oh, hardly. Everybody keeps themselves to themselves, really. It's not very sociable at all."

"No coffee mornings with the girls then?"

"Oh, God, no. Everybody is much too stuck up to be the first to suggest such a thing."

"How long have you lived here?" I asked, noting that the first house, which we had now reached and were passing, had only a low gate-less palisade fence dividing it from the path.

The garden itself was unkempt, almost an extension of the copse, with mature bushes obscuring most of the house and providing privacy.

"Nearly nine years now," she replied. "Time flies," she added as an afterthought.

"Time flies," I repeated. "We're no sooner here, than we're gone."

The second house had full-height close board fencing that looked to be almost new. At its centre was a solid looking gate of the same well-finished wood with heavy-looking black iron bolts and fittings and a large medieval style ring handle to its latch.

"That sounds a little fatalistic," she said.

"What does?"

"What you just said: "we're no sooner here than we're gone.""

"Oh right, yes. Fatalistic. That's me." I smiled at her.

House three was fenceless, with the garden screened from the path by a neatly trimmed beech hedge set with an arch-topped wrought iron gate.

The hedge and gate had been staked along their bottoms with a line of now rusty chicken wire, no doubt to keep dogs in or foxes out. A sideways glance through the gate as I passed showed a long expanse of lawn broken up in places by islands of rose bushes.

Then we were at the rear of the Booth's place, and already one of my questions had been answered: the same dense beech hedge continued across the rear of the Booth's garden, the only break in it being a high closed-board oaken gate. Its wood was greyed with age but solid looking. After the gate ran more beech hedge, behind which were the outbuildings, their pitched corrugated asbestos roofing just visible over the unkempt hedge.

I was certain now. The photographs could only have been taken from inside the outbuildings. There was no way they could have been taken through the hedge, and shooting them over the gate would never have matched the low angle.

"That's Stephen Booth's house," said Jane, breaking into my thoughts. "You know? Stephen Booth, the MP?"

"Oh, right, yes, Stephen Booth," I replied, feigning sudden recall.

"What's he like?"

"Well..." she paused.

"You don't like him," I stated.

"I didn't say that..." she replied guardedly.

I waited for the inevitable "but".

"...but I don't agree with him."

"Does anyone?" I smiled.

"Yes," she frowned "unfortunately they do. You would have hoped the world could move on, but people like Mr Booth seem to thrive on raking over old bones."

"Patriotism being the last refuge of scoundrels, and all that?"

"Yes, indeed," she replied, smiling ruefully up at me.

"He always looks a bit of a creep to me. Isn't his wife a lot younger than him?"

"Well yes, she is. She is very nice though. Although, she's not often here now."

"No?"

"No, not now. Not since Simon died."

"Simon?"

"Simon was their son."

"And he died?"

"Well yes. It was inevitable, really."

"Why?"

"He was - well - he was brain-damaged. Paraplegic. He was barely alive."

I stared out over the stubble rather than look at her.

Poor Susan.

"How old was he?"

"Seven or eight, I believe."

"When did he die?"

"Oh, it would have been - let me see, nearly four years ago now."

"So his wife doesn't live here with him?"

I could look at her again now.

"No. Apparently, her parents were quite wealthy, and when her father sold his company, some years ago now, he bought a small farm down in Cornwall. Near Bodmin, I think. She spends most of her time down there."

She leant a little closer to me and whispered conspiratorially, "I'm not sure that the marriage is all that, to be honest."

"Really?" I said, with my best politely interested voice. "You mean, he's playing away?"

"Oh God no, not him; he's much too straight-edged for that, but, well - it can't be happy can it? With her down there most of the time, and him in Parliament. And of course, as you said, she's that much younger than him as well."

"Are you still in contact with her?"

"No. We were never really friends as such. But, you see. That's what it's like around here. Everybody keeps themselves to themselves."

I nudged her gently with my elbow and grinned at her "You know, you're a dreadful gossip when you get going, Jane."

She put her gloved hand to her mouth and laughed like she'd just remembered how to.

"Well, perhaps I am." She took the hand from her mouth and touched my arm. "It's your fault though. You're the first human being I've spoken to in the last 48 hours."

She looked suddenly shy. "I'm so sorry." She tucked her hand into the pocket of her jacket.

"For what?"

We had stopped outside her gate. She stared back along the path. "Oh, for prattling on."

I winked at her and smiled. "Take no notice of me, Jane," I touched the back of her waist briefly: "I was only pulling your leg. It's been a pleasure."

She looked at me for a moment, then made great play of looking past me and calling Casper to her, opening the gate for him and shooing him into the garden.

She pulled the gate closed behind him.

"Right, well, perhaps we'll bump into each other again, Jane," I said.

"Yes. If you like walks, there are some beautiful ones around here, if you're passing."

"Perhaps if you let me have your phone number, we can share one when I am."

Casper began barking from behind the gate.

"Yes, why not. That would be nice – but, I'm afraid I don't know my mobile number though - " she paused " -can we go inside for a moment? Casper won't be quiet if I stay out here now he's in."

She pushed open the gate and I followed her into the garden. Casper ran away from us across a large expanse of open lawn towards the house, and she led the way after him.

I followed, trying to see what I could of the rear of the Booth's house.

Which wasn't much.

Most of it was obscured by a high beech hedge that ran the length of the gardens and disappeared between the two houses. Only the very top of the brick and flint dormers of the house with their glossed black soffit boards showed above it.

Beneath them, the top foot or so of Georgian framed windows were just visible. An alarm box blinked slowly above the window closest to me.

Above that, almost out of sight in the apex of the roof's bargeboard was the blunt nose of an all-weather camera, angled to cover the garden.

I followed Jane onto aged algae stained granite flagstones, under a solidly built pergola gripped by vines that had been neatly cropped back ready for the new year's growth.

Once through the pergola lay a plain paved patio area laid with the more granite flagstones. Jane chose a key from a small bunch she took from her pocket. She turned to me with the key in the door.

"Bear with me, please Joe, I'll have to get to the alarm before you come in."

I watched her as she leaned against the wall and took off the first of the hiking boots she wore. She felt me looking at her and glanced over her shoulder, then away, fumbling with the laces of the second until slipped from her foot onto the granite slab.

She unlocked the door and walked into the depths of the house. A moment or two later she returned and smiled at me.

"Would you like a coffee?"

I checked my watch. "I'd love to Jane, but it will have to be a quick one - I've really got to get going. But let me have your number, eh? We'll do that walk when I'm back this way."

"Yes, of course." She smiled thinly. "I'll get my phone. Come in, but please Joe, do take your boots off?"

I sat on the step and unlaced my boots and left them outside, and while coffee was being made we swapped numbers.

"Need to make a quick call, Jane," I said, and I leant back against the worktop and dialled my own number.

"It's not working." I stared at the phone. "The signals dropped right out."

"Oh, yes, it can be tricky here. Would you like to try out the front? It's sometimes a little better there."

I walked through into the front hall, staring at the phone as I went. She followed me, leaning against the door to the kitchen.

"Nope. Nothing. Would you mind if I tried upstairs Jane? That sometimes does it."

"Of course, help yourself."

She answered without moving. I knew if I was too long she'd get her courage up and follow me. I didn't intend to give her time.

I stepped upstairs two at a time and went into the bedroom at the rear of the house. As I'd hoped, the broad windows gave an unrestricted view over most of the Booths back garden.

The outbuildings had probably once been stables.

They were bluff and basic, cheaply built of unevenly mortared flettons. Green paint peeled from a steel-framed casement window that was set into the end facing the house.

I looked along the base of the building. Almost at the corner of the wall, low down and less than a foot from the ground was a double airbrick. Its grating had been broken through.

Pleased that I'd found out where the photographs had been taken from, I flicked my phone onto camera.

I was about to take a picture of the building when a dark tousled head appeared momentarily above the gate at the end of the Booth's garden. A second later it appeared again, and this time a pair of black-gloved hands appeared on top of the gate on either side of it.

The face hung there while its owner studied the Booth's back garden.

Well, well.

Phillipa Phapetis.

I returned downstairs, where Jane was sitting at a scrubbed pine table with two coffee cups and a plate of biscuits laid on it.

"No luck," I announced. "Sorry Jane, but I'm going to have to skip coffee and get somewhere I can make this call from."

"Oh, I am sorry."She looked crestfallen."Well, we have each other's numbers anyway." She added hopefully.

"Yup. Don't worry, I'll give you a ring next week. I'm out here again soon, and we'll line up our walk for then, eh?"

I walked to the door past Jasper, who stood up and watched me expectantly. Jane picked him up and carried him out to the hall and shut the door on him.

I opened the back door, sat down on the step and began putting my boots back on, wrapping the laces quickly around them and tying them in untidy bows.

"It's been lovely meeting you Jane." I stood up on the step and smiled. "I'm sorry, but I better get off. I shall, as they say... be in touch."

I held her shoulders and kissed her on the cheek, close enough to her mouth for our lips to touch. I felt her tremble slightly as she held the kiss for just too long. I pulled away. "I'll see myself out. You stay in the warm. Speak to you soon."

I walked as quickly as I could down the garden to the back gate, opened its latch silently and stepped out onto the path.

11

Phillipa Phapetis looked like she was doing press-ups on the mud of the path, trying to keep her clothes out of the muck while she looked under the Booth's gate.

I pulled Jane's gate shut with a bang, and she stared up at me as if she'd seen a ghost. Before she could say anything I made my eyes wide and put my finger to my lips. She nodded in agreement.

I pointed back down the track towards the car park and began walking while she got awkwardly to her feet.

She caught me up and fell into step beside me.

"What are you doing here, Danny?" she hissed at me.

"I'm working, Phillipa. What do you think I'm doing? You think I wade through wet horse shit for the crack?"

"Fuck you and your wet horse shit, look at me! At least you're wearing boots - I'm in trainers!"

I glanced down at the damp darkened legs of her jeans and laughed. "Nice one."

"Danny -" she sounded suddenly serious "- you know, you being here is giving me one of my hunches?"

"You get hunches?" I looked down at her, and she grinned at me mischievously from under the mop of hair. "Lots."

She stroked her hair away from her face and I saw her eyes in proper light for the first time. They really were sea green, almost turquoise.

"Shall we find somewhere warmer to talk?"

"OK, yes," she said, still looking at me and nearly slipping over. I caught her under the arm.

"Whoops," she said, not looking at me anymore.

I let my hand fall from her arm and slipped it into the pocket of my reefer.

We'd walked a hundred yards before either of us spoke again.

"I didn't get a chance to thank you, Danny."

"For what?"

"For what you did at the award ceremony."

I shrugged. "The blokes a fucking idiot. Who is he, anyway?"

"His names Toby Cash. He works for Associated."

"What was it all about?"

She walked in silence, but I didn't get the impression she was cooking up a story. Rather, she was working out whether she wanted to talk about it at all.

We were almost back to the sports field before she spoke.

"I may as well tell you everything. It makes no difference now. It involves Stephen Booth."

"Stephen Booth the MP."

"Yes."

"Stephen Booth, who lives in that house you were trying to break into?"

"Yes. No. I wasn't trying to break into it. How do you know he lives there?"

"Because. And think yourself lucky you didn't get over the gate."

"Why?"

"Because it's camere'd up. You'd have been filmed. Anyway, you were saying...?"

"How do you know it's got cameras?"

"Trust me, it's got cameras. So what happened?"

She took a deep breath. "Well, it began when I was sent some details on a company by someone. I did the homework on it and it all checked out. There were two directors: Susan Booth, Stephen Booth's wife, and another man, Gavin Durrant. Toby Cash is Stephen Booth's nephew by the way."

"I got they were related. Go on."

"Well. The company was weird. It never bought or sold anything, and yet every week it would receive set amounts from separate sources. And every year, those amounts would increase, but always add up to being just under the VAT threshold. When the VAT threshold changed, so the amount received each week went up, and the total amount received over the year changed. But the company never invoiced anybody."

I let her into the passenger seat of the X3 then climbed in the other side and started the engine to warm us through.

"Who did it pay out to?"

"Tradesmen. Always the same ones. There were nine of them."

"What sort of tradesmen?"

"There's a plumber, an electrician, a car mechanic, two gardeners, and the rest are general trades, painters, decorators, odd job men, all one-man bands."

"How were they paid? Cash? Transfer?"

"Transfer." She sniffed. "I think I might be catching a cold. So anyway, a couple of months after that, the person got in touch again. This time he told me he'd heard that Stephen Booth was buying a house in France under an assumed name."

She looked up at me. "Of course, by now I was getting a little wary of what he told me, because although it would check out, it hadn't ever been anything concrete I could use, and also, it seemed obvious to me it was some kind of personal vendetta he was running against Booth."

She raised a finger as if to stop me from speaking. It was small but perfectly proportioned, if just a little chubby, and tipped with a short unpainted nail like a sliver of mother of pearl

"Now that in itself is not unusual. Lots of stories come from those kinds of sources. In fact, most of them. So I wasn't going to dismiss it. But I told him, I wanted more than just tittle-tattle before I would do anything."

"What's your contact's name?"

"He tells me his name is Timothy. I don't know his second name."

"Could Timothy be his second name?"

"It could be. I really don't know." She looked up at me again. "I've always assumed it's a pseudonym. Anyway, I didn't hear anything for, I don't know, perhaps a month. Then he got back in touch and said he had everything that I needed now. Copies of the contracts; details of the property; a photograph of Booth leaving the Notaire that administered the sale, plus a signed declaration by the Notaire's secretary that she had been at the sale and witnessed Booth buying the house."

"OK. But why was that a big deal? Booth is allowed to buy a house in France, no?"

"Not under a false name, and only then if he can legitimately afford it. And he couldn't. The house cost a small fortune, and he paid cash. No mortgage. And when you looked at his declared earnings and outside interests and expenses, there was absolutely no way he should have had enough cash available."

"The money from the business account?"

"That was my first thought as well. There would have been enough. But obviously, I couldn't prove it, and I couldn't find any connection between Booth and the company, so it was a complete dead end."

I looked into her eyes.

The wide black pools inside the sea-green matched the deep almost black brown of her tousled fringe. A tiny blush of rose came to her cheeks. She took a sigh of a deep breath, then carried on.

"But. Regardless of that. I thought-" she raised the perfect little finger again. "-it's enough that he buys under an assumed name and cannot on paper account for having that kind of money. It must be worth running with, even if it only acts as a flush."

"A flush?"

"It flushed other people out. You know. There was the company, that was getting cash from who knows where, and here was Booth, buying a house that he couldn't afford, in a name that wasn't his. Well, perhaps it would flush other interested parties out, with more information. Or make someone nervous. It had to be worth a go."

"If you could prove it was Booth buying the house under a false name."

"Exactly, Danny. And that was the difficulty. Ultimately, it came down to this one woman, the Notaire's secretary, who had sworn that he had, and had supplied the document. Well, OK, that was enough for a first hit. But to really get him, I needed to be able to prove that Booth was not only living there, but that he paid the bills there, and then, together with the paperwork and the proof from the Notaire's secretary, I had pretty much him.

"So what did you do?"

She shook her head.

"Well. That's where it started to go wrong. Richard is, really, well, as you saw for yourself, he's not well. Let's be honest, slowly but surely, he's dying. We have never had that much income from advertising or anything, and it's always been uphill. A lot of the time we survive on small donations. But as he became more and more ill, so the stress of everything got to him, and he functioned less and less, and I ended up pretty much doing his job as well. Then, he couldn't afford a secretary anymore and had to let her go. Then she took him to a tribunal for redundancy."

She laid her hand on my arm.

"Don't get me wrong, Danny. I don't blame her. She was entitled to the money. But, he simply didn't have it. So, he had to sell his house, for an absolute pittance, and moved into those digs you took us to, and she was paid off. I even got some of the money he'd owed me, which, by that time, well, I was behind with my rent and things. But, you know, it was impossible for him. It was all too much, the whole thing, everything on top of the illness. It's completely broken him. He simply sits there most of the time now. Sometimes, he'll do nothing for days on end.

"Why have you stayed, babe? You have other people you could work for, don't you? Natalie said you were getting work from, what was it, the Guardian? Other places?"

She chewed at her bottom lip and looked away from me. I saw her eyes fill with tears.

"Hey come on Phillipa. Come on." I put my hand over hers where it lay in her lap. She didn't move for almost a minute, then I felt her fingers close around mine.

"I stay because I owe him. Because he helped me, believed in me. Gave me my break, and gave me chances. Even if I messed things up, and I did, he always said "a mistake is only a lesson" and kept me on, kept helping me, kept showing me things. Teaching me. Because I love him, for what he does. What he has always tried to do."

She wiped her face with the heel of her free hand. She half-turned to me, looking somewhere over my shoulder as she spoke.

"It would have been so easy for him to have become just another hack. To take sides. Become a devious shill for one party or another, but he never has. He has always been about showing them all up for exactly what they are without fear or favour. And because of it, he has spent his whole life being shot by all sides when he could so easily have made a small fortune on the back of his reputation.

But he's never, ever taken the easy way out and compromised on his principles. He's always bitten every hand that could feed him.

"Rather than be fed."

"Yes. Yes, rather than be fed. But there used to be enough. Usually. There are still people who admire what he stands for."

"Admiration doesn't pay the bills."

"No. And you know, with the internet, there's very little advertising anymore these days. We had a few regulars, but nothing big. Hardly enough to cover costs, really. But breaking Booth would have given us so much more publicity.

Richard isn't in the least money-minded, but it would have taken the weight off his mind. I know he's dying and I know that Auspex will die with him, but I just wanted to help, give him a last - I don't know - maybe a feeling that it hadn't all just been a waste of time, a waste of his life. A final, undeniable victory to go out on.

So I took the story to him, and I said, we can do it in two stages. Well, to be honest, we had to. I couldn't afford to go to France and spend I don't know, a week, perhaps a fortnight checking everything out. There was no money to pay me to go. As it was, I would have to pay my own fares and lodgings. But that didn't matter. All I could see was that we just needed to break this story, and we could turn the corner.

So I suggested we ran it in two parts. We would go with what we had about Booth having bought the house in a first story, and I would go to France on the back of what we earned from the interest shown in that, while Richard could sell advertising for the second instalment."

"And what happened?"

"He said no."

"Why?"

"Because he knows his job, and I don't."

"Sounds to me like you had the right idea."

She shook her head.

"No. Anyway. He went into one of his bad phases. He drinks. Gets stoned. It stops the pain, but of course, it means that he simply disappears for days on end."

"So what happened?"

"I ran the story."

"And?"

"And it worked."

She looked up at me. The tip of her nose was pink from crying.

"We sold nearly three times what we would normally. I had to get re-runs printed, and I did a piece for the Mirror and another for the Guardian so that I could afford to get to France because I knew, I had to get to France and close the story properly before the dailies sent people over. If I didn't, we would just be left with second prize and absolutely nothing to show for it."

"What did Richard say?"

"Not very much. I'm sure that he was angry, but he didn't show it. Not to me anyway. He was just - sad. He withdrew, completely, and wouldn't speak to me. That made it even worse, in a way."

"And you went to France?"

"Yes, I went to France. I took photographs of Booth at the house, in the garden. I'm a dreadful photographer but I couldn't afford to hire anybody. And I went to the Marie and asked if Booth was paying the taxes on the house and they said yes.

I went to the Notaire's and asked if the woman, the secretary, had worked there and they said yes, but she had left. It was all exactly as Timothy had said. I had contacted her, the Notaire's secretary, before I went and she had agreed to meet me. She didn't speak English but I speak good enough French, and I would tape her anyway and then have what she told me translated.

I went to the meeting and she told me that she wouldn't allow any photographs, but that isn't unusual, and it would only have looked strange anyway, she was so obviously disguising herself, wearing dark glasses, a headscarf. But it didn't matter anyway. I had everything I needed then, so I came home."

"And?"

"And I got back and Booth had taken out an injunction and begun a case for libel."

"That's a bit quick?"

"An injunction for libel is easy when you have access to QCs and satisfy them that you have grounds."

"And did he have grounds?"

Her eyes filled with tears again.

She nodded. "It would seem so. He denies having bought the house. He denies having been at the Notaire's and claims to have been in Germany on a private matter when the deal was signed. He states that he can corroborate his story with witnesses."

"But hold on. He is living at the house and paying the bills."

"But on its own, that doesn't matter Danny. It's not a crime to live in the house and pay the bills."

"But what about the woman, the Notaire's secretary, her testimony and the paperwork. Surely that would be enough to prove the case was real or at least that it wasn't - what's the word - frivolous? "

"Perhaps, if we were in court, it would, but we're not. Richard has no money to go to court. He has no energy and he has no will to go on, and it's my fault. I did it. He knew it was wrong to go to press before having the testimony. He sensed that Booth would pull a stunt like this. He told me, no, but I thought I knew best and I did it anyway, and out of my utter stupidity and pigheadedness I have ended up costing him everything."

"That's not being fair on yourself though, is it? You had everything you'd need under normal circumstances, and you were trying to do your best for both Auspex and Richard, and for whatever reasons, it's Richard who has kind of taken his eye off the ball. If you hadn't been alone, you could have got stage two wrapped up before breaking stage one.

And anyway, Booth hasn't proved what you wrote was wrong or libellous, let alone proved himself innocent. All he's done is used his money and his bullshit QCs to buy his way out of the situation."

She stared at our hands in her lap.

"It boils down to the same thing, though. Auspex is still ruined, and Booth has won."

"Perhaps." I squeezed her hand. "Or perhaps we can find something that trumps him, mm?"

"No Danny. Look, I'll admit it, I know what you do. Natalie contacted me and said I should speak to you. I told her, I can't afford to pay you. I have no money. Richard has no money."

"Natalie contacted you? What did she say?"

"You didn't know?"

"No."

"She contacted me last week, to see how Richard was. She gave me your number and said I should ring you. That perhaps you could help. But I never got around to calling you."

"Perhaps she's right, and I can help."

"We have no money, Dan. Do you understand? I had to buy petrol with the rent for my flat to even get here today."

"Then why did you come?"

"Desperation. I thought perhaps if someone was there, I could speak to them.

"Booth?"

"No. Not Booth. His wife. Someone. Anyone. I have no idea, really, and God alone knows what I'd speak to them about anyway." She sniffed. "It was a stupid idea. I'm not really thinking straight at the moment."

I thought about the cash I had on me, maybe a hundred, but perhaps it wasn't the right time to hurt her pride by offering her money. That could wait a few days. Let her get some balance back.

"Phillipa. I must go, babe. I have things to do. You've still got my number?"

She nodded. "Yes. I kept it."

"OK. Then text me so I have yours, and I'll call you if I dig anything up you can use, yeah?"

"Danny, thank you, but you do understand what I've just told you, about us having no money?"

"Yes, I know. You can't pay me. But text me your number anyway. Listen -" I lifted her chin so she had to look at me. "I will do a deal with you. You ask if you need me to do anything, and I'll tell you whether I can do it, OK? And I'll tell you what it will cost you. And whatever it costs you, you can owe me. OK?"

She looked as if she would argue.

"No buts, Phillipa. Natalie wouldn't have given you my number if she didn't want me to help."

She nodded.

"I see. Yes. Thank you, Danny."

I smiled at her. "Well, I haven't done anything yet Phillipa."

"Perhaps you have, without realising it. Thank you for letting me talk, and allowing me to clear things out like that. I'm sorry that I got emotional. That wasn't fair."

I winked at her. "I'll tack it on the bill. Now, go home and get a ton of Vitamin C inside you and kick the shit out that cold before it starts."

She opened the door and climbed down, then stood looking at me a moment. The breeze pushed at the thick mop of her hair.

The sea-green eyes looked up at me.

"Take care, Danny."

"And you, babe."

She closed the door, and I pulled away. I got to the main road, drove a hundred yards or so down and pulled over. I watched her in the rearview mirror as she crossed the road and got into a scruffy little red Toyota. I flicked into drive and pulled away.

Sir Galahad, indeed...

I was hardly through the door an hour later when my phone rang. It was Phillipa, and she sounded stressed.

"I had a text message from Timothy earlier. Firstly, he tells me that he has something really important for me, and could he bring it over to me. I said yes, but it reminded me. He told me a week or so ago that he thinks he is being followed, and that his house is being watched by someone."

"Watched by who?"

"He doesn't know. He told me that different cars have been parking across the street from him. As if someone was taking it in turns to watch him."

"Old Bill?"

"Sorry?"

"Do they look like police?"

"No. I asked him that, and he said that they look too nasty to be police."

I took that with a pinch of salt. Timothy was obviously jumpy, and everyone looks like a thug when someone's got the wind-up.

"Fair enough. How can I help you with it?"

"Well, I wondered, perhaps if you could go over there, and then when he comes across to see me later on, you could see if he gets followed? I know, it's a lot to ask, but..."

"It's OK, Phillipa. I can do that." I pulled a pad of sticky notes from beside the laptop. "Where does he live?"

"Ready?"

"Yep, fire away."

"55 Morninton Road, Greenford."

I got as far as writing 55, then stopped.

"Say that again?"

"M-o-r-n-i-n-t-o-n Road, Greenford. Number fifty-five. The postcode is UB6 9HN."

I stared at the sticky note.

"Wait a mo."

I pulled the folder that Malcolm had given me from the drawer and took out the photographs. The headshot of Susan and Durrant was top of the pile. I turned it over and picked up the phone again.

"OK, Phillipa. 55, Morninton Road, UB6 9HN?"

"Yes."

"Have you got a phone number for this contact of yours?"

There was a pause, and I knew she was thinking about how much information she wanted to give me.

"Phillipa, if you want me to help you, you have to help me."

"Yes. I know. Wait." I heard her move some papers. "OK. I've got two mobile numbers. Do you want them both?"

"Yes, fire away."

I wrote them down.

The second one she gave me matched the mobile number that Malcolm had given me.

"OK. Do you know what car Timothy drives?"

"Oh God, that was stupid of me. I'm sorry Danny, I should have asked him. I'll find out for you and text you it with the registration."

"No, don't worry about that now. You said he was called Timothy. I bet you won't tell me his real name, will you?"

"I swore that I wouldn't."

I let it go quiet on purpose.

"No. I swore that I wouldn't Danny. He is already frightened, and I need to be able to look him in the eye and deny it if he asks me if I've told anyone. People must trust you implicitly in this line of work."

I turned over the photograph and stared at Susan and Gavin Durrant.

"Are you still there, Danny?"

"Yes, babe. What time did he say he would be over to you?"

"Seven o'clock tonight."

I checked my watch. It was just gone five.

"And he has your address?"

"Yes. I sent it to him before I rang you."

"Did you ever actually meet up with him? I mean, you know what he looks like?"

"Yes. Why?"

"I just wondered. Leave it with me, babe."

"Thank you so much, Danny."

"No worries."

I killed the call and went back to staring at the photograph.

It was pretty obvious that Timothy was Gavin Durrant, using a false name to cover himself.

Or rather, it had been. Even if he hadn't been dead, he was going to struggle to text anybody with fingers like his.

I opened my phone, took a snap of the picture of Susan and Durrant and cropped the shot to include only Durrant.

I sent it to Phillipa.

A minute later, I had my answer.

The message said simply: "Where did you get that?"

I rang her. She answered.

"Where did you get it from?"

"Never mind that. I'm right in assuming that it's Timothy, yes?

"Yes."

"When did you get the message from him?"

"Not long after we left each other earlier today. Why?"

"And what did it say?"

"He asked to meet with me. He said he had something else for me, something very important, but that he was scared about his house being watched, so he would come over to me."

"And you gave him your address."

"Yes."

"Are you there now, Phillipa?"

"Yes. I've just got home."

"Where is home?"

"Fulham."

"OK. I'm coming over now. Text me your address when you hang up. Lock every door, and shut every window. Pack a bag for a few days. Bring your passport, and bring every last thing you have on Booth with you."

"Why?"

"I'll explain everything when I pick you up. I'll start out now. Lock the place up, then send me your address, then get packed. I'll be there as soon as I can."

"I'm sorry, Danny. But I have other things I -"

"Just do it Phillipa, and don't answer the door to anybody, even if it's Plod with all their blue lights flashing. The man you have been getting your info from couldn't have sent you a text today if he tried."

"What do you mean?"

"I've seen your contact, Timothy."

"What? Where did you see him?"

"At his house."

"I don't understand. Why were you at his house? How did you know where he lived?"

"It's not important now, Phillipa. What matters is he'd had his fingers broken and his throat cut, and if my hunch is right, the same people who topped him are going to rock up at your place at seven. So just humour me Phillipa, and do as I've asked. Send me the address. I'll be there as soon as I can."

Her message came through as I hit the M4. Ringmer Avenue. I was there just after half six.

She let me in, her eyes filled with un-asked questions. A little crimson hardshell suitcase was parked in the hallway, along with a nylon holdall and her laptop case.

"Have you got another computer?"

"Yes, my main one through there, in the living room."

"Go and disconnect it and bring it out."

"Where are we going?" The sea-green eyes were wide and frightened

"My place for tonight."

"What about Richard?"

"We'll talk about that later. You need to disappear until we get to the bottom of what you're on to."

"I told you. It's about the house. The company."

"Phillipa, I don't know whose bucket of shit you've kicked over, but when people start getting topped, it's odds on that it's not just some wanker of an MP dodging declaring a house in France. Now go and get the computer, and I'll take this lot out."

I picked up the suitcase and the holdall and took them out to the car. The back opened and I slid them inside, and I watched as Phillipa walked down the path towards me with her computer in her arms, concentrating on not tripping over anything.

I guess that's why neither of us noticed the woman approaching, but suddenly she was there on the footpath.

Phillipa stopped dead at the garden gate.

"Phil! Are you moving out?"

She was tall, maybe only an inch or two under my height. Straight shoulder-length blond hair framed a face that had too much jaw to be pretty, and from the set of her mouth, it looked like she knew it.

"And who's this then?"

She tilted her face down as she looked at me, just so I'd see her eyes looking up at me. Like her jaw, they were a bit too big.

They also showed too much white, but she must have practised whole evenings on how to trap cock with them.

"Hi. I'm Joe. I'm Phil's boyfriend."

"Phil! You didn't say you had a boyfriend! When was that?"

"Oh, we've known each other a while. No need to show off about it is there." I smiled sweetly at her.

"Oh, I think I would, Joe. So where's he taking you?" " She grinned at Phillipa, and her hand slid around my bicep and squeezed. Phillipa stared sadly at us from over the case of the PC.

"Bring it to me, babe," I stepped forward so her hand left my arm, and Phillipa passed me the computer. "We're going away for a few days, going down to my place in Brighton, aren't we Phil."

"Yes," whispered Phillipa.

I turned to put the computer in the car and looked directly into the too-big eyes. They stared back at me like we ought to share a secret.

"We'll be back next week." I winked at her and put the computer on its side in the car and shut the lid.

"Ooh, you are a lucky girl, Phil."

"Is that everything, Phil?" I asked her.

"Um, no, wait, my bag and things." She turned and went back inside the house.

Before she'd reached the door, the hand was back on my sleeve.

"I'm Karen, by the way. I have the flat upstairs from Phil."

"Yeah, she told me about you."

The Bambi on Heat look left her eyes for a moment as suspicion flickered across them, then it was back.

"Well, I can be a bit loud sometimes."

She bit her bottom lip, just like she ought to be going, and sure enough, she let go of my arm and walked to the gate. She turned around as Phillipa came out of the front door with her arms full of handbag and laptop case.

"Drop in if your passing, Joe. We're all friends here." She walked slowly into the house and closed the front door.

I took the laptop from Phillipa and held the passenger door open for her.

"She seems nice," I said as she climbed into the seat.

She pulled the bag onto her lap and I shut the door on her.

I started the engine and pulled out.

"Before I forget Phil, give me your phone."

"What? Why?"

"Don't ask questions, babe, just give me the phone."

She rummaged in the handbag and handed me the phone. I prised the back cover off, shook the battery out and handed it back to her.

She stared at it glumly for a moment pushed it into the handbag and stared out of the side window.

I pulled out onto the Palace Road.

"What's the matter?"

"Nothing." She spoke quietly without looking at me.

"OK, then tell me everything you know about Timothy. Every little detail you can think of. Start right at the beginning, and let's work our way through it together."

She stared ahead of her. I wasn't sure if she was thinking or sulking about the phone, but I let her get on with it while I fought the traffic.

Eventually, she spoke.

"I don't mind about the phone, but can you not call me Phil, please. She only does it because she knows I hate it."

"She's not your favourite, is she?"

"She's -." She thought about it, then decided to say nothing.

"Let me help you. She's a dim-lit supercilious fuck monster who's tried to blag everyone you ever brought home?"

She said nothing.

"Admit it. I'm warm, aren't I?"

She shrugged.

"Nobody said opposites had to attract. What should I call you? Phillipa?"

"It's my name."

"But you don't like it."

"Not much."

"Well, I'll think of a cute nickname to call you, and you can tell me if you like it."

"I can't wait."

"How about Frilly?"

She looked away from the window, scowling at me. "Don't you dare. Just call me Phillipa. It's fine."

"OK, Phillipa it is."

"Or I could call you Pip because I get on your pip?" I grinned at her.

She let out a big sigh.

"You don't. Honestly. I'm just, completely, stressed out."

"I know. It's OK, babe."

We drove in silence for a few minutes, then she made a big deal of rearranging the bag on her lap

"Pip is nice."

I smiled at her.

"Pip it is then. Why don't you start at the beginning and we'll go over it all together."

She took a long breath in and nodded.

"OK. As I told you earlier. I got an email about the companies."

"You never said it was an email, but go on. Just talk, babe, I'm listening." I scanned the road in the rearview mirror, trying to make a mental note of which vehicles were behind us.

"OK, I got the email from Timothy."

"Gavin Durrant."

"What?"

"Gavin Durrant was Timothy's real name."

"His real name is Dean Thompson."

"His real name was Gavin Durrant. He's on the Electoral Roll at 55, Morninton Road. There's no such person as Dean Thompson."

"Gavin Durrant is one of the directors of Duct Four. He lives in Barnet. I checked. Dean Thompson lives at 55 Morninton Road. I checked."

"When?"

"When he first contacted me. I checked the Electoral Roll."

"So, two or three months ago."

"It's longer ago than that. More like six months."

"I don't understand. I thought you said he sent you the accounts a couple of months ago?"

"I did. But they weren't the first time he'd been in contact. Months before that, he offered to send me some photographs of Stephen Booth's wife with a man, saying she was having an affair, but that kind of thing isn't our line so I passed on them."

It was my turn to go quiet for a minute.

"Did you recommend that he took them somewhere else?"

"Yes. I recommended that he send them to Colin Luscombe, from the Mail."

"OK." I couldn't think of anything else to say.

"So, she continued. "Timothy, Dean Thompson, Gavin Durrant, or whoever he was, contacted me, and we met -"

"Where?"

"In Ealing. On the Common, and -"

"So you met him how many times?"

"Only the once."

"So you never went to his house?"

"No. But as I told you, I did the usual, checked his address and so on, obviously, and that it all tied in. But I didn't go there. Anyway. He gave me to believe he could get me some really good stuff on Booth. I said that I was interested, and a few days later his email about the accounts arrived. So, I followed it up, and it all checked out."

"How much did you pay him?"

"Nothing. He said it was personal, and he'd be happy if it dropped Booth in it."

"Did he say why it was personal?"

"No. I asked him, obviously, just in case he let out something interesting, but he just said that the reasons weren't important, he wanted to drop Booth in it. I didn't push it. You'd be surprised how many leaks, even the biggest political ones, boil down to petty personal spite one way or another."

"And you're 100% sure that it was the same Dean Thompson from the photographs that you met?"

"Yes."

"How old are the accounts he sent you?"

"The ones he sent me were from the year before last. The rest I got myself from Companies House."

"The company is still running?"

"Yes."

"What's it called again?"

"Duct Four Limited."

"And Gavin Durrant is a director."

"Yes."

"And you said that you think Gavin Durrant is a false I.D. of Stephen Booths?"

"Yes. Well. I thought."

" What made you think it?"

"Because Thompson said it was, and it makes sense."

"In what way?"

"Because Duct Four would enable Booth to obtain money from somewhere without having to declare it, and using a false name on the company means that it can never be traced back to him."

I turned onto the A4 and headed into town. I took it slowly on the slip road, watching the mirror. Only two other cars pulled out after us heading east. If one of them was following us, when I changed tack and headed west in a few minutes, it was going to make it hard for them to not show their hand. "Tell me about France and the house. How did you find out about it?"

"He emailed me about it."

"How did he know it had happened?"

"I didn't ask. Why would I?"

"I would have, but that's me."

"I know what you mean, but when you're on to something in our field, you're not interested in getting bogged down in the how or why of things, and you have to be careful not to ask too many questions, or you run the risk of scaring your source away. So all I asked for was the proof."

"And he did what?"

"He got me the proof. Or what I thought was the proof."

"So he got you what? copies of documents?"

"Yes, copies of documents, a copy of the Compromise, a picture of Booth dated the day of the contract that proved he was there, and the name and testimony of the secretary to the Notaire at the time the contract was signed."

"What's a Compromise?"

"A Compromise is a pre-contract contract. When you buy a house in France, you sign the Compromise and that fixes the price and all the details of the property between the buyer and seller."

"But it's not a contract of sale?"

"It's part of the contract. You would never sign a Compromise unless you intended to buy the property, and you can't finalise without a Compromise. What the Notaire does is formalise the sale based on the Compromise. They will check to see that the sale is legal, that the land is the right size and so on, so the Compromise is the whole basis of the sale. Then, there is the fact that the Compromise was months old, and Booth was actually living in the property, which means the sale must have been completed."

"So on the face of it, you had it all, Grade A Undeniable?"

"Yes. Except for one thing, of course. The documents were all signed in the name of Gavin Durrant, not Stephen Booth."

"And if Booth signed for the house as Gavin Durrant, you had him bang to rights on fraud, right?"

"It's not that simple. The false name is one thing, but leave that aside, and imagine he had not used it, and instead signed everything as Stephen Booth. He would still not have done anything openly fraudulent in the UK, and if he got called on it, it would be one of those cases where all he would lose was face because of his anti-European reputation.

He would have done absolutely nothing wrong in France. In France, even with the false name, if I could prove that it was him that signed as Gavin Durrant, all he would have done, or could claim he had done, is put the property in someone else's name, which is allowed in France under certain circumstances.

Not the circumstances that the documents allude to, perhaps, but that's by the by if he has an alibi and denies signing as Gavin Durrant. But, the more important point is how he paid for the house. Where did he physically get the money from?"

"How much was it?"

"370,000€."

"Must be some place."

"It is. It's very beautiful."

"So, about what, six or seven years MP salary?"

"He has other earnings, outside of Parliament, of course, directorships and so on, but even assuming that he had the money, he didn't move that amount to France."

"How do you know?"

"Well, I don't, exactly, but he can't have done. If he did, he would have had to register it with Parliament. They have to if a property value is more than a year's parliamentary salary."

"I can see why he took out the injunction. You kind of had him checkmate."

"Exactly. The only way he could get out of it was by flat denial, and daring us to meet him in court to prove he was lying. Whether we could or not is beside the point. We simply couldn't afford the legal costs, and that was my fault. I took it for granted that we would be able to scrape together enough money, but it turns out we were even worse off than I imagined."

"Which Richard knew, but didn't tell you, and if he had, you might well have just had to give up the story to someone else, but then you wouldn't have made Auspex money and helped Richard go out with a bang. Right?"

She was silent for a moment, then she said quietly "I know you're right, but it doesn't make me feel any better."

"Well, it should. You did your best, with the best of intentions."

"I still messed up, and Auspex is still finished."

"Only half right. Yes, you messed up, but Auspex is only finished if we let Booth win. He's acting out of fear, and as you say, he could bat away your accusations and front it out. But he's not doing that. That means that he's afraid of something, so what we need to do is find out what it is that's scaring him."

I could feel her looking at me, but she didn't speak.

"What exactly does his affidavit for the injunction say? Have you got a copy with you?"

"No. I don't have a copy. It's Richards, not mine. I've only read it once, and then only quickly. Danny, you know, what I told you earlier was the truth. I can't afford to pay you. Auspex is broke and I'm broke."

"And you told me that Natalie told you to ring me. That means your credit is good."

"I don't have any credit. I know Natalie, but only vaguely. I expect she knows me as much as I know her, just from her work."

"Phillipa, I've known Natalie since she was seventeen. She's her father's daughter and she's a closed book, but I probably know her as well as anybody. Have you ever thought, that she might genuinely actually admire you as a journalist, and want to help you?"

She spoke quietly. "No."

I glanced across at her.

She looked ready to cry.

"Let's go back to Booth's Affidavit. Can you remember any of what it said? Not the legal bullshit, but in terms of what he says you got wrong?"

"Well. Pretty much as you'd expect. He denies being at the signing, he has witnesses and testimony that he couldn't have been, and he's denied signing the documents."

"Denied signing the documents, or denied signing the documents as Gavin Durrant."

"Denied signing the documents. I think. I'm not sure now. Sorry."

"But you have photographic evidence and testimony that he was there."

She blew between her lips.

"Yes. For what it's worth."

"And what about the Notaire? Did you try and contact him?"

"The Notaire died a few months after the sale."

"Really?"

"According to the secretary, he had been ill for a long time. There was nothing suspicious."

"Sure?"

"Yes. I suppose so."

"And where is the Notaire's secretary now?"

I hung a left up towards Shepherds Bush.

"Still in France."

"Sure?"

"I assume so. She lived there."

"Have you spoken to her recently?"

"Just that time I told you about, after we'd run the first half of the story."

"Could you contact her if you needed to?"

"I expect so. I still have her details. Why?"

"I'm just asking. Did you go to the Notaire's and check up on her?"

"Yes. She had left the company, but I knew that. She left not long after the Notaire died."

"But like, you walked in there and said "Does Missus Smith still work here?", and they said "no, she left" - or what?"

"Exactly that. I went in and asked if a Josephin Lacroix had worked there. They confirmed that she had. I asked when she'd left, and they told me the month, but they began to become suspicious when I asked why she had left. They said it was personal information, and I should write to them if I wanted to discuss the matter further. I don't know that there was anything else I could do."

"No, you did enough. You proved she worked there."

I didn't push the point.

It seemed to me that all she had proved was that someone called Josephin Lacroix had worked there.

If I'd wanted to con her into thinking I'd been a secretary who'd left a Notaire, all I needed was the name of a secretary who'd left a Notaire.

If the aim was to cause problems for Booth, then forging the Compromise and a photograph of him was easy, and tacking on about the secretary was easy enough when your forged documents said they came from the Notaire you knew that a secretary had left.

That way it all added up.

What she hadn't done, was ask when the Notaire had died.

She had only the secretary's word for that, and if she'd only asked if the Notaire was dead, not when he'd died, it added to the Secretary's story.

If the Notaire hadn't died, it blew it apart.

If he'd died in the wrong time frame, it blew apart.

She either hadn't been thinking, or she'd been completely gulled by the secretary.

Nobody gets gulled unless they want to be, but she'd wanted to be, and badly.

"Have you seen any advertisements for the house before Booth bought it?"

"An Imobbillier's flyer came with the papers that Thompson sent me."

"Did he send you them by post, or email them?"

"Email."

"You've still got the email?"

"Of course."

"Did you go into the Immobillier and check if Booth had ever been in there?"

"No. No, I didn't."

"How do you know that the picture of Booth was taken at the Notaires, and on the day he signed the deal for the house?"

"Because he is standing outside the Notaires. The time and date are date-stamped on the photograph."

"You know that that means absolutely nothing, right?"

"I know. It can be changed easily enough. But with the paperwork and the testimonies, the balance of probability says it's genuine."

"Yeah. I think you're right."

I thought it had more holes than a poor man's pants, but there was no point in giving her grief about it with my twenty-twenty hindsight.

We drove in silence for a while.

When I hit the Westway I looked across at her.

She had rested her head against the window.

When I looked again a few minutes later, she seemed to be asleep.

I left her alone.

She didn't need me knocking her down any further.

She was an expert at it herself.

We were off the A40 and the other side of Uxbridge before she spoke again.

"Can it be my turn now?"

"What?"

"To ask questions."

I smiled at her.

"Yeah, go on then."

"How did you find out that Dean Thompson was dead?"

"I saw him. Yesterday morning."

"Where?"

"I told you. At the house. In Morninton Road."

"Why were you there?"

I paused. It was a good question. Why had I been there?

"Honestly Phillipa, I don't know. I mean, I know why I was there, but I have no idea why I was asked to go there."

"Who were you asked to go there by?"

"A client."

"Malcolm Denning?"

"No. A client asked me to look into a situation for them.

"What situation?"

"I was told that - let's call him Dean Thompson - was seeing a married woman and being a nuisance. I was asked to persuade him to stop being a nuisance."

"To beat him up?"

"No. I'm not muscle. I was asked to be, kind of, like a diplomat. With very persuasive arguments."

"What, like he would be beaten up if he didn't listen to you?"

"I doubt it would have gone like that."

"Were you working for Booth?"

"No, I wasn't."

"Who?"

"If I knew that, Phillipa, I would tell you."

"But it was Booth's wife that Thompson was having an affair with?"

The iron gates of the compound began jerking open in the headlights. I drove through and swung around into my parking space.

"Yes. It was Booth's wife." I switched off the lights and killed the engine. "The backdrop I was given was that Thompson was making waves, and needed putting back in his box to protect Booth from any unwanted –"

She broke across me, an edge of anxiety in her voice. "Where is this?"

"I live here. Let's get your stuff upstairs and we can compare notes properly."

12

We rang out for a Chinese, and while it was on its way we began to spread everything she had on Booth out across the living room floor.

There were photographs, old press cuttings, copies of Booth's Army medical records, copies of his discharge papers, his birth certificate, copies of receipts for dinners and other things he'd bought, from petrol through to flowers to medicines. You name it, she had it. God alone knows where she'd dug half of it up from, but there it was, useful or not.

I sat back and surveyed the floor full of crap she'd collected on him while she served up the Chinese onto two plates.

"This is a full-time hobby for you, isn't it Phillipa?"

She passed me my share of the food. "Please don't misunderstand me. I hate the bastard."

"I'd never of guessed."

"So now you can tell me, why were you up at the Booth's house?"

I put down my meal on the coffee table, went over to the desk and brought her the pictures of Susan and Thompson.

"Here's something else for your collection."

She pulled the photographs out of the envelope.

"Do you think these are the photographs he sent to Colin Luscombe?"

"Do you think he sent them?"

"He said that he had."

"Well I was given these as a way of identifying Thompson, and I wanted to find out where and how they were taken, because they were very professionally done, and they wouldn't have been cheap, but something about them just didn't add up."

"What?"

I stirred my noodles while I thought through how to explain to her.

"Right from the off, when I got these photos, it was obvious they weren't either taken quickly or by an amateur. The way they are shot, and the way Susan and Thompson are clear rather than just vague people behind reflections on the patio doors. Whoever took them really knew what they were doing.

On top of that, the angle they are taken from is prone, not standing, so it couldn't have been someone poking a camera over the back gate or shooting them over the hedge from half a mile away. They must have been taken inside the property.

So, then I checked out the property on Google Earth, and it looked to me that the obvious place was from inside the outbuildings at the end of the garden, and that's why I was there.

I wanted to see if I had it right, because if I did, it meant that someone had either broken into the property, or they'd been allowed in.

"This is where you get your inside job theory from?"
"Exactly. And something you said to me earlier made me think about what the woman living next door to them said to me, about how Susan Booth was hardly ever there now. She said that she hadn't lived there full time for a couple of years.

But, if she was only there on and off, someone must have had to stake the place out, maybe for days, to catch Thompson there with her.

So, on the face of it, they must have been taken at a time she was living there, because what are the chances that someone would be there, all set up and waiting to take pictures, just at a time when she made a random visit, and she had a random visit from Dean Thompson at the same random time?"

She looked at me from under her fringe.

"So what are you thinking?"
"Well. How about, someone commissioned them knowing that Thompson would be there on a certain day?"

"OK. So who would know that both of them would be there on a certain day?" she raised the perfect finger: "Susan Booth".

She looked at me.

I held up two fingers. "Stephen Booth."

She grimaced. "Only if Booth was tapping into her phone or her emails or however it was she contacted Thomson."

"Perhaps it was a lucky guess? He knew Susan would be there on x day or days, and figured she wouldn't pass up on a chance to see Thompson, so he had the photographer camp out."

She shook her head and spoke through a mouthful of noodles. "Motive."

She wiped her chin.

"Why would Booth have the photographs taken, and then send them to Thompson? That's like he was blackmailing himself. It doesn't make sense."

"On the face of it no. Unless he aimed to use them to discredit Susan, as an excuse to divorce her?"

"That doesn't make sense either. They'd lived apart. He didn't need the drama of her having an affair to divorce her, and the reason you got the photographs in the first place was to put a stop to the affair."

"But Thompson gave them to Luscombe to publicise them. Exactly the opposite reason."

"Yes. So we can rule Booth out."

"No."

"No?"

"No. Maybe, but not yet. Who else?"

She chewed thoughtfully then swallowed. "Thompson?"

"Motive?"

She took a deep breath.

"How about, he wanted to split the Booths up? He loved Susan Booth and wanted her to leave Booth, but she refused, so he had the pictures taken. Then he offered them to me, thinking that even if I didn't use them, I'd move them along to someone who would, but I wouldn't touch them, so he took them to Luscombe. Then, when it got out that Booth's twee little wifey had been screwing the tradesmen, Booth would divorce her."

I had to give it to her. It was the most plausible explanation.

But, there is always a but.

"But..." she stirred her noodles thoughtfully. " -these pictures could only be used to blackmail Susan Booth, not Stephen Booth."

"How so?"

"Because she's going to be the loser, and blackmail is ultimately always about someone losing something."

"Sure, but Booth loses his rep, he gets sniggered at, he gets a messy public divorce that likely drags on for a couple of years. What does Susan lose?"

She shrugged and took another fork full of food.

"I don't know. Maybe I was just throwing the question out there because I'm not convinced that Thompson would set Susan up – especially if he loved her. That kind of goes against everything, doesn't it. How can you love someone and publically humiliate them? That's not love, that's an obsession, controlling someone."

"Alright. So let's look at that point: did Thompson love Susan?"

"That's what you were told, isn't it: that he wouldn't leave it alone."

"That's what I was told, but it doesn't always follow that what I get told is the truth. Plenty of times, what I get told turns out to be complete bollocks.

So what if Thompson didn't love her. What's his motive for having the photographs taken and passing them on then? And if he didn't get the photos done, what's his motive for hanging around like a bad smell if he didn't love her? Money?"

She took a sip of her wine and raised her eyes to look at me.

"Money?"

"Could be."

She put her glass down.

"But no, that doesn't fit with what I knew of him, Dan. He was never, ever in the least bit mercenary about it with me. The exact opposite. He didn't want a penny."

"But why then? Why was he contacting you at all, if it wasn't for love and it wasn't for money?"

"Probably, exactly as he told me: to damage Booth. To discredit him. But wait," She stared at the floor for a moment. "No. That re-states that he loved Susan – leaving aside the odd chance that he was just doing it to be a pain in the arse. And anyway, him blackmailing Susan would be pointless. The only person who could be damaged by her having an affair with Dean Thompson and it being made public would be Stephen Booth, and from what I can work out, on a personal level, I don't think he'd care a jot."

I picked up a press clipping containing a photograph of Susan and Booth from the floor.

"What do you know about their marriage?"

She held her fork up while she chewed, then swallowed.

"Not very much. They've kept it very private. She has been the dutiful Tory wife, him the proud Shires MP husband. Behind closed doors, of course, we can see something else was going on, but that's hardly surprising given the age difference."

"What do you know about the kid?"

"What kid?"

"There was a child. Simon. He died."

"He can't have been Booths. She must have been married before."

"Why do you say that?"

"Booth is sterile."

Something cold slithered around my insides.

She put down her meal and knelt on the floor, searching through papers and documents.

"Here." she handed me a clear plastic folder. In it was a photocopy of headed paper from a Harley Street practice.

I glanced at it without reading it and handed it back to her.

"I believe you."

She got back up on the settee and picked up her meal again.

"Do you know how and when the boy died?"

"Not exactly. The woman next door told me it was inevitable because he was badly brain-damaged."

"How long ago did he die?"

"About three or four years ago apparently."

"Well, I've never heard anything about it, or him, which is weird, when you think about it. You'd expect the premature death of an MP's only child to be reported, even if it was only in an obituary column. Perhaps we should check the Parish Records or something?"

"Forget it. We need to concentrate on finding out who's behind Thompson's murder. There has to be a tie in between my case and your work on Booth, and there has to be more to it than some dodgy little company. People don't get their throats cut for fucking MP's wives or emailing accounts to journalists."

She was looking at me, like, well, like a woman.

I put my dinner on the table, stretched and leant back into the settee.

She was still looking at me.

"What?"

"How well do you know Susan Booth, Danny?"

"I don't."

"OK, well then, " She raised her eyes to the ceiling. "how long is it since you knew Susan Booth?"

"Twelve. Thirteen years."

I sensed she wanted to ask me more but thought better of it. She turned away from me, fiddled with her food for a moment then put it down on the table.

"OK, what do you suggest we do?"

"I don't know, yet, but I do know that I need to keep an eye on you."

"I can look after myself."

"Sure, in the normal run of things, but this isn't normal. The bloke they topped was your contact, and they followed that up by telling you porkies to get into your home. I don't want you on your own Phillipa. You're only dead once, yeah? There's no second chances."

"Well there's certainly no point in me following you around everywhere, and I'm not going to stay here alone. I'll go doo-lally. Also, I will need to check up on Richard over the weekend and find out how he is."

"Phillipa."

"What."

"Fuck Richard."

"Well you would say that, wouldn't you."

"Yes. I fucking would. Remember what happened when you didn't listen to him, and now, listen to me."

I went over to the desk and tapped the laptop awake.

"That was really, very unfair of you, Danny."

I answered her without looking up. "Not as unfair as you getting your throat cut."

I brought up Google and typed in "Simon Booth".

Nothing came back. Odd names. American Linked-In pages, a couple of Facebook pages.

I tried again: "Simon Booth death". Nothing.

Nothing to suggest that Simon's death - or even his life - had ever happened.

She came and stood beside me. "What are you doing?"

"Trying to find any mention of the son. There's nothing. Not a birth, not a death. Nothing."

"Start the search again, and add "mort" to it."

"What?"

"Just a hunch." She nudged me aside and took over the laptop. She cleared the search and typed in "Simon Susan Stephen Booth mort inhumation" and hit return.

The page filled with French links.

"Bingo." She clicked on the first link. "Can you speak French?"

"No."

"OK. Well, this is a bit like a French version of a Parish Record, a list of births and deaths, marriages and burials. I will leave you to go through it. Use Google Translate if it helps. Can I have a shower?"

"Only if you stay here, and don't go and see Richard."

"Where is it?"

"Out to the hallway and on the left."

She walked through the lounge to the door before turning back to me. "I know you're right Danny. I'll think about it."

She pulled the door shut behind her.

I turned back to the screen and started moving down the links on the page.

When she came back from her shower I handed her a printout of what I'd found out.

"So, this is poor little Simon; and burying him in France is how they managed to keep it out of the media here." She handed me the papers back and sat down on the settee. "And now, you will go and see Susan Booth alone. Correct?"

Having my thoughts read was an uncomfortable feeling, but I realised that was the most obvious next step from a journalistic point of view.

"I think it will be best. On my own, I will be able to get under her guard if I need to. But I want you to stay here Phillipa. Please."

"I know what you want, and I know you're right, but I really should go and see Richard. What if they go after him?"

"I think Richard is safe, for now." She began to speak, but I raised my hand and stopped her. "I can't be everywhere at once Phillipa, and what exactly are you going to do if they do go after Richard?"

"Why can't we call the police, and tell them that we believe Richard might be in danger. At least then he will get some protection."

"Because then they will know you are with me, and I want you right out of the way while I'm gone."

"But we don't have to tell them where I am."

"They will know where you are within a few minutes of us calling, Phillipa. It's not like Dixon of Dock Green these days."

"Why would they bother?"

I looked at her for the best part of a minute before replying, trying to put it in a way that wouldn't be a challenge she needed to rise to.

"You know Phillipa," I said quietly "I've got a lot of respect for you. A fucking shed-load of respect for you and what you do, but, you need to understand that I know my business as well. Do you remember seeing a report of Dean Thompson's murder on the news?"

"Well, I don't know. I suppose not. No."

"No. Doesn't that strike you as strange? A man gets tortured and murdered in broad daylight in his own home, in West London, and it doesn't make the news?"

"Well. Perhaps, but I'm fairly sure Thompson lived alone. Perhaps nobody has discovered the body yet."

"They fucking well should have by now, Phillipa, because I stopped on Greenford Broadway five minutes after I saw him and told the police."

"You think his death is being covered up?"

"Well, there's only two reasons it's not been reported, aren't there. Someone nipped in and disappeared a slaughterhouse before Plod arrived, or ..."

She shook her head. "Christ. It's unbelievable."

"As I said to you earlier, babe, whatever it is you've kicked over fucking stinks. I think Booth and his company and his house are peripheral now. My gut feeling is the game has moved on in some way, and now the Establishment is involved.

I don't think we're only talking about a bent MP anymore, because if we were, they'd throw Booth straight under the bus without blinking rather than risk other stuff getting dragged up. It's got to be something more. Something about what you and Thompson started has got the movers and shakers feeling threatened."

She sat with her arms wrapped around herself, her eyes wide.

"You're beginning to really frighten me now."

"Phillipa, I'm not saying you should be frightened. What I'm saying is that right now, we need to be careful, which is why I want you to stay put and drop completely out of sight. If I can get to Susan, I might be able to get stuff out of her that cracks open Booth's defence for you, and then they will throw Booth under the bus if only to stop things escalating. Losing some handyman's corpse is one thing. Losing a well-known journalist's, when she's just nailed a bent MP to the floor and he's had to drop a libel case? That's a whole different matter."

She stared ahead, thinking things through.

"Jesus Christ. What have I done, Danny?"

"You've been a proper journalist. There's few enough of them around these days."

She didn't look at all well. "Come here." I lifted my arm.

She looked along the couch at me, then away again. Then she moved next to me and rested against me.

"While you're here, you're safe Phillipa. You know what I mean?"

She nodded. "I understand how you feel about Richard. I have a spare mobile. You can ring him on it and tell him you're OK, but don't tell him where you are, or that you're with me, and don't offer to go to him, even if he begs you to."

"He wouldn't. He's too proud."

"Exactly. So if he did, it would mean you were walking into a trap, and there's no point in you both..." I paused. "You know what I'm saying."

She nodded again. "Yes."

I pressed my lips to her hair. "I'm sorry. I can sound harsh, I know."

She shook her head. "No, I know that you're right. I can be rather pig-headed at times." She drew a deep breath. "You go and see her, and I will wait here for you. While you're gone, I will try and get in touch with a guy I know who works for La Monde. Perhaps he can throw some light on what Booth has been doing in France, and who he knows and has dealings with over there. At least that will be something positive."

"That's the ticket. Don't give up on it, but use my lappy, and get a new email to contact him with. Yours might not be safe now, so don't log onto it."

She sighed deeply. "Jesus Christ."

I let the words hang there, allowing the silence to grow.

It was a few minutes before she spoke.

"Have you worked out how much I owe you so far?"

"Yes."

"How much?"

"Half the Chinese. And don't think I'll forget, either."

13

We'd tidied everything Phillipa had on Booth up into two piles on the coffee table and sat next to each other on the couch, gradually filing everything she had on him.

Photos with photos.

Reports with reports.

Receipts with receipts.

Other stuff we sorted into personal, business or politics.

Everything was put in date order.

Most of it went back over a decade, with a few other odds and sods even further. When we'd done, we stacked it all beside my desk, ready for her to scan if she needed to send anything to her contact at Le Monde.

She stood staring out of the kitchen window while she rang Richard from the mobile I gave her. I was relieved that it seemed to be a one-way conversation. He didn't seem to be at all interested in the few questions she asked him, and after a minute or two she rang off.

"He's completely out of it." She put the phone on the coffee table and sat down next to me.

"Drunk?"

"Drunk. Stoned. Full of painkillers." Tears filled her eyes. I held out my hand to her. She turned her face away from me.

"I'm going to bed, Danny. I need some time to myself. Sorry. Goodnight."

She got up and left the room without looking at me.

The half-moon shuttered watery light across the lounge.

The ceiling glowed faintly from the yellow street lights out on the main road.

The faint chocking of the kitchen clock was the only sound.

I lay awake on the couch under a duvet, ticking off the things I might need, what I should pack, the logistics of a thirty-hour, eight hundred mile round trip.

It was maybe an hour after she'd left the room when I heard her get out of bed. The door opened behind me.

"I need a drink." she half-whispered, as if unsure whether I was awake.

"Go for it," I said.

She padded past me to the kitchen.

I watched her backside moving under the oversize T-shirt of mine she wore.

On the way back she stopped in front of me, the T-shirt not disguising her body, her nipples pushing at its fabric.

"Feeling better now?" I asked.

"Yes. Thanks."

She squatted down beside the couch. The moon shadow slid between her thighs and under the hem of the T-shirt.

"What are you thinking about?"

"Not much. The driving tomorrow. What to pack, what time to leave, all that bullshit."

"You like to be organised, don't you."

"Not really. Just – prepared, that's all. You know, knife fights and spoons."

"You're not expecting trouble with Susan, surely?"

"I don't know."

I rolled over on my side so I look at her properly. Her eyes were pale under the unruly bob.

"Anything is possible. I haven't seen the woman for nearly thirteen years. She could be a raving lunatic."

"I doubt it."

She said it like she hoped she would be.

I smiled at her.

"Or, she could be living with a raving lunatic."

She smiled back wanly, then moved her hand to me and ran the back of her fingers down my cheek.

"Danny, don't take this the wrong way, but, you don't have to sleep here. Not if you don't want to."

I took her hand and kissed the mother of pearl nails.

"I'm fine here, Phillipa."

Even as I spoke, I felt her draw back from me as if bitten.

I sensed her looking at me from under her fringe, her eyes now hidden in shadow. She gently took her hand away and stood up.

"OK. Well. Goodnight then."

When she'd gone, I got onto thinking about what I'd said to her about Thompson, and why the murder hadn't been reported. I racked my brains and explored all the angles, but I couldn't come up with a better explanation than the one I'd given her.

Someone somewhere was worried, and had worked behind the scenes to tidy up loose ends, and whether she'd meant to be or not, Phillipa was now the loosest end of all. Hiding her would last at best for a day or two.

I had to in some way or other divert attention away from her. If I could open up what she was doing and get someone else to show an interest, it would give them another fire to fight, someone else to worry about. They might even fuck up in public, and make whoever had secretly pulled strings over Thompson unable to help them

I got up and went out into the kitchen and rang Natalie.

"Hallo stranger. I'm in the bath."

"Lucky bath. How are you?"

"Wet."

I knew she wanted "How wet" or "Where" but I had other things on my mind.

"Nats, it's a bit urgent. Do you have a mobile number for that Colin Luscombe geezer you were talking about? I think I might have something for him if we're quick."

"Oh, I see. It's something important. Unlike me."

"I've told you before, Natalie Denning: learn your place."

She laughed. "Give me a while. I'll send it to you as a contact."

"OK thanks, Nats. You're a star."

"Yes, I know. I'm great, aren't I? How are you anyway? You sound stressed."

"Nah, I'm alright. Just got a lot on at the moment, that's all. Trying to get too much done at once."

"Oh, you poor thing." I heard her move in the water. "I was thinking about you, just before you rang."

"We must be telescopic."

She ignored me.

"I think it's the hot water. It makes me all puffy. And then I think really filthy thoughts."

Jesus fucking wept. Not now.

"I see. About what?"

"You."

"Well, that's nice. It's a shame I haven't got a bath, or I could join you."

"It's only nine-thirty. I'm at the Hidey Hole. You can be here by ten. There's wine."

"I can't babe. I've got to be out the door at sparrows fart tomorrow on a case."

"You're such a liar. Have you got a woman there?"

Now, there are two stark truths in life:

One is that at some point, for some reason, you're going to die.

The other is, you won't ever fool a woman who has feelings for you.

Not even if you're innocent.

"Nats. Why, would I be ringing you, about work, if I had a woman here?"

"Oh, I really don't know! Forget I said it."

And there's the third truth.

Every so often, a woman will make you want to smack her arse for her, just so she knows you still care.

"It's OK Nats. I better go, babe, alright?"

"Yes, fine."

"I'm up to my eyes in it, trying to get ready."

"No, it's OK. You do what you have to do, Missssssster Very Busy."

"Will do. Don't forget to send me Luscombe's number, will you babe? It's really important."

"Don't worry. I won't forget."

She didn't forget.

She just forgot to send it until past eleven o'clock, and when the message came, that's all there was. Just a contact card.

It was late, but what the fuck.

I sat upright on the settee and rang the number.

"Hi, Colin Luscombe."

"Hi, Colin. I'm sorry it's so late, but.."

"No worries. Who's this?"

"Danny Massey. We met outside the awards the other week. I was there with Natalie Denning.

"Christ yeah, I remember. How's it going, Danny?"

"All good mate, all good. Sorry to ring you so late, but I spoke to Natalie and she gave me your number. We think I may have something that'll interest you. Are you around tomorrow morning?"

"Well. Um. Tomorrow could be awkward. I'm out on a little mission already."

"Where?"

"What?"

"Where are you out tomorrow? I'm up to my eyes in it as well, but maybe we could meet up for half an hour in the morning, I can give you what we have and let you get on with it."

"Could be. What's this is about, this information?"

"A bent MP. Bang to rights. I don't want to say anything else right now, Colin."

"Fair enough."

The line went quiet for a moment.

"Look, tomorrow, I've got to be in Elstree at around 2 o'clock. Before that, I promised I'd go round and see me old Mum in Borehamwood. Not sure exactly when the train gets in, but how about you pick me up from Borehamwood station somewhere around eleven? We can have a natter about it, then you can drop me over Mums afterwards? If you wouldn't mind, of course?"

"No, that's great mate. Sounds like a plan. Text me tomorrow, say, around nine, and let me know on the train time, OK?"

"Sure, no problem. Look forward to it, Danny."

I killed the phone and lay back on the settee and snugged under the duvet.

If he was half as good as Natalie reckoned, what I gave him on Booth and Duct Four ought to make him start poking around and take the spotlight off Phillipa.

Hopefully, it wouldn't cost him any broken fingers.

Slowly I came round.

My phone was ringing on the coffee table.

I picked it up and checked who it was.

Sneed?

What the fuck did he want at six in the morning?

I answered.

"Sneedie? What's up?"

"Danny. That case Malcolm gave you. The one with the photographs of the bloke and the MP's wife."

Suddenly I was wide awake.

I pretended not to be.

"Er. Oh, yeah. Yeah. What about it?"

"Drop it. Lose the pictures. Forget all about it."

"Sure. No problems."

"Good. Do we owe you anything on it?"

"Nah, don't worry about that. I hadn't done anything on it."

"OK. All good. Take care, matey."

"Yeah, you too Garry."

I lay the phone down on the table, stared at it for a moment then got up and walked through into the kitchen.

I switched the kettle on.

Technically, if the case was off, I shouldn't go and see Susan.

That in itself wasn't all bad, because if something was kicking off, staying here with Phillipa was the most sensible thing to do.

But when I weighed it all up, I knew I had to go. Whether through the photos or the bent company, Susan was involved, and she might hold the key to nailing Booth once and for all.

So.

If I didn't go there about the photos, I could still go there, because Nats told Phillipa I would help her.

There was another reason, of course, but I didn't want to think about that.

The kettle boiled and clicked itself off. I left it and went and lay back down and pulled the duvet over my head.

Phillipa was in the kitchen with her back to me.

She was wearing my dressing gown, standing on tiptoe looking out of the window, her little round backside pushing against the silk of the robe.

She must have sensed my eyes on her because she turned around.

"You're still alive then?"

I pulled my arm out from under the duvet and looked at my watch. It was nearly nine. "Just about. How long have you been up?"

"Not long. Ten, fifteen minutes. Would you like a coffee?"

"Yeah. Thanks."

I was busting for a piss, but with her watching from the kitchen, I had to wait for my Morning Glory to go down first.

"Did you sleep OK?"

She leaned on the doorframe, her hands in the pockets of the robe.

"Yes, thanks. What time do you think you'll leave?"

I checked my phone. A text from Luscombe had arrived almost an hour earlier. "Will be there at 11.30."

"About 10.30. But we need to get some shopping in for you before I go."

"Well, you better get a move on then." She smiled.

I rolled off the couch wrapped in the duvet and left her to it.

When I'd shaved and showered she was sitting on the couch.

"Do you want to write me a list of what you want food-wise? I haven't got a clue what you like."

She pushed a list across the coffee table to me and smiled sweetly.

"OK. Right." I drank down the lukewarm coffee and left.

When I got back she was dressed and waiting for me, her hair a mass of loose damp curls from the shower.

I went into the bedroom and dragged a holdall out from under the bed. I threw pants, socks, a pair of jeans, a couple of t-shirts and a spare jumper into it.

I opened the bedroom door and pushed my fingers down on its top edge. A piece of the door's wooden core popped up. I lifted it away, stuck my fingers in and pulled the little Smith and Wesson from the hollowed-out section I'd created for it. I tucked it into the back of my belt. I dumped the holdall out into the hallway and lay my leather reefer jacket over it.

She'd sat on the couch in silence, allowing me to do what I needed to do. I went over to the desk and brought back the spare mobile. "This is for you. Don't whatever you do turn your phone on for any reason. Even to get someone's number."
She nodded and took the mobile from me.

"My number is on it. Keep it with you and ring me if you get suspicious about anything. I will ring you tomorrow at the latest." I pulled out the snub. "And this is for you too. Have you ever shot anybody before?"

She looked at me wide-eyed.

"Now listen, I'm leaving you this just in case. The thing to remember is that if you have a gun, mostly you won't have to use it, provided you look as if you know how to use it. Stand up, babe."

I broke the little gun open and knocked its shells out into my hand.

"OK, empty." I showed her the cylinder before flipping it back into place. "Here."

I held the gun out and she took it from me.

"Hold it with both hands, with your arms outstretched." She did so.

"Straighten your elbows. Plant your feet more. A bit wider, so you feel balanced. Try and imagine that your right index finger is the barrel and point it where you want the bullet to go."

She frowned down the gun's barrel.

"That's good. Keep your elbows straight. Now, squeeze the trigger. Harder. Keep pointing that imaginary finger."

I watched the hammer edge slowly back, then it snapped forward.

"That was good. You didn't drag it off target. Do it again, but one smooth movement."

Again the hammer moved back and snapped forward.

"Much better. But don't aim head high. Aim belly high. Imagine, you're some bloke who's broke in here, and instead of a woman

145

scared out of her wits, he's faced with a woman ten feet away pointing a gun at him. She not aiming at his head, which means she'll probably shoot high anyway, and he can duck down and charge her. No. She's aiming it at his guts, where he can't duck and he knows even a pulled shot is going to hit him.

Remember, he's not just seen gunfights on TV, where people get hit in the leg and limp about a bit acting all heroic. He's seen what guns can really do. He knows what gun you're holding. He knows it's a Smith and Wesson. He's counted the cylinder holes and he knows it's a .38. He knows what a .38 can do. He knows if you hit him in the leg and he's unlucky, he'll bleed to death in minutes.

If you hit him in the chest or guts he'll probably die, even if it's slowly. If you hit him in the head, he'll die instantly.

That's why it's vital, that he thinks you know what you're doing.

That if he moves towards you, you don't look like you'll turn your face away when you pull the trigger 'cos you're scared of the noise.

If he thinks that, he'll face you down. He'll keep moving at you to make you lose your nerve, and when you do turn your face away he'll take the gun off you before you can fire it.

But, if he thinks you'll keep the gun pointed like your finger and looking straight down it, that whatever he says, however he acts, whatever he does, you're in control of the gun and not afraid of it, he'll respect that, and he'll make a choice."

"What choice?"

"To shoot you first, or fuck off before you shoot him. But he's only going to have a chance to shoot you first if he's come in here with a gun ready, and the chances are he won't have done that because he thinks you're a frightened woman armed only with your favourite hairbrush. And if he had come in here with a gun, you'd already of shot him."

I nudged her.

"Wouldn't you, because it would have been him, or you."

I looked at her. She stared resolutely down the gun.

"Wouldn't you, Phillipa. Because that's the only way to overcome his gun and his expertise. Shoot first. If you see a gun or a knife, don't ask questions and don't give yourself a chance to be outnumbered or out-psyched.

Shoot, and always fire twice for each target. Aim Bang Bang. Aim Bang Bang, always keeping the gun aimed. That way if you miss with one bullet, you'll likely hit with the other, and it's more noise and more deterrent.

She looked up at me.

I touched her waist gently. "You've got to be first, Phillipa. Let's try it. I'll come in the room, and you react. You put the gun up, just as you are, and be ready to react to what I do and what I have in my hands."

I walked to the door and went out, pulling it closed behind me.

I called through the door.

"Blam blam blam, I just kicked the front door in. Now I'm checking the bathroom. Now the bedroom. Under the bed. In the wardrobe. Now I know, you're going to be in here."

I let her wait, just to see how she would react under tension. I gave her thirty seconds, then set my fingers in the shape of a gun, threw the door open and rushed straight into the centre of the room at her.

She wasn't there.

Then she stepped out of the kitchen and the Smith and Wesson snapped at me twice.

I stood there staring at her, as dead as a Dodo.

"Was that OK? You had a gun, right?"

I grinned at her. "Yes, I had a gun, and you got me."

She smiled proudly, the first time I had seen the blue-green eyes bright with happiness.

I held my arms open: "Come 'ere, killer!"

She ran to me and came into my arms.

I kissed her hair.

"You'll be fine. I'm not going to worry about you at all."

She turned her face up to me and smiled thinly. I kissed her fringe.

"But really, you should be OK. Nobody knows you're here, and nobody you've been dealing with knows where I live."

I took the gun from her and reloaded it, then lay it on the coffee table.

I faced her again and felt her arms slide around me.

"Don't worry. I won't stay down there any longer than I have to, and I'll ring as soon as I'm on my way back."

I held her close to me, feeling the warmth of her against me, her firm little breasts, and the pressure of her stomach against my crotch.

I stroked the unruly mop of her hair and she turned her face up to me, kissed my cheek, and I felt my lips finding hers, felt them part, tasted her, felt her tongue warm against mine, felt myself swelling, felt her trembling, her hands gripped me, the perfect little fingers dug into my back as she writhed against me and I imagined her wetness, opening, spreading beneath my fingers and I drew back and pulled away from her.

Not like this, then I'd leave her and go to Susan.

I stared into the dark pupils then drew her head to my chest. She deserved better than that.

Maybe we both did.

I kissed her hair and let her go, picked up the holdall from the hallway and left to meet up with Luscombe.

14

He was waiting outside the station for me when I drove up.

"Got anywhere we can go for a natter Colin?"

"We can go to my Mum if you like, she's got a back room and she won't bother us."

"Nah, mate, somewhere else. I don't like risking getting other people involved in stuff. You never know when things might get out of hand."

If I'd been testing him, he would have passed.

He didn't bat an eyelid at what I'd said.

"Fair enough. There's a pub on the estate that should be open. We can get something to eat."

A few minutes later we were pulling into a pothole and gravel car park. The two-storey flat-roofed pub itself sulked at the far end, up a couple of steps to a paved patio that ran in front of its peeling Georgian style wooden windows.

At the top of the steps, a pair of half barrels sat, one each side, both with a dead-looking leafless shrub of some kind poking out, and beyond them were a pair of metal half-glazed doors with steel mesh tack welded over the glass.

We pushed through them into the bar.

Freshly lit logs smoked in a brick-built central fireplace but did nothing to warm the stale air in the place. It smelt as if it had been flooded and never dried out properly.

The low ceiling was crossed by faux blackened timbers. Rough plastered walls were hung with ancient-looking sepia photographs of farming scenes in a variety of tatty frames.

Behind the bar, the Queen smiled down from the early 1960s. The chicken wire tacked across the lower half of the windows saved sweeping the patio on Sunday mornings.

"Nice place," I murmured to him.

"Innit. The new landlords really turned it around."

I followed him up into the far corner, and we sat down under the windows on either side of a chipped and ring stained table.

A thin woman with lank bleached hair appeared behind the bar.

"Oh. Right!" she croaked. "Thought I heard something. Be with you in a minute."

"Even the local minge is hot." I grinned at him. "I'll have to let you take me out again."

"I'm spoiling you today." He winked. "Not everywhere I go is this good."

The woman appeared again and hobbled across the pub's threadbare carpet to us. "What'll it be?" she demanded.

"Can you do us one plate of chips, and a coke each love?" asked Colin.

The woman turned her mouth down at him. "Is that it?"

"That's it."

She flicked her pencilled-on eyebrows upwards, snorted quietly and left us. Colin watched her go. "Beauty, grace and a sweet personality."

"You can fuck off. I saw her first."

He grinned at me.

"So what's the big secret then? Who's the MP?"

"Stephen Booth."

He pulled a face at me.

"You fucker. I take you out for a top lunch, and you give me Stephen Booth? Remember I told you, the old man made it ab-so fucking-lutely clear, I was to stay right away from Booth. Er ist verboten."

I stared at him, smiling like I knew something he didn't. He stared back for a good ten seconds before he cracked and closed one eye. "Go on then. What have you got?"

"Well, you know that wicked rumour about Booth having bought a house in France?"

"Yes."

"Well, let's just imagine, just for a minute, that it's true. How do you think Booth might have afforded to buy a four hundred grand house in France that he didn't have to declare to the House of Commons?"

"Serious question?"

"Serious question."

The woman slapped a tray down on the bar and clattered knives and forks onto it.

"Well. They're only allowed to buy a property worth a year's salary, so, I'm going to guess with money that couldn't be traced to him."

"How do you think he could get money without it being traced to him?"

"This is coming back to Phillipa Phapetis, isn't it."

"Yes, it is. She worked it out alright, but she didn't quite get all the evidence together in time. But Booth knows he's bang to rights, and that's why he set the law on them. He needed to break them before she could nail him. Do you know the background to that piece they put out?"

"Not really. All I know is what they published."

"Remember the photographs you got sent, that got taken off you? They were part of it."

"In what way?"

"They were offered to Auspex first, by the same bloke that gave them the info about the house in France. They turned them down because dogging's not their angle, but it was Phapetis that recommended he sent them to you. You said your old man got edgy about them and took them off you. Did you find out what happened to them?"

"No, I didn't. I've had a sly dig around, but they're gone. My guess is, he shredded them."

"Can you describe them for me?" I spotted the woman slouching towards us with our drinks and moved my head to alert him. "Wait up."

She placed a glass of cola in front of each of us without speaking and walked back toward the bar.

"Can you describe them?"

"Ok. They were colour. There were seven, maybe eight of them. I forget now." He lifted his glass to me "Cheers" and took a sip. "They were taken through some patio doors, I assume at the Booth's place."

"We're they time-stamped?"

"No. No, they weren't, but they were well taken. A top job."

"How did you get them? Through the post?"

"Yep."

"Addressed to you personally?"

"Yep."

"Postmark? Was there anything else in there? A note?"

"They were sent registered. From a Portsmouth address, but I checked it back and it was moody. There was a printed note pinned to them that said, I can't remember exactly, but, words to the effect, "Sir Stephen Booth's perfect wife, with her big black toyboy.""

"Did the note and the envelope disappear as well?"

"Yep."

The woman dropped a plate of chips on the tray and started over towards us.

"Grub up, this is my shout."

I pulled my wallet out as she got to us and waited for her to lay the tray between us before handing her a tenner, telling her to keep the change. My reward was her baring her long, yellowed teeth in an ingratiating smile.

"Is there anything else you'd like?" she begged.

I knew if I looked at Luscombe, he'd be looking at me and I'd laugh, so I smiled sweetly up at her and said no thank you, then concentrated on getting something out of my inside pocket for him.

I slid the folded photograph to him under my hand.

He forked a chip into his mouth and picked it up, lay his fork down and unfolded it. I didn't have to ask if he'd seen it before. He swallowed the chip almost whole.

"Where did you get this?" he asked.

"Can't remember," I replied, looking straight at him.

"Phapetis?"

I shook my head.

"Nope. Not Phapetis. She reckons she's never seen the photographs."

He turned the photograph over and looked closely at its corners, then handed it back to me. "This is one of the ones I got sent. See the corner? There." He pointed at the bottom left corner. "That little crease? I marked them all with my fingernail when they first arrived."

"Oh yeah, I see it now," I said, purposely not looking at the photo and putting it back in my jacket. "Why'd you do that then?"

He shrugged and lifted another chip into his mouth.

"Habit. If you get something arrive you're interested in running with, you can prove it's yours if you need to, if some other fucker nicks it."

"So you're 100% sure, that's one you were sent?"

"Absolutely nailed on, Dan. That's one of them."

I took a swig of coke and thought about where I should go with things next.

"What do you know about Booth, Colin? All I know is he's one of the swivel-eyed Europe haters. What's he really about?"

He shook his head slowly and smiled as if he pitied me.

"Danny, mate. I warned you before when we were at the awards, and I meant it. Don't get too close to Phapetis."

"What makes you think I'm working for Phapetis?"

"You think you're not. You think you're working for what's right. But there is no right. There's only them up there, and us down here.

And from time to time, people like Richard Hemming or Phillipa Phapetis are stupid enough to think that them up there, should have to obey the law like the rest of us. They'll get this -" he waved his fork around his ear "- mad fucking idea that them up there should play by the rules.

They forget, these are the same set of bastards who've been running this place for hundreds of years. They're the same set of fuckers who made their fortunes out of slavery, then paid themselves fortunes in compensation when slavery got abolished. There's been civil wars and world wars, but they've never, ever lost their grip. They culled a generation in World War One to keep what they have, then they fought Hitler, not because he was a maniac, but because if he'd won, they'd have lost their power.

So they went along with Churchill and armed six million men, the sons of the generation they'd culled twenty years before, and when Hitler was gone, they had to give those six million men they'd trained a land fit for heroes, or those men would have risen up and taken their power.

So they gave the taxpayers their own money back as the Welfare State, and for thirty years they pretended to give a fuck. But only so they could keep their power.

But slowly but surely, they've spent the last forty years taking it all back again, bit by bit, working their way back into the saddle and taking back control. Then along comes Phillipa Phapetis, bless her, and she honestly thinks she can dob one of them in and get away with it."

"Is that it?"

"Not quite. But I'm hungry, so you can do the talking." He winked at me and forked a chip into his mouth.

"You know that I agree with everything you say, don't you?"

"Good. But there's nothing you can do about it. Phapetis has given them the means to finally get rid of Auspex, and believe me, they've been waiting fucking years for that show to hit town. So it's best you just let that happen, Dan, because make no mistake, they will make your life a fucking misery if you don't. I've seen how these people work. Close up. They can shit on you in ways you never dreamed possible, mate."

"OK, let's say I accept what you say about Phapetis and Auspex and not getting involved. But tell me what you know about Stephen Booth."

"Why don't you tell me what you know Dan, because you're the one who said you had something on him."

"I have."

"What?"

"I've got enough on him to make the rest of them chuck him under the bus."

"Like what?"

I looked at him for a moment like I needed to make my mind up.

"Alright, I'll tell you what I've got." I leant forward and spoke quietly, looking directly into his eyes. "I've got proof, and I mean absolute nailed on proof, that he bought the house in France using a false name, using a fake passport, and he paid for it using a front company which he's a director of under the same false ID, and he runs it to launder money coming in from abroad." I picked up a chip from his plate and sat back.

He speared another chip but didn't lift it. "Where did you get all this from?"

I wrinkled my nose at him. "It's like your photos, mate. Can't remember."

He put his fork down on the plate and wiped his hands on a napkin.

"I thought you were hungry."

"It'll wait. Where can I see this nailed on proof?"

"At my flat. With the rest of your photos."

He watched me for a moment, then:

"You don't have to tell me where you got it, but tell me if you got it from Phapetis or not."

"I didn't get it from Phapetis, or Auspex, or who sent you the photos."

"Closer to home?"

I held his stare and shrugged, then let the silence lie between us, letting him think.

It took him a minute, then he asked quietly. "What do you want to know?"

"Anything and everything. Start where you like."

"Alright. Stephen Booth is a horrible cunt, who has some very shitty friends in high places."

"People like Booth usually have." I agreed. "Is that why you weren't allowed to follow up the story about him having a place in France?"

He stared at me for a moment.

"How do you know I wasn't allowed?"

"Because I can't believe that you wouldn't want to trumpet that a leading Brexiter secretly owned a second home in France and hadn't listed it in his interests?"

He shrugged. "Fair comment."

"So what happened? Why didn't you?"

"Honestly?"

"Honestly."

"OK. You're right. I wrote a piece that trolled along with what Auspex said they had on Booth and his house, more or less to keep a fire under it, you know what I mean? But the Old Man bottled out, and I honestly don't know why, because I know he rates Richard Hemming, and it's not as if we were doing anything other than kind of, poking the nest, to see what else flew out.

We're not Auspex, Dan, you know what I mean? If Booth wanted to play rough, we've got big shot QCs of our own, so, worst case for us, Booth would have demanded an apology, we'd have said sorry on page 328 and it would have all been buttered over. The worst it would have done is shown him up as a hypocrite over the EU."

"What happened? with the Old Man?"

"What happened was, I got dragged all the way upstairs, and the old fucker didn't just carpet me, he stood me there like a soldier on a Courts Martial. Never even offered me a fucking seat. Told me that if I even so much as thought about writing anything about Booth again, I'd never get another job in the media anywhere."

He stuffed the chip in his mouth and waggled his fork at me as he chewed and spoke. "And the thing is Danny - he didn't say "because he'd see to it". He didn't even say it like he was pissed off with me. He wasn't. I could tell. He said: "This is something out of my hands." Exactly that: "This, is something out of my hands." And from the look on his face, I believe it was."

"You mean he looked - what? Scared?"

"Not outwardly. Not to me, or in front of me. To my face, he was more like, resigned. But he's Old News to end of his todger. He knows a story when he sees one, and he and Hemming go back donkey's years. And he knows me. He knows I was careful, and he knows there was nothing Booth could do, because it was, really, just trolling, you know what I mean? Just asking questions about questions, like I said, just to keep a fire under the story. But then -" he stabbed another chip "- what with the court case against Auspex, maybe with hindsight, I can see his point. It's pretty obvious now that Phapetis dropped a bollock somewhere."

"She didn't. She just didn't manage to get everything she needed in time, and the only reason she didn't was because the poor little cow has been running Auspex on her own and unpaid for the last six months. She's not even been able to pay her rent. She had to freelance to earn enough to get to France to back up the story."
He raised his eyebrows.
"I didn't know things were that bad there."
"Mate, the only way she could afford to get the rest of the story together was to run with what she had and hope she could get the second half printed with the money the first half brought in.

Hemming has been out of it for nearly a year. He's living on weed and booze to kill the pain. They're working out of a rented house in Dulwich, they don't even have anyone to answer the phone. They haven't got a pot to piss in, Colin, which is why Booth felt safe setting his QC on them. If he can shut them up for just a month or two, then they'll be gone, and the truth about what he's been up to will go with them."

He looked at me for a moment, then nodded.

"Tell me everything you've got, and tell me everything you know."

I checked around us. The skinny woman sat on a stool at the bar with her back to us, thumbing through a magazine. Apart from her, it was just him, me and the fire that had given up smoking and gone out.

"OK, I'm going to tell you everything, OK?

I could see that he doubted it, but he nodded.

"It started out, Phapetis got sent a file by email by someone she trusts. The file was a set of accounts and scans of a bank account for a limited company called Duct Four, with the info that Stephen Booth was a director. She checked it all through, and it's a pukka firm, all set up properly at Companies House. The company number checks out, proper accounts are posted that are all up to date, but there's no Stephen Booth as a director, and nor has there ever been.

So she went back to her contact and said Stephen Booth isn't listed, and the contact said Stephen Booth is the director called Gavin Durrant, that Gavin Durrant is a pseudonym, a false identity of Booths, with a passport, bank accounts, you name it.

As you would, she said prove it. The contact came back to her and gave her all the paperwork on a house in France bought by Gavin Durrant, including a picture of Gavin Durrant, a k a, Sir Stephen Booth, leaving the Notaire on the day of buying the house. He gave her a witness, a secretary at the Notaires, who had signed a statement that Stephen Booth, a.k.a Gavin Durrant, had been the buyer."

"Have you got a copy of this Gavin Durrant's passport?"
I liked his mind. It went straight for the case's throat.

"No, she doesn't have a copy of the passport. It's the one thing missing. That, and a direct link to the money from the company, which on the face of it, is the only way that Booth could have afforded to buy the house.

He doesn't have enough earnings declared to Parliament to have that kind of cash laying around, and he has never declared the house or anything to do with France. Those two things taken together point to an outside source of cash, which fits with Gavin Durrant being the way he washes the money he gets for whatever he does into his own pockets."

He nodded. "Sure, but if, and only if, it's proved that Gavin Durrant is Stephen Booth. Without some kind of bullet-proof evidence, and I mean, like a passport in Gavin Durrant's name with a photo that's Stephen Booth on it, it can't be proved that the two men are the same, and Phapetis is clutching at straws."

"Spot on. But leave that aside for a moment, and go back to the company, because I need to explain to you how it works. As I said, Phapetis got hold of all the company accounts, and she checked them all through, and they all checked out. Or at least, the figure work looks right. But something didn't add up. It's a real live company with real turnover, making a real profit, and paying real tax, but it doesn't actually sell anything that she can find."

"So what is it? Some kind of long firm?"

"No, it's not a long firm. It's absolutely on the level and squeaky clean, and it's been trading and putting up pristine accounts for the past six years, but while it supposedly trades in things, because it gets money in, there are no things. It has no product. Nothing. It has no premises either, except some outbuildings at Booth's house it claims as office space."

"Why would Booth tie it to his house if he's using a false name?"

"There are two directors: one is Gavin Durrant, the other is Stephen Booth's wife."

He nodded. "OK, that works. Nothing suspicious about the offices.

How much turnover are we talking about in a year?"

"It varies, but not by much. Every set of accounts she got for them, going through all the years, it's always just a few bob under whatever the current VAT threshold happened to be. If the threshold changed, so did the income."

"But they paid tax on that?"

"Yes, they paid tax, but the important thing is, they never hit the VAT threshold for turnover."

"Nobody does if they can help it. It's a pain in the arse."

"Exactly. Once VAT's involved, you have to start explaining what you sold, and like I said, the company doesn't seem to sell anything."

"Maybe it sells services?"

I shook my head. "It doesn't seem to do anything, Colin. She, Booth's wife, is some sort of artist, but she's not really selling much as far as I can make out, and according to the accounts, we're not talking payments here and there like a painter selling the odd picture. We're talking about regular weekly payments.

On the Tuesday of every week like clockwork, money arrives in the account. It's then paid out to various other bank accounts, with payments covered by invoices from trades-people, all one-man bands. Plumbing, cleaning, decorating, you name it, until the company is barely breaking even.

It never buys petrol for a car. It's got no assets, not even a photocopier or computer. Nothing. Just money in, and money out, all neatly calculated to leave it paying minimal tax and to creep just under the VAT threshold."

"Where does the money come from? You said it's transferred in from a bank account. Who does the bank account belong to?"

"There's the next funny thing. The bank account, according to the IBAN in the accounts, doesn't belong to a company, it belongs to a private individual living in Luxembourg."

"How did she find that out?"

"I don't know and I didn't ask. She'd obviously done enough spadework to get that info, so that is good enough for me. The money comes in from Luxembourg, and it's laundered out using a bunch of small traders in the UK.

Every month, each trader sends the company an invoice for something, let's say, to fix a tap. The invoice is paid through bank transfer so it's all neat and above board, but what's odds on is that the tradesman just takes a cut for his trouble. He writes Duct Four an invoice for £300, and he'll earn half for writing and sending it.

When he's paid, he draws Booth's half out in cash and pays it into another account that belongs to Booth. It's fucking perfect. From the Duct Four end, everything looks above board, and as long as the books are squeaky and they pay tax like clockwork, nobody is likely to start sniffing around or digging too deep. And even if they did, they would just end up speaking to a list of tradesmen who all carried out properly invoiced work for Duct Four.

They could all verify that the right money was paid into their bank account, and there, the trail would end."

He frowned. "What the fuck is he doing it for? Why not just declare the money coming in from Europe as – whatever – consultancy fees, or a directors salary, and have done with it?"

"Good question. One, it might be because he doesn't want to answer questions about earning money in the EU what with being a big-time Brexiter. Two, it might be because he can't admit the source of the money because it's a kickback of some sort.

The truth is, Phapetis doesn't know, and now, she doesn't have the time or the ability to dig further because of Booth's court case. But Booth got enough cash to buy that house in France from somewhere, and it looks pretty much nailed on that by working these payments from Luxembourg through Duct Four is at least part of where he got it."

He nodded slowly, then: "OK, I'm interested."

"I thought you might be."

He picked up his fork, looked at the chip on it but laid it down again.

"Tell me something, because I have a sneaking suspicion that you'd know. How easy is it really, to get a moody passport?"

"Very. You can go at two levels. One, it looks like a passport, you can use it for getting a bank account, a credit card, buy a house in France and so on. Just don't try and use it at a border, because the biometrics won't work and you'll throw a flag up.

Or two, it's a full-on passport, use it where and how you like. The first will cost you but is relatively easy to get if you know where to ask. The second is silly expensive, and you have to know someone right high up the food chain to get one.

But for Booth's purposes, the first type was all he would have needed. No backwoods Notaire is going to do anything except photocopying it to cover his arse."

"OK. And straight up, Danny, how sure are you, your gut feeling, that Booth really is this director Gavin Durrant?"

"Straight up Colin, for a very, very good reason I'm not going to tell you, it's nailed on that he is.

He pulled out his phone. "What's the company name again? Duct Four?"

"Duct Four Limited."

He tapped at his phone.

I took a sip of coke.

The door opened and a man of about 30 stepped in and walked to the bar. He was lean, but his shoulders were broad and he held himself properly. Somewhere in my senses, an alarm went off.

He was casually dressed, but the jacket he wore over faded jeans was an expensive leather piece, Italian cut.

And I mean Italian Italian, not Leicester Italian.

His shoes were newish looking Doctor Martens. There was a glint of a heavy gold watch at his wrist as he leaned his hands on the bar and waited for the woman to walk around to serve him. I checked the fall of the jacket under his arms where it wrapped around his torso.

For some reason, nearly a grand's worth of schmutter with a shooter had just walked in.

He might have been the local drugs baron, but if he was, he wouldn't have been alone, and he would have been known. The skinny bottle blonde showed no sign of recognising him.

So what were the chances of a well-known journalist, a private dick working for a crime boss and a useful looking geezer, who just happened to be dressed like a prince and carrying a gun, all turning up in the same shithole pub on a council estate on the same day?

Let alone the same hour.

The barmaid put a tall glass of what looked like lager on the counter in front of him.

He'd have to drink it quickly or leave it to follow us.

Colin spoke: "Alright, Company House says -"

I kicked him lightly under the table.

"Drink up, we're leaving."

I saw the question form on his lips.

"Don't argue. Don't say a word. Put the phone away. Act normal. Just get up and leave, right now, and follow me out to my car."

I spoke quietly, but in the same tone I'd use if I'd just won the lottery and was asking him to come shopping with me.

The pub was silent, and the tone of a conversation carries even if the words you use don't. Whoever the blond was, I didn't want him to know he'd tripped a wire before we were outside.

"I need a piss," Colin complained.

"You can piss in the car," I said in the same quiet singsong voice while grinning at him. "Follow me, right now Colin. Colin, it's really fucking important that you do exactly as I say."

I stood up and walked to the door without checking if he followed me. He caught up with me in the car park as I got into the X3.

"What the fucks going on?"

"Get in and I'll tell you." When he pulled the door shut I reversed out of the parking place and pulled slowly to the car park's exit. Blondie didn't show himself, but if he was part of a pro mob he wouldn't have to. He'd WhatsApp voice message someone who was waiting outside, probably parked down the road.

I stopped at the entrance to the road and checked both ways. Left headed into the estate. Turn right, and within half a mile I could be on the A1. I turned left and pulled slowly away, letting the X3 loiter around 20mph, driving with my eyes on the rearview mirrors. I'd gone maybe 200 yards and a Range Rover pulled out of the line of parked cars behind us and drove into the pub car park. I flattened the accelerator and the X3 sat its arse down and spurted forward. We came to a junction and I turned left.

"You know this estate, Colin?"

"Should do, I grew up on it. What the fucks going on?"

"Did you catch the face that came into the pub? Blonde cropped hair, leather jacket."

"Yeah, why?"

"That's why we left. Take a look back and tell me if a silver Range Rover turns onto the road behind us."

He moved round in the seat. "No. Nothing. Wait. Yeah, now."

"Are there any shops near here?"

"Shops?"

"Shops, a parade of shops."

"Yes. Go next left. The parade is about 500 yards on."

"Can you drive around the back of it? Is there trade entrances behind the shops?"

"Yes."

I got to the junction, let two cars pass then pulled out. The road was long and straight, and as Luscombe had said, a parade of eight or so shops lay on the left.

"When we get to the shops I'm going to drive round the back, and you bale out the second I stop. Get out of the way in case they come round after me, but I'm going to try and stop them doing that if we're quick enough."

I swung the X3 into the service road behind the shops and stopped. His door was already half-open.

"Ring me in an hour, Colin. If I don't answer, forget we ever met." He got out. "Don't go to Old Bill, and drop the story. Door, mate."

He slammed the door and I stamped on the loud pedal and hammered along the back of the shops then back out onto the road. The Range Rover was just arriving at the shops. I jammed my foot down and pulled out in front of some poor woman who must have thought her last moments had come. She didn't even have time to brake.

I floored the X3 going back the way we'd come, past the Range Rover with the driver staring at me, thick-set, balding, Blondie in the passenger seat mouthing something at me as I went past.

In the mirror, I saw the Range Rover swing across the road and begin to three-point turn. I went back the way I'd come. Foot still hard down, I slewed into the road that led back to the pub almost sideways. A glance over my shoulder as I turned told me the Range Rover was stuck for now. Someone had pulled forward across it after the driver had reversed back into the shop's service road.

They'd be clear soon enough, but it was a few more precious seconds between us.

I hammered it down the road past the pub, then swung a left out onto the main road, ignoring the horn of a car who I cut in against. After that, I had no choice but to go with the flow of the traffic as best I could. The road curved, but as I lost sight of the road to the pub in the mirror, I couldn't see any sign of the Range Rover.

Since I'd joined the road the traffic had been doing a fairly steady 30 and I'd moved forward 300 yards or so. Already there were a dozen or so cars behind me. At best, I figured the Range Rover would reach the road in another half minute. Assuming that the driver guessed I'd turned left, that would mean the best part of a mile, and maybe 20 or 30 cars between us.

I was fairly sure if there were no hold-ups ahead I'd lost them.

I followed the A1 out of London, then pulled off at South Mimms and took the scenic route to Watford. It was slower, but if I was being tailed it was easier to spot and I had more options than on the M25. Past Watford, I carried on to Maple Cross then joined the M25 for the last leg down to the M4.

Luscombe rang me.

"Colin, did anybody know you were meeting me?"

"Only Natalie. She rang this morning to see if you'd been in touch. She said you were acting a bit weird last night."

"I was in a rush, that's all."

"That's what I said. I said you sounded OK to me, but you had something urgent for me. Is everything OK between you two?"

"Couldn't be better, mate. She just worries sometimes."

He didn't say anything, and I used the pause as a chance to break off talking to him.

"OK Colin, I've got to get gone mate. I'd suggest you play it low key with Nats, avoid her if you can, and I don't have to say, don't tell her what we talked about."

"No, sure. But before you go, Danny. Who were those geezers today? Anything to do with Booth?"

"Nah, that's something else and I didn't want you getting caught up in it."

"Alright. I just thought they were connected, because of what you said about dropping everything if I couldn't get hold of you."

164

"Nah, I only said that because I wouldn't be able to give you the stuff I have on Booth. I'll be back in a couple of days and we'll sort out a meet so you can take it all off me, but you've got the Duct Four angle to be getting on with. Like you, I've got a lot of time for Auspex and what they do. You crack it, Colin. Crack it for Richard Hemming. Take care, mate."

I dabbed the screen and killed the call.

Natalie, poking around.

And who the fuck had Natalie told? Sneed? Why would she do that?

No.

Natalie had rung Luscombe because she was worried that I'd sounded strange on the phone.

Luscombe had put her straight. That was that.

So that left them being the team that had topped Thompson and tried to get to Phillipa.

We'd been found at the pub because I'd been too casual. I didn't know where they'd picked me up from so I had to assume from home, which meant they knew where I lived, which meant they might go back there.

But that was a long shot.

They either didn't know, or didn't care, that Phillipa was there, or as soon I'd left they would have gone in after her instead of following me.

They must have tailed me to see if I was meeting her, but instead, I met up with Luscombe.

That was good for Phillipa.

It might not be quite so good for Luscombe, but I couldn't allow myself to worry about that.

I picked up the M4 and let the X3 eat up the miles, took a brief stop for coffees to take with me at Bristol, and then on.

The first snow showed up as I reached Honiton, light flurries from a bruised looking sky. By the time I was past Taunton it was falling thickly, flakes the size of pennies spiralling into the windscreen, and the further west I travelled the more the weather socked in.

The A38 became a white tunnel in the growing dusk, and when darkness fell properly, it turned into a long snake of tail lights that rarely got above forty.

Finally, through Bodmin, I pulled over into a lay-by and took final bearings for Lowthesall. Still another nine or ten miles. After that, Tretalas itself lay a couple of miles down a B road about a mile after Lowthesall.

I checked the clock. It was nearly seven. Later than I'd wanted, but I'd made good time given the weather. I sipped lukewarm coffee and watched the snowflakes hitting the windscreen and settling, before being swept away by the intermittent wipers.

Despite the caffeine, I felt sunken and exhausted.

I checked my face in the mirror.

I looked how I felt.

Half an hour later I turned into the lane that led to the farm and stopped. God alone knows who'd handed it B road status. It was narrow, not much wider than a single vehicle.

Furrows left by a previous vehicle had filled with fresh snow, leaving little more than smudges for me to follow on an otherwise smooth surface that twinkled innocently under the headlights.

I let the window down and listened to the snow crunching under the wheels as I pushed on with the engine at little more than tick-over. The road curved gently around to the right and then up a shallow incline. The steering felt vague and disconnected, and I could sense the transmission shuttling between wheels as it tried to keep the car moving.

At the summit of the incline, the road forked.

Two unreadable road signs on a single post pointed in different directions. Either way was a featureless undulating whiteness.

The sat nav told me to turn around. Its last destination had been Lowthesall, the farm itself being unrecognised.

I sat and listened to the hum of the air conditioning and the faint pattering of the engine.

The Moor rolled away ahead of me, silent and bare except for vague furrows of ditches alongside snow smothered dry stone walls.

Here and there a twisted skeletal tree clawed at the darkness above the car's lights.

I tossed a mental coin and took the right-hand fork.

The road curved right, then sharply left, then right again. After that, it was virtually straight for almost a mile, then left again, and suddenly a pair of pale yellow lights glimmered in the blackness on my left just ahead of me.

The tyres scrabbled up an incline, and a curved dry-stone walled entrance opened up on the left. I slowed to a crawl and half turned into it before stopping.

A driveway, perhaps seventy yards long, sloped down past a low barn on the right, its frontage hung with canvas sheeting instead of doors. Lying at right angles 30 yards to the left of the barn was a long, squat two-storey farmhouse with a snow-blanketed roof that was a jumble of different levels.

Thin smoke rose like a pencil in the windless moonlight from one of its chimneys. The yellow lights I'd seen glowed from its downstairs windows.

In front of the house, to one side of an enclosed porch, what looked like a long-wheelbase Land Rover sat thickly blanketed in snow.

I nudged the X3 through the entrance and let it find its way down the driveway at tick-over.

As I got close, I saw a figure move across one of the windows, and then the front door opened within the porch. She stood and watched me park and turn the engine off.

I got out and walked towards her, shielding my face against the snow. When I reached the porch she brought her arm from behind her, and I could see the side-by-side shotgun she held.

She called through the closed half-glazed door to me.

"What do you want? Are you lost?"

I felt like saying something ironic but stopped myself.

It was too fucking cold for smart-arsed comments.

I let my hand fall from my face.

Snowflakes fluttered against my cheeks.

"It's Danny, Susan. Can I come in?"

15

She stood for a moment and looked at me, then opened the porch door and stood back, the shotgun still in her hand.

I stepped inside.

"Hallo, Susan."

Her eyes took me in for a moment, questions shuttering across them.

"Come in."

As she spoke, she turned and went back into the house.

I shut the door of the porch behind me and stepped through the front door into a stone-floored kitchen.

She lay the shotgun on a broad wooden table that with the chairs placed around it took up most of the room.

She turned to face me, leaning herself back against the table.

I closed the door behind me.

"What's with the pop gun?"

"I live here alone. One never knows."

"No. I suppose not."

I looked around me, trying to think of something to say. Low oak beams and rustic looking cupboards over newer looking marblelite worktops made up half the room.

In the far right corner, an aged pastel green AGA stood by a closed door. A large cream enamelled kettle sat on the AGA with steam writhing from its spout.

"Don't spose you've got any coffee, have you, Susan?"

"Yes. I'm sorry. Come and sit down. I'll make you one."

She didn't need to add "before you go" - it was just there, in her attitude, that same old imperious upper-middle-class thing.

It wasn't that she was much too polite to say it - more that she didn't see why she should. She lifted the shotgun off the table and took it with her over to the AGA, leaning it beside the closed door that I presumed led outside to the back of the house.

I sat down in the first chair at the head of the table.

She moved the kettle across the AGA onto a hot plate and came back, opened a cupboard and took out a jar of coffee and a pot I assumed contained sugar.

"White?"

"Please."

From a fridge she took milk and brought it to the table, standing the sugar and milk in front of me.

Now recovered, she decided to at least be polite.

"Well, this is an unexpected pleasure. What brings you to Cornwall, Danny?"

"I'm here on business. I saw one of your paintings for sale yesterday, although I didn't know it was yours at the time. I went into the shop and asked about it, and they told me about you. I said we'd known each other years ago. They said you lived here, so I thought why not?"

"I see."

She spooned some coffee into a mug and walked back over to the AGA. "And which shop was that?"

"I don't know, I think it was in Bodmin. Or maybe Wadebridge. I forget."

"Probably Wadebridge. I have a friend who has a shop there. She puts my paintings on display for me."

"Yeah, probably Wadebridge."

"Probably." she brought the coffee over to me. "Except that I don't have any paintings out for sale at the moment. So why are you here?"

I poured milk into the coffee and stirred sugar into it. "Why don't you sit down, and I'll tell you."

"I'm perfectly fine standing up, thank you."

"Got any biscuits?"

She pursed her lips, turned on her heel and walked towards the cupboards.

I was across the room and had picked up the shotgun before she realised I'd moved.

"Now -" I broke the action and pulled the shells from the gun. "Sit your stroppy arse down at the table and stop talking to me like I'm shit you just trod in. Then I'll tell you why I'm here."

She glared at me. "How dare you..."

"Shut the fuck up, Susan, and sit down. I'm shagged out, and I didn't drive to the middle of fucking nowhere, just to be talked down to by some stuck up - ." I left whatever I was going to say to her imagination.

She crossed her arms and walked - almost flounced - back to the table and sat down on one of the chairs at the opposite end to me.

"Right, I'm here now. So, say what you have to say, drink your coffee, and then go."

"Thank you."

I snapped the gun shut and leaned it against the frame of the front door.

"How well did you know a man called Gavin Durrant?"

She shook her head. "I don't know anybody called Gavin Durrant."

"OK then. How well did you know a man called Dean Thompson?"

Her eyes widened just slightly, but she controlled herself well.

"I don't know anybody called Dean Thompson."

I spooned another sugar in and stirred.

"He's a tall geezer. Some sort of handyman. You were fucking him."

She looked away from me.

"I told you. I don't know anybody called Dean Thompson."

"Susan, I've seen the pictures."

She glared at me.

"And I have told you, I don't know anybody called Dean Thompson! Is this what you came here for? Are you jealous? Good god! It's bad enough having a husband who sees men behind every tree without some - fool - from a lifetime ago!"

I tapped the spoon on my mug and dropped it on the table. "I'm not jealous, and if I had been before I got here, I fucking wouldn't be now. I don't believe you, Susan. I've got a photograph of you together taken in your house at Whistbury. There was a blackmail attempt. I was asked to stop it. When I got to Dean Thompson, he was dead."

I saw her chin quiver a moment before she could cover its betrayal. Her eyes stared at me. She looked down at the table a moment, then looked back up at me.

170

"When?"

"A couple of days ago."

She drew a deep breath. For a moment her eyes filled with tears and I thought she would cry, but she fought them back.

"Are you a policeman now?"

"No."

"What are you then?"

"Never mind that. I think you're in trouble Susan. I want to help you if I can. That's all."

She nodded, and now, finally, her mouth squirmed and her eyes filled.

She gave out a sob, a lonely little sound that died in her throat.

I dropped my voice.

"Why don't you tell me about Thompson, babe. Let's start there."

She made herself some kind of herbal tea, one of those insipid things in a bag that you hang in the cup, then came back to the table.

This time she pulled out the chair to my left and sat down next to me.

She drew an ornately carved wooden box from under a newspaper, opened it and started to roll herself a joint. She stopped and looked up at me.

"You don't mind, do you?"

I sipped at my coffee.

"No."

"Dean..." she concentrated on the joint, heating the block of resin and crumbling some of it onto a paper she'd laid in front of her.

She got up and pulled a drum of tobacco to her from the other end of the table, opened it and filled the paper before continuing.

"I met Dean when he came to do some work on the house. I know, it is a dreadful cliché. It - just started. Out of nothing, really. Just..."

She finished working on the joint, put it between her lips and lit it, then drew on it heavily and inhaled. She let the smoke out slowly. I watched it curl from her nose and drift upward, through her hair and away towards the beams.

"Just sex?" I offered.

She cut me a glance, watching to see if I meant it critically.

I shrugged.

"It happens."

She pursed her lips and looked away from me, then shook her head.

"No. I don't know. To begin with, yes. I suppose so. I suppose I tried to think that it wasn't, but it was. But as I got to know him, no. It was more than that."

She drew on the joint again, then offered it to me.

I shook my head.

"No thanks. When did it start?"

She took another draw, a smaller one, more like she was smoking a cigarette.

"Oh. The first time? or when did it really start? I mean, to be an affair." She widened her eyes as she emphasised the word.

"Both."

She blew out her cheeks and wiped the tip of the joint into a dull red point on the edge of a deep brass ashtray.

"Around, four years ago now. Four years ago this summer. The day before Daddy's birthday. July the eighth."

I grunted and took another sip of coffee, blotting out the mental images of sultry summer heat and sly suggestive comments.

"And after that?"

The joint glowed red again, the paper shrinking inwards as she drew the smoke into her mouth. She wiped the ash from it again in the ashtray. Then she smiled and shrugged.

"It just grew."

"Grew?"

"Yes."

She paused, and I said nothing, knowing from her eyes that the dope was kicking in and she would speak when she had formed what she wanted to say. "It was Dean that started me on this stuff." she lifted the joint from the ashtray and took another pull. "I'd never done it before."

I watched her, waiting for her to properly unwind.

"The work he was doing finished. And I didn't see him for a while, I thought, well, that was it. I was just a screw and overall it was best that way. But it was really good." she gave a little giggle,

172

then bit her lip and touched my arm, just above the wrist. "I'm sorry..."

I gave her a jokey old fashioned look, then winked at her.

"Get on with it, you slut."

She wrinkled her nose and gave a little laugh.

"I was. I know. But, well. Nobody was hurt. Stephen didn't know, and he wasn't interested anyway. Well, he would have been of course, if he had known, but he didn't know, so that was -" She took a final draw on the joint and stubbed it out. "- alright."

"No harm done." I prodded.

She exhaled a long plume of smoke.

"Exactly." she agreed "I did feel a bit, well, silly about it for a while, but I thought, you know - that it was just me. Being prudish. I am a bit of a prude really, Dan. You know I am."

"Yes, Susan, I know."

"But I didn't hear anything from him for weeks; and I thought, that was it, over, just a silly stupid thing that happened; and I got over it, and Stephen was busy with things and I got involved in those - would you like some rum in your coffee? I have some rum. Wait."

She got up from the table, went to one of the wall cupboards and came back with a quarter-full bottle. She unscrewed the top and began tipping it into my coffee.

"Say when."

I let it run for a second.

"Thanks."

She poured a good dose into her tea, then squeezed out the bag with a teaspoon and dropped it in the ashtray.

"So what happened next?"

"Mm, well he called around. Out of the blue one day. He said that he thought he'd left a tool with us. It was just an excuse, of course. He hadn't. He came in and pretended to look for the tool, and -" she sipped her tea "- well, it started properly then. Sometimes, he would come to the house, but most times we met at his house."

"Where did he live?"

"In London. Well, sort of London. Barnet. That isn't really London, is it? I never think it is, not really. It's sort of outside London, isn't it? - "

"Yes, I suppose so." I cut across her. "Did you meet often?"

"To begin with, yes. Once a week, sometimes twice a week."

"Did you stay over?"

"Sometimes if Stephen was away I would, but not often."

"Do you still have his address in Barnet?"

"I could find it if you want it. What do you want it for? He doesn't live there now. Didn't live there, now." She shook her head as if you clear her thoughts. "He had moved, about two years ago."

"Where to?"

"I don't know."

"Weren't you still seeing him?"

"No, not really. He - well I think he was not - you know what they say? - never stop a traveller? - and Dean was a traveller. Nothing was fixed about him; he was a man who lived for the present, for today. A free spirit."

"But he said he loved you?"

"I, yes, I think he did. In his way." She took a couple of mouthfuls from her cup. Her eyes were suddenly full of tears and she put the cup down smartly and flapped her hand in front of her face as if waving away fumes. "I'm sorry."

"No need to be sorry, Sue," I said softly. "It's OK."

"It is OK. I know." she pursed her lips and forced the emotion back. A single tear slid through her lashes and ran down her face into the corner of her mouth. She cuffed its trail away and stared down at the cup, holding it in both hands. "How did he die, Dan?"

"Let's not get into that right now babe. Tell me about the break-up. Did it end suddenly, or - what?"

She shook as a sigh wracked through her.

"It. Sort of just - fizzled out."

"How?"

She shrugged.

"Oh, he was always busy. I would call, but he wouldn't answer. Then he would call me. Days later. Sometimes weeks later."

"And you always went back?"

She nodded. "He was like a child in some ways. He could never face up to things. I had to help him with things."

"With money?"

"Sometimes."

She let go of the cup, unscrewed the top from the rum and poured more of it into her tea. "A lot of the time, to be honest. He never had any money. His business was going wrong, too many East Europeans he always said. God, but how Stephen would have loved to hear him talk about that. I went over a few times when he wasn't expecting me and he was never working. He never seemed to have any work."

"Was he good at what he did? The work he did, I mean.." I winked at her, but she just nodded, a little tilt of her chin to acknowledge my weak attempt at a joke.

"Yes. Well, it was OK. He did decorating, plastering, some plumbing. That kind of thing. It was fine."

"But he never had any work?"

"No. Well. Not enough."

"Did he have a family?"

"A wife, and a little girl. I never met them."

"Divorced?"

She shook her head. "Separated."

"What was her name?"

"Carol."

"Can I get myself another coffee?"

"I'll get it..."

"No, it's OK. I need to stretch my legs. I've been driving all day."

I passed behind her and lay my hand on her shoulder, allowed my lips to brush the hair on the top of her head.

She covered my hand with hers.

"It's nice to see you again, anyway Sue," I said.

"And you too, Dan. Thank you."

"For what?" I moved away and fixed myself a coffee.

"For coming."

I shrugged. "Why wouldn't I?"

"Well..."

I came and sat back down.

"Well, what?"

"I was horrible to you."

"You were who you needed to be for yourself, Susan. It didn't work for you. So you got out. I understand why." I shrugged. "It happens. That's life."

"I've often thought about you. Wondered how you were. What you were doing."

I looked at her. She looked away, fiddling with the cup. "Really. I did. I felt - really, so bad. About everything."

"Well, don't let's talk about that. It was a lifetime ago."

"Was it?"

"Yes."

She shook her head. "You never thought of me?"

"Of course."

"Very often?"

"Sometimes. When did you last see Thompson?"

I saw her eyes move under her lashes. She took a swig from the cup. "Nearly two years ago now. November. The week before Guy Fawkes Night."

"Where?"

"Just, out. We met for a walk."

"Where?"

"I don't remember exactly. I think it was somewhere near Watford. Along the canals."

"Was he still living in Barnet?"

"No, he had moved by then."

"But you didn't know where to?"

"No."

She drank again.

"He wouldn't tell you?"

"No."

"Do you think he'd gone back to his wife?"

She shook her head slowly. "No. I don't think so."

"What makes you say that? Something he'd said?"

"I just don't think so." she sighed. "It was a long time ago now Dan, and I have - put it all away. Do you understand? All the emotions of it. I don't remember what I felt, and because I don't know what I felt, I can't remember all the details."

She looked up at the ceiling and took a deep breath through her nose.

"It's not important to me now. It is behind me, and it is gone, and I am here now."

I looked at her profile. Her eyes were narrowed as if staring at something far away. Without looking at me, she asked: "How did he die?"

"He'd had his throat cut."

"He was murdered?"

"Yes."

"Did you see it?"

"I didn't see it happen. I saw him not long afterwards."

"But - who?"

I left the question open. "How much was he into you for Susan?"

"Pardon?" She looked at me, puzzled.

"How much money, had he taken from you?"

She stared into my eyes for a moment, then back to her hands cradling the cup. "I don't know. Five, perhaps six thousand pounds."

"Are you sure Stephen didn't know about the affair? Or about the money?"

"The money was from my account. He knew nothing about that. Whether he knew about the affair or not, no. At least, I don't think so. He didn't say anything about it. But then he wouldn't. He is too clever for that. But we were always very careful. Always discrete."

"But you used to meet at the house in Whistbury"

"Yes. But not very often."

"How often?"

She pulled the box towards her and began rolling another joint.

"Do you do a lot of that?"

"Sometimes. It helps me relax. Helps me create."

"How often did you meet at the house?"

"Five, perhaps six times."

"That's all?"

"Yes. Not including the first two times that I told you about. It was too risky. Stephen might have come home, or that nosey woman next door might have cottoned on."

"What nosey woman?"

"The woman who lived in the house next to ours. Janet. No, Jane. Always wanting to talk."

"Did you ever think Stephen might have bugged the house?"

She shrugged.

"I don't know. I mean, there was an alarm and cameras outside. We had to do that for the police; but no, I don't think he would have done anything like that."

"Why not?"

"Because." she licked the paper and rolled the joint, smoothing it together and twisting the end closed.

"Because what?"

"Because, Stephen and I had an agreement." she lit the joint and inhaled, then blew the smoke out. "He wouldn't interfere in my life, and I wouldn't ever cause him problems or embarrass him."

"Had?"

"I'm sorry?"

"You said you had an agreement with Stephen."

"Had and have. We live completely apart now. I have nothing to do with him at all. I haven't seen him since - " she thought "- since before last Christmas. And that was the first time since the Easter before."

I sipped my coffee and she beat me to the next question.

"So what about you? What are you doing now? That looks a rather expensive car for a council estate hooligan to be driving." she grinned, her teeth showing white and her nose wrinkling. "Did you steal it?"

"Yes. Just to impress you."

She laughed. "I can believe it." Again she put her hand on my arm, but this time, she let it slide down past my wrist and squeezed my hand. Her eyes were narrowed, the pupils wide.

She was as high as a kite.

"And are you married?"

"Nope. I never married."

"Why not? Because of me?" she giggled and took her hand from mine and put it to her mouth like a naughty child. "Sorry!" she whispered.

"No. I never wanted to. It's never been an issue."

"So, nobody special?"

"No. Nobody special. Is that clock right?" I asked.

She turned her head to look at the clock that hung beside the Aga.

"Yes, why? Do you have to go?"

I took a deep breath. It was getting on for nine o'clock, and I was socked in, in the middle of Bodmin Moor, without a clue where to find a room.

"I should have asked earlier. Do you know where there's a hotel?"

She leant towards me and smiled. "Don't be ridiculous Dan. You can't possibly go out in this weather. I won't hear of it."

And then, right then, that was when I knew I should have stayed at home, and not because I was worried about Phillipa.

I went outside to get my bag. She stood at the door with a heavy woollen coat around her shoulders, her arms folded in front of her.

The sky had begun to clear and the moon dropped milky grey light onto the hardening snow. I started the car, cleared the snow from both its screens and reversed it back within the barn.

The snow crunched and collapsed beneath my feet as I walked back to her.

"Why did you do that?"

"I was worried what the neighbours might think."

She giggled.

"I'll need to be away early in the morning, Sue. Fuck having to clean it when the snow's had all night to freeze on it."

"You really are still so coarse, aren't you."

"I'm almost house trained these days."

"You were, always coarse. It was always, fuck this and fuck that and everybody else was a See You Next Tuesday."

I pushed the porch door closed behind me.

"Most of them were."

"And you were always so hard done by, waving your bloody background at me like a flag on the slightest excuse."

She rolled away from the doorframe and walked into the kitchen. She hung the coat on a hook by the door. It missed the hook and fell to the floor.

179

She seemed not to notice and sat down at the table again, took a swig from her rum tea and eyed me like a child who's seen chocolate as I dumped my bag on the floor and closed the front door.

I took off my jacket and hung it over the back of my chair, then picked her coat up from the floor and hung it on the hook she'd missed.

"Can I eat something Sue? I'm bloody starving."

"Of course, help yourself." She waved her hand vaguely at the kitchen worktops. "There's a chicken, I cooked it earlier in the fridge."

"That will do fine."

"Bread is there." she waved again in the general direction of the worktops. "There's pickle and stuff. In cupboards."

As I walked past her she reached for the wooden box again and began to roll another joint. At this rate, I'd just have to chuck a blanket over her where she slept.

"Don't you think you've done enough of that for one night?"

"Pffft."

Obviously not.

I opened the fridge and lifted out a chicken. It was missing one leg and some breast but otherwise looked as good as it got.

I carried it past her and lay it on the table. "Glad you finally learned to cook in the end, anyway."

"I could always cook." She was concentrating on the joint, slowly rolling the paper around and over itself. "I just never cooked for you."

"Where's the knives and forks?"

"In the drawer."

"Give me a clue. Which one?"

She licked the joint and closed it carefully. Satisfied with her handiwork she put it in her mouth and lit it.

"Knives? Forks?"

She exhaled.

"In that." She pointed at a drawer.

I sorted myself out a knife and fork, found a half loaf of sliced bread, some butter in a stoneware dish and on the way back around spotted salt and pepper.

She pulled slowly on the joint, inhaling deeply, watching me put myself a sandwich together.

Then she exhaled and said loudly "Oh no!"

I stopped with the sandwich halfway to my open mouth. "What?"

She wagged a finger rhythmically in the air, like she was scolding an invisible child.

"Logs."

"What?" I took a bite of the sandwich.

"Logs need in. I forgot."

"Logs," she repeated, looking at me.

I chewed on my mouthful of sandwich and spoke with my mouth full.

"Let me eat. I'll get them afterwards."

She smiled at me, leaning towards me, her eyes half-closed, her pupils deep and liquid. The pungent sweetness of the resin merged with the chicken. "Thank you," she whispered.

I nodded at her, still chewing.

"I must pee," she announced. She lifted herself away from the table and half walked, half tottered to the door beside the AGA.

"Want more coffee?" she asked.

"Yeah, in a bit."

"K". She opened the door and closed it behind her.

I took another bite of the sandwich. I looked at the tobacco tube. Lucky Strike. "Fumer Tu". French. I looked at the rum. Negrin. French.

I put down the sandwich and was about to go to the fridge when the door opened and she came back into the room. She smiled blandly at me as she walked across to the table and sat down heavily in her chair.

She emptied the last of the rum into her cup, took a sip then looked at me curiously. "What do you do Dan."

"I'm an estimator."

She lifted her chin, then let it fall in a nod. "Oh. I see." she sipped from the cup, her eyes still on me. "And what do you estimate?"

"Costs, outlays, times. For projects."

"Oh. I see. What kind of projects."

181

"Building projects mainly."

"Building projects?"

"Building projects. If someone is expanding, they are maybe opening a new branch. It all needs costing and checking through."

"Uhuh." she nodded again, then shook her head. "I don't understand."

"It's not important." I pushed the last of the sandwich into my mouth and took my coffee cup over to the AGA. "How often do you sell paintings?"

"Oh, well... enough."

She was looking a lot worse for wear now.

"I think I'll get those logs in before I drink this. Where are they?"

"In - barn. Right side."

"OK."

I brought the coffee back to the table and put my coat on. "Is there anything to carry them in?"

She thought for a moment. "Yes, a barrow. It's there."

I assumed she meant in the barn. "OK."

I opened the door to the porch and the shotgun caught my eye. I lifted it, tucked it under my arm and closed the door behind me.

I watched her through the glass.

Her hands were cupped around her mug, and she stared wistfully into the middle distance. She wouldn't hit the barn, let alone me. I broke the gun and reloaded it, slid it onto the rafters of the porch and went for the logs.

16

She sat watching me stack the iron stove in the living room.

I'd made her a coffee and forbidden her any more dope, and after some sulking and a long meandering lecture about bloody men always telling her what to do, she seemed to see sense and had given in.

After the coffee, she seemed a little bit more with it, although she was still pretty much bat-shit and had needed steering onto the couch, where she now sat with her legs coiled under her.

I lit the fire, made sure it would take and went at sat down at the other end. I stared into the window of the stove, watching the logs spit and smoke and flames begin wriggling around and in between them.

She rested her cheek against the back of the couch and looked along it at me.

"What did you do when we split up, Dan?"

"Do?"

"I mean, did I hurt you badly?"

"I think we hurt each other, didn't we? It wasn't only you, was it. I was a right arsehole at times."

"But, did you love me?"

"Yes. But I didn't know what to do about it."

"What do you mean?"

"I didn't think I was good enough for you, so, I don't know, I tried not to get involved."

"You took my virginity and then you fucked other girls."

"I did not fuck anybody else. Ever."

"Didn't you?"

"No."

I looked down the couch at her. "I've had a few years now to think it all through, you know? and - we would never have worked. Your parents would've had a fit if you'd brought me home. That's just how it was. I knew it back then, inside, I just didn't know how to express it. I took it all personally."

"Daddy would have loved you."

"Don't be daft, Sue. Daddy would have fucking hated me. A council house toe-rag like me banging his only child, and leading her astray?" I shook my head and looked away from her.

"Mummy would have understood. She would have talked to him."

I looked at her. She was demented. Worse, she was perfectly serious.

"Well, there we go. Such is life."

She wriggled along the couch to me and lay her head against my shoulder, sliding one arm underneath me and laying the other across my waist. "I've missed you."

"Good. I missed you too."

"Have you?"

I looked down at her. Her eyes looked up at me from under her hair, child-like and serious. I lifted my arm and let her slide against me. "Course. You're my Sue, aren't you."

I felt her trembling against me, heard her breathing change and knew she was crying. I stroked her hair and pushed my lips to her head.

Christ.

And I thought I was a fucking mess.

I stared into the stove, watching the logs glow and flare and begin to crumble. I didn't have the heart to ask her about Simon while she was like this.

It seemed obvious what had happened anyway. Simon had died and she had been fucked up by it. Booth was an absent husband, and Simon wasn't his anyway. Into the vacuum had walked Dean Thompson, and she had fallen for him.

From what she'd told me, about the unanswered calls, the calling round to see him unasked, it looked as if she had chased him, been a pain in the arse until finally, he dodged her altogether by moving on without telling her where he had gone.

Eventually, she stopped crying, and her breathing grew slower as she fell asleep.

I stared into the fire and soon nodded off myself.

I awoke with her moving against me. She sighed and pushed closer to me, kissing my cheek and then my neck, her hand squeezing me and stroking me, edging downwards until she met my belt, sliding along it, then her fingers pushed under it.

"Sue?"

"Mmm..."

"Bed."

She nodded, her face rubbing against my chest. "OK."

I followed her upstairs and she led the way into her bedroom. Moonlight through two tall sash windows draped pale grey rectangles across the unmade bed, the small wooden cabinet beside a chair hung with discarded clothes and the large old fashioned wardrobe that took up most of the right-hand wall.

She turned to me and slid her arms around my neck, pushing her mouth against mine, moving it to my neck, one hand pushing upwards through my hair while the other ran its nails down my spine.

I steered her gently to the bed. She broke away from me and undid her jeans, sliding them down her thighs, taking her knickers with them.

She sat down on the bed and finished taking them off, then reached out and grabbed my belt and pulled me to her and began unbuckling it.

"Sue."

She struggled with the belt, tugging at it, then finally freeing it.

I grabbed her hands.

"Sue."

She looked up at me.

"Yes?"

I shook my head, reached out and stroked her hair.

"Let's not, Sue. Not tonight."

She moved my hand from her head.

I let it fall to my side.

She sat staring down at her jeans where they lay at her feet.

I sat down on the bed next to her.

Her voice was small when she spoke.

"What's wrong with me?"

"Nothing."

She shook her head.

"Nothing is wrong with you Sue. I've been driving all day, yeah? And the past few days have been - spent - finding out all kinds of things about you and your ex -" I thought about how to put it tactfully and decided that to say nothing was best.

"It's because of him, isn't it."

"Who?"

"Dean. Because he was black."

"Don't be daft."

"Yes, it is. You think because I said it was good. You don't want to be second best."

"Or second biggest?"

She shrugged. "Well? It's true, isn't it?"

"It never crossed my mind. I'm hardly hung up about the size of my cock."

"You shouldn't be."

"I'm not. You're the one with the problem, not me. You slept with a black bloke and I've slept with black women. Big fucking deal."

She looked directly at me:

"You really don't care?"

"No. I really, don't care." I nudged her with my elbow "You sssssslut."

She rested against me.

"It isn't funny."

"What isn't?"

"That."

"What? You being a slut, or me sleeping with black girls?"

"Shut up."

"OK. I'll shut up."

I put my arm around her shoulders.

"Come on, let's get you into bed, Sue. You're out of it."

I lay down on the duvet next to her.

She stared out of the window, her face half in shadow. Her hand found mine, squeezed it and drew it across her so it was under her chin.

She spoke without looking at me.

"Will you sleep here Dan? Please?"

186

"Course. Is there another duvet or something?"

"I mean, will you sleep here, in bed, with me. Just hold me. Nothing else. Please?"

"If you want."

She nodded.

"I really do."

"OK, babe."

"But don't call me that. Please."

"What? Babe?"

She nodded.

"You always called me that."

"Sorry."

"Don't be. Just, don't call me it now, please."

I slid into bed beside her and lay on my back, feeling the warmth of her close to me, the soft pillow under my head.

Sleep began pulling me away.

I studied the shadows cast by the window frames, the creamy moonlight cut with dark straight lines.

The last thing I remember was thinking was how silent it was.

I woke with a start, lifted my head from the pillow and looked around.

The moon had shifted across the sky and the room was now almost completely dark.

I stared at my watch, trying to make out the time. It was just after four.

Susan lay on her front, her hair spread across the pillow, one hand raised and half-covered by it. Her breathing was slow and deep.

I needed a piss.

I slid out of bed, crept across to the door and managed to open it silently. To my left, another window at the end of the hallway looked out over the drive. Straight across from me, the stairs fell away into darkness. To my right, a short corridor with a door on either side ended in another window.

I opened the door on the left. It was another smaller bedroom. A single metal framed bed took up most of, its bare mattress piled with clutter. I pulled the door closed and opened the one opposite.

187

An old cast iron bath with a shower curtain took up most of the far wall. To its left a basin with aged looking taps sat beneath a pebbled glass window, to its right a toilet under a high mounted cast iron cistern.

I couldn't find a light switch, so I pissed by what little light came in through the dappled glass of the window.

I looked in on Susan on the way back.

She had spread herself over to my side, her arm outstretched.

I went downstairs to the kitchen, found myself a glass and filled it with milk.

I sat down at the table. There was a quarter-inch of rum left in the bottle. I poured it into my milk.

I looked at the bottle's French labelling.

I pulled the box of tobacco to me.

She said she hadn't seen Booth since last Christmas.

Then why had she been in France?

I went to the fridge and moved stuff around, checking labels. There was nothing French.

I looked through the cupboards. A few tins were French, but the sell-by dates were still long. They could have been bought anytime in the past couple of years.

There were two more full bottles of Negrita.

I drank the milk down, went back upstairs and slid into bed.

She moved against me.

"Where have you been?" she asked drowsily.

"For a piss and a drink of milk."

She giggled and slid both her hands down inside my boxers and gripped me, pushing my foreskin firmly down and squeezing and kneading the exposed flesh.

"Is he clean enough to eat?"

Despite myself, I responded, feeling myself thickening and forcing her fingers apart.

She slid her face down my stomach and I felt her hot greedy mouth around me as she forced me into the tight undulating roughness at the back of her throat.

I sensed her get up in the morning.

She padded out of the bedroom and quietly pulled the door to, leaving me to sleep.

The next thing I heard was the clatter of the Land Rover's engine kicking into life outside.

I rolled over and checked my watch. Nearly eleven.

I slid out of bed and looked out of the window.

She was sweeping the Land Rover clear of snow with a broom.

I sat back down on the bed.

I was hoping I'd feel something.

Anything.

Even guilt.

But there was nothing.

Not even the memories, that had once meant everything.

Only two strangers, from two different lifetimes ago.

I pulled on the basics and went downstairs barefoot.

As I stepped out into the porch. She saw me and smiled, brought the broom to the door and stood it against the side of the porch.

She opened the door.

"Good morning."

She stood waiting for me to react.

I shivered at the cold.

"Aw, come inside, you'll catch your death." She pushed in past me and closed the door, then put her hand behind my head and kissed me on the lips.

She drew her face back.

"Thank you, Dan."

"For what?"

"For being here."

She let her hand fall, doubt across her face, her amber eyes wary. "Are you OK?"

"I'm freezing cold, and still asleep."

She smiled and walked into the kitchen.

I followed her.

"I'm going into Bodmin. Shopping. Will you be staying tonight?"

I sat down at the table.

I hadn't got that far ahead, but I heard myself say yes.

"Good."

She wrinkled her nose and ran her fingers through my hair.

"Then I'll get some stuff for a roast and we'll have a feast and get your strength up for tonight."

I looked up at her.

"Don't I get a night off?"

"Yes, in another 12 years or so. Now I've found you again I'm going to wear you out."

She walked to the cupboards and pulled a mug from a hook.

"I'll make you a coffee and then get going. I'll probably go and see my friend Libby while I'm there. The one who has the shop I told you about, so, I don't know. I'll probably be back at three."

She filled the mug from the kettle on the AGA and brought it over to me.

"You know where everything is, just help yourself."

She stroked my hair, then bent and kissed my cheek.

"Right. I will get off."

I sugared the coffee and sipped it, hearing the doors to the house closing behind her.

The Land Rover's engine clattered as she manoeuvred around, then she drove it slowly up to the road.

I heard the engine roar briefly as she pulled out, then fade away.

With luck, I had an hour or two.

17

I shaved and showered, threw down another coffee, and then began to take the place apart.

I started downstairs in the kitchen. In cupboards, behind cupboards, on top of cupboards. Taking drawers out, checking the backs and bottoms for anything taped to them, checking for false bottoms. I moved onto the living room, the same routine, with the same result. Nothing but drawers full of trash. Dead batteries, half-empty boxes of matches, candles, the type of junk you find in any home.

From the living room, I went into a smaller room next door.

It looked as though Susan used it as an office. It was almost bare, just a single filing cabinet, a desk and a computer, a late model laptop.

I switched it on and it booted to a password screen. I turned it off and checked through the filing cabinet. Nothing except household bills and documents.

I went out into the kitchen to my jacket and brought back a USB drive. I plugged it into the laptop, went into BIOS and booted it from the USB. When it had started, I opened search and typed in STEPHEN

While it searched I looked through the desk drawers. Once again, nothing out of the ordinary.

The search had returned a list of 30 or so files. I copied them over to the USB drive, cleared the search and typed in "Duct Four" and hit return.

A door next to the desk opened into what was Susan's studio. Two empty easels stood like naked scarecrows. A few paintings, landscapes, seascapes, a view that must have been of the moor from the rear of the house.

The pictures were formulaic, but would be attractive and effective for the market she no doubt sold to, foreign tourists and the like.

I checked back on the computer. The Duct Four search had found nothing. I cleared the search box, typed in SIMON and hit return.

Immediately pictures began filling the search window.

A head of unruly dark hair, a lopsided untidy smile, Susan's eyes but brown. Half-round but vacant.

Lost.

Susan and a baby.

Susan smiling.

A child in a cot, brown eyes smiling.

A pause.

More pictures vomited onto the screen.

From somewhere above, through glass, a dark wood window.

A garden, a broad gravel drive.

A wheelchair, it's back to the camera.

Dark tousled hair barely showing over the back of the wheelchair.

Booth, tall, bending, speaking into the wheelchair.

Sneering.

Holding the hair.

Pulling the hair towards him.

The punches.

The wheelchair, on its side.

The sprawled helpless body on the gravel.

I sat at the kitchen table watching the second hand of the clock jerk silently round its blank face, the minute hand flicking once each time the second hand overtook it.

I unlocked my phone and rang my landline, but as soon as she answered I knew it was a mistake.

"Danny?"

"Hallo babe. Everything alright?"

"Yes. Thanks."

Silence.

I couldn't think of anything to say except the last thing I wanted to.

It sat on my tongue, begging to be spoken.

"Is everything OK, Danny?"

"Yeah, sorry. I was watching something outside. It's all OK here. She's gone out so I thought I would see if you were alright before I started looking through things. I better go. She'll be back soon. Take care babe."

I went upstairs and lay on the bed, smelt Susan there.

Tasted her again. Felt her hot slick insides gripping me. Her eyes half-round, childlike, looked up at me again.

Sunlight broke through the window and mocked my tears.

I needed to keep it together.

I had an opportunity here, while she was out, to get anything else I could find, anything that would nail Booth, without having to ask her for it, without her ever knowing.

I realised, though, that I no longer cared if it nailed her too.

She cared nothing about me.

She couldn't even tell me about Simon.

Not then.

That, I understood.

Eighteen years old and afraid, in trouble, pregnant by a useless waster like I'd been then.

But last night, when she was in my arms and talked in the safety of having slept with me, knowing that I meant her no harm.

Then she could have.

Then, she should have.

Instead, she'd told me he was Booths, born prematurely.

And the worst thing was?

I'd wished I could have believed her.

I got up and started with the chest of drawers, lifting the clothes and checking to the back of each drawer in turn. Nothing.

I pulled out the under-drawer to the wardrobe. Blankets. Duvet covers. I lifted each of them, lifted them all out. Pulled the drawer out and looked underneath it. Looked behind it. Nothing.

I pulled the drawer of the bedside cabinet open.

Rubbish, papers. Receipts. Lighters. A candle. I slid my hand to the back of the drawer and hit cold metal.

I gripped the frame and drew it out.

It must have been a family heirloom.

A top break hammerless tank crew Enfield.

I broke it and half-opened it. Six rounds began to eject.

I closed it again and pushed it back into the drawer under the papers and other crap.

I checked under the bed. Dust bunnies. A single pink cotton sock.

I clambered up onto the bannisters, lifted the hatch to the loft and slid it away. Using my foot against the wall I levered myself up through the opening. I shone my phone light around looking for a switch and found it down beside the hatchway. I flicked it and a dim bulb came on at the far end of the loft.

A narrow dormer window hung with an old sack for a curtain faced out onto the front of the house. I tore the sack away in a cloud of dust and immediately saw twice as well. The place was a jumble of crap - old boxes, bags of clothes, old toys, picture frames. God alone knew what.

I began at one end, systematically opening the boxes and searching through the contents, then carefully replacing them in the reverse order.

Books, photographs, the paraphernalia of several lifetimes; an ancient needlework box. Old ornaments and mementoes. Ugly vases. A cardboard box full of ancient car and motorbike magazines.

I stood up and checked my watch. Nearly two.

She said she would be back by three, and if Susan had one trait I believed would never leave her, it was punctuality. She might be early, but she would never be late.

I opened my phone and set an alarm for 2.45.

I checked around the dormer window to see if I could open it a crack - at least I would hear the Land Rover if she came back early. It had been nailed shut. I went back to checking the boxes, but I gave up trying to be tidy about it. I had less than an hour to go through everything. I'd just have to take the chance that she hardly ever came up here.

Another half dozen boxes later I found some of her university stuff, and with it mementoes of our time together. An empty box from some chocolates I'd bought her. A CD of mine. Photographs. I realised that she had kept everything.

I opened an ancient shopping bag, and there was a jumper of mine that had been at her place when she left me.

I pulled it out. It was neatly folded in a clear plastic bag, but there was something else apart from the jumper. I split the bag and pushed my hand inside. Inside the folds of the jumper was a flat metal cigar box. I drew it out and opened it carefully. A lock of brown hair. A ring I had given her. A length of cine film.

I pulled the film free and carried it to the window. I tried to make out some of the frames but the sunlight was too weak. I knelt, laying my phone on my leg and held the film over its light.

Naked men. A smaller man, perhaps a youngster, was being held by two other taller men, while a third man stood behind him.

I wrapped the film around my fingers and drew it tight, then put it back in the cigar box and shut the lid.

The kitchen door creaked open downstairs.

I froze.

I lay the phone and the cigar box down, stood up and padded silently to the hatch.

Footsteps tapped slowly across the kitchen's flagstones then across the foot of the stairs towards the living room.

I heard the slight scrape of the living room doors hinges and sensed it being pushed open.

The footsteps returned, stopping at the bottom of the stairs.

A voice called up the stairs, American with a Germanic accent. "Anybody here?"

This must be a friend of hers. Perhaps a neighbour checking up on her, seeing if she was OK.

I took a deep breath and thought through how to play it.

If I just came down out of the hatch now and said hello, I could put the hatch cover back in place, dust myself off and be having a chat with the neighbour when she got back.

All totally innocent.

She would never even know I'd been in the loft unless he said something.

If he did, I'd say I thought I'd heard rats to try and fob her off.

Then I heard the clatter of the Land Rover's engine as it breasted the rise in the road that led to the house. She gunned the engine to change gear, the transmission whining as she slowed to swing into the driveway, and from the bottom of the stairs, I heard the unmistakable sound of a gun slide being pulled back and released.

I thought of the Enfield in her drawer.

The Land Rover squealed to a halt outside and its engine died.

This was going to be all about timing.

If I fucked it up, she was dead.

I dropped through the hatch until I was hanging on my elbows.

The door of the Land Rover creaked open then slammed shut.

Give me time.

Get shopping out.

Check a tyre.

Anything.

I held my weight for as long as possible, lowering myself as far as I could before I dropped onto the landing.

I was sure he must have heard me, but if it put him off, all the better.

Another of the Land Rover's doors slammed.

I ran into the bedroom and dragged open the drawer to the bedside cabinet. It opened inches and stuck.

I pictured her happy and smiling as she propped the bag of shopping under one arm and reached for the porch door.

I was going to be too late. I shouted: "Susan stay outside!"

I shoved the drawer back in and pulled it again.

It came completely out and spilt its contents onto the bedroom floor.

I grabbed the Enfield and ran through the bedroom door, firing a round blindly down the stairs as I went.

My ears rang and whistled. Now he definitely knew I was around, and hopefully, she would stay outside.

I double gripped and turned the corner of the stairs with my back to the wall.

Plaster showered away from around my head from a round I hadn't heard him fire.

I threw myself down the stairs, firing towards the kitchen doorway as I went.

Through the grey haze of smoke, I saw him as I fell, short cropped blonde hair, a thin determined face, leather jacket.

I saw him turn towards the kitchen door, level his gun and fire twice at Susan, glass from the door disintegrating around him as I landed on my knees at the foot of the stairs and fell headfirst against the wall.

There was a splintering thud as the frame of the living room door was hit behind me. I lifted the Enfield and fired wildly, trying to get to my feet before he could close in on me and finish me while I was prone.

Through the smoke I saw him backing away from me into the kitchen, the fat muzzle of the gun's silencer held in front of him, lining up for a clean shot.

I dived onto the floor at the doorway into the kitchen with the Enfield held out in both hands, firing as he dropped his aim towards me again.

He screamed as his right leg was knocked inwards.

He was crouched now, his left hand gripping his thigh as he levelled the silencer at me single-handed.

I fired again and hit him low in the chest.

He let out a gurgling howl.

Blood fell from his mouth as he crashed forward into the back of the kitchen chairs, struck his head on the table, then hit the stone floor face down.

I crabbed across the cold flagstones to him and pulled the gun from his hand; his fingers flexed, slowly, gripping and releasing something invisible.

I stood up, pulled open the kitchen door, and ran through the porch.

Susan lay face down beside the Land Rover in a sea of shopping, but as I reached her, she moved and pushed herself up onto her elbows.

As I knelt down next to her I heard the transmission whine of a car as it reversed down the drive towards us. I stood up and double-handed the Enfield over the Land Rovers bonnet.

The driver's door of the silver Range Rover opened and the big bald driver I'd seen in Borehamwood half got out, looking at the house.

Then he saw me.

I fired the Enfield at him. The door glass beside him crazed to blue-grey and he leapt back inside and slammed the driver's door shut in a shower of glass.

I fired again but the hammer clacked down on a dead case.

The Range Rover lurched forward, stopped, then its rear sat down and the wheels sprayed slush and gravel as it careered up the driveway towards the road. He accelerated out of the entrance, scraped the car's rear corner along the dry stone walling opposite and was gone.

I knelt beside Susan.

She was squatting, her head low, almost between her knees. As I lay my hand on her shoulder she retched and vomited.

"Are you hit?"

The back of her head shook in denial.

She retched again, but nothing came up.

"Stay here."

I went back into the kitchen.

His hand had stopped flexing. His breathing was shallow, a rasping sobbing sound. I turned him over.

"Who sent you?"

Wide terrified blue eyes stared at me.

His lips were open and quivering. His tongue licked slowly in and out at the blood congealing on them.

"Tell me, and I'll help you: Who sent you?"

His eyes closed.

He tried to swallow but choked instead.

Fresh blood bubbled from his mouth.

I lifted his eyelid with my thumb.

The eye rolled downwards until it centred on me.

"Who sent you?"

The eye lost focus.

His tongue lay still between his lips.

She sat at the table, gripping the mug of coffee and rum as if it was all that kept her upright. Occasionally she would tremble for a few seconds, but she was calmer now he was covered by a blanket and she could no longer see his face.

Blood had run out from under the blanket and begun to congeal in the cracks between the flagstones. I'd opened the doors and windows, but the stench still hung in the air from his body letting go.

I watched her lift the mug to her mouth and take a sip. She looked pale and cold, even with her coat and the duvet I'd wrapped around her.

I went into the living room and took a packet of firelighters and matches from beside the stove, went upstairs and clambered up into the loft again. I tipped the contents of some of the boxes into a heap in the middle of the floor, broke the firelighters open and shook some of them onto it, threw a match into the pile and waited while it began to burn.

One of the firelighters took hold. I piled more paper onto its flame. The low roof space began to fill with smoke. I looked around, spotted a heavy brass curtain rail and smashed through the dormer window with it. Within seconds the flames had risen higher as the fire drew fresh oxygen up through the hatch. I picked up my phone and the cigar box and levered myself back down onto the landing.

I stuffed everything of mine into my holdall and threw Susan's jeans and t-shirt that she had left beside the bed on top of my clothes. I opened the wardrobe, lit a firelighter and threw it inside.

I lit another and dropped it into one of the boxes in the storeroom. The muted roar of flames coming from the loft hatch told me it was time to get her out. I went downstairs.

"Drink up, Sue. We're leaving."

I threw my holdall down by the front door, and dropped the Webley and the Beretta into it, along with a spare clip I'd found in his pocket. I took his wallet from the kitchen table and threw it in after them. I looked back at her.

She still stared into her coffee.

"Susan!"

She jumped.

"Come on, sweetheart."

I pulled the mug from her fingers.

"Come on. Now. Get out to my car."

She picked up her dope box and the tube of tobacco from the table and walked slowly and unsteadily out of the door, the yellow wellingtons she'd worn into Bodmin scraping on the flagstones.

I went into the study, lit another firelighter, opened the bottom drawer of the filing cabinet and dropped it in.

I picked up her laptop, took it into the kitchen and slid it into the holdall. I lifted the shotgun down from the eaves, tucked it under my arm, picked up the holdall and left the porch.

Susan was almost to the barn, but she'd collapsed and was lying face-down on the ground.

I took two steps toward her and the rear window of the Land Rover exploded in my face.

I ducked instinctively against its bodywork and there was a loud impact, the tyre beside me flattened and searing pain bit into my lower left calf.

I heard the low growl of the Range Rovers engine from the road as it pulled away.

I looked across at Susan.

Crimson snow was blooming around her shoulders.

18

I reached the A30 as dusk fell.

The wound on my calf was a quarter-inch deep furrow across the back of the muscle. It had stopped bleeding, but it burned and ached.

Worse was that I couldn't stop shaking, and I couldn't get warm, and when I turned the heating up my throat would tighten and I would almost vomit.

I knew I was in shock, that I should stop and at least eat something to raise my blood sugar, but I had to get as far from her and the farm as possible.

As close to London, and safety, as I could.

I needed protection.

I needed Malcolm.

But Malcolm wasn't there.

Only Sneedie.

My stomach ached, and my clothes felt tight and damp.

I tried to pull myself together, taking deep slow breaths.

Over-concentrating to keep my mind occupied, checking the shape of headlamps behind me, trying to identify cars before they passed me.

I was in a race.

In a race between getting home as fast as I could, while not being stopped by some ticket happy traffic unit for hitting 80, while allowing cars that came up behind me too fast to pass so I could know they weren't following me.

I was past Okehampton now, the road a gloss-black ribbon snaking through the snow-shrouded landscape above my knuckles gripping the wheel, staring into the white tunnel the headlights stabbed through the darkness.

A services sign.

No.

Keep going. You can make it.

Swindon. Get to Swindon, then you can have a break.

Who did I know?

Who did I know who I could go to that I could just hole up with for the night?

Get cleaned up. Get some food in me. Sleep.

Cry.

Susan's head.

Broken.

Open.

Her eyes.

Half-round.

Staring at me through the blood in them.

I felt tears scald my eyes and the road ahead blurred. Let yourself cry.

It will help you.

Let yourself cry.

I lowered the window and breathed in the icy wet air.

My throat tightened and I retched, knew nothing would keep it in, pushed my face out into the slipstream and vomited, then again, and I almost immediately felt myself centre, felt the vice around my ribs and stomach easing.

I stared ahead into the headlights and felt bile rising inside of me again, but this time I knew it helped and pushed my face into the clean cold air and let it go.

I pulled over into the far corner of Exeter services and parked up.

My leg still ached and stung, but I felt whole again.

Calmer.

I now longer shook.

I checked around.

Nobody was parked near me.

I slid out and pulled a pair of jeans from the holdall and sat in the back seat and changed, before limping across to the services building and buying two coffees, a burger and chips, and some chocolate.

I took it all back to the car and sat and stuffed my face and swilled one of the coffees down.

I pulled the phone out of the holdall.

Two missed calls.

Sneedie.

Home.

Phillipa. What the fuck did she want? I rang her.

"Danny, are you OK?"

"Let me guess. You had a hunch."

"Yes." her voice sounded small and fearful. "Are you OK?"

"Yes. I'm fine. Some other people are not quite so fine. But I'm OK."

"What's gone on Danny?"

"Never mind now. I got what you need to finish Booth. I'll call you later when I'm closer to home."

I thought about ringing Sneedie but decided it could wait until I'd cleaned myself up.

I booked into the Travel Lodge.

I stood under the shower for a good ten minutes, letting it scald me and unknot my body.

I dressed the leg wound with the First Aid kit from the car.

The wound was deep but hadn't ripped any muscle.

I dropped four Paracetamol from the kit.

I turned on the TV, tuned it to BBC and left it talking to itself while I worked.

I emptied the gunman's wallet.

80€ and £130 in cash. A German bank card, and a German health insurance card in the name of Dieter Uwe Schroeder.

He'd had a mobile on him but it was switched off. When I turned it on it locked me out of the SIM with a code. I switched it off again.

I checked over the guns.

The Enfield was now empty, all six rounds used. I would have to lose that somewhere. The ballistics would link it back to Schroeder.

The gun Schroeder had carried was a silenced .32 Beretta, ideal for close-in executions with the suppressor fitted.

I cradled the compact weapon in my hand, wondering at the way tiny details, not even mistakes as such, could make the difference between life and death. With its flip-up barrel design, the Beretta could carry a round ready to fire for its first shot.

If Schroeder had loaded that first round, he wouldn't have needed to work the slide.

If I hadn't heard him work the slide, I would have dropped out of the loft smiling and he'd have killed me before I was halfway downstairs.

I dropped the magazine out. It was empty. The gun could hold seven rounds in total with the one in the barrel.

I tried to think back through the gunfight.

One, perhaps two at me as I'd come down the stairs. One in the door frame. Two through the kitchen door at Susan.

He must have missed me with another shot somewhere.

What was clear, was that at the point where I'd leg shot him, Schroeder was already holding an empty gun.

If he'd carried a full magazine, with one up the spout, even wounded, he could hardly have missed me once I'd dived onto the kitchen floor in front of him.

He had arrived to lay in wait for an unarmed woman.

As she'd walked in with her arms full of shopping, he would have carried out the perfect hit: two rounds in the side of her head, point-blank.

Two rounds.

That's all he would have needed.

He was dead because he'd assumed.

Such a trivial detail - you couldn't even call it a mistake, given what he had to do - had cost him his life, and saved mine.

It was now nearly four hours since I'd left the farm, and I had to assume that Susan and Schroeder had been found.

It was odds on that the fire brigade would be there well within an hour of my leaving. Even in that remote area, someone would have seen the smoke, gone up there for a look and then called them.

I had to assume that the police would have arrived shortly afterwards, and by now it would have hit the local news.

I Googled her name and got hits on the BBC Cornwall news site and other sources.

I opened the top report. She'd been murdered. Her body had been found in her barn. A fire had almost destroyed her farmhouse. I opened another report. Same story. Found in her barn. No mention of Schroeder anywhere.

The question now was whether whoever had topped Susan and Thompson wanted to take it further with me.

If they did, it was a matter of whether I could get back to London before they managed it.

I turned the TV off and rang Sneedie.

When he answered his voice was low and guarded.

"Danny. Where the fuck are you?"

"I'm down west."

He paused, just long enough to make me wonder.

"Where?"

Just long enough to trigger my guard.

"Cornwall."

I thought of Schroeder, pointing an empty gun at me as I killed him.

"Whereabouts?"

"Near Penzance."

Again, that half a heartbeat pause.

"Listen, Danny. Find yourself somewhere out of the way, a guesthouse or something, and when you know where you are, call me back. OK?"

"What's going on Sneedie?"

"Never mind. Just do as I say, and everything will be fine, OK?" He cut me off.

That told me several halves of several stories.

It told me Sneed knew that I was involved in something in Cornwall.

The only thing I'd been involved in was killing someone sent to kill Susan.

The only people alive who knew about it were me, and whoever had tidied up at the farm.

And now Sneed.

I must have trodden on someone's toes who had access to Sneed.

That meant Schroeder had been working for someone big.

If Sneed was going to protect me, he would send me a shield, then contact them: "We're sending a bloke who looks like this and he's driving this car."

Unspoken would be: "This man will protect Danny Massey. If you go against our man, you'll be going against us."

I couldn't think of anyone from the UK who would take MDH up on that offer, but from Europe? Perhaps.

Some Eastern European outfits wouldn't give a fuck. If there was any kind of blood vengeance involved, they'd top me and the shield and worry about what happened afterwards.

That Schroeder carried a German ID I took with a pinch of salt.

He could be a Russian who'd lived in Germany for long enough and was legitimately German, or from one of the Polish families that settled in the Ruhr after WW2.

More likely, it was a fake ID. A couple of German businessmen would fly under the Border Agency's radar far easier than any Eastern European.

I got myself a rum from the mini-bar and sat and thought it all through again, but to be honest, I didn't like it any better when had.

It was what it was, and from any angle, what it was, was shit.

I got onto Google again and found a guesthouse, then I rang Sneed.

This time he sounded breezy.

"You found somewhere, matey?"

"Yeah. It's -" I read from Google. "Westview, Alexander Rd, Penzance TR18 5LZ. What do you want me to do?"

"Say again?"

"What do you want me to do?"

"No, the address."

"Westview, Alexander Rd, Penzance TR18 5LR. What do you want me to do?"

"Stay there. We'll send someone down to you."

"Who? Weasel?"

This time he answered too quickly: "Not Weasel. We'll get someone local."

"Yeah, right." I thought.

"OK, thanks."

"You stay there."

"Will do."

Like fuck.

I booked two berths on the morning sailing for Dieppe from Newhaven, grabbed another rum and rang Phillipa.

"Danny? Is everything OK?"

"Everything will be fine. Have you spoken to that bloke from Le Monde?"

"Yes. He's asked me to -"

I broke across her.

"Good. We're going to France. Grab a piece of paper and a pen. I'm going to give you a list of things to bring with you. Ready?"

"Danny, what -"

"Phillipa, not now. We can talk everything through when we meet. Ready?"

"Yes. Of course." She sounded angry. I didn't blame her.

"Phillipa, I'm sorry. Just trust me. Please. It's vital, we get our skates on, OK?"

"OK."

"One. Take the right-hand drawer completely out of the desk. Look into where the drawer was and you'll see a bag stapled inside under the top of the desk. It's got a passport, cash and some other stuff in it. Don't open it. Bring it all.

Two. In the left drawer, you'll find a set of keys to a white Fiat van you'll find in the car park. The reg ends in BVO.

Three. Get your suitcase and put as much of your stuff about Booth as you can in it. Don't worry about clothes, we'll buy new when we get there.

207

Four. Bring this mobile. Make sure it's charged.

Five. You'll need your passport.

I want you to head for Newhaven, via Brighton.

Work your time back to find out when you need to leave, you want to arrive in Newhaven at nine-thirty tomorrow morning latest.

You'll find a sat nav in the van's glove box. I will ring you at nine tomorrow and give you the final destination. That's all of it."

"OK. Well, what can I say?"

"Not a lot. I'm sorry, but time is short, sweetheart. One last thing: if you think you're being followed tomorrow, find a roundabout, and go slowly all the way around it. Watch what happens in your mirror. I've got to go now, babe."

"OK, Danny."

"Pip?"

"Yes?"

"Take care of you."

I set an alarm for 2 am and swigged down a third rum.

I lay my head back on the crisp white pillow and tried to sleep.

It took me an hour of blotting out the hole in Susan's head, but I got there in the end.

19

I dropped off the road near Honiton and hid the Enfield and Susan's shotgun deep in a hedgerow down a narrow track.

By eight-fifteen I was parked in a lay-by on the A26 outside of Newhaven.

I rang Phillipa.

"Follow the A27 then A26 to Newhaven. When you're in Newhaven, the road you're on ends in a T-junction that's a roundabout. It goes right for the port, but turn left. There's a Mcdonald's further on, on the right. Go into the Mcdonald's and park up. Stay in the van, keep it running, and watch the clock. Wait exactly five minutes, then go out again, turn left, going back the way you came. When you get back to the roundabout, go right around it and come back to the Mcdonald's. Park up as far as you can from anybody else and wait in the van. I'll come to you."

I drove to the McDonald's, had breakfast and a couple of coffees, and waited.

At just gone nine, she pulled in and I watched her park up. A grey Renault pulled in a few seconds later and parked nowhere near her. A man and woman got out and came into the Mcdonald's.

I checked my watch. Two minutes to go. A white Insignia pulled in. It parked up. Nobody got out.

I checked my watch. One minute.

Still, nobody had got out of the Insignia. I pulled out my phone and rang her. She answered almost immediately. "Stay there Phillipa. Don't drive off."

"What's happening?"

"I don't know. Maybe something, maybe nothing. Just hold on a minute." I rang off.

I gave it another two minutes, but there was still no movement from the Insignia.

I rang her back.

"OK, do as we said. Go to the roundabout and come back. This time park up and come in the Mcdonald's, order something, but don't sit at my table. When you've sat down, leave your seat and go to the toilets. Take the van keys with you in your hand. Got that?"

"Yes."

I watched the van reverse out of its parking place and slowly drive towards the main road.

The Insignia didn't move.

She waited for traffic then pulled out and drove away.

I watched the Insignia. Still no movement.

I looked across at the X3. It was in clear view of the Insignia's mirrors, and whoever was in the Insignia had a clear view of the entrance to the restaurant. There was no way I was getting out without being seen.

I rang Phillipa.

"Yes?"

"Don't come back in. Go to the port, park up near it and wait for me."

"OK."

I cursed myself.

I'd been too cocky. Too controlling. I hadn't allowed for anything except the logical assumption that Phillipa would be followed by a rank amateur who would follow her again when she left.

I should have left the X3 somewhere and walked to the Mcdonald's.

Could have, should have, would have.

Now I was stuck in a dead-end with nowhere to go but out through the Mcdonald's kitchen, and then what? If I was them, I'd have someone on the back door anyway.

I'd fucked up.

My Schroeder moment.

I checked my watch. We still had an hour until the ferry sailed.

I rang Phillipa.

"Everything OK?"

"Yes. I'm parked just outside the port. There are some industrial units on a road on the right after you turn into the port. I'm down there. What's happening, Danny?"

"It's not your fault, but it looks as if one of us was followed. A car came in not long after you, and instead of following you when you left, he's just sat there. Odds on, he's watching my car."

"The only time I had any thought I was being followed was about half an hour after I'd left your place. But I did what you said and went right around a roundabout, and when he followed he was stopped by the police."

"What kind of car was it?"

"It was white. A Vauxhall. I don't know what model."

"Go through exactly what happened for me, from beginning to end."

"I did what you said. I tried to look two or three cars behind me. I noticed that a car had been behind me for a long way. Maybe fifteen miles. So I did what you said. I came to a roundabout and went right around it. He followed me. So I got to another roundabout and I stopped. I waited until a car was coming and I pulled right out in front of it, then I went right round and back on myself again. The Vauxhall was two cars back in the queue to get onto the roundabout when I got around.."

"Did you see who was driving it?"

"No. There were railings between the carriageways and I couldn't get a clear enough view."

"Was it one man? Two?"

"Honestly Danny, I have no idea. I'm sorry. I was frightened and there was traffic all around me and I was in the inside lane. I just saw it was a Vauxhall."

"What about the registration?"

"Danny I have no idea. I couldn't see. Honestly."

"OK babe. I'm not having a go. So what happened next?"
"Well. I think he must have got impatient or something? I don't know. I was trying to see if he was following in the mirror but I had to drive as well. I had gone perhaps half a mile when I saw blue lights so I slowed down. We were on a sweeping bend, and in the mirror, I could see a white car had been pulled over into a bus stop that I'd gone past perhaps 30 or so seconds before. I assumed it was the Vauxhall. It looked the right shape. That was the last I saw of it."

"You did well, babe."

"I was scared bloody witless."

"I know. It gets your adrenalin going, doesn't it?"

"You could say that."

"I think he's got here anyway. Either by luck or judgment, he's turned up and seen the X3 and now he's waiting for me to come back to it. I'm stuck in McDonald's."

"What are you going to do?"

"I don't know yet, but you've given me an idea. Stay put and keep your head down for now and I'll ring you when I can."

I went and ordered another coffee and took a seat close to the window. From my new seat I could see the roof of the Insignia, but because of a Volkswagen parked by it, not its registration. I would have to hope the other car moved.

Nearly half an hour and a second coffee passed, and I was getting to be a fixture. The same waitress had cleared my table twice now.

I was a strange man with a bruised face and a limp carrying a holdall. I was half a mile from a port, and I'd been here the best part of two hours. The last thing I needed was for them to get suspicious and call Plod. They'd look in the holdall, find the Beretta and the jig was up.

My feet wouldn't touch the ground.

Another ten minutes went by before, at last, a couple walked up to the Volkswagen.

They opened the boot and put something in it. The boot closed and they looked across at the Mcdonald's. For a moment it looked as if they would come across, but the woman waved her hand and they got into the car. As they pulled away, I texted Phillipa the Insignia's registration number and then rang her.

"OK. Here's the plan. You've got the registration. It's a white Vauxhall Insignia. Wait for exactly three minutes after we end this call, then ring 999. Give them the name and address of someone you know. If they ask for your car and registration, pick one from a car you can see, and give them that, not the van.

Tell them you are in McDonald's car park. You've just seen a man acting aggressively to a woman he was with. He was pushing her around and shouting at her, then he pulled out what you think is a knife and forced her into the back of his car. You had followed them at a distance. When you got near the car, you could see the man in the driver's seat. He was injecting himself in the arm with something. You could hear the woman crying. You are there now in the car park and very worried. Got that?"

"Yes."

"OK. With luck, I will see you soon."

I rang off, walked outside the restaurant and stood just to one side of the entrance.

I waited 2 minutes, then dialled 999.

A few minutes later a Police Volvo estate car with no lights or siren running weaved its way through the traffic on the dual carriageway that ran past the entrance. It drove past and I lost sight of it.

A minute or so later a Police van followed it.

I moved to the corner of the restaurant and looked across the car park. The Volvo sat just inside the entrance. The van pulled up blocking the way out. A Policewoman got out of the passenger side of the van and walked to the Volvo.

Another policewoman got out of a side door to the van and began walking along the road and waving traffic away from the entrance to the car park.

The van moved and a second Police Volvo estate stopped next to the first. The van reversed until it blocked the entrance again.

The drivers of the two Volvos held a brief conversation through their open windows, then moved forward into the car park and drove slowly through two different lanes of parked cars towards the Insignia.

Then, in perfect synch, they accelerated, and as one screeched to a halt behind the Insignia the other pulled into the parking place in front and shunted into it, knocking it back a foot.

In seconds four coppers from the Volvo's had jumped out and surrounded the Insignia.

I picked up the holdall and walked across to the X3, started it up and reversed out.

One of the policewomen ran past me, flat-footed and babbling breathlessly into her radio.

I pulled away and joined the end of a short queue of cars that were being waved out onto the main road.

A few minutes later I found the Doblo.

I pulled into a side street a hundred or so yards past it and parked up, pulled the holdall off the front seat and began walking back to Phillipa. The wind was getting up and the sky looked bruised and leaden. It was not going to be the smoothest of crossings.

I threw the holdall in the Doblo's side door and got in the passenger seat. Her arms went around my neck and she held me in silence for a minute. Then she whispered in my ear.

"Remind me, to never, ever trust you. You are the slyest, most conniving bastard I have ever met."

"Thank you!" I said with mock gratitude.

She laughed, then pulled away from me and saw me properly for the first time. "Oh! Jesus!" She looked my face over "Are you OK? What on earth happened?"

"I fell downstairs."

"When?"

"At Susan's. But look on the bright side. When they shot me, they nearly missed."

"What? You've been shot? Where? What the hell has been going on Danny?"

"I'll tell you when we're on board. Right now -" I reached behind me into the holdall and pulled out the Beretta "we need to hide this and get on the ferry."

I got out of the van and tipped the passenger seat forward.

I pulled some clips free at the bottom of the seat's vinyl backing and pushed the Beretta up inside it until I felt the silencer snag between the seat's springs and foam padding.

I got back in and pulled the door to.

"OK, let's get going."

The ferry wasn't busy, not even a quarter full.

We took over a bench seat by a window for ourselves and settled down for the journey. I lay my reefer over me and put my arm around her. She snuggled against me under her coat, and we sat in silence and watched the rain running down the window beside us.

Now, finally, I could relax for a while.

We'd arrived only minutes before the cut-off point and had been the second but last car in the queue.

The last car had been an elderly couple who we'd left behind on the car deck, bickering about whether they should take a picnic basket with them or not.

I felt the warmth of her against me. The ferry tipped and wriggled against its moorings. Somewhere far below us, deep within the ship, a vibration began. I allowed my eyes to close and felt myself falling asleep.

I opened my eyes once and looked around the deserted saloon.

When I came to we were underway.

"How long was I out for?"

She kept her head on my chest. "Not long. Twenty minutes."

"I'm starving. You fancy anything?"

"Better not. I'm not very good on the water."

"Chocolate?"

"Chocolate's different."

"I'll see what they've got." I pulled my jacket on. "Do you want a drink of anything?"

"No. I'm OK." She pulled her coat over her. "Why does it take so long for these things to warm up?"

"Don't know," I said.

I looked down at her. Just her nose showed between the collar of her coat and the mop of hair. "Has anyone ever told you? You're really pretty."

She shifted slightly so her eyes peeked from under the mop of hair.

"There's a joke coming, isn't there."

"No."

She narrowed her eyes at me.

"Pretty chubby? Pretty short?"

I smiled at her.

"No."

"No?"

215

"No."

I walked away to find the buffet.

The deck shook and shimmied under my feet as the ferry got out into the Channel proper. I walked through a maze of carpeted corridors that all seemed identical until eventually, I pushed through a set of swing doors that opened into a bar.

A wall of display cabinets divided it from an identical bar on the opposite side of the ship. Gaps under the cabinets allowed the staff to see through to both bars, and a walkway at the far end of the bar allowed them to serve both sides.

The side I'd entered was empty except for a man and a woman.

They were perched on stools, their elbows on the bar's high polished wood counter, peering into a mobile phone together and talking in whispers.

I walked past them and leaned against the bar. A swarthy man with slicked-back thinning hair appeared in the walkway.

"Yezzir?"

"Know where the food buffet is?"

"Yezzir, go here -" he pointed down a corridor - "then up the stairs and you directly will see it."

"Thanks."

A voice called to the barman from the other side of the ship.

"Have ye got any crisps?"

I stood stock-still, unable to believe my ears.

The barman turned with his standard "Yezzir." and went back through the walkway.

I moved sideways a little and tried to see through one of the gaps under the cabinets.

Nothing.

I glanced across at the couple along the bar. They were still deep in conversation over the phone., so I ducked down lower than the bar just in case and left the way I'd come.

Once through the doors, I straightened up and walked down the corridor until I came to another pair of doors on my right. I pushed through them and walked across the ship to the other end.

The doors were held open by hook stays.

I checked behind me.

A couple of lorry drivers were walking towards me.

I leaned back against the wall and waited for them to go through the doors. They turned right. Perfect.

I ducked out behind them and scanned the bar.

It was empty except for one tall well-built figure.

He was eating a packet of crisps and watching a television that was mounted on the wall beyond the bar.

His back was to me, but I'd know Trevor Halland anywhere.

I backed into the corridor to be sure he didn't turn around and spot me, then walked as quickly as I could back to Phillipa.

I only got lost once before I found her again.

She had lain sideways on the seat with her coat completely over her.

I crouched down next to her and lifted the coat. "Phillipa?"

She blinked awake. "What?" Her eyes searched my face, and then she frowned. "What's happened now?"

"There's someone on board who will be after me. I haven't got time to explain it all now, but I want us to stay apart." I moved over to the holdall and dug my passport out of it. I slipped it into my inside jacket pocket.

"Why are you taking your passport?"

"Because I might need it, babe. Listen, we mustn't be seen together. You don't know me, OK? I'm going to sit over the other side of the ship where I can keep an eye on you, but if you see me, don't look at me, and if I talk to you, treat me as if I am a stranger. Whatever happens, OK? And whatever you do, don't call or text me or contact me at all."

I checked behind me. No sign of Halland.

"Look after the holdall, Phillipa. Everything you need is in there, so whatever happens, carry on with getting to Paris, OK? I can look after myself."

I leaned forward and kissed her on the cheek. "Take care of you."

She watched me as I stood up, the sea-green eyes searching my face, then she bit her bottom lip and pulled the coat over her face.

I crossed to the other side of the ship and sat down at a round table surrounded by leatherette-covered chairs.

I couldn't go anywhere, and there were hours of the journey left to go. It was either coincidence, or he was here on business. If it was, fat chance, a coincidence, it didn't matter if he found me.

If it was business, it could only be police business, in which case it was better I knew whether or not it was to do with Susan. If it was, I didn't have to do anything. Halland would find me.

I put my feet on the table, shut my eyes and waited.

It took him well over an hour.

He kicked the leg of my chair.

I opened my eyes as he took a seat opposite me.

"Aren't ye going to ask what I'm doing here?"

"The best booze trips go from Dover."

"Very funny. Denning sent me to watch over you."

"That was nice of him."

"You're in something too deep."

"Am I? And what might that be?"

"Well. Let's see." he glanced around him. Nobody was sitting anywhere near us. "A Missus Susan Booth was found raped and murdered at her farmhouse in Cornwall."

"Sounds bad. What's it got to do with me?"

"Well now. DNA."

"What about DNA?"

"Your DNA. It's everywhere. In the farmhouse. In the barn." he smirked. "In her."

I knew he was bullshitting, but I couldn't say anything. It would take longer than overnight to get a DNA sample even if there was one, which after a fire and the Fire Brigade hosing everything down would be unlikely.

As for any DNA from Susan, it was still far too soon. He either knew or was guessing that I was involved.

If he knew, it could only have come from Sneed.

"Trot along, Trevor. You're going away, you've seen me and reckoned you'd have a bubble. Where are you off to, anyway?"

"Oh, you carry on, son." He said, grinning a slot mouthed leer of a smile at me.

I laughed.

"Trevor, if I was in the shit, you'd be the last person Malcolm would send to help, and if he did, he'd have called me and apologised." I grinned. "Anyway –" I winked at him. "- we'll find out when he gets back, won't we?"

"There was no need to call you. Garry Sneed already told you he would send someone. Except when he got to Penzance, you'd fucked off."

I looked at him.

He put his face a bit sideways to me, his doll eyes daring me to deny it.

I sucked my teeth.

"OK, Trevor. Let's hear it."

He stood up.

"I'm gasping for a fag. Come outside and we'll talk where nobody can listen in."

We pushed our way through a heavy bulkhead door out onto the stern deck.

Eventually his cigarette lit.

"Look, Danny. Let's talk turkey for a minute. I know what you think of me. And, let's be fair, you know what I think of you. But we're on the same team over this. The Man says do, and it's up to us to make it work, right?"

"Go on."

"You're in a sea of shite son, and it's getting deeper by the hour. Now, I don't know what you went to that farm for, but I do know that Sneed had told you to drop what you were doing, and what you were told to stop doing was connected to this Susan Booth.

But even after you were told, you still poked your nose in. And now you've pissed off the wrong people. You've pissed off some big faces on the continent, but worse, you've pissed off the UK Establishment, people that Sneed and Denning can't help you with. If it was some British firm or other, we both know Denning's name would protect you.

But these people can ruin Denning. And he knows that. So." He took a deep draw on the cigarette. "I will tell you as much as I know, and as much as I can guess.

You were there. You fucked her. She was killed. Your car will end up being found with the gun that killed her in it. You'll go to trial and the ballistics from the gun and the DNA will put you right there. My guess is it will be rape and murder. You'll get off on the rape because it's your word against hers, but you'll be bang to rights over the gun, and the DNA will be enough to make the jury convict you even if they can't do you for the rape.

The same Establishment fuckers as fitted you up will make sure you get life with thirty minimum. You'll wake up with a couple of fellas in your cell one night, and that will be the end of any tales you can tell." He stared out at the ship's wake and drew on the cigarette again.

"I don't know, because I booked sick to come here, and I can't be seen showing too much interest, you know? But, I suspect that there will be a European Warrant put out for you already.

As much as I do know, is that the Devon and Cornwall CID are all over the farm and dabs and DNA are everywhere in spite of the fire. Now, you and I know it's too soon for them to say officially it's your DNA and dabs, but we both know it is. And someone, I don't know who, has made sure you're squarely in the frame.

So, Denning and Sneed have talked it through. They'll look after you as best they can. It's not about caring, because you disobeyed Sneed and got yourself and them in the shit, but the last thing they want is you banged up and getting lemon because you're facing a thirty stretch, then gobbing off just to spite them.

They know that they can't take on the Establishment, so they've come up with this. This way they cover all the bases. If there is a Euro Warrant out on you, I have you under arrest. While it's just me against some French woodentop at the port, I can blag our way through. You're my nick and it's enough you're in cuffs and I'm by you. We have to assume they either have a Euro Warrant on you by now, or the French police are looking out for you anyway."

"Why would the French police be looking for me if there wasn't a Euro Warrant?"

"I'll come to that. Denning's idea is to get you back to the UK. Then you lay low while we cover your tracks. There's plenty we need to cover, but we can do it over a month or two unless you're in custody. Stuff gets lost. DNA gets contaminated. Someone over cleans a gun before it's tested. Enough silly shit to make the CPS unwilling to go through with anything, and even if they do under political pressure, you'd get acquitted by a jury, but -." he took a draw on his cigarette, pulled the smoke in deep then blew out. "- once you're in custody, and once there's a trial to be planned, it's too late. They'll ring-fence the evidence and we'll never get near it. At that point, you're fucked. You'll go down, then they'll make sure you don't come out again."

He shrugged. "Rapist gets topped by other inmates. Happens all the time."

He drew on his cigarette again, looked at it and got another out of his pack. He lit the new cigarette from the old and flicked the stub away.

"So, that's the UK side of things. You asked me why the French police would be looking out for you. You have to understand the level of the people you've been playing with. These are not some two bob UK firm that Denning can scare away. They're top kiddies from Europe.

In France, Germany, Belgium, they have the Police in their pocket. You topped one of theirs, and they want you for it. They will already have dropped your name and the French and Belgian police will be looking out for you. It would make sense from their point of view to make sure that the Police at the ports are in the know. Then there's no fuss. They pull you for a customs check, then hold you on sus until they collect you on a moody warrant."

"OK Trevor, let's say I buy all this. How are you going to make any difference?"

"Because I'm a British detective and you're in my custody. You are under arrest in connection with the rape and murder of the wife of a British MP. Then, a Euro Warrant works in your favour. You're under arrest, and their job is not to interfere but to assist me in returning you to the UK. In short, they can't take you away from me."

"And once we're through customs and in France?"

"We give it a day, then get a ferry back. Again, they can't stop me. I'm executing an EW. They have to assist me."

"What if I want to stay in France?"

"I'm not to allow you to."

"Says who?"

"Says Sneed. If you come back to the UK with me, you get helped. If you try and get away from me, I'm to let you go and call in the French police."

"So you're my pass back through into the UK?"

"I get you back into Blighty. Then Denning will hole you up while the evidence is made unworkable."

"Alright. You've been straight with me, now I'll be straight with you. I need 48 hours in France, and if you give me those 48 hours, I'll give you the nick of your life, and everything you need to put the dead woman's husband inside."

"What for?"

"Fucking kids"

He blanched, then stared at me. "What?"

"Fucking kids. Him and someone else, even bigger. If you give me 48 hours once we're in France, I'll set the whole thing up for you. All you'll have to do is walk in and nick him."

He thought about it for a moment then shook his head.

"No. You and me are getting back on the next boat. Those are my orders, and that's what we'll do."

"Do you understand what I'm offering you? I'll give you Stephen Booth MP, on a plate. Bang to rights. Video evidence. And who knows who else around Parliament you might scare into the open. You'll be fucking Met Commissioner before you're through."

He stared out at the horizon, but I could see from his expression that he wasn't buying it.

"You do understand what I'm offering you here, Trevor?"

He nodded, then looked right at me.

"Aye. I understand what you're offering alright. You're offering me a shallow grave at worst or jail and no fucking pension at best." he shook his head. "You were warned. You were told to drop it, but you carried on. You turned this stone up, all by yourself Massey. And now look what's crawled out from under it.

These cunts run the country, and they won't think twice if keeping their place at the top means snuffing out the likes of you and me. If you want to die a fucking hero, that's your business. I don't."

"I knew you were bent, Trevor, but I never had you down for a fucking coward."

His face coloured and his eyes became slits.

"You're really fucking stupid, aren't you Massey. Do you not understand? So far, at least three people, maybe more, have died to keep a lid on whatever has been going on? And now you want me to get involved? You want me to put the jaws on an MP when people have been killed to protect him? You hand me as much evidence as you like. The fuckers will close ranks. None of it will ever see the light of day, and I'll be fucked. Not you, because you're fucked already. But me."

He pulled on the cigarette.

"No, Massey. You can fuck right off."

"Then don't get involved yourself, Trevor. But let me go, because I don't want anyone else to end up dead before these cunts get what they deserve. Let me go and give me 48 hours and I will come back, you will have done your job, and no one will know you haven't. I'll take my chances with the French filth. Just, let me go. Please?"

He looked at me, his doll eyes bright and wide again, thinking it through.

"OK." He chain lit another cigarette. "OK. Here's what we'll do. We'll get off this thing together. You put cuffs on and I'll drive in case they have been tipped off and are waiting for you. They booked us into a place just outside Dieppe in case we needed to wait overnight. We'll go there. Then, I'll give you 24 hours. If you're not back in 24 hours, I'll tell them that you said you were sick so we had to wait an extra day, but you fooled me and got away."

"OK, 24 hours. Just as you say. But I'm not putting cuffs on."

"You'll put cuffs on. You're my prisoner, a fugitive from a murder in the UK and I need to be able to show them I have you. If you're sitting there like we're off for a dirty weekend together it won't add up."

I shook my head and was about to argue, but he turned and grabbed my sleeve.

"Listen to me, Danny, and stop thinking you always know best. I'm a copper, and we're the same the world over. If they're looking for you and they stop us, it doesn't matter what fucking country, no copper holding a murder suspect would have him sitting in the car as free as a bird so he could hop out at the lights and be off. It wouldn't happen, OK? We try that, and they'll smell a rat. They'll take you in and they'll be nothing I can do about it."

He let go of my jacket, shaking his head.

I had to admit, what he said made sense.

"Alright, we do it your way. I'll wear cuffs. But you give me a key."

He lifted his face to the sky as if asking for divine assistance.

He turned back to me.

"No. I won't give you a fucking key. How do I explain you having a key if they pull you out of the car and search you? Which - " he held up the two fingers holding the cigarette at me to still any argument "- they are entitled to do."

He took a last pull on the cigarette before flicking it away into the ferry's slipstream.

"Your only chance if we're stopped, is that we look exactly what I tell them we are. That way I can blag my way through."

He walked past me and pulled the door open.

"You're just going to have to trust me."

20

While we were queuing to get down to the car deck I saw Phillipa.

She looked straight ahead, the suitcase behind her, my holdall over her shoulder.

A man offered to help her with the suitcase. She thanked him and they disappeared together into the crowd. If she saw me, she made no sign of it.

Halland led the way through the bowels of the ship to his car. "Take your jacket off and have it over your lap. That way the cuffs won't show." He clipped one cuff to the door pull and the other to my left wrist and we sat in silence, waiting while the queue began to inch forward.

Halland's Insignia was nowhere near the Doblo.

He must have flashed his ID and they'd found him a place towards the rear of the ship. With luck, we'd be one of the last cars off and Phillipa would be long gone. He hadn't mentioned Phillipa, even though his number plate proved it was him in McDonald's, and it must have been him that had followed her down and been pulled over.

"How did you know I was on here?"

He looked across at me, then back to the slowly moving queue of cars. "I'm CID. I can get a check on any name. Just takes a phone call."

I nodded. Like fuck.

"What do you want me to do or say if they stop us?"

"Just act normal unless they don't. If they start poking around, let me handle it."

We moved forward off the ship and onto dry land and Halland accelerated after the car in front, following the narrow concrete-walled driveway until we met the end of the queue waiting to get through the kiosks.

"Give me your passport. The check will be on my side."

He took his passport out of his jacket pocket and handed it to me. That was one problem solved. He didn't get to look at mine.

I looked along the lines of traffic, trying to spot the Doblo. A pair of Douane walked slowly down the line of cars, one a tall thin-faced man with glasses, the other a girl of about 25 with her blonde hair in a plaited ponytail.

"Fit." said Halland.

"She's all yours. I'm not keen on blondes."

"Really? What's your poison?"

"Don't know really. I don't mind blondes. I just don't go mental about them."

"Know what you mean. Some blokes would fuck chickens if they had blonde hair."

"Eyes, arse and intellect for me."

"Aye. Got to have something between their ears."

The girl stopped as she drew level with us. She was even prettier up close. Her large brown eyes moved across the interior of the car. Halland looked back at her.

I nodded to her.

She ignored us both and walked across the front of the car.

"Och, fucking hell," said Halland under his breath. "Piss off, you nosey cunt."

The car in front moved forward. Halland put the car in gear, and as he did the girl raised her hand.

"Bollocks," he whispered.

She walked slowly to his window and motioned him to let it down.

"Ouvrir du coffre, si vous plais."

Halland pushed a button and the boot clacked open behind us. She walked towards the rear of the car. Halland took his seat belt off, got out and followed her.

"Ouvrir." I heard her say. I assumed it was a suitcase or bag Halland had in the boot.

The car in front was twenty yards away now. The other line moved forward, and there was the Doblo, right beside me. I stared at Phillipa's profile, willing her to look at me.

She rolled her window down a little. Then she turned and saw me.

I shook my head at her. She stared at me. I dropped the passports in my lap and waved my finger in the only way I could think of to tell her to keep going to Paris.

The boot slammed shut behind me. The car in front of Phillipa moved on. She gave me a last look and pulled forward after it. The car rocked on its springs as Halland got back in.

"Everything OK?" I asked him.

"Aye, yeah. Fucking busy body cunts." he spat.

The two Douane walked past my window. Halland started the car and pulled up behind the queue.

We were only a handful of cars from the kiosk now.

In the other queue, Phillipa was next in line. She had to be scared stiff with everything she was carrying.

The Doblo moved forward and stopped behind the kiosk. I could only see its rear doors. The two Douane walked along the line of cars towards the van.

A minute or so later we moved forward a car length, but the Doblo still sat there.

I let the window down, more for something to do than for any fresh air I needed. The two Douane reached the kiosk. I lost sight of them as they walked between it and the Doblo.

We moved forward another vehicle length. Just one car to go now, then us, and now I couldn't see the Doblo at all.

Half a minute later and the car in front had its passports handed back through the kiosk window. Its brake lights went off and it pulled away.

Halland pulled forward and stopped by the window.

I stretched out my right arm with our passports. I had to almost get out of the seat so the Gendarme could reach them. He looked at me strangely for a moment, took in the bruising on my face, and then his eyebrows raised and he took the passports from me.

Perhaps he was thinking I'd had an accident and had a broken arm. He opened the passports one by one, ducking lower to check our faces as we sat in the car. Then he got up and moved further into the kiosk.

A few seconds later he appeared again in front of us, this time at the doorway at the end of the kiosk. He motioned Halland to drive forward. As we stopped beside him he handed me the passports.

"Merci, Monsieur Gregory."

He waved Halland through and walked back into the kiosk.

Halland put the car in gear and we moved off. We came to a junction, slowing momentarily while traffic passed us.

I watched the door mirror. The Doblo still stood at the kiosk. Phillipa stood between the kiosk and the van, talking to the female Douane who stood with her hands resting on her gun belt. We turned right and pulled away, and Phillipa and the Doblo and the Douane slid out of view.

I handed Halland his Passport. He took it and threw it behind him onto the back seat. "So who's "Monsieur Gregory" then?"

"Fuck knows. Never heard of him. You can give me the key now."

He turned for a second and leered at me then looked back at the road.

"You reckon?"

"Don't be a cunt, Trevor."

"Ah, but I am a cunt, as well you know. And you son, are a mug."

"We'll see. So tell me again how you knew I was on that ferry?"

"I don't have to tell you anything. Right now, if I was you, Monsieur Gregory, I'd shut up and enjoy the ride."

"Where are we going?"

"You'll find out." He turned to me and winked. "Don't worry. I'll make sure we have a wee while alone to talk things over between us before you get picked up. I'm looking forward to that."

"Picked up by who?"

"Some people you know."

I watched the traffic ahead. Under the jacket, I flexed my hand against the cuffs and tried to break the door pull free. I soon gave that up. There was no give in at all, and all I achieved was cutting the clasp of the handcuffs into my wrist.

Realistic options seemed limited to in some way causing him to crash the car, but even if I managed that, I would still be chained to the wreckage, and any impact that was bad enough to disable him was at best going to break my arm.

And I still wouldn't have the key.

I'd let myself get mugged by Halland to keep him away from Phillipa, and now, judging from the Douane's body language and the delay at the kiosk, she looked likely to have been pulled anyway.

The whole thing was fucked up, but it was what it was, and there was no point in going over it. Instead, I tried to get an idea of where we were going.

Halland had the sat nav on but he hadn't put a destination in, and he didn't look to me to be heading anywhere pre-planned. It was more as if he was looking for somewhere suitable to stop.

I assumed from what he'd said that he would then call someone else in to take me off him.

We passed through an industrial area, over a large roundabout then under the N27.

Past more industrial units, then the road ended at a campsite.

Halland turned the car around and went back towards the N27. He pulled over before we reached the flyover and dragged at the screen of the sat nav. Satisfied, he pulled away again and joined the N27 heading south.

A few minutes later we reached a roundabout and took the first left. The road led between some houses and agricultural units, after which we were mostly driving through open fields. We came to a crossroads and he stopped and swiped the sat nav again. He grunted, then put the car in gear and drove across the junction.

Across another junction, then around a sweeping left-handed bend, Halland slowed the car and turned off onto a track on the right that ran into a forested area.

The car lurched across the uneven ground as he picked his way along, the trunks of the trees growing closer and the track becoming less and less well defined. In the end, it was no more than a strip of unkempt knee-high grass between the trees.

After another 20 yards or so, he stopped and looked around him then nodded to himself before turning the engine off.

He turned in his seat and faced me.

"That's a pretty bruise you've got there, Massey."

His right fist shot out and he punched me directly on the bruise.

"Now that, Monsieur Gregory, is just for a warm-up."

I raised my right arm, my elbow out.

"Have another pop Halland. Let's see if I can't break a few of your fingers."

He put his hand under his seat and pulled out an old-style wooden police truncheon that had been sawn off about a foot long. He slipped his fingers through its leather strap.

"You won't break anything son, but I'm going to break both your fucking arms, and you have to believe me, I'm going to enjoy doing it. This -" he brought the truncheon down across my elbow "- is for a lady I knew. Well. I say, lady." He smirked. "But this -" he brought it down across my forearm "- is for her as well. But the rest of it, it's all for me, you sneaky little cunt."

He brought the truncheon down across my arm again and then leant into me and brought it down across my forehead. My face felt as if it had burst and I partly blacked out.

"You and your shitty little Golf, following me around for Denning, you cunt."

The truncheon came down again, this time across my shoulder. I'd tried to move my arm to cover myself, but it hadn't responded. It just hung there, like it didn't belong to me anymore.

Halland got out of the car, walked around to my side and opened the door. I half fell out, dragged off balance by the handcuffs but pinned to the seat by my seat belt.

He brought the truncheon down across the inside of my left elbow and I fell a bit further out of the car. "You mug Massey. You fucking mug."

He brought the truncheon down across my lower arm, close to the wrist. I felt it, and I knew he'd done it, but it was as if he'd hit someone else.

I sagged, suspended by the handcuffs and the seatbelt, my face laying in the grass, almost against the ground. Everything had gone far away now.

I stared between the blades of grass under the open car door.

There was a twig.

A thin, dark, brown twig.

I wondered how it had got there.

It lay as if the blades of grass supported it. Held it up.

Up to heaven.

Hallands voice was faint now.

I ignored it.

It was easy to ignore.

The grass grew darker.

The sun must be going in.

"You fucking cocky little -" he whispered and something bumped against my bicep again. "-cunt. You fucking -" I hung there, my face close to the ground, waiting for the blow, knowing it didn't matter.

 The twig shivered on the grass blades.

A silvery-bronze beetle scuttled across the dark earth between the grass.

Where was the beetle going?

What did it know?

Train doors slammed. Far away, from behind me somewhere.

I wondered where we were off to.

Halland's cursing grew louder, but I didn't feel the blows anymore.

My shoulder and my ribs began to hurt.

"You cunt. You - cunt!" Halland was crying now.

Sobbing.

I tried to get upright.

The door opened wider, moving away from me, and I almost fell further out, but the seat belt still held me.

I pushed down against the door with an arm that didn't belong to me and finally got enough leverage to lift my foot out of the car and push myself upright in the seat.

"You cunt!" Halland cursed again.

I turned my head as far as I could, but I still couldn't see him. I fumbled at the seat belt with numb fingers. It slipped free.

I lifted my other foot out of the car so I was sitting sideways in the seat and could see him.

He was sitting on the ground holding his lower leg.

Phillipa stood to one side of him, pointing the Smith and Wesson at him with both hands, just like I'd showed her.

She looked at me.

I tried to focus on her eyes but couldn't.

"Key. He has the handcuff key."

"Give me the key," she said.

"Fuck you." Halland spat at her.

"Shoot him in the other leg. We don't have time to fuck around with him."

She lowered the gun toward him.

"No. No." Halland held a hand up to her. "Alright. My jacket. In the car."

He'd hung his jacket behind his seat after we'd got in. I levered myself back into the car and pulled the door closed. I could just reach the jacket with my fingertips. The pain almost made me pass out. I pulled it from the hook and onto my lap and went through the pockets until I found the key and freed myself.

I pushed the door open and got out.

Halland still sat on the grass, scowling at me. His left trouser leg was wet with blood, but she'd not hit an artery. If she had, he would have already been dead.

I walked past him to the back of the car. Moving made my head swim, and I had to rest a moment on the boot of the car.

"Oh God, what has he done to you?"

I realised that I could feel blood on my face. I put my hand up to my brow and it came away wet. "Just keep your eyes on him."

She nodded.

I went to the other side of the car and flipped the keys in the ignition, opened the boot then took the keys with me.

Halland had a holdall similar to mine. I opened it and tipped it out on the floor of the boot. Socks, pants, a couple of shirts. Shaving gear. A pair of walking boots. I picked up one of the boots and threw it at him. Pain seared across my shoulder, but Halland flinched as the heavy boot hit him under the chin.

"Get a lace and tie your leg off."

I went through the pockets of the holdall. More socks, a French phrasebook, his insurance documents for the car and an old model Samsung mobile phone. I switched it on. Went into contacts. There was a single entry:

S.

I looked over at Halland. He was pulling the lace from the boot. I moved around the car so he couldn't see me. I went into the phone's messages.

"Onboard. He's here."

"Update me when you've got him."

I went back into Contacts and selected "S".

I rang the number. It rang four times before it was answered.

"All sorted?"

I rang off without answering and turned the phone off.

I pulled Halland's jacket out of the car and went through the pockets.

His warrant card, a wallet, cash, credit cards, his Driving Licence and Health cards. I threw the wallet onto the floor of the car. Another later model mobile phone. I slipped that in my pocket too. I went back to the rear of the car and shut the boot.

Halland had lifted his trouser leg and was probing the wound. She'd hit the calf muscle and it had gone right through. It seemed to have stopped bleeding.

"Get up and get in the car, Halland."

I took the gun from Phillipa. "How many times did you fire it?"

"Twice, exactly like you told me. I missed him with the second one."

I smiled at her. "Well done, killer."

Halland was struggling to his feet. "Come on, you fucking prick. We haven't got all day."

I backed away and allowed him to limp to the car. He sat down heavily into the driver's seat, his face ashen and sweaty.

"There's your keys." I threw them away into the long grass beyond the car. "I've got both your mobiles. What I suggest you do is find yourself a hotel, and get cleaned up, then book a ferry home."

He stared sullenly at the dashboard of the car.

I bent closer to him and lowered my voice, whispering to him.

"But, Halland. If you cause me any problems from now on, any at all, and if you even fucking look at me the wrong way again in your entire fucking life, I'll make sure that old mobile finds its way to Malcolm, and if you think Sneed will still be around to protect your fat fucking arse, you're even stupider than you look. Just remember what I have on you Trevor, and think on how many new playmates a bent pig finds inside."

I stood up and away from him.

"D'ye kenn meh, Trrrevah?"

He nodded.

"Good. So long as we understand each other."

I slammed the Insignia's door shut on him and walked back to where Phillipa waited.

"Come on, let's get gone.

I eased myself gingerly into the passenger seat of the van. Just reaching the seat belt across me and clipping it home was agony.

"Are you sure you're alright?" she asked. "You look a mess."

"Thank you. You say the sweetest things. Where exactly are we heading?"

She started the van and began an expert three-point turn.

"Montrouge, in Paris. Jacques has an apartment there. He's brought everything he has on Booth home and we'll work there until we're ready to take the story in. We talked about it, and it seemed a better place to work than travelling into the newspaper every day."

"Who is this Jaques?"

"His full name is Jaques-Victor Billaud. He's a very experienced investigative journalist. He's been responsible for breaking some of France's top stories down the years.

"Like what?"

"Oh, loads. He's done stings on organised crime in France, and another of his scoops involved exposing French troops operating in Afghanistan when the French Government denied it."

"I thought the French were there as part of the UN forces?"

"They were part of ISAF, but that wasn't formed until after the Twin Tower attacks. This is before that, in the late nineties. It was to do with Jaques Chirac's presidency.

He was already under pressure at home over domestic policies and corruption, but on top of all that, he was suspected of wanting France to rejoin NATO simply to cut French military spending.

But having French forces under foreign command has never been popular in France. Deployment of French troops against the Taliban would be seen as Chirac currying favour with America, so it was being kept a closely guarded secret. That was until Jaques and a cameraman went into Afghanistan and filmed French Special Forces operating there."

"He must have made some interesting enemies."

"I'm sure he has, but the French still take journalism seriously, and French public opinion brings its own special protection. That's why the Charlie Hebdo attack attracted so much sympathy here.

It wasn't that the magazine was particularly popular, in lots of ways it isn't. Many people see it only as a deliberately provocative comic, and it's often gone too far. It was shut down at one point for mocking de Gaulle's death. But in France, freedom of expression is important. People might not like what you say or how you say it, but you shouldn't be silenced."

"I thought Hebdo was like a French Private Eye?"

"No. That would be Le Canard enchaîne. Le Canard and Private Eye are very similar. They are both satirical magazines that do serious investigative journalism and don't care who they go after. Hebdo is more of a shock comic that doesn't care who it offends."

"Our media is shit."

She shrugged.

"Most of it has lost any purpose. We've never had it taken away, so we've forgotten how much it was worth."

"How do you mean?"

"Oh, I don't know, as with so many things with the UK, it comes back to the War. Everybody else in Europe was invaded and lost things like having a free press and the right to discuss politics, to investigate and openly criticise governments.

The war made them realise how important those things are. Even with the internet, France still has long televised political debates. They take being governed, and the right to object to being governed seriously. We seem to have lost all that. Our politicians don't even pretend they're telling us the truth these days, because they know there is nobody that will hold them to account.

They lie to us, blatantly, and people are angry about it, but there is nobody to give a voice to that anger. Instead, the politicians are owned by the same people who own the media, so when they lie, it's ignored and public opinion is simply blotted out. It's just a mouthpiece for the same old feudal elite."

"You sound a bit like somebody else I was talking to recently."

"Who?"

"Doesn't matter, nobody you'd know. When did you tell this Jaques Billaud you'd be arriving?"

"I didn't, I left it open. I just said I would get there as soon as I could but within the next few days."

"How long do you think it will take to screw everything together?"

"I honestly don't know. I don't know what Jaques has got, or how it will dovetail with what I have. It could be a day, or even a week if there's cross-checking to do."

"Have the paper laid on any security?"

She looked at me then back at the road.

"No. The only people who know we are working on the story are Jacques, his Editor and the managing director of the paper. We talked about it, and thought it best to keep it that way."

"That might have been OK yesterday, but now Halland knows you're here."

"Well, we did the best we could."

"I know. I'm not blaming you. I just wish you'd done as I said and gone straight there."

She said nothing and stared straight ahead at the road, but I noticed that her head had dropped slightly.

It was like a bull dropping its head to charge.

It made me smile that I was getting to know her mannerisms.

I put my hand on hers where it held the steering wheel.

"I'm sorry. You did well. Really."

"I know what you said, and I know that it was the right thing to do, but I had a hunch." She looked at me and smiled thinly. "You know what I'm like about my hunches."

"Yes, I know. And I'll take more notice of them in future. What the hell went on at the port? I thought you'd been pulled in."

"Well. That was part of it, my hunch. I saw you when we were queuing to go down to the cars, and I didn't like the look of your body language.

Then I saw you in the queue, and it seemed strange to me, the way you waved. You were behind me, so I did a bit of a blonde on them. First, I pretended that I couldn't find my passport. Then I asked them how to get to Paris, but made sure it took until you were through before I understood."

I laughed out loud.

"You're carrying two loaded guns through customs in a van not registered to you, and you fuck around with the French police asking how to get to Paris?"

"I was worried about you!" She turned and frowned at me. "Stop laughing at me!"

"OK, I will. It's fucking killing me anyway. But thank you, babe. It was really brave of you. I'd have been shitting bricks."

And I would have been.

"So then you followed us?"

"I tried to, but the problem was, I couldn't get too close because I was almost sure he must be the car that followed me, and I knew he knew the van, so I hung back and hung back and then I lost him.

But we had a lucky break. It was near that roundabout onto the motorway. To be honest, I'd given up, and I thought about what you said, about getting to Jaques being the most important thing, so I reversed back into a lane to turn around and go back the way I'd come, but I stalled.

As I started it up again, you drove past. If I hadn't stalled, I would have pulled out going the other way and he would have spotted me. Instead, I pulled out after him again.

I saw what road you went down from there, but the sat nav showed it was straight, so I held back, and it was just as well I did because he stopped. I thought at first he had spotted me, but then he kept going, so I just followed slowly.

I wish I could have got there sooner but I had to get the gun from where I'd hidden it, and then find you through the trees."

"It's all good babe. Perfect timing. Look, there's a village up ahead, let's see if there's a chemist. I can get some painkillers, and if there's a shop I can buy some water and stuff and have a clean up."

Twenty minutes later we were underway again, stocked up with water, Coca Cola, chocolate, four beach towels and bandages and a pack of Paracetamol.

I decided to travel in the back rather than sit in the front. I could lay down rather than being sat upright, where even the normal movements of the van shook me around and jarred my injuries.

Four paracetamol and half an hour of lying down later, the edge had gone off the pain enough for me to try cleaning myself up with the water and a towel, and take stock of what was left of me.

It wasn't looking good.

My calf was swollen and raw from the bullet graze, but that was the least of my problems. The bruising from Halland's handiwork had started to kick in, and every movement I made while trying to clean myself set off shooting pains that made me wince.

The only positives were that I didn't seem to be concussed and that the worst of the damage was to my left side. My right arm and shoulder were bruised and painful, but still usable.

"Are you feeling any better?" She asked.

"Not much."

"Danny?"

"What?"

"You're in so much pain. There's no need for us to get there tonight. We could stop off somewhere, go to a hotel. You could get properly clean and get a good night's sleep. You haven't eaten anything, either. If you don't eat and rest properly, you really will suffer for it tomorrow. Why don't we find somewhere?"

"I'm bothered about Halland, Pip. I don't understand who he's working for. I don't know if what he told me on the ferry about there being a Euro Arrest Warrant out for me is true or not.

If there is, and you're caught with me and a van full of artillery and I've shot a copper, we'll both be fucked, and so will any chance of you getting to Paris and getting the story out."

"I shot him, not you."

"No way. If it comes to it, we tell them I did it. You pointed the gun at him and stopped him whacking me about, then I got free, then I took the gun off you and got my own back on him. That's what happened and we both stick to it."

She didn't say anything and I started to clean myself up again. I dabbed one of the welts Halland had given me on my left arm with a wetted towel just as the van hit a bump. I had to stop myself from screaming and a wave of nausea racked through me.

I knew she was right. Another few hours without food and rest would do for me.

"How long do you think until we're there babe?"

"Perhaps two hours, two and a half. It really depends on how the Periphique is. We could have been quicker but I thought it best to avoid the Peage."

I dabbed gently at the bruising. "Let me think about it."

"OK."

We drove in silence for a few minutes.

"I forgot to ask you." She said. "When you left me on the ferry, you said that everything I needed to get Booth was in your holdall. What did you mean?"

"Yeah, I'd forgotten about that. I'm pretty sure I know why Thompson and Susan were killed. It's a long story, but it boils down to a roll of cine film that Susan had. I found it while she was out and brought it with me. It's in the holdall."

"Film of what?"

"Some men, and I think they're raping another man. Well, more of a boy, I suppose. Maybe a teenager."

"Oh my god. And one of the men is Booth?"

"I'm fairly sure it's him. It's old film, twenty or more years old, so he's younger, and it's 16mm and I only got to look at it against the light. Do you think Billaud can get hold of a projector we can use?"

"I'll ask him. Wait." She went on hands-free and sent Billaud a voice message in French.

"OK. I've asked him to try and sort one out. So you think that this film is why Thompson was murdered?" she asked.

"In a roundabout way. I think he got topped because without knowing what he was doing, he accidentally tipped someone off as to where the film was."

"Tipped who off? Booth?"

"No. OK, there's a lot you don't know yet because we haven't had a chance to talk about it. This is probably not perfect, but here's the best I can come up with as to what's happened."

As I was about to begin filling her in she got a reply from Billaud.

"He says they have 16mm projectors at the offices and he will have one brought across to him."

"Excellent. Can you ask him, what is parking like there? Is it off the street? Private? We need to get the van out of sight."

She sent him another long message in French. Within a minute he had replied.

"The parking is in an underground car park. He says it is very secure. He says that there is a spare bedroom and he will make it ready."

"Well, that's that. Forget the hotel idea and don't spare the horses, missus."

We finally hit the Periphique and crawled around it until we came to the Porte for Montrouge. Once in Montrouge proper, Phillipa pulled over and rang Jacques to let him know we were almost there while I climbed out of the back and got into the passenger seat.

I'd had visions of us being lodged in a flat facing onto a main road, but Phillipa explained to me that Jacques would have to open gates to the building and the shutter for the underground car park to let us in.

88 Rue Boileau was a block four storeys high and built from dark grey stone in the shape of a shallow chevron with apartments on each side. A windowless central spine ran down the middle of the chevron. It was set back by a few feet, like a notch to an arrow between the two halves of the building. At the base of the notch, up a flight of four paved steps, was a glass-fronted foyer door.

In front of the foyer stood a tall thin man with collar-length wavy hair. He aimed something in his right hand at the gates and they opened slowly in front of us. Phillipa drove in, and the gates shimmied on their hinges before closing again once we'd passed through.

As we got closer, I could see Billaud properly.

He was older than he'd looked at first, perhaps in his early fifties, with a broad broken nose over a wispy cavalier goatee. As we pulled to a stop outside the building, white even teeth appeared in a smile.

Phillipa dropped the window and Billaud walked down the steps, rested long-fingered hands on the van and leant down to peer inside at us with smiling brown eyes.

"Hallo Phillipa. It is charming to meet you, finally."

"Hallo Jaques, yes, it's lovely to meet you too. Let me introduce Danny, Danny Massey."

I stretched a hand across in front of Phillipa. "Hallo Jacques. Nice to meet you."

He shook my hand with a grip that his hands hadn't looked capable of.

"Hello, Danny. Please Phillipa, drive down to the garage slowly. The door will rise automatically. If you drive to the left, you will find two places marked seven, please park there. The exit is marked. Take the stairs and I will meet you in the foyer."

He stood back from the van and we drove down the slope towards the garage, and as the van got close, the shutter door began lifting itself. Behind it, yellow fluorescent lights were flickering into life.

We pulled around to the left and nosed the van between rows of parked cars.

I hadn't expected the garage to be so full, and didn't like the idea of having so many people to keep tabs on.

"How come everyone is home? Is it a holiday or something?" I was speaking to myself more than asking Phillipa.

"No. Public transport in France is way better than in the UK," she said. "These are pretty upmarket flats. These will mostly be weekend cars."

I took her word for it. They didn't look the sort of cars you'd want to use as a daily driver in the lunacy we'd just driven through on the Periphique.

Most of them were new looking, late model Jaguars, BMWs and Audis and high-end Citroens and Renaults. In one bay, the beautifully understated Americana of a Simca Vedette lay under the gossamer of a lightweight dustsheet.

The sleeping cars ended in a sharp left-hand turn that made the Doblo's tyres squeal on the floor's shiny urethane surface.

As Jacques had promised, two empty spaces each marked with a large yellow figure seven came into view on the right, and Phillipa turned the van onto one of them and switched off.

While she began moving our luggage out of the Doblo, I stood and took stock of the garage and how it was laid out. It was almost L shaped, with the roller doors beginning on its lower stroke and the upright of the L running back underneath the building.

The walls and ceiling were of grey-white concrete with thick concrete beams spaced every ten feet or so overhead. Set into the wall, almost opposite where we stood, was the heavy looking fire door into the flats themselves.

Phillipa passed me my holdall and hung hers over her shoulder, extended the handle of her suitcase and waited for me to retrieve the Beretta from inside the Doblo.

We walked together to the door, pushed through it, and concrete stairs covered with black rubber matting led us up to the foyer where Jacques waited.

I thought about possible ambush points while Phillipa and Jaques exchanged pleasantries in French as the lift carried us up to the top floor of the building.

Jaques led us down a broad corridor to a mustard coloured door on the left, slid a key into it and pushed it open to allow us inside.

We entered a large high ceilinged apartment, its walls washed with pale oatmeal grey and hung with vibrant prints. A large oval dining table was set centrally in the first half of the room surrounded by white leather-covered chairs. A piano wood sideboard took up most of the right-hand wall.

Beyond that, a half-open door led to a bedroom, with the foot of a double bed showing through it. The bed covering was pulled back and the pillows and sheet were crumpled as if Jaques had recently been asleep. Beyond the bed, doors led out onto a narrow balcony.

The far end of the main room ended in full-height glass doors that led out onto a larger balcony. The doors were hung with crimson floor-length sheer curtains that were pushed to the sides of the window. Far away, the silver spec of an aircraft crawled slowly across the blue sky leaving a thin trail behind it. To the left of the window, a deeply padded brown leather settee against a plain white wall, facing a wide flat screen on the wall opposite.

On the left were three more doors.

Jacques pushed the first of them open and went through it. A mix of coffee and fresh bread wafted out to greet us.

"Would you both like coffee?" he asked from inside the room.

"Yes please," replied Phillipa. She looked at me and shrugged, then smiled.

I reckoned I understood what she meant: that Jacques wasn't all faux jolly and friendly. Instead, you got the feeling that life was going on the same as ever, except you happened to be there.

"Danny, you look as if a bus ran over you," he said from the kitchen door. "You take my bedroom." He motioned across to the open bedroom door. "There is a shower. I suggest you fix yourself up and then get some sleep, and Phillipa and I can work. The sheets are clean, although, forgive me," he grinned "I admit, I had what you call a nap earlier."

"Thank you, Jaques," Phillipa said before I made any arguments about standing guard "Come, Danny."

She moved me gently. I gave up and obeyed. The thought of falling asleep on that bed beat any ideas of caution. I told myself there was no way Halland could get anyone here tonight anyway.

She followed me into the room and closed the door behind me. I lowered myself gently until I was sitting on the bed, and she helped me off with my jacket, jumper and t-shirt, making me grit my teeth and moan as my arms were moved.

"Oh my god," she whispered when she finally saw the extent of Halland's work. "Wait here, I will see if Jaques has any ice or frozen peas or anything."

She went out and closed the door again, and I heard them conversing in French. She opened the door again, and I could see behind her Jaques was shrugging himself into a heavy woollen coat.

"Jaques will go around the corner, there is a supermarket. He'll buy some ice." He came to the door and stood behind her.
"Is there anything else you want Danny? Cigarettes? Whisky?"

"Rum, Negrita will do if they have it, Jaques. That'll knock me out. And some dark chocolate. Is there anything in to eat?"
"There is a delicatessen on the way. I will order pizzas and bring them back with me. Take a shower, Danny, I will be perhaps thirty minutes."

She came back in and shut the door. I started to reach forward to untie my boots but she stopped me, knelt at my feet and began to pull at the laces.

I lay myself slowly back onto the bed, closed my eyes and let her get on with it. One by one she pulled them free, peeled off my socks and then stood up.

"Can you do your jeans?"

I looked up at her standing over me.

"Don't you want to undress me then?"

She coloured.

"How much more do you need beating you until you stop being lewd?"

"Depends what part you beat." I winked at her.

She pursed her lips.

"I'm going to drink my coffee." She turned on her heel and went out, shutting the door behind her.

A moment later the door half opened and my holdall was thrown through it.

The door clicked shut again.

The shower was a godsend.

After a few minutes on almost scalding, the aching across my shoulders eased and with it some of the pains down my sides and across my chest. The wound on my leg was sore, but I guessed it must be scabbing over because the water didn't sting it.

I cooled the water down and checked myself in the mirror that filled most of the opposite wall. No wonder she'd looked shocked when she'd taken my shirt off. I had to hand it to Halland. He knew how to beat the shit out of someone.

I killed the shower and dried myself on a thick towel that hung from the door, then checked my face in the mirror. I wasn't pretty, but nothing looked permanent. I touched at the bruise on my forehead, but raising my arm set off pain in my shoulder.

Shaving could wait.

I padded out into the bedroom, lifted the holdall on the bed and unpacked it. The jeans I'd worn when I was shot. Susan's jeans, one last clean T-shirt. A clean pair of socks. The cigar box. I lay it on the bedside table, then went back into the shower room and rummaged through Jaques' cabinet until I found a pair of nail scissors.

I sat on the bed and cut a half-inch slot across the inside of the waistband of my jeans, then opened the box and took out the film. I cut a strip eighteen inches long from the end and spent the next five minutes pushing it slowly through the slot in the jeans so it lay flat inside the waistband.

As I finished dressing I heard Phillipa greet Jaques as he got back. I stood still and went over everything in my mind. The snub I'd laid under the mattress of the bed. The Beretta lay on the bedside table. Everything else was back in the holdall except the tin. I wound the film and put it back in, closed the lid on the two locks of hair and dropped it into the holdall.

Phillipa tapped on the door. "Danny? Food."

I came out and sat on the first chair I came to.

Jaques came in from the kitchen with plates and glasses and laid them on the table.

"Feeling better Danny?"

"Almost human."

Phillipa smiled and sat down opposite me. She passed me a plate and laid another at the head of the table between us for Jaques.

Jaques returned from the kitchen again, this time with a bottle of wine and a de Gaulle. He sat down and began stripping the neck of the bottle while Phillipa laid a pair of Pizza slices on each of our plates. The smell hit and my stomach lurched as I realised how hungry I was.

I picked up a slice and started eating, while Phillipa put a tumbler by my plate, unscrewed the top of the Negrita and poured me two fingers worth.

"More." I slurped at her through the pizza. "You two can talk all evening, but I'm going to be rude and eat then sleep."

"Best thing after what you have had happen Danny. Sleep is the best doctor there is," said Jaques.

He poured himself and Phillipa a glass of wine, placed the bottle down and lifted his glass towards me. "Salut." He turned to Phillipa. "Salut. You are a great team. It is an honour to know you both."

"Salut Jaques." I lifted my glass to him. "And to Phillipa, without who we wouldn't be here."

She blushed.

"Did she tell you, Jaques? she's not only a journalist, she's a gunrunner?"

"No?"

"Danny, be quiet."

"No! I must hear." He grinned. "That someone so modeste is really a Queen of the pegre intrigues me."

"I will let her tell you later if she wants Jaques, but seriously, without her guts, we wouldn't be here. She's got more bottle than most people I know." I raised my glass to her. "And I mean that, Phillipa Phapetis."

She blushed again and battled with her pizza for a moment, then asked Jaques if he had a knife and fork. "Of course, wait –"

"No. I will get it. In the kitchen, yes?"

"Yes. The drawer next to the basin."

She got up and went into the kitchen, and he looked at me and raised his eyes to heaven. "Women" he mouthed, looking at me pitifully, then he winked and held his glass to me. "Bonne Chance" he whispered. I tapped him with what was left of my rum. "Salut." and necked the rest of it.

As Phillipa returned from the kitchen, Jacques's mobile rang from inside his coat. He licked his fingers clean and retrieved it.

"Aha! Claude!" he dabbed at the phone and held it to his ear.

While he spoke, I poured myself another glass of rum and tried to catch Phillipa's eye across the table. She wasn't having any of it and concentrated on cutting up her pizza.

Jaques sat down at the table again, still talking on the phone. Then he said his goodbyes and switched the phone off.

"That was young Claude. The projector will be here tomorrow morning. He will drop it by on his way in. He took it with him tonight but his wife telephoned him and was feeling unwell. She expects their first baby in a week or so. So he went directly home." He topped up Phillipa's glass and his own with wine.

He looked at me and winked.

"I had told him that I found some old cine film of my family and want to view it during my days off, so I am afraid he did not think it was quite as important as we do. But he is a good kid. He will have it here a little after 8.30 tomorrow."

The rum was kicking in properly now.

I gave up halfway through a third slice of pizza and sat nursing the last finger of the second glass I'd poured myself, listening to Phillipa and Jaques talk shop about European politics.

Gradually English gave way to French, and I gave up trying to understand what they were discussing.

I poured myself another smiling finger for luck.

After another ten minutes, I felt my eyelids dropping and tipped what was left in the glass down, excused myself and hit the sack.

I undressed and lay down in the bed, shifting the Beretta under the mattress so its grip fell into my hand at head height. I pulled the duvet up over my ears, and even the faint murmur of their conversation disappeared.

I smiled as alcohol shifted the bed slightly, a boat tethered to a silent riverbank, moving on a gentle swell. The smell of grass, shaded from the early evening sun by catkin smothered branches.

21

I came round about 4 am.

A fully clothed Jaques snored softly from the far side of the bed, his back to me and his arms wrapped possessively around a pillow. Beyond him the dull sheen of the curtains glimmered, reflecting the sleeping city's faint yellow glow. I slipped out of bed and picked up my jeans on the way across the room.

I put my shoulder against the door and pushed down on its handle until I felt the catch give then backed out of the room, pulling the door gently closed behind me.

The wreckage of the meal lay scattered across the table, empty plates stacked together, two empty wine bottles and another half full, the harsh stale smell of an ashtray wriggling somewhere under the cheese and cold grease from the pizza.

I slipped my jeans on and padded across the shadowed floor of the lounge to the spare room and once again opened the door silently before backing in and pushing it closed.

I waited for my eyes to adjust to the darkness, then turned.

A wardrobe lay along the left wall, and where it ended, a small window was hung with curtains that were drawn. Halfway under the window, a single bed took up the right-hand wall.

In the corner, Phillipa sat hunched at the pillow end of the bed, her knees drawn up against her chin, her arms wrapped around her legs. Her eyes were pale against the darkness, open, unblinking, staring past me. I moved towards her, and as I drew closer, I could see she had been crying.

I sat down next to her.

"What's up, babe?"

Finally, she looked at me, but she didn't speak. Then she dropped her eyes and shifted away from me, leaning herself against the wall.

"What's the matter?"

She shook her head slightly. "Nothing you can help with Danny."

"Come off it Pip." I reached out and put my hand over hers. "What's the matter?"

"Please don't call me that."

"I thought you liked it."

She shook her head slowly.

I took my hand back. "I don't understand."

"I know you don't. And if I told you, you wouldn't understand either. So let's just forget about it. Forget about explaining things. Because there's too much to explain, and I'm not sure that I could anyway, and even if I could," she turned her mouth down and shook her head. "You wouldn't understand."

"Phillipa, you're talking in riddles."

She nodded slowly. "I know."

I lay down on the bed next to her. "OK, whatever it is, we won't talk about it. But you come here and let me put my arms round you, and if you want you can put yours around me, and we'll both sleep, because tomorrow you have a busy day."

She laughed, but it was humourless, a low, cynical sound.

"I don't know whether you are blind or you think I'm gullible. Do you honestly think that I could just lie next to you in bed?

Do you know what you do to me? How you make me feel? How you've made me feel since the moment I first saw you? As if that wasn't enough, you are with somebody, and so was I.

The things you said. The way you looked at me. They were easy for you. Just a part of the game you play with every woman. For me, they were the end of everything, and for nothing, because I would have meant nothing. You would have walked away like a dog that had marked a gatepost and I would have had to face him."

"Phillipa, really, you've lost me."

She sniffed.

"I never had you. I never would have. I would have broken his heart and you'd have walked away thinking you'd done nothing, thinking you were wonderful and clever and gone back to Natalie as if nothing had happened."

"Broken whose heart? What are you on about? Natalie and I are just friends."

"Shut up, you fool."

"OK. I'm a fool. I'm lots of things. Now what the fuck are you on about, woman? Broken whose heart?"

"You're the detective."

"I haven't got a fucking scooby. Either talk to me properly or sit there and feel sorry for yourself, because I have better things to worry about."

She sat in silence after that.

It lasted a good ten minutes, then she straightened her legs and slid down until she was laying next to me. I felt her arm move up my stomach until it rested on my chest. Her head found its way onto my shoulder, the mop of her hair soft against my cheek. I let my arm fall around her shoulders.

"Talk to me."

I felt her take a deep breath. "Richard."

"What about him?"

"I rang him last night. When you were asleep. He wasn't there, so I rang his mobile. A doctor answered it. He's in Guys Hospital, in Intensive Care."

I bared my teeth in the darkness.

"You rang him from the mobile I gave you?"

"No. I tried, but there was no service. Did you have roaming turned on?"

Shit. "No. My fault. Where did you ring him from?"

"I borrowed Jaques's phone."

"His mobile?"

"Yes. I thought it was best. If I had used the landline someone could trace it, right?"

"What did the doctor say?"

"He said Richard had been brought in during the afternoon. He had had a minor heart attack, but mostly he had difficulty breathing. They had sedated him, and put him on a ventilator."

"What was the doctor's name?"

"I think he said, Mohammed. He had quite a thick accent. I asked him what he thought might happen, and he said that he had to be honest, that he believed that Richard did not have too long left."

"What time was this?"

"I don't know. Perhaps eleven, somewhere around that."

"So he's in intensive care at Guys and you spoke to them what? Five, maybe six hours ago?"

"Yes."

"OK. We'll try again later and see if there's been any change. I understand why you were upset now. Sorry."

"I don't think you do understand, Danny. But it doesn't matter now. I said things I shouldn't have. I'm a grown-up. I'm responsible for me, and I'm responsible for how I treat other people. Blaming you is cowardice."

"You're no coward. You know that."

"Believe me, I am. I am frightened of things that most people simply accept as normal. Things that everybody else would see as a part of life to be accepted and enjoyed absolutely terrify me."

"Like what?"

She took another long sighing breath.

"Like, lying here, with you. My face against your skin. Hearing your heart beat. Feeling your arms around me. Feeling safe. Protected. Wanting you. Wanting you so much that I ache just to feel you inside me, when I know, I would have no idea how to please you and I would be the worst lover you had ever had.

I am more scared of those things than you could ever imagine. And what scares me most, more than anything else, is not only do I want them, but that I can admit to you that I want them. That I have to admit them to you, because I know you, and I know it's the only way I can stop you.

I know that if I admit these things to you, you will say that you want me, and you will mean it. But afterwards, you will be frightened, too. You will feel responsible for me. Then you will feel guilty. Then you will run away, just as you always do. Because for different reasons, you're as terrified of me as I am of you.

In the end, the fear would always win. Anything we built, it would destroy." She stroked my shoulder, and I could feel her fingers, those perfect little fingers, trembling. "I don't want that for either of us. We both deserve better, whatever better is. I'm 28 years old and I've slept with eight men in my entire life. The first was everything to me, and when he left, I fell apart. The next four were me learning that I couldn't replace what I had with him. The sixth was me learning that I can't pretend to love someone, and that however horrible living alone might be, it would never be as bad as hating myself.

The seventh was years later, and I slept with him twice, because I had some mad idea, that he would help me get a job. It was stupid and naive, but at least I learned that I wasn't good enough in bed to try that again. So you see, I am the worst of all worlds. I'm a whore who is rubbish in bed."

"Nothing you've said makes you a whore Phillipa. You just, learnt about yourself, same as we all do. Some things we do, we don't like. Some things make you cringe when you remember you did them. But that's normal. We all do it."

"You don't need to make excuses for me, Danny. That's how it would begin. But it's not going to begin. I have never wanted any man the way I want you. You make me someone I've never been.

You only have to look at me and I'm wet. From the moment I first saw you, it's been that way. And the more I know you, the more I want to be with you, the more I feel us growing closer, the more I know I could never be with you. You would own me, completely. And because of that, you wouldn't fear me. If you couldn't fear me, you couldn't respect me. It would irritate you, that I couldn't see another woman wanting you without being afraid of losing you.

Then you would hurt me, to see if you could make me retaliate, so that you could respect me. But when I couldn't, when all I could do was forgive you, you'd be even more irritated, and the more irritated you became, the more you would hurt me, and the more guilty and trapped you would feel."

"You've got me all worked out, haven't you."

"Not you. Me. As you just said, we learn about ourselves. And I know me. You need an equal, or at least, somebody you can believe might beat you. Then you behave yourself.

But I can never be your equal. If I ever allowed myself to begin, I would love you too much, so much, that I would forgive you anything. Because you're everything I could ever want in a man, on every level. But I would destroy you, and then us both."

"You realise, that you talking to me like this, being able to express yourself and knowing how I am makes you different. It nullifies what you are saying?"

"Danny, this is not a debate. It's not a chess game you can win with clever moves. It's my heart, and I have already broken it so that you never can. I will get over loving you, and you will get over wanting to be the best fuck I've ever had, just so I can never forget you."

"You think that's what I care about?"

"I don't disbelieve that you could fall in love with me. But I know that you wouldn't stay in love with me, because we are who we are. And yes, I totally get the irony that I can see you for who you are, but that doesn't mean I should be with you, just on the off chance that the utter wonderment of fucking little fat Phillipa Phapetis will trigger a Damascene change in what makes you tick."

"You're not fat."

"I'm certainly not thin."

"So?"

"Oh, shut up Danny, please. It's got nothing to do with it."

"Hasn't it? I bet you wouldn't be afraid of me," I poked her gently in the ribs "if you thought you looked like a model."

"No, but then you would be afraid of me, so we wouldn't have to worry about it."

She had me there.

"So who was number eight?"

She moved her face against me and I felt her fingers tap at my chest a moment. Then she spoke softly.

"Number eight was me allowing someone to love me for all the wrong reasons, for all the right reasons. Because I know that it helped them, and I could never bear to hurt them. Because, in a way, however wrong it might have been, I love them, and most of all, I love them for giving me the strength to be true to myself."

"Richard."

She nodded.

22

While Phillipa rattled things about in the kitchen making coffee, I sat at the table and found the enquiries number for Guy's Hospital on my phone. The door clicked open behind me and a crumpled version of Jaques tottered past me and sat down. He squinted at me through one bloodshot eye, scratching slowly at the greying stubble under his chin. "Morning." I winked at him.

"You slept well." He stated.

"I had no choice." I grinned.

"I fell over, in the dark. You did not even move." He said with a hoarse chuckle that turned into a short cough. "I need a cigarette." he croaked.

He lifted himself out of the seat and carried his cigarettes through the lounge and out onto the balcony.

Phillipa carried a tray in with three coffees. She looked down the lounge to where Jaques stood leaning on the railing of the balcony. "Is he OK?"

"He says you tried to get him drunk last night, and it worked."

"He didn't need any help from me. I get the distinct impression that he's quite a handful for his girlfriend."

"Who's she?"

"Her name is Meike. She's a social historian, from Germany. They bought a place on the Nordsee together to renovate. He packed her off there when he knew we were coming."

She lifted one of the coffees from the tray.

"I'll take this out to him."

I watched her walk to the windows and out onto the balcony.

He turned to her and took the coffee from her, the cigarette wobbling between his lips as he spoke to her. He said something to her and I heard her laugh, her hair a mass of dark curls that shimmered in the morning's pale sunlight as she replied to him.

I knew she was right.

I knew that we would only be happy in a different world, in a world that would never exist; one where she would never need to forgive me.

She laughed again, then stepped back in through the hazy crimson curtains. She pulled the door half-closed and walked back to the table.

"I'm going to take a shower." She announced.

"Well, I wasn't going to say anything." I pulled a face.

"I'm not that bad, am I?" she looked at me wide-eyed.

I rolled my eyes at her.

"It was a joke, woman."

She frowned at me.

"Anyway. Soon I won't stink."

"You don't stink. Much. Do me a favour before you go, write down Richard's full name, his address and date of birth. I'll ring Guys and check on him."

"Hello, my name is Colin Luscombe; I'm from the Daily Mail. Do you have a Mr Richard Thomas Henning? I believe he is in intensive care."

I watched Jaques walking through the lounge towards me.

"Wait a moment please, I'll put you through."

"OK. Thank you."

Jaques pointed at my coffee cup. I nodded and moved it towards him with my free hand. The line clicked and someone said something indistinct, then I heard a telephone receiver being replaced. "I.C.U."

"Hello, do you have a Mister Richard Thomas Henning? I believe he has been in intensive care since yesterday afternoon."

"This is Intensive Care. Wait a moment and I'll check for you."

I heard the rattle of a keyboard, then a pause.

"Say the name again please?"

"Henning. Richard Henning."

Jaques came back to the table carrying two coffees and placed one in front of me.

I gave him a thumbs up.

I heard the keyboard clack again.

"No. No, I'm afraid we've had nobody of that name admitted. Are you sure they're in intensive care?"

"That's correct. Richard Thomas Henning, date of birth 31st October 1955.

"Yes, I heard you. We've had no admissions under that name."

"And how is he?"

"I'm sorry? I've told you, nobody of that name has been admitted."

"Oh, that's great. Better than I was expecting. Thank you. Thank you for your time and sorry for calling so early. Thank you, bye."

I killed the call.

Jaques covered his mouth and yawned.

When Phillipa had finished showering, I asked her to get dressed and come back to the table. I'd decided that it was better to tell her in front of Jaques. That way I could impress on both of them that time was probably short, and they needed to work quickly and methodically.

When I'd told them, she had gone pale.

"Then who was it I spoke to last night?" she asked.

"No idea."

"And what about Richard? What have they done to him?"

"Nothing I would think. They don't need to draw attention to themselves. They will have just pushed him around a bit, taken his mobile, and warned him not to do anything stupid.

They won't have told him it's about you. They'll have warned him to keep his trap shut and not get any ideas about opposing the court case."

This was nonsense, but for now she was beginning to buy it.

Jaques wasn't, but he'd been in enough sticky situations to realise that having Phillipa freak out wasn't going to achieve anything.

"Danny is correct Phillipa. They won't hurt a sick old man. They don't need to. All that they wanted was the mobile phone so that they could trace you when you called him."

"He would never have given them the mobile phone for that!"

"They wouldn't have said anything about you, babe. They'd have told him they were taking the phone so they have a list of his friends and relatives.

That's how it works. When they know from the phone he has a young niece, for instance. They'll tell him what a shame it would be if someone broke a glass in her face in a nightclub."

Her eyes widened, and she stared away from me like she'd lifted a sheet and seen my rotting corpse.

"Yes, I remember now." She said quietly. "What you told me. How it was your job to persuade Dean Thompson."

"Then trust me, Phillipa. Richard will be fine. They won't have hurt him."

Jaques looked at me, then lifted his cigarettes from the table and lit one. He leaned back in his chair and spoke to her gently.

"We should put these things aside and begin Phillipa. We have much to do, and perhaps, less time than we hoped."

I left them to it.

I decided I would shave.

I felt filthy enough now, without looking it as well.

By the time I got back things were in full swing.

Papers and files were stacked on the table and the sideboard and between them. Jaques's easy nature and having her mind occupied seemed to have cheered Phillipa up.

A buzzer sounded from around the front door. Jaques went across and lifted the intercom from the wall.

After a brief conversation, he replaced the handset and took his coat from the hooks beside the door.

"Claude has brought the projector for us. I will go down and take it off him."

He pulled on his coat and left the flat.

As soon as the door closed behind him, I got up from the table and collected the Beretta from the bedroom. I threw my reefer jacket on and tucked the gun down inside its sleeve so that the grip lay against my chest.

"What's the matter?" asked Phillipa.

"Nothing. I just want to see how the gates operate."

"Why do you need the gun?"

I ignored her and stepped out into the passageway.

Where it ended in front of the lift was a large window. From it, I could see out across the compound to the front gates. A white saloon was parked to one side of them, only its boot visible, the rest of it hidden behind the high stone wall.

A fair-haired man waited behind the car, blowing into his hands and moving from foot to foot to keep himself warm.

Far below me, Jaques walked towards the gates and they began to swing inwards. He greeted the man, who walked forward and shook his hand.

Jaques stayed within the arc of the gates, I figured to stop them from closing, while the man returned to the car, opened its boot and lifted a large oblong black box from within it.

He walked to Jaques and passed the box to him, then returned to the car and shut the boot. He turned back to Jaques and they talked for a minute, the to and fro of their conversation marked by the pluming of their breath in the cold air, then the man waved goodbye and got back in the car.

Exhaust spurted from behind it and writhed on the road, dissolving as Jaques walked back towards the flats.

The gates swung inwards, closing behind him.

I waited until he disappeared out of sight beneath me, went back into the flat and took my jacket off.

The Beretta I took into the bedroom and slid back under the mattress.

I went back into the dining room and sat down.

"Well? Anything interesting?" she asked.

"Not much. The gates take a count of ten to fully close and they're controlled from inside by some sort of sensor."

"Is that important?"

"Might be. It means that if someone could climb the wall, they could open the gates from inside without anybody in any of the flats knowing they had. If they were high tech, they could send a cheap drone over and drop something over the sensor that would open the gates."

"Would somebody do that?"

"I don't know. If you wanted to get in without anybody knowing, that's the sort of options you'd have, but a drone would be overkill.

The walls are maybe nine or ten feet high. Two fit men with the right training would get over easily enough, then the one who got in would trigger the sensor to open the gates."

Jaques pushed in through the door and we cleared a space on the table for him to drop the projector onto. He pointed it at the wall and ran an extension cable he brought from the spare bedroom to it from a socket beside the piano wood sideboard.

I brought him the cine film from the bedroom, watching as he expertly wound it onto one of the projector's reels. While he worked, he spoke conversationally to us.

"These are old machines, but believe it or not, people still use 16mm today for filming, especially in combat zones. Once it is developed, which is easy to do even in say, a hotel bathroom, it is so much more robust than video, or even digital in some ways.

I have films from Syria and Afghanistan we took I can show you later, if we get a break." He fed the film through and fixed it to the other reel. "If you would be interested, of course."

He smiled at me.

"There. Voila. We are ready. Somebody get the lights."
I moved to the door and switched the lights off, and our end of the room fell into shadow.

Jaques threw the switch on the projector. It hummed briefly then clattered into life, and a blurred oblong of light danced on the wall above the piano wood sideboard.

He adjusted the focus, and there, suddenly in crisp detail were three men, two of who were holding a thin boy down by his arms while between them a third fucked him savagely.

The boy's face twisted towards the camera, fear and distress and agony distorting his features, his mouth a sobbing gash under terrified eyes.

The man on the left leant forward and crushed downward onto the boy's shoulder, looking directly into the camera and speaking, then the oblong on the wall turned white and the film slapped around the reel.

Jaques hit the projectors off switch and the room fell silent.

23

"So. It was true, after all." Jaques said flatly.

"What was?" I asked.

"What Ménard had hinted, about a film, before he died."

"Who is Ménard?"

"Of course!" exclaimed Phillipa. "That's Pierre Ménard! But younger."

"Who is? And who the fuck is Pierre Ménard?"

"Turn on the lights Danny, we'll go through it again, and I will explain who these men are."

I did as he asked, then came and sat down at the table while he reset the projector. He ran the film through again. This time the image on the wall was barely visible, but as it played through he spoke over the muted clattering of the projector.

"On the left, this man is called Pierre Ménard. On the right, who you can half see, is Robert Booth. Behind the boy, that is the reason we all now have big problems. That is Walter Samsel.

Who operated the camera we can only speculate. The boy is, or was, Sebastian David Melrose."

As if on cue, the film ran out of the machine and the ghostly images disappeared leaving a lighter shape on the wall. Jaques reached across and switched the projector off.

He stood up and went out to the kitchen, returning with an ashtray and a packet of cigarettes.

He took one out and put it in his mouth and lit it, then sat back down.

"So, this film. I had heard once, a rumour that it existed, but never seen it. I can tell you now, that this is almost certainly the cause of many fatal problems for many people, not least, the men in it.

The boy, the victim. This is Sebastian Melrose. He committed suicide under curious circumstances in 1992. There were objections from his family about the case, accusations that the coroner had been in some way coerced into deciding a verdict of suicide when the verdict should have at least, have been open.

Perhaps, the distress of the family was understandable, because Melrose was, I don't know how you would say, but, a delicate man, who had a history of paranoia and drug use from his twenties.

He was from a good family and was well educated. After attending Cambridge University he began work in the British Foreign Office, something minor, but would be expected to rise, naturally, with - what do you say? - school tie?"

"Old School Tie Network."

"Yes, quite, just as with the tentacles of our own demi-mythique Two Hundred families. But at some point, and for some reason, Melrose began to involve himself in drugs and become what you say is a loose cannon.

Eventually he lost his job. It is not clear why exactly. However, at that point it seems, he became also abandoned by his family. Perhaps they were attempting to discipline him, more than actually disliking him, because after all, they were so concerned for him after his death. I can only speculate."

"You said it was suicide, but how did he die?" I asked.

"An overdose, but no ordinary overdose. Barbiturates, heroin and other medication, mixed with alcohol."

"Barbiturates? In 1992?"

"Yes. This I also find interesting. He must have obtained them privately. He was prescribed Flunitrazepam, and had enough to kill himself with that alone, had he wanted to. Why he would also need barbiturates? It is a mystery."

"And heroin. By injection?"

"Yes, he injected heroin according to the autopsy, but, his family were particularly angry about this. They believed that he never had used heroin."

"What is Flunitzepan?" asked Phillipa.

"Flunitrazepam," I answered. "I could do with some now. It's a very strong painkiller and sedative."

"It is also a common date rape drug." Said Jaques. "As Danny says, it is very strong. So strong, most doctors will only give it to people who are in a very bad way, and then only for a very short while."

I looked at him.

"Are you thinking what I'm thinking might have happened, Jacques?"

"I suspect that we are on the same road. Perhaps, he was forced to take too many Flunitrazepam with some alcohol, and the evidence of him having taken heroin was in reality an injection of Amytal Sodium as a truth serum, followed by the heroin to create a cocktail that would reliably be lethal, but at the same time perhaps deter a better analysis."

I nodded. "Yes, the same road."

"So you think he may have been murdered after somebody tried to get information from him?" asked Phillipa. "Information about what?"

Jaques gave a classic Gallic shrug and stubbed his cigarette out. "I doubt we will ever know. About the other men. Robert Booth MP is also now dead. He died in 1998, in a driving accident in Germany while he was on what was described as a business trip. What business he was involved in is not clear, since he listed no business interests anywhere in Europe with the British Parliament.

He was, in fact, one of the earliest and most noisy and implacable Europhobes of that era in British politics, and especially hated Germany, who he blamed still for the death of his father during the war.

However. There he was, in his hated Germany, on a business trip where he had no business, dead in a ditch near Frankfurt when a wheel exploded on his car."

"Exploded?"

"Ah, perhaps my English. Not exploded. The air came out."

"OK, I see, he had a blow-out."

"A blow-out, at quite some speed on the autobahn."

"Being chased?"

"There was no suggestion of him being chased, including from cars he had passed who then arrived at the accident. It was night time and the autobahn was almost empty. Many men in those days would speed their Jaguar. Now, it is not so easy. But then, yes."

"But you've no idea what he was doing in Germany, or who he was meeting with?"

"It isn't something I have tried to investigate, because well, it was almost certainly an accident, and to go beyond that is nearly impossible. All we can say is that here, in this film, Robert Booth is holding down a young man called Sebastian Melrose, and with him, on the left are Pierre Ménard, and our friend Walter Samsel."

"Robert Booth is related to Stephen Booth, I take it?"

"Yes, he was the older brother of Stephen Booth. I believe, although I cannot be sure, that this film we have was taken at a party. Although, a party is perhaps not a good word. A meeting of like-minded individuals is perhaps better, three of who were connected by their attendance at Cambridge."

"Samsel was at Cambridge as well?"

"Samsel attended Cambridge at around the same time as Robert Booth and Melrose, although as we see, Melrose was much the younger of them. At the time of the film, I would estimate he was eighteen, in his first year, the others, between four and six years older."

"You say like-minded individuals, but it doesn't look like Melrose is enjoying himself."

"I do not know. Perhaps it was playing a game. Melrose was in his sex life bi-sexual and took part in ritual sex, domination and sado-masochism. It seems, if it could be described as sex, he would do it, so perhaps, even if he looks unwilling, he also enjoyed this rape by Samsel, and perhaps also by the others. But that is empty speculation and beside the point."

"What about Samsel? Which way does he swing?"

"Samsel was married but is now divorced. He has two children with his wife, and a third by a lover some twenty years ago. He is an intensely secretive man and protects himself and his family vigorously. Clearly, though, his tastes were once for other men. Perhaps they always have been and the marriage and affair little more than charades for public consumption."

"Who was his wife?"

"Like Samsel himself she is Swiss. Little is known of her. She was probably well paid for her trouble, and now, she has disappeared."

"And the lover?"

"The same. Disappeared. A Belgian journalist interviewed her around fifteen years ago. There was nothing of any weight to it, very drab, nothing even vaguely sensational, but we can assume that Samsel made sure that she wasn't tempted to talk further."

"She's alive?"

"Yes, as far as anyone knows, but where? It is a mystery. Perhaps on some private island somewhere. Samsel detests publicity and extends that dislike to protecting people he has close contact with. He is not outwardly interested in politics, except as a means of controlling countries' governments for his business interests, and what political interests he has he fronts with people like Ménard.

He sits like a spider and controls his web quietly using influence, blackmail and bribery, and I believe this is why he feels so threatened by the film.

I doubt he feels any shame or remorse, or even embarrassment about it. It's simply that its release would cause revulsion among the people he relies on corrupting, and thus, lose him influence.

Without influence, he could no longer corrupt people to gain lucrative contracts."

"What kind of contracts?" asked Phillipa.

"Samsel has his fingers in many pies, in many countries. From manufacturing, to weaponry, newspapers, construction. There was a famous instance here in France some years ago of a bridge that was built in the middle of nowhere, a bridge joining two tiny villages near Alençon over a non-existent road. A year later, another of his companies was involved in constructing the roadway under the bridge. It is a rare example of something going wrong. Normally, he would not be so careless."

"What happened?"

"Nothing. When the media picked up on the story, nobody who could say what happened would say, and nobody you might think would want to ask them, asked. As often happens in cases where the corruption is too widespread, the story appeared to quietly die of neglect.

But his companies are involved in far dirtier things, particularly the further east in Europe you go. In the old communist countries, the machinery of government is – shall we say – less mature, and more malleable. The communist regimes were every bit as corrupt, so it's expected, and therefore the scrutiny is less."

"And who is the last man. Pierre..?"

"Pierre Ménard. Well, Monsieur Pierre Ménard and I, we had a history. In fact, he once told me he had put a price on my head."

He smiled, almost to himself.

"Perhaps if I had known that he was so intimately involved with Walter Samsel, I might have taken him more seriously."

"So who is he?"

"Ménard was many things, but most famously, he was a politician of the extreme right-wing. I was instrumental in him being in jail, after myself and a journalist from a German newspaper – do you know of Helmut Kraus, Phillipa? – "

She shook her head.

"- he is with Spiegel. Working together, we exposed Ménard's corruption, some of which also pointed towards Samsel, but unfortunately, never directly enough.

Ménard though, was a criminal before he went into politics. There were rumours of his being involved with Mafia organisations. He was a Corsican by birth, although not by lineage.

On Corsica, organised crime is like fine sand. It finds its way into everything. Like Samsel, Ménard was said to have had homosexual relations before he married a Vieux riche socialite, who coincidentally was some years older than himself, and again, coincidentally, died not long after the marriage."

"I assume by you saying "he was", that Ménard is dead?"

"Yes."

"How?"

He laughed, but the laughter didn't quite reach his eyes. "Another unusual suicide."

"What happened?"

"He hanged himself in his cell, while supposedly having been placed in solitary confinement for his own protection."

"Protection from who?"

"I expect he could have told us, but it could have been many people. It quickly became clear that the rumours of him having sung for a lighter sentence after his conviction were more than likely true. People began to be arrested for crimes that only a man like Ménard would have known about. Not that he was required to testify against anybody himself of course, but, well, if you put yourself in the shoes of a man who has been corrupted or is otherwise a criminal. And suddenly, something from years ago is unexpectedly brought to light. You might be forgiven for thinking it was not coincidence."

"When was all this?"

"He was convicted four years ago. Seven months later, he was dead."

"And nothing ever came of his threats against you?"

"No."

"But you said you might have taken him more seriously if you'd known he was mixed up with Samsel."

"Perhaps yes. Samsel is a different kind of man to Ménard. Ménard was corrupt, but almost as a sideline. His politics, his racism, this was the passion that drove him into the corruption that trapped him, in order to fund them.

However inhumane his views, in a way, he was proveably human because he held them. His threats against me were him screaming at himself. He was a broken man, and they were the very human response to my having helped finish his dreams of how he could, as he believed, purify France."

He pulled out another cigarette and tucked the packet back into his shirt pocket.

"But Samsel has no such human frailty." He lit the cigarette. "Samsel is a machine, as heartless as he is remorseless, as remorseless as he is relentless.

With a man like Ménard, well, you can make references to such men throughout history. Men who operated from a genuine belief that what they did was right, even while they must have realised what they did was wrong. You know of a man named Pierre Laval, Danny?"

"Yes."

"Who was he?" asked Phillipa.

"He was part of the Vichy Government in World War Two. In a lot of ways, he was the power behind Petain's throne."

Jaques took off an imaginary hat to me.

"Danny is correct Phillipa. I would describe Laval as a man, so corrupted by his own inner workings, that he destroyed everything that France really was, in order to save a France that was only in

266

his head. Ménard, had he ever gained enough power, was I believe, such a man also."

"And Samsel? What kind of man is he?" she asked.

"Almost the complete opposite of Ménard. Ménard was charismatic, a persuasive orator, even though offering only the kind of simple solutions that will always appeal to simple minds, and whose rhetoric would always be wrapped in the Tricolour as a dare to anyone to oppose it. "Le Patriote plastique" as one of my colleagues used to describe him. You have these men in the UK also, of course. Your Mister Farage is one. Mister Johnson another.

Every country has them these days, and they all seem to be connected by that common thread of racial and social conflict which they use to attack their real enemy, liberal democracy.

Or to describe it more accurately, our free choice not to give them the power they want. But -" he drew on his cigarette, held the smoke in and exhaled slowly before continuing. "- it always seemed to me that Ménard was overly important to Samsel, and I always had thought that it was because Samsel used him as a political sock-puppet, because Ménard was everything that Samsel could never be.

Eloquent, charismatic, politically adroit. So, it made sense for Samsel to pay Ménard to be the monkey, while he played the organ in the background.

But now, with this film, I can see why I might have been wrong. Far from Ménard being the monkey, perhaps all along he had Samsel dancing to his tune."

"Do you mean that Ménard was blackmailing Samsel into supporting him?" asked Phillipa.

"I would put it this way."

He paused for a moment and thought.

"While I'm sure that Samsel holds no love for structures such as the European Union, I think it is possible that Samsel's support for Ménard was more from knowledge of what Ménard had on him, than any great interest in undermining it."

"Then why does Samsel still support those things?" Phillipa asked, "even though everyone in the film except him is conveniently dead?"

"Perhaps they aren't." I said. "Somebody must have shot the film."

Jaques put his cigarette between his lips, clicked his fingers on both hands and pointed them at me.

"Oh shit! Of course!" said Phillipa.

"Right at the end - " I said "- did Ménard speak to whoever was filming?"

"I think you are right, Danny." said Jaques, and stood up and began to reset the projector.

When he was ready he motioned towards the light switch.

I stood up and flicked the room into gloom.

"OK, I will slow it down when it is half way through," he said, and the projector clattered into life again.

As Melrose turned towards the camera Jaques pushed a button on the projector and the image on the wall slowed.

"Look," Phillipa said. "do you see the way his bottom lip goes behind his teeth. That has to be either an F or a V. It can't be anything else. And the sound before that, where the lips make that shape as if he is blowing, but his tongue is there."

"Wait." Jaques broke across her. He reversed the projector and rewound the film for a few seconds.

The men jerked as if frozen for a moment, then the scene flickered against the wall once again.

"Look! There!" said Phillipa excitedly. "It is an S. Then a V. He's saying Stephen." She thumped her fist on the table, as if daring either of us to argue. "Stephen Booth was the cameraman."

"It works." said Jaques and turned the projector off.

"He stops filming because Ménard tells him to, because Ménard is afraid something, incriminant is filmed."

He moved around me towards the door and turned the lights on.

"Then afterwards, when Booth develops the film for the others to enjoy, he cuts these last seconds and keeps them to himself. Nobody will notice them missing, but, just these few seconds, they are enough to give him power over the other three men."

I left them to it. I carried one of the white leather chairs from the table outside and set it up beside the window where I could watch over the gates and the street.

After what felt like a thousand years, I checked my watch. Almost two o'clock. They'd been at it for nearly five hours.

I knew nothing about journalism, nothing about writing up a story, but plenty about screwing a case together, and when I'd gone in for a coffee an hour before, it didn't feel to me as if they'd even scratched the surface.

I realised I was stressing.

I had to trust them.

They knew what they were doing, and I had to leave them to work and concentrate on my job, and my job was to protect them, or at least warn them.

The truth was, I felt on edge. I wasn't happy with the whole set-up, and the more I thought about it, the less I liked it.

With only the stairs or the lift down to a single easy to block exit, if Samsel's troops arrived we were caught like rats in a trap.

Not if.

When.

Whatever they had or hadn't done to Henning, by now Halland would have told them we were in France, and Phillipa's phone call would have got them Jaques's phone number.

Trace the number back to him, and from there it was child's play, a casual phone call to an unwitting receptionist, to check if he was at work.

Getting a home address would take time, but if you could gull the name of the district he lived in out of someone, it wouldn't take long before you'd narrowed it down to a street and then a house number.

In the UK, I'd be confident of cracking it inside a few hours, maximum, however well someone had covered their tracks.

I stared out at the street beyond the high wall, trying to map it out in my mind, every tree, every parked car, every shadow, every window in the buildings opposite so I could recognise if or when anything changed.

The other side of the street was dominated by walled villas.

No doubt the flats we were in had been similar, until the original building had been redeveloped.

Most of their front gardens were filled with bushes and trees with meandering gravel pathways that led to secluded seats or small areas of lawn.

Their frontages were fancy, and typically French, all louvred widows and twisting intricate ironwork painted in blue-greys and pale lemon yellows, tall narrow upper windows, each with small railed balconies.

Beautiful homes, for no doubt beautiful people, with beautifully paid jobs in Paris.

Alongside the walls pollarded trees paraded, their clubbed branches beginning to bud, and their thick trunks seeming to push up rootless through the pavements.

Parked against high kerbstones, cars lined most of the street on both sides. At the end of the road, traffic flowed constantly on a busy through-route.

On the right-hand corner, the faded red front signage of a shop over plate glass windows ran for several yards into the road until it met the first villa.

On the left, the wall was blank brickwork, the windowless side of a three-storey building, probably a shop with its frontage on the main road. High up on the brickwork, an ancient blue and white painted advert had faded to almost nothing.

A car passed, a tiny sans-permis with cartoon bodywork, its 2-stroke engine rasping loud enough for me to hear through the thickly glazed window.

An old man in a raincoat and a battered shapeless fedora walked a little white dog along the other side of the road to us. He stopped and watched the sans-permis go by while his dog squatted and made a puddle.

Nothing, at all, seemed out of the ordinary.

I began working through possibilities.

What would I do?

Would I get into a villa on the other side of the road, with a silenced rifle?

No.

It was a two hundred metre shot through double glazed windows that were tempered, and probably laminated. They might be able to scare someone, but not reliably kill them. It was too indirect.

And they needed the film.

Once they had the film, all that Jaques and Phillipa were left with was a good story that wouldn't fly. It was back to the Auspex scenario, but there was no way La Monde would let Jaques wag the dog like Phillipa had, especially not with this Walter Samsel in the frame.

In the end, then, it came down to the film, and that meant that some way or another they were going to have to get into the building, and then into the flat.

So how would I get into the building?

With the right training, two fit men could scale the wall, but that would attract attention.

There was only one realistic option. They would come through the main gate in a vehicle.

That left them with finding a way to open the gates remotely.

That left them with hacking the lock with a decoder.

I could feel in my water that time was getting short.

An hour, maybe two, maximum, and they would arrive.

And they wouldn't fuck around taking chances this time. They'd be mob-handed, and the best I would manage would be to warn Jaques and Phillipa, then slow them down getting upstairs to the flat. We needed a way to let them think they had everything, while keeping as much as possible. If they could come in, thinking they'd surprised Phillipa and Jaques and found everything they wanted all laid out and ready to scoop up, we'd make it easy for them.

There'd be some slapping about for effect, but if we were lucky, nobody would get seriously hurt. Nobody would need fingers breaking, nobody would need killing.

They could take what they wanted and go. It wasn't what I'd call a great Plan B, but it would be the best of a bad job.

I stood up and stretched.

Pale sunlight shone from an innocent blue sky.

I took a last look out along the street.

Phillipa sat down on the settee, and Jacques perched on its arm alongside her.

" Jacques, how much of your material have you got scanned? or is it all on paper?"

"Scanned? Well, some. Mostly it is paper. That is normal. It is evidence. A scan can be messed with."

"OK, I understand. Phillipa, what about you?"

"Much the same, as you know."

"OK, then gather up as much as you can of what you know will definitely have to be paper, key documents. Put them to one side, and use your phones to photograph everything you won't be able to replace. My guess is that they will come straight up here to get what you have. I'm going to try, but we've got to be realistic, I doubt I will be able to stop them, only slow them down a bit.

The way I see it, there is no point in trying to hide the documents. It's better that you act surprised they are here, and then with luck, if they get a load of documents and the film, hopefully, they won't look for your phones.

When you've finished photographing everything, switch your phones off, and find something like a plastic shopping bag and put them in it.

Jaques, if you have an old mobile anywhere, switch your SIM card over to it, then they at least find a working phone with the number they have for you. If they don't, they're likely to wonder why and start searching.

Start now. We don't know how long they will be."

I pulled the reel loose from the projector.

"Jacques, I need scissors. Kitchen?"

"The drawer by the sink."

I took the reel into the kitchen and spooled a couple of feet off it then cut it through. I took the reel and put it back onto the projector. I cut a pair of single frames from the film and left them where they fell on the table.

I went through the bedroom and opened the broad sliding doors out onto the balcony. As I'd hoped, there was a gully running around the edge of the balcony and a drain hole in one corner that took water away.

I looked down the road again to check it was still clear then called Jacques into the bedroom.

"Jacques, when you have finished taking pictures, or if I warn you they're here, turn both the phones off, wrap them in a plastic bag, like a bin liner or a shopping bag or something, and stick them down this drain. Push them down far enough that they can't be seen, but not too far, so we can get them out with a coat hanger or something after they've gone.

I beat down the urge to crouch and cling to the floor that vertigo always brought on in me and stepped out onto the balcony.

I checked the street both ways then stepped back inside and leaned my back gratefully against the solid wall beside the door.

Phillipa passed me and walked out onto the balcony. She rested her body against the spidery iron railing and stared out at the skyline. I turned away from her rather than fight the nausea that watching her brought on.

Jacques sat down on the unmade bed and leaned back against the wall.

"You do not like heights Danny."

It was an observation, not a question.

He tapped a cigarette from a packet that was on the bedside table.

"I was the same. I still am if I allow it to control me. It was part of the reason I took this apartment. To prove who controlled who."

He grinned and lit the cigarette.

"I told you I covered Afghanistan. There it is very mountainous, and once, I found myself, and my friend Alain who was my cameraman, in a situation where I could be afraid of heights and we would be captured by the Taliban, or –" he lifted a glass ashtray from beside the cigarettes and rested it in his lap "– or, I could run for half a kilometre along a dusty path no wider than my shoes directly over a sheer 200 metre drop."

He looked past me for a moment, nodding to himself slowly, then looked back at me.

"I found it an educating moment. A realisation that I could actually choose, to conquer a fear, even a fear I had all my life, if something I feared even more, made me choose."

He smiled and took a deep pull on the cigarette and looked at Phillipa. I could see from the corner of my eye that she had turned and leaned her back against the railing.

Jaques blew the cigarette smoke out.

"Learning about ourselves is a never-ending journey, is it not? But, in such knowledge, lies wisdom."

He stood up and put the ashtray down on the bedside cabinet. "Come Phillipa, let us begin."

I'd been on watch again for less than an hour when Phillipa came out to me.

"Come back in the flat Danny." she said quietly. "There's something I think you ought to see."

I picked up the coffee mug I'd brought with me and followed her to the door.

As we got there, Jaques pushed past me into the corridor almost apologetically, careful not to catch my eye.

"I will look out for a while, Danny."

I watched him walk to the chair and sit down, then I felt Phillipa's hand under my arm.

"Come in and sit down, Dan."

I sat at the table and stared at the piles of paper and photographs the two of them had been working on. A silver laptop lay open opposite me. I took a sip of the cold coffee.

Phillipa came back, and laid two closed files full of papers in front of me. She pulled up a chair and sat down next to me.

"These files are some information that Jaques received from a contact of his that works for a regional newspaper.

The regional had sent them to Jaques some time ago, and he had simply filed them away because although he was already suspicious of Stephen Booth, he felt that to go after him using what is in here would not serve any other purpose than to alert him that Jaques was investigating him.

But, when I explained a little of what you told me about you and Susan, and, I am sorry, Danny, but when I saw your reaction to me telling you that Booth couldn't have been Simon's father, I - well, while you were in Cornwall, I felt that it couldn't hurt to ask Jaques if he could find anything out, and he remembered these."

I looked across at her.

The sea-green eyes were serious and held my stare.

"Did Susan tell you anything about Simon?"

I pictured Susan laying in the snow, her blood a crimson halo. The way her feet in the oversize wellingtons had their toes turned in. Like a child. Like her child eyes.

I felt my insides curdle, and wished I had a bottle of rum and a dark room to disappear into.

Stress, I told myself.

Shock.

Coming back to get me again. You'll get through it.

I shook my head.

"No. We never spoke about him."

I took a deep breath, but it felt like none of it got down into my lungs.

"I expect we would have, except, we never had a chance to."

"Of course." Phillipa said.

I bared my teeth and tried another deep breath. It ended up as some kind of sigh, but at least it got further down than my throat.

"She wasn't anybody that I knew anymore."

"I'm sorry." she said, with a choke in her voice.

I looked up at her, and her eyes were filled with tears.

I touched her cheek and felt the warm wetness as a tear fell against my fingers.

"I'm sorry." she said again, and the tears were gone with a wipe of her hand. She tapped her finger on the pink cover of the top file.

"This is a copy of a French police report. Now, I know you won't understand it, so I will explain it to you. We want to use it now, because with everything else we have, we consider that it's best just to hit Booth with everything at once.

On its own, it won't ruin him, but hopefully it will isolate him, and that's going to be important. Anyway. I told Jaques that I wanted you to see it before we make it public."

She opened the file and thumbed through a few pages, then flattened the sheets of paper with the heel of her hand.

It was a photocopy of some kind of police form.

At the top were boxes that had been completed with a mixture of handwriting and typing, and below them a section of typed text with a signature and date scrawled underneath it.

She looked at me for a moment, then she spoke, and her voice was almost a whisper.

"Danny, this is a report made by the French police in the case of Simon Daniel Booth." she pointed at the name where it appeared in the lower text section.

"It explains that Simon was admitted to a hospital here in France, in Laval, six years ago. It states -" she ran her finger down the text and I watched its perfect little mother of pearl nail without really seeing it, my mind already somewhere else.

"It states, here, that Simon had fallen down a flight of stairs at home and fractured his skull."

She slid the top file upwards, drew out the lower one from under it and opened it. Another photocopy, this time of a letter a few pages long.

"This is the report to the police on Simon's injuries from the hospital. It describes the extent of his injuries, the possible repercussions, the condition Simon was in on admittance, the ongoing treatment and early tests confirming that he had suffered brain damage, and that in their opinion, he could not be expected to recover."

She looked at me before continuing.

"OK?"

I nodded.

Well, someone, somewhere outside of me nodded, anyway.

She looked at me carefully for a moment before swapping the files over again and flicking through a couple more pages.

Then she flattened the file again.

"This is a follow on from the initial police report. The detective in charge, here - " she tapped a name filled into a box - "an Inspector Tomas Lefort, states that he was called in by the local police after an ambulance woman who spoke some English reported that she over-heard an argument where Susan was hysterical, and accusing Booth of having beaten Simon around the head with a leather belt.

From what the woman said she overheard, Simon had tried to get away from Stephen, and had fallen down a short flight of stairs - " she stopped running a finger along the page "- the stairs were in two parts, a short section to a landing, then a longer flight down to a stone tiled floor.

The ambulance woman said that Susan had accused Booth of kicking Simon across the landing, then throwing him rest of the way down the second flight of stairs. And here - " she ran her finger along the typed text towards the bottom of the paper "-

Inspector Lefort concludes, that in his opinion, the injuries Simon sustained would be unlikely to have been caused by a fall down the shorter flight of stairs, because the wood panelling that Simon would have fallen against was fairly flexible, and would have almost certainly cushioned any impact, even if he had hit his head directly against it.

But, he states, that Simon's injuries could," she tapped the perfect finger under some words to emphasise them "without doubt, have been caused by a fall down the main flight of stairs onto the stone floor - exactly as the ambulance-woman claimed that Susan had said."

She closed the file and slid the two together.

It was a minute before I spoke.

"So. What happened?"

"In essence, nothing. When Lefort had interviewed Booth, under caution, as we would say, he had denied that the argument with Susan had ever taken place.

It was Booth's word against the word of an ambulance-woman, who a police translator had reported spoke very poor English, and had in any case had only overheard what she claimed from outside the room.

Ultimately, it was felt that there wasn't enough evidence for the investigation to go any further.

"What about Susan? Did Lefort interview her?"

"Susan wasn't there when Lefort visited the house. By the time the ambulance-woman had reported it, and convinced the local police that she knew enough English to support her story, Susan and Simon had gone home to the UK so that Simon could receive treatment there.

Inspector Lefort tried several times to call Susan in the UK, and when he finally spoke to her, she denied that there had been any assault. She said that at the time, she was distraught and hysterical, and admitted that she had shouted at Booth, but that the ambulance-woman was mistaken. There had been no argument between them."

"So, Lefort dropped the case?"

"Yes. From a police point of view, there was no case, unless Susan was willing to make one."

"You said, Booth was interviewed under caution. Is there a statement by him in the file?"

"Yes. It says exactly what you would expect: that the ambulance-woman was mistaken, there was no argument. Susan was upset, and what the ambulance-woman overheard and took to be anger was hysteria."

I stared at the files.

"Shall I leave you alone for a while?" she said gently.

"No."

I shook my head.

"No, it's OK. I'll get back out there. You and Jaques carry on."

When I stepped out into the corridor, Jaques was standing at the window. He turned, and smiled sadly as I reached him.

"I am sorry, Danny. That cannot have been nice to learn."

"No. Has there been anything happening out there?"

"Nothing not ordinary. People. Cars. The same as always."

"Have any cars come in that you didn't recognise?"

"No, nobody at all has come in."

"OK Jaques, I'll take over. You and Phillipa crack on. Let's get this done as quickly as possible."

"Sure. But, would you like it, if I was to try and speak to this Inspector Lefort, on an unofficial basis? Sometimes, you know, well, a policeman doesn't put everything he thinks in a report, only what he knows he can defend."

He was right, of course.

Especially when dealing with someone like Booth, someone with money, and probably enough local influence to make Lefort's life a misery if he crossed him, the man could be forgiven for only reporting the bald facts, not his gut instinct.

He was pushing his luck by mentioning the wooden cladding, and a fall down the longer staircase being more likely to have caused Simon's injuries.

"Yes, thanks Jaques, why not. When you get chance, but not now. Get the rest of it tidied away. Lefort can wait."

He nodded.

"Danny, between only us, what do you think has happened to Richard Henning?"

I took a deep breath and leaned back against the window so I would see if Phillipa came out.

"I think he probably committed suicide, Jaques, like Melrose did. They had the perfect alibi for not leaving him alive as a loose end after getting his phone. The pain from his illness, money worries, the court case.

So long as they hadn't whacked him about and given him any injuries, I doubt anybody would suspect anything."

He nodded.

"I think this, also. Danny, my phone number. Is that traceable?"

"Yes. It's traceable, if they have the right contacts within your phone supplier. Sometimes it's enough to Google it. Linked In, websites. It's surprising where people put their number down without thinking."

"I believe I am guilty. That number is on our website, naturally, as a way for people to contact me."

"Well, we can guarantee that they know whose phone Phillipa used, then. Getting your address would hold them up, but not forever."

"How long?"

I shrugged. "Hours. Half a day. It's difficult to say, Jaques. But it's spilt milk. They'll be here; it's just a matter of when."

He slapped me gently on the shoulder. "I will get back."

"Sure. One thing though. Use the spy hole before opening the door, and don't open it to anyone except me, and then only if I knock like this."

I rapped my knuckles on the windowsill: Rap, rap-rap, rap.

He smiled at me thinly, like I was a drunk he'd been humouring but had begun to lose patience with.

"OK Danny. I will do that." and walked back into the flat.

I watched him go.

I'd admired his calmness to begin with, but I was beginning to wonder whether it wasn't guts, but blissful ignorance.

Maybe his idea of shit going down was someone kicking in his door.

Mine was something else. Mine was what I'd seen them do to Durrant and Susan.

A car swept past without slowing. Just somebody out and about, minding their own business.

Down the far end of the street, a scooter pulled in between two cars that were parked alongside the glazed window of the store. The rider got off and dragged it back on its stand.

He watched the car I'd just seen drive past him as he unbuckled the full-face helmet he wore.

It didn't slow down. He dropped his right hand from the helmet and gave the car a thumbs up.

Then he crossed the road and began walking away from the flat. The car waited at the junction at the end of the road then pulled out left.

The scooter rider walked quickly along the street until he reached the junction. Then he turned left and disappeared from view.

Coincidence?

Another few minutes went by, and the scooter rider returned.

He pushed the scooter back off its stand and sat on it. A puff of grey smoke left the rear of it, and he used his legs to back it out of the parking spot. Then he rode slowly down the street towards me.

Sixth sense made me draw back from the window.

When he was almost level with the flats, he pulled over and dragged the scooter back on its stand again. This time, he crossed the road and disappeared from view behind the wall.

Whatever he did to the gates took him less than two minutes.

They swung open and sat waiting for a car that never arrived.

As they began to swing closed, the rider appeared again from behind the wall and crossed over to the scooter. He dragged it off its stand and left a plume of grey smoke behind him as he rode off. The gates shook slightly as they met, then closed together.

I rapped on the door to the flat and waited. I sensed someone on the other side checking the peephole, then Jaques opened the door. "They're on their way. I need to keep an eye on the road while we talk," I walked past him to the far end of the room and stood by the window. "OK, listen. When the door next gets knocked on, one of you check to let the other know what to expect. If you can't see me, then you know that I can't help anymore and it's down to how easy you make it for them.

Remember, we want them to think that you weren't expecting company, you had no chance to hide anything, and that everything they see is everything you've got. Jaques, take the phones and stash them where we said."

He held his hand out to Phillipa and she passed him her phone. He moved away into the kitchen and I heard him pulling a drawer open.

I checked up and down the street.

A large silver car pulled into the road from the direction the scooter had gone.

Gut feeling told me this was them. They'd have waited for the scooter driver to decode the gates, then ride to them and hand the zapper he'd coded for them over. The car grew larger, then slowed and stopped.

I stepped away from the window.

"Phillipa?"

I reached the table and stood checking the Beretta over.

She laid a piece of paper on a pile and looked up at me.

"Yes?"

I slid the Beretta down the inside of my jacket sleeve and buttoned the jacket halfway.

"Come here, babe."

I held my arms open and she came to me, laying her head against my shoulder with her face turned away from me. I pressed my lips against her curls.

" Just do as they say, and let them do what they want and take what they want. And whatever you do, Phillipa, this time, don't be brave."

"I'm not brave." she whispered. "I'm shit scared. All the time, and I wish we weren't here."

"So do I babe, but we are. So let's just do our best to get through it in one piece."

I kissed her hair.

"When was the last time you had a holiday?"

"What's a holiday?"

"It's a quiet thing, with sunsets and sandy beaches. Let's get through this, then we can try one and see if you like it. What do you reckon?"

"Don't talk about such things."

She pushed away from me and walked back around the table.

"I told you everything last night. None of it, was in any way a joke."

She picked up a stack of folders and held them to her chest.

"Please, Danny. Just go downstairs and hide somewhere. If I don't have to be brave, neither do you."

I took the stairs down to the car park and edged my way through the fire door.

I'd thought about waiting for them on the stairs, but the Beretta was a better tool for sniping and dodging than a head-on shoot out. If I could pick one of two of them off while using cars as cover, I at least stood a chance.

If I was stuck in the stairway and one of them could force their way in through the foyer door, I'd be back shot, and it would all be over.

It was better to have it out before they got into the main building.

I let the fire door close against my back then moved sideways with my back to the wall.

If I could keep out of sight of the light sensors, so much the better.

Flattened against the wall, I thought it through.

If anyone was going to get up there they would have to go through the fire door. It was maybe 25 yards from the back wall of the car park to the fire door.

From the opposite wall, I stood a fair chance of hitting anyone who went near it.

The Beretta wouldn't stop anybody at that range unless I got really lucky, but it would wound them, and with the silencer and the shadows between cars, with luck I could wing enough of them before they worked out where I was and went for me mob-handed.

Once they did, I was fucked of course, but I pushed the thought out of my mind.

I kept my back against the wall and moved slowly along it to the corner, then along the wall towards the first of the parked cars, peering into the blackness and praying that the lights wouldn't trigger.

When I was finally behind the car, I crouched down behind it and moved silently along its length then behind it.

I slid the Beretta out of my sleeve and brought the slide back, then let it silently forward. Still crouched down below the body of the car I moved slowly along the wall behind it.

There was an empty parking place, and then the Doblo, and behind that, a dark coloured estate.

I edged my way across the empty place until I was behind the Doblo, then past it until I was behind the estate.

Next to it was parked a BMW, and between the estate and the BMW the green and white exit sign above the fire door glimmered in the darkness.

It was as good as it was going to get, and I was as ready as I'd ever be.

The roller shutter hummed and clattered into life and yellow light chased its way down the far end of the car park. A car pulled in, its tyres squealing as it turned into the first part of the garage, and then silence except the low thrum of its engine at tick over.

They would be sitting and planning, talking through what they would do. Soon they would park, and then the doors would close and it would be game on.

The roller-shutter squealed and clattered closed again.

After a good five minutes, the car finally moved.

The engine revved and its tyres squealed as it pulled into a parking spot and the engine shut down.

I heard the doors shut, quietly pushed to rather than slammed. Four of them. The boot unlatched, and after a pause, was shut.

I held the gun across my lap and waited.

I heard a sound from the left, where the garage dog-legged. The echo of a scuffed step.

I rose up a little, trying to see through the glass of the BMW.

Nothing.

Then another scuffed step, closer now, over by the doors, the opposite side from me.

Yellow lights flickered on around me. He must have moved into my area of the garage and be heading for the fire door.

I peered through the back screen of the BMW, the gun lowered and my arm straight, ready to lift it on to target.

Then I saw him.

Broad-shouldered, short dark hair, a bomber jacket over dark combat trousers bloused over thick-soled boots. The trousers had dust on their knees. He must have crawled to the corner and then stood up, and he was now only five or six steps from the fire door.

He looked around him, then began walking slowly, almost comically, on tiptoe towards the fire door.

One step.

Two step.

I lifted the Beretta and braced myself, moving to the corner of the car with the Beretta double-handed out in front of me.

Three steps.

He stopped and coughed, as if he'd breathed in dust.

Then he stepped forward again.

I moved further down the side of the car.

One more step, and he would show between the BMW and the door.

He took another tip-toe step, and now, I could see him, just.

I needed one more step.

Instead, he took half a step, still not giving me a clear shot, and stood looking around him.

I either popped up, and shot him now, or I risked him seeing me before I had a chance to shoot.

I braced myself, crouched on my knees with my upper body straight and the gun held outstretched in both hands, my heart in my mouth, trying not to breathe.

After three.

I breathed in deep and held it.

One.

I steadied myself.

Two.

I felt the cold nudge of metal behind my ear.

"Keine Bewegung."

The metal prodded me again, pushing my head forwards.

"Fallen lassen."

The metal was pushed harder into my neck.

"Fallen lassen, sofort"

It's funny how quickly you pick up another language when you need to.

I dropped my arms and let the Beretta slide from my sweating hands.

It fell with a rattle onto the floor of the garage.

"Auf dein rucken!"

A hand went under my chin and half pulled half pushed me onto my back over an outstretched leg.

He'd stepped to the side as he tipped me backwards.

No chance of grabbing at him, even if I'd been stupid enough to try.

The fat muzzle of a silencer pointed at my head.

The face behind the silencer was bland and emotionless.

No hatred.

No emotion.

The worst kind.

I heard rather than saw the Beretta picked up, and somebody kicked my foot. I looked down my chest.

Combats, a bomber jacket, topped by a broad face with a half-inch crop of reddish blonde hair, pale skin that looked like it had been out in the sun too long.

Pale eyes stared down at me from either side of a flattened nose.

"Wer bist du?"

I thought of Schroeder. How he must have felt.

How I'd held his eye open.

The helpless terror in it, as his life drained away.

The third man, the Noisy Walker, appeared beside the blonde man.

"Ich werde die Eingangshalle im Auge behalten."

He looked down at me, then at the Beretta in the other man's hand.

"Gebb mo her?"

The man handed him the gun, and he briefly examined the silencer.

"Beretta und Wasp. Wie beim Schreoder."

He looked down at me, handed the gun back and walked away.

The man stared down at me.

"Where did you get this?"

Irish. Southern Irish.

I cleared my throat. "I found it."

Well, what the fuck else could I say?

He was going to top me with it anyway. Poetic justice, and all that. Pop me off with his oppos gun, for popping off his oppo.

People like that sort of thing.

Let's be honest: if Schroeder had been my mate, I'd have liked it too.

"Where did you find it?"

I could have said "Up your mother's hole" or something, and gone out in style, but life is precious.

Every last minute of it counts.

In another minute, Weasel could come running out the fire door shooting and blow them both away.

Or John Wayne and the seventh Cavalry would rock up.

Which on the face of it was more likely.

I said nothing.

"Show me your right hand."

'What?'

"Your right hand. Hold it up. Show me the back of it."

I held it up.

"Spread your thumb out"

Now I understood. The gun wasn't enough. He wanted to be sure he was topping the right bloke.

Suddenly he was angry and his accent thickened.

"Spread your fucking thumb!"

I spread my fucking thumb.

He stood over me and peered at my hand.

I could have kicked up between his legs and - but I didn't.

He looked directly down at me.

"Answer me this, Danny Massey, and don't fuck around. Use your intelligence. Who stitched that hand up?"

'Manny'

"OK. That'll do."

He took a step back from me and nodded to the man beside me.

"Das ist er. Massey."

The man grunted and leant back against the car behind him, unscrewing the silencer from a Walther.

"Get up, Danny. My name's Sean. This -" he pointed to the bloke behind me - "is Markus, and Denis is out front.

Mister Denning sent us. When we get upstairs I'll tell you more and you'll get your gun back."

I stood up and dusted the arse of my jeans off.
"Ah, and I almost forgot."

He dropped the magazine out of the Beretta into his palm and checked it.

"I was to tell, you who else got themselves stitched up that night."

"Go on then."

He slid the magazine back into the Beretta and pushed it home with the heel of his hand, then drew the slide back. The unused cartridge spat out of it and rattled dully on the garage floor. He let the slide go and it clacked home.

"Paulie Croxford."

He had me almost believing him now.

He nodded over his shoulder towards the door.

"Let's go."

You know that thing where you have loads of brilliant ideas, and all of them are really shit?

Well that was me, walking upstairs, with about seven feet of Markus, silent and three steps behind me, and Sean's arse three steps up in front of me, his fist making the Beretta look like a toy.

We got to the foyer and Denis gave Sean the thumbs up through the glass panel of the door.

Sean motioned to the lift and we filed in, me first, right at the back, then Markus and then Sean filling the doorway.

"Which floor?"

"Four"

Sean pressed the button and the doors slid closed on us, three big blokes packed in a shiny little stainless steel box.

I looked into Markus's face.

He stared back at me, calm china-blue eyes under a brown Grade 1 crop.

I got the feeling he'd look the same whether he was slitting throats, blowing brains out or eating schnitzel.

The lift shuddered and slowed, inching the last few feet to the landing. The doors slid open behind him and he stood aside and motioned to me.

"Raus." he said quietly with a hint of peppermint.

Sean waited for me on the landing.

"OK, tell me now Danny, cos we don't want any dramas. Do they have any guns?"

"No. That's it." I nodded at the Beretta, "but they're going to panic if you knock the door. If you let me knock and they see me through the spy-hole, they'll open up."

"Makes sense. We'll hang back."

He spoke briefly and quietly to Markus. Markus nodded.

"OK Danny, give 'em a knock." said Sean with a wink.

I headed down the corridor to the flat and stopped outside the door.

I looked around at them.

Sean nodded, smiling. Behind him Markus squeezed a fresh gum out of a packet into his mouth.

I turned and knocked.

24

I sensed movement behind door, and the lens showed light as its cover was slid away. There was a murmur of voices and then a rattle as the safety chain was unhooked.

The door swung open and Jaques stood back from it, smiling at me.

I took a step forward, and as I did I saw Jaques face change as Sean and Markus appeared behind me.

"Jaques, this is Sean. He's here from my company in the UK."

He didn't look re-assured, and stepped backwards until he stood by the door to the kitchen.

His eyes shifted from them and back to me as they moved into the flat behind.

He was looking at me like I'd insulted his mother.

Markus pushed the door closed behind us.

I smelt peppermint and knew he was stood behind my left shoulder.

"Well, now," said Sean, "It looks as if Mister Billaud isn't very pleased to see us."

Jaques looked at him, raised his head and snorted. As he did, I felt the cold metal of Markus's Walther tap my ear.

"You see, Danny," said Jaques quietly as he leant back against the wall. "This is Walter Samsel. This is how he works."

"Sitzen." said Markus, and tapped my ear with the Walther again.

"Sit down at the table, Danny," said Sean without taking his eyes from Jaques, "keep your hands on the table in front of you, so Markus can't make a mistake."

I did as he said.

Everything looked exactly as I'd expected, the table covered in papers and files. The hunched body of the projector was directly in front of me, its black eye watching me.

Everything was there, except Phillipa.

"Jaques Billaud," said Sean flatly, and as he spoke, he raised the Beretta until it was under Jaques chin.

"Greetings, from Monsieur Ménard."

The bullet took Jaques directly through his windpipe. He straightened against the wall, his eyes rolled upward.

His mouth fell open and blood spilt from it.

His knees gave and his body slid down under its own weight until he sat untidily against the wall.

His head lolled forward and his body followed it, leaving him lying face down, hunched over, a man at prayer.

Sean had followed him down with the Beretta.

He grunted and pushed Jaques body over with the flat of his foot. It lay with blind eyes staring at the ceiling.

He nodded and turned to me.

"One's usually enough. Get it right and you take out the brain stem.

Miss the brain stem and it ends up in the skull and blats around."

He sniffed and spoke to Markus.

"Er stinkt. Zieh ihn ins Küche und die Tür zu."

He pulled out a chair and sat down beside me.

"Where's the girl, Danny?"

"I don't know. I thought she was in here."

He nodded and laid the Beretta on the table between us.

"I expect Markus will turn her up, but meantime, you and me need to do some talking. As y'man Billaud said, I work for Walter Samsel.

We'd met briefly before, and he knew me as soon as I walked in. A very clever guy, he was, but to a man like Samsel, an un-ending pain in the arse.

But, egal. I'm here from Samsel, and he sends you his regards."

Behind him, Markus dragged Jaques into the kitchen.

"Now, I know what you're thinking. How did Samsel's man get to know those things, about your hand, about this guy Croxford? There's only one place they could come from, right?

And of course, that's where they came from.

Your man told my man, because they figured between them it was the only way to handle you. Now, the thing is Danny, you know that this film is the problem."

Markus pulled the kitchen door closed.

"Markus, finde das Mädchen. Aber tu ihr nichts."

He spoke without taking his eyes from mine.

"You know the problem with the film and you also know the rules. If you allow this film to get out, your man Denning will have to allow my man Samsel to do for you. On the other side, if anything happens to you, Samsel has to let Denning do for me. It's a deal between two bastards, Danny.

Top table shit, and you and me, we're just the hired help, stuck in the middle and expendable.

So, we have to work together, not against each other, right?"

He waited for me to respond, his blue eyes searching mine.

Behind him, Markus came out of the spare bedroom and loped across the lounge towards the main bedroom door.

"What about the girl."

"Ah, well. The girl is another problem, isn't she Danny. She's trouble.

She knows everything, except how to keep her fucking trap shut."

"She's our problem."

"How so?"

"Because you have to come through me to get to her."

"Now, that's not what Denning and Samsel have agreed, Danny."

"I don't give a fuck, Sean. This is between you, and me. Anything happens to her, and either I'll do you, or you'll do me to stay alive. And then the rules kick in. Your choice."

"Danny, you're not muscle, and there's three of us onto one of you. For sure, you can go for me, and that big mad German bastard in there will tie your arms in a bow like shoelaces.

He knows the rules. The rules say you're not to be killed. That doesn't mean he can't make you a cripple if you fuck around."

He stood up and took the spool from the projector.

"And he's an artist Danny. And he fuckin' loves his work."

Markus appeared at the bedroom door. He leant against the frame, chewing slowly.

"Zeest draussen, auf'd Balkon. Hat über da Zaun geklettert." he grinned.

Sean sat down again. "She's out on the balcony." he said without looking at me. "She's climbed over the railing."

He pulled a length of the film from the spool and held it up to the light.

"Jesus fuckin' wept." He breathed. "Have you watched this?"

"Yep. You can see why he wants it."

He nodded.

"How did you get it?"

"I beat Schroeder to it."

"I heard about that. So it was down in Cornwall?"

"The wife had it."

"Any idea why?"

"Not really. Only theories."

"Like?"

"Later. Let's get the girl in before she freezes and falls off."

"If she falls off she falls off."

He threw the reel of film on the table.

"If she falls off, Samsel won't get the last couple of feet of that film."

He looked at me, his eyes smiling.

"Now look Danny, don't go trying to be a tricky bastard with Samsel. He always gets what he wants. Right now, you've got the best of both worlds. You've crossed him, but you get to walk away. Take it while it's offered, because you never know when things will change. Where's the rest of the film?"

"Get the girl in and we'll talk about the film."

He picked up the Beretta. "Was this Schroeder's?"

"Yes."

"How did you get it?"

"He left it in Cornwall."

"You killed him?"

"It was me or him."

He nodded slowly.

"He was always too clever for his own good, Schroeder. Never thought things through properly."

"He took too many things for granted."

He widened his eyes, staring at the gun.

"You can't afford to do that."

He laid the Beretta back down on the table.

"Is this everything, Danny?" he looked around the table. "I mean, is this everything the girl and Billaud had?"

"I don't know. You'll have to ask the girl."

He nodded.

"Go and get her in." he picked up the Beretta again, dropped the magazine out of it and held it out to me.

"Take this and show her you've got it, so she knows she can trust you."

I stepped out on to the balcony.

Phillipa stood shivering on the left side of it, her hands white, clinging to the yellow-painted steel railing. Her eyes were wide and fearful.

"It's OK Phillipa," I spoke softly to her. "You can come in now. Nobody is going to hurt you."

Her teeth chattered as she spoke.

"Are you sure?"

"Yes, I'm sure. Look." I opened my jacket and showed her the butt of the Beretta. "Everything is fine. Come back in and we'll talk everything through."

"Where's Jaques?"

"Jaques is in the kitchen. Come on, get back indoors before you freeze your tits off."

"I think they've already gone." She chattered.

She lifted her left leg to try and get it over the railing but it was too high. She stood on the bottom rail of the railing and tried again, but she still couldn't reach.

She looked at me helplessly. "I'm too short. Help me get over."

"How?"

"Well, lift me."

I moved towards her, trying not to look at the horizon, trying to concentrate on her face.

"Danny."

Sean spoke from behind me. I looked around.

"Forget it. Let Markus do it."

Markus moved from behind him and the balcony trembled under my feet as he walked onto it. I went the other way, making an effort not to grab gratefully for the doorframe as I made it back inside.

"I can't stand heights either," said Sean. "let the fuckin' Fallschirm-jaeger do it."

I looked back as Markus lifted Phillipa up under the armpits. She kicked her feet over the railing and he let her down. She pulled her T-shirt demurely down over her hips and smiled wanly as he grinned down at her.

"Thank you." She shivered, not looking up at him.

"Bitte." He chewed back down at her.

"I need a coffee," she complained. "I'm frozen through."

I dragged the duvet from the bed and draped it around her.

"What the fuck did you go over the side for? What were you going to do? Jump?

"I was scared. Where's Jaques?"

"Come through into the living room and sit down. You need to listen carefully and make sure you understand."

"Danny? Where is Jaques?"

"You want to see Jaques? he's in the kitchen, dead."

"What?"

"Dead."

The colour drained from her face.

"What? Why?"

I took a deep breath. "You know why. He told you."

"No. What? When did he tell me?"

"He told you, that Ménard had warned him. Well, it happened."

"Who did it?"

"Who do you think? Phillipa, please, shut up and go and sit down on the couch in the front room. We've got a lot to talk through, and most of it is about keeping you alive."

She scowled at me and I saw her head lower.

I put my finger up directly in her face.

"Don't - bother getting stroppy." I hissed at her. "If you don't listen to me, you'll end up in the kitchen with Jaques. You've pissed off this Walter Samsel and you're on your last chance. Now, get through there, sit quietly, listen and agree to everything."

She sat huddled in the duvet at the end of the couch.

I sat at the other end.

Sean sat facing me astride one of the dining chairs with his arms resting on its back.

In the dining room, Markus was stuffing everything from the table into black bags.

"There'll be an ambulance along shortly." Sean said to me. "Well, not really an ambulance, but, you know what I mean."

I watched Phillipa out the corner of my eye.

"I want us to be out of here and gone by the time they get here, so we need to get ourselves agreed on things. Danny, you have a length of the film. Walter Samsel wants it. We also need to talk about – Phillipa. Now, Samsel gave me clear instructions, but so far, I've not carried them out. What have you got to say?"

"On Phillipa, I'm shield. I told you earlier: you take her out, and either I'll top you or you'll top me. Either way, you go to war with MDH.

I'm shielding her because whatever history there was between Samsel, Ménard and Billaud, she was not involved. She was after Stephen Booth, not Samsel.

Stephen Booth was blackmailing Samsel over the film for years. I got on the end of something between Booth and his wife in the UK that brought me into the situation, and I found the film.

None of that was her doing, and until I brought the film into this room, she didn't know it existed. She would have nailed Booth, and Booth alone, not Samsel, without the film.

She had nothing to do with Samsel, and what she was working on with Billaud was nothing to do with Samsel.

Samsel either accepts that, or he doesn't."

"Fair enough. But there's two of us, and your guns empty Danny. You couldn't kill anybody."

"Go and look under the mattress in there, Sean."

I pointed my thumb over my shoulder towards the bedroom.

"There's a snub Smith and Wesson. While you were sitting on your jacksee waiting for us in here, I could have plinked Markus through the bedroom door and then we'd be one on one.

And we'd have woken the whole street. Even if you'd survived, you'd have stood fuck all chance of sneaking four corpses out. But I didn't do that. I played it straight. I've proved my goodwill.

What I want Samsel to do is to play it straight as well. Leave her out of it. I will personally guarantee to him that she will forget everything that's happened here. She won't speak a word of it or write a word of it, ever, and if she does, Samsel can take me.

And you know, Sean, that I am going outside MDH on this. This is my call, on my honour, and Denning will have to allow Samsel to take me if she does. Do you understand that Phillipa?"

I looked down the couch at her.

"Do you understand what we are talking about here?"

She nodded without looking at me.

"What, Phillipa?" I asked her again.

"Yes." She looked up at me. "I think so."

"Well, let's spell it out and make it one hundred per cent clear you understand, lady." said Sean, looking across at her.

"Danny is guaranteeing, with his life, that you will forget everything. The film. Billaud. That any of it happened. That any of us were ever here. If you don't, he agrees to take the blame. If you let him down, ever, he ends up like your friend Jaques, and so do you, and if there is any suspicion that you break this bond, to avoid conflict, his organisation will likely dispose of both of you before we even hear about it.

Now - is that crystal clear enough for you, lady?"

"Yes."

She looked ashen.

He grunted and looked back at me.

"OK, now that's all said, I will go and speak to Samsel, and we'll see what he says."

I nodded.

He got up and moved to the other end of the room, spoke quietly to Markus then left.

She looked down the couch at me for a moment, then looked away.

Whatever was going through her mind could stay there. I needed all the peace and quiet I could get to think.

Markus leant against the wall watching us, his tidying up finished.

A pair of black sacks bulging with the angular shapes of files lay on the other side of the door to him, ready to be moved out. Phillipa hadn't said a word. I hadn't interrupted her.

Another ten or so minutes passed before Sean rapped on the door and Markus opened it. As Markus pushed the door closed, Sean spoke quietly to him.

Markus nodded, closed the door and walked toward us.

"Danny," Sean motioned to me to join him at the table.

I stood up and passed Markus. He moved past me and took my place on the couch without looking at me.

Sean had sat at the table and pointed to the chair next to him.

As I sat down he looked into my eyes and spoke quietly, almost a whisper.

"I'll put it simply to you. Samsel has spoken to MDH and agrees to what you propose about the girl. He says to tell you that you have his word that nothing will happen to her."

He put his hand into the thigh pocket of his trousers. He drew out the clip from the Beretta and laid it on the table in front of me.

I picked it up and turned it over in my hand. "Good. I'm glad that's settled."

"Me too. And now the film you have. Samsel told me to make it clear to you that MDH know nothing about the film or what I am about to tell you.

It's a private matter between you, and him. You have the last of the film, and he would like to bring the matter to a close. He is realistic. He knows that we cannot force you to tell us where it is without bringing in MDH against us, and that's not what he wants.

He also realises that if you get the film back to the UK, it's odds on to fall into the orbit of y'man Denning.

So, he is prepared to offer you, personally, 50,000 Swiss Francs for it, to be paid into any account of your choosing."

I shook my head.

"For what I've been through, for what she's been through," I nodded towards Phillipa "and for killing Susan Booth, who was an old friend of mine, you can tell him, he doesn't offer enough.

But, I understand he wants to close the issue, and I don't want to profit from his situation. I want to go away for a couple of days, take some time to myself over here. R and R, Sean, you know what I mean?"

He nodded.

"Yeah, I can understand that."

"So, here's the deal on the film. You take Phillipa, and get her on a flight home today. Samsel can donate the fifty grand to Auspex, her magazine. Booth has fucked them over, and they haven't got a pot to piss in.

Tell Samsel he'll find a donation link on their website. I'll check with her the day after tomorrow. So long as she's home, and the magazine has the money, I will contact you and tell you where you can pick the film up from."

He shook his head at me and grinned.

"You're as bad as he is."

"I doubt that. But you can tell him from me, I take his word that no harm will come to her, and he has my word that he'll get the film."

This time Sean was back inside five minutes.

When he knocked the door, Markus nodded from the couch and I let him in. He pushed the door closed and leaned back against it.

"You've got your deal. I'll give you my number when we're downstairs, but now, it's time we were all gone. Get your stuff together, and get the girl to get herself ready. Ten minutes, and we're out."

25

I drove south out of Paris on the A6.

After an hour, with dusk fast falling, I pulled over into an Aire and had a quick meal and a couple of coffees.

I hadn't seen him come into the Aire after me, but the tail picked me up again as soon as I left. He was driving a white Renault Laguna, and keeping doggedly half a dozen cars behind me.

After a while I got bored with him and pulled over into another Aire for a piss. I drove right through, almost out onto the slip road again. I watched him in the mirror.

He killed his lights as he entered the slipway and pulled over immediately, stopping before he got properly onto the Aire.

So he had a tracker on the van, and he probably had an infrared sight of some kind so he could see me from a distance.

I tucked the Beretta into my jacket sleeve and walked across to the toilet block. I stepped inside, then stood by the door and looked around it.

A row of vehicles parked along the main roadway blocked my view of the Renault. If I couldn't see him, he couldn't see the toilet entrance. Now I needed to get across to the van and into the trees and bushes that ran along the length of the Aire. The cover would take me to the Renault.

The problem was I had twenty yards of open ground to cover, and someone who would be watching for me. And if I didn't show up soon, he was going to smell a rat.

Then I woke up.

I walked across to the van and got in.

He was four hundred yards away in the pitch dark. Even with the best equipment, he might be relying on the interior light of the van coming on to tell him I was on the move.

I reached up, prised the cover off the interior lamp and stripped the bulbs out of it.

I opened the door, got out crouching and slipped into the wooded area that ran the length of the Aire.

Traffic passed by on the Peage as I made my way along, throwing sweeping shafts of light through the trees. I stayed as low as I could, only moving when no traffic was passing, slowly edging closer to him.

Eventually I was thirty yards away, and could faintly hear music coming from the Renault.

This last part was going to be the trickiest.

I really couldn't trust the Beretta to hit the narrow grille of the Renault at more than ten yards, not in darkness and with a silencer blocking the sight. It was going to have to be point blank.

I paused, wondering if I wasn't making it more difficult than it needed to be. The weak point was the gun. Take that out, and what other options were there? Keep it simple stupid.

I dropped back further into the trees, moved closer to the motorway and worked my way along until I was sure I would be past the Renault. Then I made my way up through the trees towards the roadway.

I looked down the motorway.

Traffic was sparse. Nobody had driven in since we'd arrived.

Across the far side of the Aire, a row of Artics were parked like a chain of sleeping elephants. Lights shone dimly behind some of their cab curtains.

In the main roadway, the half dozen vehicles that had shielded the entrance of the toilet block were mainly large vans, Sprinter size long haul wagons.

Like the Artics, their drivers would be sleeping or watching crap on their phones.

I crept to the edge of the trees.

Loud music thumped inside the car.

Praying that no one had walked their dog, I flattened myself and rolled silently across the ground and down the kerb onto the roadway behind the car.

I moved quickly to the passenger side rear wheel and felt around it for the valve. It was about as far from me as was possible, but by laying half under the rear of the car I could reach it.

I unscrewed the cap, and working by feel reversed it in my fingers. I gently pushed the point of it into the valve. I felt resistance, then heard a faint hissing as the air from the tyre blew around my fingertips.

Slowly, slowly, slowly, I told myself.

Gradually the tyre began to deflate, then the Renault's door opened.

He stepped out, and I heard him groaning over the music as he stretched and yawned.

I silently drew my feet in as far as possible and tried to wriggle further under the car. I started to move my arm in and heard the leather of my jacket scrape on the ground.

I froze.

A spattering noise started somewhere by my feet.

I dug my chin into my chest and looked down as best I could.

He was pissing into the roadway beside the car.

The song began to fade and a French voice took over for a few seconds, then another song began.

He started singing along to himself quietly, off-key and too high.

The spattering stopped. Began again. Stopped.

After a few seconds I heard his zip go up.

The car lurched as he sat back in, then the door was pulled shut.

I found the valve again and pressed the cap into it. Air hissed and the tyre sank lower. The tone of the air coming out deepened as the pressure in the tyre reduced and I pushed the cap as far in as it would go.

Half a minute later the tyre was flat.

I squirmed out from under the car and sat up, looking around me.

I could go back through the trees, or with luck, I could roll across the roadway and get up behind one of the vans without him seeing me.

I lifted myself up and looked over the boot through the back screen. He was tapping his fingers on the steering wheel, not taking a blind bit of notice.

I crouched down and duck walked along the side of the car until I was level with the passenger door. I slid out the Beretta and tapped the butt of it lightly against the car.

Nothing.

I tapped louder, and this time the music went off.

I tapped again.

After a few moments, the door opened and the Renault lurched as he got out.

I stood up and pointed the Beretta directly at him across the roof. "Bonjour."

He jumped and his mouth fell open. I stepped along the car keeping the gun on him, raising my left hand and saying "Up. Up."

Like me with Markus, he picked up new languages real fast.

His hands shot straight up above his head.

He was a chubby guy, maybe fifty and narrow shouldered. His eyes were wide and his face pale and sweaty in the light from the car. He was either muscle and a great actor, or just a motor-man and no threat.

I was his side of the car now. "Allay," I said, motioning with the Beretta he should move away from the car.

He took a step sideways.

"Allay." I waved the gun again.

He took two wide steps backwards and on the second one tripped on something and nearly fell. Panic shot across his eyes but he kept his hands straight up as he righted himself.

I glanced inside the car. Sure enough, a tablet was fixed to the centre console. Sean had stuck one on me.

I passed the Beretta to my left hand and moved inside the car door, keeping my eyes on him while feeling around behind the steering wheel until I found the keys.

I pulled them out and stood back up, moved around the door and pushed it shut with my backside. I pushed a button on the key and the locks of the Renault whirred. I found another button and pushed it, this time they whirred and I heard the locks go home.

I under-armed the keys over his head into the trees and passed the gun back to my right hand.

I began slipping it back into the sleeve of my jacket.

If he was going to try anything, it was now he'd try it. His hands never moved, apart from shaking.

I moved along the side of the car and back onto the roadway, watching him. His wide frightened eyes under his thinning hair followed me, with the rest of him being super extra special careful to stay exactly where it was.

I pulled back onto the A6 and followed the sat nav to Orleans.

By nine-thirty I'd parked the Doblo up in a back street, loaded the holdall and was trekking across town.

I found an anonymous travel lodge and booked in for the night. In the foyer I checked out hire car brochures. One of them had a map on the back and made a big deal out of being only a few streets away. I took it with me.

Showered and shaved, I set myself up for an early start and hit the sack.

By eight-thirty the following morning I was driving into a golden sunrise, heading for Le Mans in a 3008.

Hambais was a village that lay on one of the secondary routes running west from Le Mans and onwards towards the Atlantic coast. After a long drive where the road was one long continuous straight, it climbed in a series of sharp bends into Sille Guillame, then swept downwards towards the Loire Valley.

I drove through the narrow main street, taking in the layout of the place. Not that there was much to take in. A few shops, then a central square opened out. A few more shops then a post office, and that was that. Once through the town, the road widened and straightened again. The cemetery appeared on my right, behind a high stone wall that ran alongside the road.
I swung the car around at a forked junction and headed back, parking in a side street a hundred metres or so from where the road narrowed as it entered the town.

Walking back into the centre, I took a seat under the awning of the cafe-come-newsagents that took up the corner of the town square.

The long-faced patron loped out to me, wiping his hands on an apron.

"Monsieur?"

"Cafe au Lait, S'il vous plaît."

"Certainement."

A few minutes later he delivered a small brown tray with coffee, sugar and a tiny bar of chocolate.

"Merci."

"Merci, Monsieur." He nodded. He stepped from one foot to another for a second, as if he might ask an awkward question, then changed his mind and left me alone.

The square, perhaps a hundred meters wide, was dominated by an ancient square hewn gothic church. Almost directly across the street was my next stop, a gaudily painted Immobilier.

Coffee and chocolate finished, I dropped a pair of two Euro coins onto the tray and wandered across the street to Immobilier and scanned the properties on display.

"ENGLISH SPOKEN HERE" announced a sign.

I shaded my eyes and looked through the glass. The place was empty except for a thin-faced starchy looking woman of around fifty who was busily putting files into a steel cabinet.

I pushed open the door and went inside.

From a brief stilted conversation, I learned that the Notaire's office was across the main street and on the other side of the church.

I thanked her and walked across to it.

Properties for sale and official-looking announcements on pink A4 sheets dotted its windows. I peered between them to see inside.

The room was low ceilinged and no more than ten feet square.

A young girl with long chestnut hair wearing outsized black-rimmed glasses sat at a desk. She was studiously typing something from a piece of paper beside her into a computer.

I pushed inside the low entrance and shut the door quietly behind me.

"Hallo." I smiled at the girl. "Parlez vous Anglaise?"

She looked at me with sad brown eyes through the glasses.

She swallowed.

"I am not sorry. Patientez s'il-vous-plait."

She got up and walked around the desk, smiling demurely at me as I had to move out of her way to let her past. She disappeared through a doorway and I heard her shoes thumping as she ran up a flight of stairs.

The stairs seemed to end somewhere above my head.

Then I heard her shoes on the stairs again, and she came back through the doorway and stopped in front of me.

"Madam Balchin... will." She stalled and blushed. "Une moment, s'il-vous plait" she whispered and retreated back behind her desk.

Footsteps started down the stairs, stopped then started again.

A woman with short dyed auburn hair appeared.

She wore a white blouse tucked into a tight mid-length wool check skirt. Long slender legs in white stockings ended in a pair of flat-heeled brown slip ons. A pair of frosty lavender-blue eyes studied me from under thinly plucked brows.

"Madam Balchin?"

"Yes, I am Madam Balchin. I am sorry, Monsieur le Notaire is away today. Is there something I can help you with?"

"Well, I hope so Madam Balchin. I was passing through the area, and I suddenly realised that I have an old friend who lives not far from here.

The only problem is, I wasn't expecting to be this way at all, and I haven't got his address, and worse, I don't have an up-to-date phone number for him.

I do remember though, that he bought his house through the Notaire in Hambais, and that's you. I wondered if you could give me his address?"

She shook her head. "No. I am afraid that is impossible, Mister..?"

"James. Joseph James."

"I'm afraid that is impossible Mister James. You will need to visit the Marie tomorrow morning and enquire. We are not allowed to give confidential details."

"Oh dear. That's a pity. You see –" I pulled my wallet from my inside jacket pocket and opened it. I pulled a One Hundred Euro note half out of it "- if I can't find Gavin, I will have to spend this hundred Euros on a hotel room tonight. I believe that the hotel –" I pointed out of the door. "- is just over there?"

She thought about it for all of a second then threw a sideways glance at the girl, who was tapping away for all she was worth on the computer.

"Perhaps I may be able to help, Mister James. Follow me please."

She turned and began walking back up the stairs.

I followed, enjoying the way the white stockings moved inside her skirt and the way the tight skirt rode higher up her thighs with each step.

She made no effort to pull it down.

The stairs turned back on themselves and ended at a grey-blue door panelled door.

She pushed the door open and led the way inside.

"Close the door, please Mister James."

She spoke without looking at me and sat down on a grey swivel chair behind a desk cluttered with files stacked around a wide silver monitor.

She pulled her chair closer to the desk and tapped briefly on a keyboard that matched the monitor.

"What is your friend's name?" she asked without looking up at me.

"Durrant. Gavin Durrant. D, U, R, R, A, N. T".

She typed and hit return.

I watched her eyes scanning the screen, her lips pursed so that small lines formed around them that showed through the crimson lipstick she wore.

She moved the mouse, then clicked it with a long finger tipped with a nail that matched her lipstick.

Her eyes glanced up at me watching her.

She smiled to herself as she looked back to the screen.

I took a seat on the edge of her desk.

She pretended not to notice.

Finally, she took a sticky note from a pad and wrote the address on it in neat rounded letters.

She passed it to me.

I smiled, opened my wallet and slipped out one of the 100€ notes.

"What is your first name, Madam Balchin?"

I laid the banknote on the desk.

"Elise."

She slid the 100€ under her keyboard.

"And, is Elise married?"

She looked me up and down from under her lashes.

"Sometimes."

"Will you be married tomorrow evening?"

"Unfortunately, yes. But, I believe I will be unmarried during the weekend."

"That's interesting. I will also be unmarried then. I don't suppose, Elise, you know of any quiet restaurants where two unmarried people could get to know each other?"

She smiled and pushed the chair back, twisting slowly on her seat so I could see just how far the little skirt had climbed.

"I think I can remember one, at a hotel, in Rennes."

"Rennes?"

"It is, perhaps seventy kilometres from here."

" That sounds perfect Elise. How shall I contact you?"

She thought for a moment, then took a card from a pile on a glass holder and passed it to me.

"Call me on this number, any day between one and two o'clock."

"I certainly will."

I slipped the card and the paper she'd given me into my wallet, and went to close it, but stopped.

"Elise."

I grinned as if enjoying a private joke.

"While you have Gavin's file open, I don't suppose you have a copy of his passport on there?"

She looked at me with her eyebrows raised.

"Because if you have, I'd be interested in reminding him how much he's changed. I saw him last year, and he's gone bald as an egg."

She turned her face a little sideways to me and looked at me along her lashes.

"Well. I really don't know."

"Is it traditional for the man to buy dinner in France?"

I slipped another 100€ note half out of my wallet.

"Especially, when a beautiful woman meets him in Rennes, wearing a beautiful new dress?"

I closed one eye and looked at her, smiling.

She narrowed her eyes at me, then her mouth pouted itself into an ironic smile.

She turned back to the screen and put her hand back on the mouse.

After a few small movements and a couple of clicks, a printer wheezed into life, spat out a single sheet then fell quiet.

She reached across, picked up the sheet it had printed and held it up for me. I grinned at her, slid the 100€ note onto her desk and took the sheet from her.

"You are a star, Elise." I grinned.

She raised her eyebrows.

"Make this small please and put it away before you go outside."

I did as she said, folding it and tucking it into my inside jacket pocket. I lifted myself from her desk and held out my hand to her.

"So, Elise. Until we speak again."

26

Sille-le-Guillame seemed as good a place as any, so I found myself a hotel that did evening meals, fed and watered myself and was in bed asleep by nine.

By seven-thirty the following morning, I was on the Peage out of Le Mans and on the way back to Orleans.

I dropped off the 3008 and got a cab back across town to the Doblo. From there I drove to a hardware store, parked up in a far corner of its car park and went shopping.

I came back with the smallest roll of roofing lead I'd been able to find, a cheap home maintenance toolkit, a disposable boiler suit and some work gloves, and a tube of latex cement.

It took me over an hour to find the tracker Sean had planted. They were nothing if not professional.

Working in the van's side door with the craft knife, pliers and hammer from the tool kit, I sliced a broad strip from the roofing lead and folded and beat it into a crude box big enough to hold the tracker.

I cut another strip and made another box large enough to hold the first. Satisfied that together they would kill any signal, I piled everything back into the van and set course for Tours with the tracker on the passenger seat beside me.

Past Tours I pulled over into an Aire and sank a coffee.

I figured that this time they would be keeping me on a loose leash and using the tracker's range, and they would have stopped off a few kilometres back as soon as they saw the Doblo go stationary.

I went back into the shop area and bought myself a map of France, then ordered another coffee to take with me and went back to the van.

I stripped the battery out of my phone and put it in the glove box then sat and studied the map, tracing the route back to Hambais and circling the important junctions on the route with a pen.

Ready to roll, I took the tracker around to the side door and placed it in the smaller lead box, folding the box's crude lid shut.

I placed the smaller box upside down in the larger one and folded that box's lid shut.

I pulled into Hambais around 8 o'clock, parked the van in a side street behind the church and took my holdall to the small hotel that faced the town square.

I pushed through the heavy glass door.

A seated area on the left with half a dozen round tables and dark stained wooden chairs took up the first part of the room.

The tables were laid with pale cream table cloths. In the centre of each table sat a narrow empty glass vase.

The cream painted wall beyond the seated area ended in an arch, and a gaming machine stood guard at the entrance to the rear half of the bar, where the air was a fug of illicit cigarette smoke from a group of half a dozen men who were playing darts.

Their conversation was animated and studded with laughter.

Behind them, from high up on the wall, a television blared the commentary to some Champions League game.

A broad dark wooden bar around gut high to me ran the length of the right-hand side, ending by the door behind me with a display filled with chocolate and bags of sweets.

One of the men playing darts collected his arrows from the board and saw me waiting. He nodded to me, then went behind the bar and ducked halfway through a doorway.

He straightened back up, nodded to me again and turned back to his game.

A minute or so later a woman of around forty with shoulder-length dark hair held back by a black band came through the door and walked along the bar towards me.

She wasn't much more than five–three in the flat-heeled pumps she wore, an oval face with high cheekbones and wide-set eyes.

She had dusky complexion that you knew would be like milk chocolate within a few hours sun.

A dusting of darker freckles lay across her cheeks and the broad snub of her nose.

"Bonjour Monsieur."

She said, adjusting a loose black jumper that hinted at cleavage inside its V-neck.

"Bonjour Mademoiselle"

I smiled at her, and she gave me a wry smile back that narrowed her eyes. They were the deepest brown, so deep they were almost black.

"Parlez vous Anglais?" I continued.

"Une petit, monsieur."

She made a pinch sign in front of her face with a small, pale-palmed hand.

"You are for a room?"

"Yes, please. A double if you have one."

"I have. Five ish Euro avec petit dejeuner. "

"Fifty?" I wrote the fifty in the air between us, smiling at her.

"Qui, fifty." Her eyes sparkled at me and she chuckled.

"Superb." I tried, "I'll have it."

"Yes, Monsieur."

She reached below the counter and drew out a dark leatherette bound book and opened it in front of me.

"You name, ici, here –" she touched one of the biro drawn columns with the tip of a finger, "- and here -" she slid the finger to the next column, "- you address –" the finger slid along again "- here, you –" she tapped the book, thinking, then "- passport number."

I looked down at the book and then up at her.

Her dark eyes took me in from behind thick natural lashes.

I drew out my wallet and opened it, laid a fifty Euro note onto the open book, then slid out a twenty Euro note and laid it beside the fifty.

She looked down at the seventy Euros, then back at me and smiled.

The seventy Euro's disappeared somewhere under her jumper and the leatherette book slapped quietly shut and went back under the counter.

She opened a wooden cabinet that hung on the wall behind her, lifted a set of keys from a hook then turned back to me, holding them out to me by the tip of a key.

"Go out —" she waved her left hand while she tried to remember the word "-gauche - left!" she chuckled, that sound again.

"Then immediate, is door, for this."

She shook the keys at me.

I took them from her.

"Go, we meet us inside, and I see you room."

She thought for a moment, then nodded, obviously pleased with her English.

I smiled and nodded back to her, picked up my holdall and went outside. From above me, a tinny-sounding bell chimed down from the church tower.

I found the door just after where the window of the hotel bar ended, set deep in the wall on top of a pair of worn granite steps. I slid the key into its loose lock and pushed it open.

As I stepped inside, a low wattage bulb came on and she walked towards me through a passage alongside a steep set of carpeted stairs, her figure silhouetted by a brighter light from within the hotel. I caught a breath of lavender as she reached me.

She held out her hand.

"I am Madame Bauduin."

"Joe. Enchante, Madame Bauduin." I took her hand and gave it a gentle squeeze.

"Merci, Monsuier Joe." She bowed her head a little and looked up at me briefly from under her lashes.

"Come," She motioned towards the stairs. "Please. Follow."

The church bell clanging thinly through the window woke me. I checked my watch. Six-thirty.

After Madam Bauduin had showed me around the low ceilinged room with its avocado en suite shower from the late 1970's, she had told me that I could have breakfast at any time after seven.

The bed and its mattress were probably older than the bathroom, but they kicked the shit out of the foam and flat-pack crap you get in a travel place.

I'd slept like a log.

I shaved, showered and dressed, and by seven-fifteen I was sitting at one of the round tables with the place to myself.

Outside the hotel the town was slowly coming to life, people passing one way, then some time later returning, mostly carrying newspapers and baguettes.

The glass door clicked and a wizened old man held it open for an overweight brown dog.

It plodded in and sat by the bar panting, waiting for the man to join it. As the door closed I heard a buzzer sound faintly from somewhere, and a few moments later Madame Bauduin appeared, walking along the bar.

"Ca va, Henri " she smiled at him, and lifted a packet of tobacco from the shelves that ran behind the bar.

"Ca va, Adele." he croaked back.

As she laid the packet of tobacco on the counter and he rummaged through his pockets for money, she saw me over his shoulder and smiled.

She raised her hand, signalling she would be with me soon.

I nodded and smiled back.

The old boy finally got enough money out of his pockets and onto the counter, picked up the tobacco and tucked it away in the shapeless woolen jacket he wore.

Madam Bauduin scooped up his pile of shrapnel. The till pinged open and she dropped the money into various places as he shuffled around and pulled the door open.

The dog lifted itself up and went slowly through the door and the old man followed it.

"Au revior Henri" she called after him.

He waved vaguely and pulled the door closed.

"Monsuier Joe, cafe? Au lait? Er," she thought for a moment."Black?"

"Au Lait, please Madame Bauduin."

She nodded, then stood and looked directly at me.

"One minute, please!" she said, and nodded as if justice had been done.

I smiled, giving her a thumbs up.

"Perfect!"

Ten minutes later she brought me out a tray with a pot of coffee and a jug of hot milk, sugar and a pair of fresh-made Pain au Chocolat she must have bought specially from the Boulangerie across the road.

The sweet smell of them made my mouth water.

She laid everything out in front of me, then lastly, she lifted a single yellow rose from the tray and dropped it in the vase.

"Voila! Bon apetite, Monsuier Joe."

She smiled, tucked the tray under her arm and turned to walk away.

"Madame Bauduin. Adele. Have you coffee?" I motioned to the table.

"Come. Talk."

She thought for a moment, then nodded and walked away.

She returned with a small cup and saucer and a pot of coffee for herself.

"How long have you had the hotel?" I asked, motioning at the room.

"Ooof. It is famile, for – very long. I was – what is, Neasant? Bon? Bun?"

"Born. You were born here."

"Qui! Born. I was born here. But" she blew out the full lips of her small mouth, "I think, not long now. See?" she lifted her hand to the empty room.
"You will – fini? End?"

She leant her elbows on the table, cradling her coffee.

"Why do it? I am now, aloon?"

"Alone." I corrected.

"Alone, yes. My man, est for sanq – five annee mort. My... girl?"

"Daughter?"

"Daughter. She is gone, university. She has no interest for this little place."

She shrugged and wrinkled her nose, making the freckles across it dance.

"I am sure, I not also, when I am her."

I nodded. "It cannot be easy."

"Pfff… in winter, no monai, summer, no d'aide."

She shrugged.

314

"But, it is all what I know, so - I know, it is I shall be here, always. My familie, they are here." She moved the coffee around in her cup, staring at it, then drank it back. "Familie is here since-" she motioned to the church behind her. "Depuis l'église. Nous sommes comme des mauvaises herbes dans les jardins."

She filled her cup again.

"And you, Monsieur Joe. Why are you to Hambais? You are the city man, no?"

"Yes. London."

I looked at her dark eyes, wondering at the urge I had to tell her everything, realising that it was a warning.

"I'm just driving through, Adele. I needed a rest."

She looked at me, taking in the fading bruises.

Then she smiled. "Before, also. The Notaire."

I stared at her.

"Ooof." She waved her hand at me. "Famile! The girl, with long hair, she is the daughter of my, what is, cousine?"

I nodded, frowning.

"Cousin."

She looked at my face, then chuckled.

"Monsieur Joe, you think to be a secret? when men as you arrive un petit place comme Hambais,-" she chuckled again, "- chaque femme le remarque."

In spite of myself I laughed with her.

I really was a city boy, so used to anonymity I took it for granted.

I left her with another fifty Euros for the coming night and drove down to the cemetery. The heavy wrought iron gate squealed as I pushed it open.

A grey crushed stone path rose in front of me, climbing the slope of the hill the cemetery lay on.

On either side of the path, narrower paths laid with grey-brown flagstones led off through the ranks of elaborate marble and gilded tombs.

I had no idea where to start, so I walked to the top end of the path then turned left, scanning each monument for a name as I went. At the end of each path I turned back, and did the same for the opposite path.

Half way along the seventh path, I found him.

It was a plain monument. White and black speckled brown marble like many of the others, but where most were adorned with elaborate gilded angels or Jesus figures in painted robes with hands held open in sad welcome, on the waist-high oblong of Simon's grave stood a simple white cross.

I reached out and ran my fingers along his gold inlaid name.

Half an hour later, I laid the tin with its three locks of hair under the cross and began walking slowly down the grey stone path towards the van.

A squat little old woman, almost as wide as she was tall, pushed through the iron gate and began walking up the slope towards me, her body rolling on legs so bowed they seemed to fall from the outer edges of the heavy woollen overcoat she wore.

On her head she wore a dark blue linen scarf that was tied under her chin.

In one hand she held a small bunch of white and purple flowers, in the other an aged brown canvas shopping bag.

She bowled slowly up the slope towards me, and as she got closer, I heard her breath wheezing at the effort each step took.

I stood into one of the side paths to let her pass, and as she drew level with me she stopped and looked up at me with watery brown eyes rimmed with the grey of cataracts.

Her eyes widened and a smile began to form on her lips, then stopped, and faded.

She shook her head.

No. It wasn't him, after all.

I nodded to her.

"Madame".

She ignored me and began climbing the path again, scolding herself between wheezes for her foolishness.

Back at the van, I unfolded the lead boxes and took the tracker into the graveyard. I stuck it to the bottom of the wastepaper basket that stood inside the wrought iron gates.

I pulled the Beretta from my holdall and slid it inside my jacket sleeve, picked up the tube of latex glue and sat in the van, letting the engine warm through while I coated my fingers and thumbs with the glue, holding them in front of the air vents to dry.

When the glue had set, I pulled out of the lay-by, back onto the road to Mayenne, and set off for Booth's house.

27

I slowed down as I drove past the lane.

It was narrow, barely wide enough for two cars to pass.

Above it the trees had grown together, mingling branches with each other until the lane was almost a tunnel.

A hundred yards further on, a small lay-by appeared on my left. I swung the Doblo into it and switched off.

I walked back towards the lane like I was out for a stroll. A solitary car passed me from behind, music trilling from its driver's open window.

Across the road, maybe fifty yards beyond the lane in a plot carved out of the open fields around it, lay a low stone-built house. An elderly man in a sleeveless jacket was snipping wearily at a hedge that ran between the house and the roadside with hand shears.

It looked like every snip was an effort, and after every half dozen of them he would stop and brush away cuttings as an excuse to rest. He'd probably cut the same hedge every spring for fifty years, most of them as a chore, then a few more from vanity, just to prove he still could.

Now he looked as if he'd die doing it and be grateful.

I turned into Booth's lane.

The house was separated from the potholed tarmac by a grass-filled ditch topped with a straggling hedgerow. As I walked along I glanced through, taking in what I could of the house and the layout of the garden.

A gap a couple of feet wide opened in the hedge, but apart from a pair of chimneys and its steep slate roof, I still couldn't see the house. An island of magnolia bushes stood fifteen or twenty yards inside the garden, blocking most of it from view.

I stopped and took a step back. From somewhere behind the magnolia came the sound of slow rhythmic digging. I stepped across the ditch and through the gap in the hedge, walked to the edge of the magnolia and slowly parted enough of its glossy leaves to see through.

Neatly trimmed lawns that looked like they'd just had their first cut of the year lay either side of a broad curved gravel drive. On the other side of the drive, a man forked at an island cut into the lawn that was filled with bush roses. Close by him sat a steel barrow laid over with long-handled tools.

The house stood to his left.

It was two tall stories high and built of brick columns around grey local stone into which tall arched windows were set. It lay square to the lane and the road, with its entrance at one flattened corner.

Up two low stone steps from the gravel path lay a wide slate-roofed porch, its open sides supported by broad golden-grey oak timbers. Beneath the porch and half in shadow, was a wide, heavy-looking oak front door.

I let the magnolia's branches slowly fall and backed away to the lane again.

I stepped back over the ditch onto the roadway. It was perhaps thirty yards to the entrance now. I slipped sunglasses out of my pocket and put them on, straightened my flat cap and lifted the collar of my jacket.

The man stopped digging and turned around when he heard the gravel under my feet. He was around forty with dark short wavy hair and small, narrow set brown eyes.

I looked past him.

Beside the house and set back from it by twenty yards or so were a pair of slate roofed double garages with brown stained timber doors.

In front of one of the doors a small grey van was parked. One of its rear doors hung open. On the other, half a name was written over a picture of half a traditional wooden wheel barrow. Under the wheel barrow was half a telephone number.

A cat lay asleep under the rear of the van, its front legs stretched out in front of it.

The man turned to follow me with his eyes. As I drew level with him he cleared his throat and let out a half-hearted bonjour.

Without looking at him or changing pace I replied.

"Gutentag."

I stepped up into the shadow of the porch and laid my glue painted fingers on the bulbous brass knocker. I rapped three times and heard the sound echo away into the house.

I slowly unbuttoned my jacket.

I was about to knock again when I heard a heavy latch being lifted, and a second later the door swung open.

I didn't give him a chance to say anything. I stepped into the house past him, speaking at him with what I hoped passed as a mild German accent.

"Mr Booth, I have a film from your wife that I believe you will be interested in acquiring."

I turned to face him.

He gawped at me.

"Please act as if you were expecting me and close the door if you wish to know more."

He swallowed and nodded.

"Nice to see you." He said overly loudly. "Come in."

He held out his hand.

I ignored it and pushed the heavy door closed.

Against the wall to my right, a gilded Comtoise clock tocked slowly under the silence. Whether it was aftershave or perfume, he smelt of something too sweet, like cheap cola gone flat.

The skin on his face was oily and open-pored, and altogether too creamy to be natural, perhaps a special effort for the gardener.

I watched him from behind the sunglasses as he regained his normal haughty expression.

Then his eyes became guarded.

"You had better come through," he said tautly, and led the way across the polished stone floor of the hallway, past the ornate banister of the double-width stairway.

Mauve pile carpet climbed its golden oak steps until they ended in a carpeted landing that turned left.

Walls panelled in the same golden oak rose from the landing, topped by a broad window made up of three frames. I pushed the visions out of my mind.

He turned and opened a pair of doors to the left of the stairs and I followed him into a broad living room.

Its right-hand side was made up mostly of ceiling-high French doors. In front of them ran a long, curved burgundy leather settee at the end of which a television sat talking quietly to itself in French.

Booth walked across the smooth blue carpet, picked up a remote from a table beside the settee and the television died.

He moved to stand in front of the fireplace, a French take on an Inglenook that ate up half the wall.

Once posed, he motioned to a pair of deep matching armchairs that faced the leather settee.

"Sit down, mister...?"

I ignored him and remained standing.

"You may call me Mister Smith, but names are not important in this matter, except one: Walter Samsel, who would be very pleased to receive what I am about to offer you."

He fixed his top lip into a smile over a row of too-perfect implants and eyed me coldly while he computed how to react, then: "Very well, Mister Smith."

He rested a waxy looking hand that managed to be both large and feminine on the mantel of the fireplace and pretended to relax.

"So you have something which you think I may be interested in acquiring," he purred at me. "Could I ask, how you came by it?"

"I'm afraid if I told you, Mister Booth, I would have to kill you."

His oily smile vanished and his eyes narrowed.

It was an old joke, and besides, I ruined the punch-line by showing him the Beretta under my jacket.

"Let us dispense with small talk and pretty behaviour, Mister Booth." I continued "We are neither of us gentlemen, we are businessmen.

We, my colleague and I, have a certain sixteen millimetre film which you, rather carelessly, have mislaid.

The film is valuable, as is the knowledge that it is no longer in your possession."

Somewhere behind his imperious almond-eyed stare something flinched.

"Would you like to sit down, Mister Booth? You are looking a little, uncomfortable."

He blinked, too quickly.

"I'm perfectly fine."

"As you wish. Allow me to remind you of the item you are missing. I have here-" I took the strip of frames from my jacket pocket. "- a sample."

I held the film out to him.

He leaned away from the fireplace and took it from me, the tips of his fingers pointed and delicately manicured. It was the hand of middle-aged woman, except the back and fingers of it were pricked by sparse dark hairs like a house-fly.

He turned to the window and held the frames to the light.

"A romantic little scene, Mister Booth. No wonder it is such a popular item."

A sudden smear of sweat lay on the pale skin of his neck.

He lowered the film, staring out through the windows for a moment before he turned to face me.

The imperious cockiness in his tilted eyes had been replaced by reptile watchfulness.

I held out my hand to him for the film.

His mind was racing through possibilities, and he did nothing to disguise it.

I clicked my fingers at him.

"My gun has a silencer, Mister Booth. If you wish me to wound you before you return the film, I am happy to oblige."

He hung the film over my upturned hand.

"How much of the film do you have?"

"The film is as you left it, Mister Booth, and includes Monsieur Menard asking you to cease filming, as I am sure you remember."

His eyes lit for a moment before he could hide his elation. "And where is it, now?"

"It is with my colleague, not far from here. It can be returned to your safe keeping later today, provided, of course, that you and I can come to a reasonable arrangement."

He turned his head slightly away from me.

"And, what would you call a reasonable arrangement, Mister Smith?"

"A reasonable arrangement, Mister Booth, is one that persuades me that offering the film to Herr Samsel would not be more profitable."

I rolled the film up and put it back in my pocket.

"I believe the saying is, the ball, is in your court."

"And how much has Herr Samsel offered you?"

"Would you like me to ask him to make an offer, Mister Booth? Or would you prefer to conclude our business without Herr Samsel realising you do not possess the film?"

He lifted his lip over the implants again.

"You seem to have me trapped, Mister Smith. It's not a situation that endears you to me."

"Your personal feelings do not interest me, Mister Booth. Business is business. Once Herr Samsel realises that you no longer have the film, within a matter hours, you will be dead. Perhaps a curious suicide, perhaps a fatal accident, such as your brother experienced.

This you know. This I know, and - should anything happen to me - this my colleague knows, also."

The grimace had gone, and he glowered at me sullenly.

"Perhaps then, Mister Booth, you will make your offer known to me."

"Very well." He pursed his lips. "Fifty thousand Euros."

"I'm sorry Mister Booth. That is not acceptable. I wish you good day." I turned and walked to the door.

As my fingers touched the door handle, he spoke.

"One hundred thousand Euros."

I turned to face him.

"In cash, Mister Booth. Today."

"I – I don't have that much cash."

"How much do you have?"

"I don't know. Perhaps, twenty thousand."

"But you could transfer the remaining eighty thousand Euros online today."

He nodded.

"Yes."

He watched me warily as I walked back towards him, the creamy skin now pallid. His downturned mouth with its plump lips quivered as I stopped directly in front of him.

I looked into his eyes. No longer haughty and condescending, or even sly, they were now wide-pupilled and plaintive.

It was as much as I could do to stop myself pulling out the Beretta and beating his simpering face apart with it.

I breathed out slowly.

"So then, we have our agreement Mister Booth. We will accept 20,000€ in cash, with 80,000€ by way of SEPA transfer. Be sure that your gardener, and any other people you have working here, are not present after two p.m. today. I'm sure that with Herr Samsels' interest in the matter, you will understand the need for complete privacy."

He nodded.

"I must ask you to show me now proof, that you have the 20,000€ in cash."

He returned a few minutes later with a large bottle-green cotton bag which he carried across to the table beside the settee. He held up a neatly taped bundle of 50€ notes. "There are 20 to each bundle, Mister Smith." he said without looking at me.

"Please count out the money into two lots of 10,000€, Mister Booth. I will take 10,000€ with me now, my colleague will collect the other ten thousand when he arrives."

The repulsive hands stacked the money. When he'd finished, he stepped back from the table and watched me as I stepped forward.

I began putting the right hand pile away in my jacket pockets as I spoke to him.

"This afternoon, my partner will call on you with the rest of the film. On arrival, he will identify himself to you as Mister Brown. You will have the second 10,000€ ready for him when he arrives.

You will place it into this bag, on the middle of the bottom step of your stairs, so that he can clearly see it through the doorway when he arrives.

On receipt of the 10,000€, he will show you the film. You will then transfer 80,000€ to an account online, the details of which he will give you. Once he sees the transfer completed, he will hand you the film."

I tucked the last of the notes away and faced him.

"Mister Booth, my colleague Mister Brown will be armed. Please be sure to carry out my instructions to the letter, because he will take any changes to what I describe to him as evidence of a trap by Herr Samsel, with unfortunate consequences."

Booth's larynx bobbed as he swallowed.

"Please, tell your friend Mister Brown, that he has nothing to fear regarding Herr Samsel. He is the last person I would tell of any arrangement between us. Business is business."

"Honour amongst thieves, Mister Booth."

"Exactly".

He tried the ingratiating grin again, but it didn't last.

I stared at him from behind the sunglasses.

"Leave the bag on the stairs as we have agreed, and all will be well."

"But, Mister Smith, you have 10,000 Euros and I have nothing but your word that you have the rest of the film."

"Honour amongst thieves Mister Booth."

"Well yes, but really. Could you not leave me the piece of film you have?"

"So that you can pretend to Herr Samsel that you have the whole film after all, Mister Booth? Really, what do you take us for? We are not amateurs or cheap con-men. We are professional people.

If you doubt it, I suggest you re-read the newspapers, about your wife's death, the death of your alter ego Mister Gavin Durrant, or Dean Thompson as he was otherwise known."

I turned and walked to the door and opened it.

I turned back to him.

"Remember to place the rest of the deposit on the stairs."

"It will be done exactly as you say, Mister Smith."

I nodded.

"I wish you good day Mister Booth. A pleasure to do business with you."

I drove slowly back to Hambais, past the cemetery.

The lay-by was empty. I pulled in. I put my phone back together and switched it on.

I rang Phillipa.

"Danny?"

"Everything OK?."

"Yes. I got back in the evening. I called Natalie as you said. She came herself and picked me up."

I smiled to myself. I bet she did.

"So you're where now?"

"I'm at your flat."

"Good. Stay there. I may be a day or two more, but I'll be back as soon as I can. Before I go, go online and check the Auspex bank account."

"What?"

"What I said. Go online and check the Auspex bank account."

She took the phone with her and I heard her lay it on the desk.

The keyboard of the laptop clacked quietly, then paused, then clacked again.

Then silence, then: "Oh! Oh, my god!" she picked the phone up.

"Where did that come from? Who are these people?"

"Never ask a question, if you might not like the answer. Pay yourself, pay your rent, I will give you a call when I'm on my way back."

I called Sean.

"Sean. You can come and get the film."

"Where?"

"You on your own there? Can I speak?"

"Yeah, just me here. After you gave us the slip Samsel went right into one, but I told him you'd given him your word and he should back off and give you enough rope to hang yourself.

The deal was you'd contact me, and I said he should give you room to breathe. Cover the ports and leave you alone until tomorrow. It's just me and you now."

"Fair enough Sean. Thanks."

"No need. I knew you wouldn't screw him over. You're not stupid. Besides, you know as well as I do, people like Samsel and y'man Denning, they like to be impressed, even if someone's rubbing their nose in it.

He might have the arsehole with you, but that's only 'cos he's uptight about the film. You've done yourself no harm at all, how you've handled things. Where are you, anyway?"

"I'm in a town called Hambais. It's on the N35, between Le Mans and Mayenne. When you get close enough, you'll pick up your tracker. Just follow it. There's a lay-by, outside a cemetery. I'll meet you there. How long do you think it will take you?"

"Wait a mo. I'll check."

I heard him tapping slowly at a keyboard. "I can be there," I imagined him moving the mouse and checking the whole route. "- around three-thirty."

"Make it four o'clock, Sean. I'll be waiting for you. But make sure you aren't followed, mate. I won't bore you with it now, but I've managed to set something up on the side here for us both, and I don't want us to have to share it."

28

I drove back to the town and parked in the street behind the hotel.

As I slid my key into the door the bells above me chinged out eleven.

I closed the door behind me and stood in the gloom, allowing my eyes to adjust before treading my way up the stairs to my room.

I dropped the holdall inside the door, filled the ancient basin with hot water and began getting what was left of the latex off my fingertips.

When they were clean I dried them and drew the curtains, picked my boots undone and slipped them off, then lay back on the bed and stared into the darkness.

I heard quiet footsteps stop outside the room.

The half-hour chimed softly through the closed window.
I waited, watching as the door handle slowly turned, hearing the lock click free. I slid from the bed and tiptoed around it as the door began to open.

I took hold of the door, pulled it gently wide open and smiled at her.

She smiled nervously back, her eyes wide. .

I reached out and stroked her hair away from her face. She moved toward me and I pushed the door shut.

She looked at me from under a pile of hair as she lay across me. "I yam appy."

She smiled, then chuckled and kissed my chest.

"I. Yam. Appy."

She stated again slowly, and raised her eyebrows at me, waiting for me to respond.

"Jer sweet, hear ox."

"Merde!" she pinched me and laughed. "J'abandonne! Toi singe anglais."

"Der kell colour lee petit shat?" I intoned.

"Pas "der"! Êtes-vous un Bosch?"

She chuckled and blew a raspberry on my stomach.

"I think, in one hundred years, you will not can speak French!"

"Ach, I'm shit at languages, babe. Sorry"

"Hmmph."

She looked up at me again.

"But, you are not shit at the make love, so – hm…" she shrugged, and slid her hand up my thigh, began rubbing me gently, peeling my foreskin back and stroking me with the tips of her fingers, making me swell and harden.

She made the little "Hm" sound again and slid her face down to meet me.

"I am forgive you."

I felt the wet warmth of her lips sucking me in.

Her dark eyes watched me as I poured myself a last coffee.

We sat at the small table in the hotel kitchen, trying to be grown-ups.

Or stupid.

Or whatever it is you try to be after ships have passed in the night.

I poured some cream in and smiled at her.

She smiled back, narrowing her eyes and wrinkling her nose, making the freckles dance.

I stirred the coffee.

"Adele, can I ask you to look after something for me?"

She looked puzzled.

"What is – look after?"

"Hmm. To, care for something. Like, ah – le petit chat."

I made a movement, as if I was stroking a small cat, then picked it up and cuddled it.

"And, like you –" I opened my hands and looked around "- you look after the hotel."

"Faire? Garder?"

I smiled.

"Yes, like guard. Look."

I reached into my jacket and laid three hundred Euros in fifties on the table.

She watched me carefully.

"Adele, this is for you."

I pushed the money across the table to her.

She didn't take her eyes from my face.

"I am not, the bordel here." she said quietly.

"I know babe. Believe me. But I want you to have this, for the quiet times."

I looked around me at the simple kitchen with its worn fixtures and tired furniture.

"For when there is no money. But, also, I hope that you will look after something for me. Something important, that I cannot do."

She folded her arms on the table in front of her and watched me.

I looked into her eyes.

"You see, there is a grave. Une inhumation? In the cemetery. I would like that you, once a year, put flowers, fleur, petite fleur, on it for me."

She closed her eyes and shook her head slowly, then lifted herself from the table.

She walked across to an ancient roll-top desk that stood in the corner of the room, stood for a moment in front of it, searching, then moved some papers and picked up a pen.

She brought the pen and a piece of paper back to the table, laid them in front of me and sat down again.

I wrote on the piece of paper, a name, a date and then drew a crude map of the cemetery, with a cross halfway along the seventh path on the left.

I laid the pen down and checked what I'd done.

Satisfied, I passed it to her.

She turned it around and studied it before laying it in front of her and looking up at me.

Her eyes behind their long lashes glistened.

"Who is?" she asked quietly.

I felt my eyes fill.

"Nobody."

I felt my mouth trying to cry out and bit my lips, shaking my head.

She pushed herself up from the table and came to me, holding my head within her breasts, stroking my hair, whispering to me.

"Mon bel homme brisé… parle-moi."

I smelt the warmth of her, the faint lavender under the musk of our sex, felt my face wet against her skin and the satin of her dressing gown as she rocked me.

"Fais moi confiance, dis moi, dis moi tout."

The church clinked the quarter-hour as I left, hurrying to the Doblo and dropping the holdall behind the seats.

I drove through the town for the last time, not looking down between the church and the hotel, knowing she would be at one of the windows, watching me go.

I passed the bar on the corner, and the hotel was gone.

Sean stood leaning against a silver Peugeot.

As I arrived he stood up.

I stopped and beckoned him to get in the van.

He studied my face. "Everything OK?"

"Good as it ever is."

He nodded and looked away from me, staring up the hill at the cemetery.

"Life's a cunt, and then you die."

"That's the one."

He beat me to the next question.

"What the fuck, Danny? How did you get yourself involved?"

I looked out along the road over the steering wheel of the van. I took a deep breath.

"Booth's wife was my ex. When we were kids. Well, eighteen, she was. She was well off, I was from the boonies. It was a fucking joke, but –"

331

"You know, Danny." he broke across me. "You don't have to play the stone-hearted English bastard for me. I'm a fuckin' Paddy. We live and breathe sentimentality."

I smiled and nodded.

"She was everything to me, but, I never thought I was good enough for her. I couldn't handle it, so I treated her like a cunt."

He nodded, watching me.

"Then one night, she turned up, and told me she had something to tell me. I acted the cunt again, and she fucked off. I figured she'd just had enough. But, it turns out, she'd been pregnant."

He said nothing, but I saw his lips flatten in a tough-luck smile.

"I don't know what happened, but she ended up with Booth. He's a professional ponce, and her family had money, so I guess he was happy enough to pull a well-bred woman half his age.

But, it didn't work out. Again, I don't know what went on, but he started whacking the kid about, probably because he couldn't whack her about without losing Daddies money."

"The kid was yours."

"Yep."

I nodded.

"Then one day, he went too far, and knocked him downstairs, brain-damaged him. Made him paraplegic. Even after that, he would still whack him about. I don't know. She wouldn't tell me. Maybe he was fucking him. After seeing that film, nothing would surprise me.

Then Susan, the wife, she had some work being done at their house by a builder called Thompson, and he found Samsels' film where Booth had hidden it under some floorboards.

She hid it somewhere else, and I figure she told Booth if he touched the boy again she'd – I don't know what – send the film to the papers or let Samsel know Booth didn't have it anymore.

In the end, the boy died, as they said he would after the brain damage, and she left Booth, taking the film with her. She went to live down in Cornwall, Booth carried on being Booth, and they both kept up the show of being happily married."

I shook my head.

"I don't know why. I can only think he had something on her as well, or she was getting money off him for the film. But anyway.

At some point, she'd started knocking off the builder, Thompson, and it went on for a few years.

Then out of the blue, I get handed a job by Denning, to chase Thompson off her. Nobody knows who asked for it to be done, but you know how it goes with these things. Half the time you don't know what the fucking deal is -"

Out the corner of my eye I could see him nodding,

"- it's just your job to get the result. So, I went round to Thompson, and he'd been topped."

"Schroeder?"

"Yeah. They played snap finger with him. My guess is that they'd been called in by Samsel because Booth had whined to him about being blackmailed, and they were after the negatives of some pictures of Thompson with Susan, but then it got confused.

I reckon Thompson thought they were after the film that he'd found, and on the second finger he tells Schroeder that the wife has the film.

Schroeder wonders what he's on about, and phones home.

Samsel twigs that Booth hasn't got the film anymore, and he sends Schroeder after it, but I got there first. Not because of the film. I didn't know it existed, but because I sensed that Susan was mixed up in something that was getting out of hand.

Schroeder turns up, I stop him killing her, but his oppo does for her and leaves me holding the baby. So, I get the fuck out and head to France."

"And what about the girl, Phillipa?"

"She's incidental. Like I told you, she didn't have a scooby about the film. She was after Booth for running the money he bled out of Samsel through a front company.

But Schroeder got wind of her, maybe on Thompson's third finger, so he was going over there to put her out of her misery and get the blackmail negatives.

I got there first and moved her into my place, then went down to Cornwall. Once Cornwall blew up in my face, I couldn't protect her in the UK so I told her to get to France.

She'd already contacted Billaud, because she figured that he'd be able to help her do Booth, and that's how we ended up there."

He nodded.

"And the rest is history."

"The rest is history, Sean. Except for one thing."

"What?"

"Half of this couldn't have happened without someone inside MDH being involved."

He looked away from me, staring towards the cemetery gates.

"What's the name in MDH, Sean."

He turned back to me.

"I don't think you need me to tell you that, do you Dan."

He shifted around in his seat, so he was near enough facing me.

"Danny, y'know, things change. Nothing is forever. As I told you earlier, you've done yourself a lot of good in Samsels' eyes, the way you've played this."

He paused, watching me.

"If I was you, I'd keep my head down. Try and stay off the front line and let things play out. Then, that way, you look after your own interests."

"Is that what Samsel told you to tell me?"

He nodded slowly.

"So many words."

I stared out at the road. Then I nodded, and reached into the pocket of my jacket and pulled out the coiled film. I held it up to him.

He took it from me.

"That's all of it, Danny? Every last frame, no souvenirs?"

"No, I gave him my word, and that's all of it."

He held the loose end of the film briefly up to the light then pushed it into the pocket of his jacket.

"I think I know where you want to go now, Danny, but, you know, I can't let you, don't you?"

"I was hoping I wouldn't have to."

I put my arm behind his seat, pulled the Beretta out of the holdall and offered it to him.

He took the gun from me, checked the magazine then slid it inside his jacket.

"How do you mean?"

"Well, we're maybe 10 minutes drive from Booth's house, and I took that film there and showed it to him this morning. I told him I could give him the whole thing back, this afternoon, for thirty grand cash, which was what he had in readies."

I slipped one of the 50€ note wads out of my pocket and handed it to him.

"He agreed, so I took ten grand off him as a deposit. I told him to clear everybody away this afternoon, and to have the other twenty grand waiting in a bag on the stairs, so my colleague Mister Brown could pick it up when he arrived with the film."

He tapped the wad on his hand, smiling, then handed it back to me.

"I'm all ears, Danny."

I explained the layout of the house to him, the driveway, the porch, how the porch couldn't be seen from the entrance to the garden or the house from the road, how the door was left hung, the stairs onto the stone floor.

"Anyway, -" I finished "- the money is there, Sean. As for whether you suggest it to Samsel first, or do it for yourself, I leave that up to you. You know Samsel better than I do."

"If I tell him I've got the film, and Booth is sitting there just down the road on his ownsome, odds on he'll ask me if I think I can do him."

He grimaced.

"Problem is, if I do ask him, and he tells me no.."

He blew out his lips thoughtfully.

I nodded.

"Yup. Well. I leave it up to you, mate. Either way, there's twenty grand there. Me, I just want to get gone. Get back to Blighty and rest up for a bit. I've had a fucking gut full of it. There's a ferry from Le Harve sails at eleven, and I want to be on it."

"I don't fucking blame you. Danny -" he held his hand out to me and I took it.

"Don't forget what I said, fella. Be wise. Let the world turn."

I nodded.

"I thought about it already. You're right. We're just soldiers. At the end of the day, we have to look after ourselves."

"That's right."

He gave my hand a last squeeze, got out of the van and shut the door. He rapped on the roof with his hand and walked towards the Peugeot.

I checked the mirror, pulled out and took the road towards Mayenne, then took a right turn at a fork alongside a supermarket and followed the road uphill out of Hambais.

A mile later, I took a turning on the right and drove up a narrow road that wound its way upwards through open fields, then swung hard right and snaked its way through a tiny hamlet.

It ended at a T- junction.

I turned right and coasted down the hill until I could see the car park of the supermarket and the forked junction I'd taken.

I pulled up and waited.

By now, she would have cleared the bed to wash the sheets. She would have lifted the pillows, and found the rest of the money, with my clumsy note to explain.

How I hoped it would take her worry away, but not mentioning the peace I'd felt as she wiped the tears from my oh-so-fucking hard, sophisticated face with her gentleness and simple, caring words, in a language she barely knew.

I wanted to cling to that peace.

I wanted it to last forever.

I knew it wouldn't.

Like the man had said:
In knowledge, lies wisdom.

The silver Peugeot passed by below.

I put the van in gear and drove slowly down to the junction, then joined the main road.

I walked quickly down the deserted road to the lane, breaking into a trot until I reached the gap in the hedgerow. I jumped the ditch and sprinted across the lawn until I reached the cover of the magnolia, just as Sean knocked the door.

I ducked behind the bush and waited.

Half a minute passed, then I heard the latch grate in the door.

A second later the Beretta fired once, then again.

Dull, flat sounds no louder than gloved handclaps.

I gave it a slow count of ten then cut across the lawn until I reached the corner of the porch.

Stepping slowly up into the shadow, I put my hands in my jacket pockets and moved silently across to the open front door.

Booth lay sprawled on the stone floor, his head surrounded by a halo of blood, his eye staring down his waxy cheek.

Beyond him, Sean stood at the bottom of the stairway with the Beretta tucked under his left arm, peering into the bag of cash.

He looked up as I crossed the threshold.

"I thought you'd be along."

He smiled.

"I don't blame you. I'd want to see the cunt dead as well."

"Just thought I'd check he kept his word."

I pushed the door closed with my foot until it hit the latch..

"Looks like he did."

He lifted a wad of notes out of the bag and turned them over in his hand.

"A good man always does, Sean."

"Well, I'm not sure he was what I'd call a good man."

"He was scum."

I slid the snub out of my pocket.

"But Jaques Billaud wasn't."

The first shot hit him high in the chest, the second went lower, taking his pinkie off on its way through the money he held.

The Beretta clattered onto the stone floor as he toppled forwards, his forehead splitting open as it hit the stone floor.

I wiped the gun on my shirtfront, picked up Booth's right hand and placed the snub into it.

I curled his index finger inside the trigger guard, aimed, and fired into Sean a third time.

I let Booth's hand fall, stood up and stepped back through the door, using the cuff of my jacket on the brass knocker to pull it closed behind me.

I stood a moment in the porch, looking out across the neatly cut lawns with their stately islands of rose bushes and jumbled perennials and evergreens.

Letting the flat lemonade scent of honeysuckle chase away the stench their deaths had made.

From behind the house somewhere, a blackbird piped a feint meandering melody into the twilight.

A car hummed past on the main road.

The sound of it faded away, leaving only the breeze murmuring through the trees surrounding the darkening garden.

Susan called to Simon from within the house, her voice echoing across the still lawns.

He looked out from behind one of the evergreen islands by the entrance.

She called again, and he left what he was doing and began running up the lawn, then onto the path towards the house.

I walked towards him, down the gravel toward the road as he ran to meet me, his dark tousled hair moving as he ran.

Closer now, almost to me, his broad smile happy and his brown eyes, half-round, just like hers, filled with joy, and laughter, and innocence.

He ran right through me, and I was gone.